Still AIR

FREYA BARKER

Copyright © 2016 Margreet Asselbergs as Freya Barker

All rights reserved.

This book is a work of fiction and any resemblance to any person or persons, living or dead, any event, occurrence, or incident is purely coincidental. The characters and story lines are created and thought up from the author's imagination or are used fictitiously.

Cover Design:
RE&D - Margreet Asselbergs

Editing:
Karen Hrdlicka

DEDICATION

*There are some whose hearts are so big, there is room for
everyone. They have a tendency to carry around not only the joy,
but the pain and the struggles of everyone around them. Always
first to offer a hand, a comforting shoulder—always ready to take
on burdens and provide relief.*
*All to often they fill their hearts and lives with the care for others
to shield their own struggles and needs.*
But who takes care of them?

TABLE OF CONTENTS

CHAPTER ONE

Pam

"Are you done with that?"

After four hours on the road, coming back from New York, I had to stop for a bite. The roads around Boston were brutal. With construction everywhere, a trip that normally would take no more than five hours in total, was going to take me at least another two from here to get to Portland.

Already with a blinding headache after the day from hell, I'd needed sustenance or I'd drive myself off the road. I found this little hole in the wall diner in Lowell that was still open this time of night.

The tired-looking waitress, who looks like she's been on her feet all damn day, points at my half-empty plate.

"Sure, but could I have another refill?" I hold up my empty cup. That will make six coffees today, all after two o'clock. Not only am I never going to sleep again, but my stomach likely won't recover for days. I have to keep a clear mind, though. Another two or so hours behind the wheel and I'll be home, where I can sink into a bath and deal with my emotions. I'm done with this day.

At almost midnight, I finally pull into my driveway. For a minute I stare at the dark windows of my small bungalow. I bought it just early last year, mostly as a way to invest the savings I'd been able to stash away over the years. This is an older area of Portland and a lot of the property around here is steadily going up in value. On my street alone, eight of the original small houses were purchased, leveled, and replaced with ostentatiously big mansions. All because of the good sized lots and the location: close to the water, close to the downtown core.

For the longest time, I simply stayed in the small apartment on the first floor of Florence House, the women's shelter I've managed for twelve years now. That place still feels more like a home to me than my own house. Perhaps because it offered as much of a sanctuary for me over the years, as it does for the women who walk through the door, looking for safety.

When the new funding came through last year, I was able to hire an additional two counselors, which relieved some of the pressure, but it also meant I was free to focus on a life outside the shelter. Something I thought I was ready for, but sitting here, outside what should be my home, I still want to turn around and find my sanctuary at the shelter. Especially today.

-

"How was your day off?" Brenda asks when I walk into the kitchen the next morning.

"Peachy." I realize my response sounds a bit dismissive and to counter that impression, I smile and give her shoulder a squeeze as I reach past her for a mug. More coffee is needed. "What did I miss here?"

"Maria left last night after dinner and I haven't seen or heard from her since. She's not answering her phone again," Brenda informs me, as she sits at the table.

Maria came to us about four months ago, trying to escape an abusive relationship. At nineteen, she's the youngest resident we currently have. She's also the most worrisome, with a history of abuse growing up and little or no resistance to the draw of Christian Neve, a good-looking bad boy, who, at the age of twenty-seven had just a few months ago, taken over leadership of one of Portland's growing gangs. With a heavy hand in the local drug trade, the Seals have been amassing in numbers with the pressure of one particularly notorious gang threatening to expand their Boston territory north.

This is the third time, in the past month and a half, that Maria has disappeared on us. Just two weeks ago, we received a call from Maine Medical Center, that she had been brought in, unconscious, bloody, and beaten. Because of signs of trauma to her genital area, they'd automatically done a rape kit as part of their examination, something Maria had been upset about when she woke up.

I'd gone to pick her up the next morning and brought her back here, making it clear that she was not only endangering herself, but the other residents by sneaking off to meet the very man who landed her at Florence House to begin with. I can't say I don't understand her, because I was just as blind to reality at that age. Just as eager to believe that if only I understood better and loved harder, I could turn a monster into a man.

Maria had been warned that with one more infraction, we would no longer be able to offer her shelter, but if I'm completely honest, I don't know if I can refuse her if she comes back.

"Okay," I instruct Brenda. "Let me know if she gets in touch."

One more thing to worry about, but I can't let it dominate my thoughts; there are three other women currently living here, and they're waiting in the meeting room for their daily group session. With my coffee in hand, I make my way over there and take my seat in the group.

A long hour later, I resurface, drained and struggling to keep it together. There are days when your own demons become so loud in your head, there simply is no room to take on anyone else's. Today appears to be one of those days. That's probably why, when I walk into my office to find Viv there, I'm even more abrasive than normal.

"What do you need?" I wince at how snarky I sound and immediately follow it with: "Sorry, girl."

Luckily it's Viv, who's known me for a long time and she simply raises an eyebrow. Viv came here many moons ago, on the run from an abusive situation. Over the years, she's become a good friend and a loyal volunteer, but just last year the full extent of her abusive history came to light. One that went back much further and deeper than the relationship she'd run from. Her new husband, Ike, had been an important component in her emotional recovery.

"Maybe I should ask what it is *you* need?" she counters sardonically.

I sit down heavily in my chair and immediately pull open the top drawer of my desk, where I stash my supply of ibuprofen. Migraines are a bitch to control if you let them get out of hand, and I have a doozy brewing. "Drugs," I mumble around my mouthful of pills, three in all, before swallowing them down with my coffee.

"Not gonna keep you long," Viv says with an understanding smile. "I just wanted to see if you'd be able to come over on Sunday night for the last BBQ of the year?"

"You nuts? They're expecting snow next week!"

"I know," she says, smiling mischievously. "On Tuesday, which is why Sunday night is perfect. A final goodbye to summer. Besides, my brother and his husband are heading back to the warm West Coast. Apparently their constitutions are too weak to handle our New England winter. So it'll be their bon voyage party, too."

I lean my head back and regard Viv through half-closed eyes. She's become such a good friend, but even to her I can't unload. The role of therapist is too deeply ingrained in me to even consider sharing my own shit. What irony; I became a counselor to unburden others but have never felt right about unburdening myself. Part of me wonders if Viv sees it in me—the dark pain I've been hiding from for so long.

There is only one person who ever picked up on it, which is why I avoid him like the plague.

Dino

"Jonas! Get your ass out of bed, boy!"

Fucking brat. Every damn morning the same song and dance. I'm sick of it, but I don't know how to get through to him. He was never an easy teenager—something I can't blame him for in hindsight. But since his mother left, he's only gotten worse. Angry, confrontational, and downright challenging at times, I'm running out of ways to try and handle him.

I always thought when the kids were little, that Gina, my little princess, would be the cause of my worries. Would never have guessed that my boy, my buddy, would go from an active, happy-go-lucky kid to surly teen. At seventeen, he's already a big boy. Not quite as big as his dad, but he broke six feet when he was only fifteen and since then has just been growing more solid.

Gina looks more like her mother; small, fine-boned, and with a smile that can melt my heart. Too bad I haven't seen her smile since her mom fucked us over.

It's been a brutal couple of months since she took off. Not even a phone call to check up on her kids. Her drug infused head so far up her ass; she didn't hesitate for a second to blame our son for the stash of drugs I found in our house and the money *she* took to pay for them.

I blame myself. I knew something was off. I'd known for a long time, I just…*Fuck,* I don't know what I was thinking. I kept believing her when she denied using drugs again. Maybe it was easier to believe the lie than the reality. No wonder Jonas is pissed at me.

"Daddy?"

"Yes, baby." I shake off my dark thoughts and turn to my little girl.

"Can you make pancakes? Blueberry?"

"Sure thing," I say, prepared to do anything to try and get my baby to smile. "It'll have to be frozen berries, honey. Wrong time of year for fresh. Do you have your lunch packed?"

Gina holds up her lunch bag before disappearing down the hall. No smile, but it'll come.

When I have a stack of pancakes staying warm in the oven, I head back upstairs. "Jonas, you have fifteen minutes to get showered and dressed to make first bell." I step into his room when I don't get an answer. The lump under the blankets I presume is Jonas, although it's hard to tell in this pigsty. It reeks in here; like locker room, and something else. I pull the covers away from him.

Christ. Fully dressed, stinking of beer and weed, comatose by the looks of it. I tamp down my anger as I grab him by the arm and start pulling him up. He's like dead weight, and for a second, fear hits me like a punch in the gut, but then he starts mumbling.

"Up, buddy. Gotta get to school and you're a mess."

"Sick," he mumbles as he sways on his feet. "Staying in bed."

"The fuck you are," I bark, losing patience. "You've got the stench of bad decisions rolling off you in waves. Not gonna let you hide in your room. You're cleaning up, you're going to school, and tonight we're gonna have a serious talk because, Son, this is the end of the line for this bullshit."

His eyes start blinking and slowly open; red-rimmed, and with pupils that make it clear whatever he's been using has not quite made it out of his system. And anger—*shit*, so much anger. He forcefully yanks his arm free and I let him, my own anger and frustration is too close to the surface for any kind of confrontation right this minute.

When I hear the shower turn on in the bathroom, I take one look around the room before resolutely pulling the door shut. I rest my forehead against the frame and close my eyes. With Jeannie, I refused to see what was right in front of me; an addiction rooted so deep, that the girl who once couldn't even fib without betraying herself, became a stone-faced, cold-hearted liar. The thought the same thing might be happening to my boy, right under my nose, is unacceptable. I will not let that happen, even if it means calling in help.

-

"Morning!"

Viv's cheery voice greets me when I walk into The Skipper's kitchen. I'm supposed to be in charge of the kitchen here, but over the last few years, every time I turn my back, someone else slips behind my stove. At first that ticked me off, but it sure helped the past months when I've had to take time off until the kids and I got our routines sorted without Jeannie. Although, I'm starting to wonder how sorted we really are.

I grumble at Viv, but I can't pass by her baby girl, Francessca, sitting in a bouncy chair on the kitchen table, without taking a sniff of that downy golden head. Babies are the bomb.

They're soft, sweet, and cuddly and best of all, they can't walk away from you or lip you off. I nuzzle her little neck and blow a raspberry, earning me a happy squeal and a big smile when I step back. Her little legs are kicking out furiously, making the seat bounce over the table.

"She's gonna fall," I tell Viv, who is working on prep for the lunch crowd.

"She's not, I'm keeping an eye on her."

"Yeah? How are you gonna do that with your back turned?" I point out, heading for the pantry.

"Moms have eyes in the back of their heads, haven't you heard?" she jokes, but when she sees me walking out of the pantry with a sack of rice, she rolls her eyes.

Just like every other morning when Viv brings her little girl into work, and we have this discussion, I use a ten-pound bag of rice on the little chair's frame to anchor it.

I grab my apron, wash my hands and move next to Viv, who's made a decent start on the vegetables.

"How's the kids?"

Well, my daughter has lost her light, and my son drinks, does drugs and is slipping away—but I don't say that. "I dropped them off at school earlier," I answer with a nonanswer to divert. "I made pancakes so they missed the bus." I try to ignore Viv, who has dropped her knife and has turned to me, her hands on her hips.

"You know," she starts, in a tone that promises nothing good. "It's amazing for someone prone to grunting, how many words you can string together when you try to avoid something." A chuckle slips from my lips. She's a ball-buster, Viv. Not afraid of anyone.

"I'm losing him," I find myself confessing. Viv doesn't need an explanation, she knows who I'm talking about. Every one of my friends has seen the change in Jonas. "I just sat through a painful meeting with the school counselor, who caught me in the school parking lot. She informed me he's missed more classes than he's been present for in the past month. Apparently, he's been bringing in notes with my forged signature. I'm at a loss," I admit.

"Are you ready now to have me ask Pam for a good referral?"

This is not the first time she's suggested getting her friend, Pam, involved, but it's the first time I'm considering it. Of course, the fact that woman hates me might have had something to do with my reluctance. I can't remember doing anything to her, but since the first time we were introduced, she's taken a dislike to me. I don't care much for her either, with her bossy attitude, but for the sake of my kids, I'll deal with the devil himself.

"Yeah," I give in. "Please," I add as an afterthought and I see it surprises Viv. Her mouth hangs open in disbelief.

"Did you just say *pleeease*?" She drags out the word, harassing me.

"Just stuff—"

I don't get to finish my insult because a loud banging can be heard at the backdoor. Viv reacts faster than me and is already heading into the hallway. I can hear the sound of voices and then heavy footsteps coming this way. I recognize a hint of panic on Viv's face when she enters the kitchen, two men following behind her.

"Mr. Brachio?" The older of the two walking up, holding out his hand. I automatically wipe my hands on the towel I have tucked in my apron before grabbing his hand in mine. "I'm Detective Barnes and this is my partner Detective McCullough." I shake the other man's proffered hand, but my eyes never leave the first detective. "I'm afraid I have some bad news." I hear a kitchen chair scrape over the floor, despite the sudden roar in my ears and my first thought is *Jonas*, but his next words take me by surprise. "We received a phone call from one of your neighbors at about nine this morning. They noticed unusual activity at your place; an unknown van was parked in the driveway and they spotted a person crawling in through the kitchen window. The responding officers found a young male beside an old Dodge Caravan in front of your home and a woman inside the house, apparently in the middle of a burglary. The woman claims she lives there. Claims she's your wife. We need you to—"

"Impossible," I blurt out, unable to comprehend what he is telling me. *Jeannie*? I feel an arm slide around my waist and I know Viv is close. "She's in Springfield with friends." At least that's what she'd told me last time we spoke.

"I'm not sure what the story is, sir," Detective Barnes says gently. "We're holding her and her companion at the police station on Middle Street. We'd appreciate it if you could come with us and help clear this up."

This is going to tear my kids apart.

CHAPTER TWO

Dino

"I'd like to stop at my house first," I tell Detective Barnes when he climbs in behind the wheel of his car.

The other detective graciously offered me shotgun, since I guess it was obvious I wasn't going to fit in the backseat of the cruiser that easily.

"I'd rather we get this sorted first," he says, not unkindly. "As soon as we clarify who she is, and what she was doing at your house, we'll head over to the house. I have officers still at the scene."

"My kids, they get off the bus at three forty-five," I point out.

Barnes turns to me briefly before focusing back on the road. "We'll get you out of there as soon as possible. You may want to catch them before they get home. The woman appears to have done some damage."

Fucking great.

The rest of the drive to the police station is quiet but my head is chaos. They say imagining is worse than knowing, and right now I believe it.

I follow the two detectives into the building and down a hall, where they show me into a small room with a large window. I barely recognize the woman on the other side, sitting on a chair against the wall with her head leaning back, appearing to be asleep. *Fuck, Jeannie.*

"Is that your wife?"

I nod and swallow the lump in my throat. Unbelievable how six months can change a person. At least visibly, because she had changed a long, long time ago—I'd just been too blind to see it.

"It is. We've been separated for six months and divorce papers have been filed." I try to keep my voice even.

"I see," Barnes says. "Who filed for divorce?"

"I did. When I discovered she'd been doing drugs in our house, taking money that wasn't hers to take, and pulling the kids down with her."

"I see," he says again. "Was this drug problem new?"

I shake my head, turning my back on the window. I've seen enough. "No," I answer. "Jeannie had a hard time after Jonas, our son, was born. Postpartum depression? She was put on meds. It wasn't any easier when our daughter was born three years later. She always needed something to help her cope. I'm not sure when it went from prescription to recreational street drugs— when it started going off the rails."

A hand claps on my shoulder as Barnes leads me out of the small room. He stops me in the hallway. "Would you mind if we put you in the same room with her, so we can ask her a few questions and see how she answers with you there?"

Yes, I fucking mind, but I'm going to do it anyway because the only way out of this hell is go through it. I give him a curt nod and he opens the door to the adjoining room.

Jeannie's head comes away from the wall and her eyes grow large when she claps them on me. "Francis…" She sounds pathetic, pleading. I tear my eyes from the ravages drugs left behind on the once fresh, pretty face of my wife. She looks like she's aged twenty years in a few months. I didn't expect it to hurt but it does.

Just half an hour later, I walk out of the police station and take a deep breath in. The air inside had been cloying and thick with the full evidence of Jeannie's addiction. She'd started off saying she needed her family, that she missed us—but when Barnes confronted her with some of the things her companion had admitted to already, the conciliatory Jeannie disappeared. The guy was her drug dealer turned boyfriend, she admitted. Apparently had been for a while. That bit of news didn't sting half as much as it probably should.

Jeannie had never left for Springfield, but had hung around Portland. I'd been pissed with her for not contacting the kids, but now? I'm glad she didn't. I will do whatever the fuck I need to do to keep the kids from seeing this mess of a woman. A mother who admittedly breaks into her kids' house to steal their stuff to sell for drugs? Sickening.

Barnes walks up behind me and grasps me on the shoulder. "Sorry for the hold up," he apologizes. "My partner just informed me that the boyfriend just admitted this apparently was not their first burglary."

"Their?" I pick up on that distinction immediately.

"Would appear so. We need to get to the bottom of it, but we've got a stack of unsolved burglaries that we'll be looking at them for. Ironically, your wife—"

"Ex," I bite off.

"Your ex-wife," he corrects. "She thought hitting up your place would be risk free. That if anything happened, she could talk her way out of it."

"Yeah, I gathered that." I try to stay calm but want to put my fist through the brick wall. "That woman may be the mother of my children, but I don't know her. I have a feeling maybe I never did."

"Addiction—any kind of addiction—can change a person into someone unrecognizable."

Barnes drops me off at The Skipper so I can pick up my wheels. I should probably pop inside let Viv know I might not be back today. Gunnar, the owner and my good friend, is sitting at the kitchen table with Viv, playing with her little one, when I walk in.

"Trouble?"

I snort at the understatement. "You could say that. I just left my ex-wife and her boyfriend at the police station, strung out on drugs, and from the sounds of it, facing charges for a string of burglaries."

"A string?" Gunnar says.

"A boyfriend?" Viv exclaims at the same time.

I rub my hands over my face. Their response is nothing compared to the reaction I anticipate from the kids. I briefly consider lying to them, but decide against it. The chance this news will get to them some other way is too great, and I want to be there to deal with the fall out. *Son-of-a-fucking-bitch.*

"I'll fill you in later, but I haven't been to the house yet, and I've got to intercept the kids in a bit. Let them know what's up." I turn to Viv. "Sorry to leave you hanging like this, girl, but—"

"Get out of here," Viv says, waving me away dismissively. "I've got it covered."

"Need company?" Gunnar asks, already out of his chair.

My first instinct is to tell him I've got this, but maybe it's time to practice what I've preached to my friends for years: take a hand when it's offered. The truth is, I feel totally fucking overwhelmed, and it would make me feel better to have someone with a clear head on his shoulders back me up.

"Please," I say quietly, the unfamiliar word strange on my lips.

Barnes is already waiting in my front yard when we arrive. We have to park in the street because there are three police vehicles in my driveway. That'll do wonders for my reputation in the neighborhood.

Gunnar doesn't wait for me; he walks straight up to Barnes and introduces himself.

"Mr. Brachio," Barnes says as I walk up. "Just a reminder, there was some damage done. My guys are about done, but until then, I'd like to ask you to leave everything as is." I nod in response.

When we get in, the living room looks almost untouched, except the big screen TV that is missing. Quick cash.

"They had loaded that in the back of the van already, we'll get it back to you," Barnes says, catching me looking.

In the kitchen, the only things out of place are the tins we keep on top of the fridge for small odds and ends, as well as emergency household cash. They're on the counter with the contents spread out. Figures that would've been the first place she went to look for money. There hadn't been much, if anything, in there. The kids know I'll put twenty bucks a week in there for minor household needs or a pizza.

The upstairs is a different story. My bedroom is a mess, but the worst is not the contents of the dresser drawers, which were tossed all over the room. Nor was it the walk-in closet, where Jeannie had previously found the cash I'd been saving for a second hand car for Jonas, and spent it on drugs. The bed, though, that was a shocker. It was literally ripped to shreds. Pillows, covers, even the mattress had huge rips in it. It's clear she'd released her frustration at not finding another stash in what used to be my hiding place, on what once was our marital bed.

It's funny, standing here looking at the wreckage she left behind; I can almost feel that door slamming shut. Done. Over.

Any guilt I may have felt at the demise of our marriage disappears as I take in the symbolism of the demolished bed.

"Your daughter's room seems mostly intact, aside from some minor mess, but I think you should have a look at your son's room," Barnes says behind me.

I follow him down the hall to where the kids have their bedrooms, separated by the second bathroom. If possible, Jonas' room is even worse than mine. This room is tossed. The mattress is off the bed and every last one of the drawers have been pulled out and emptied. The contents of his closet have been emptied on the floor and his desk chair was shoved in there. Even the posters he had on the wall were torn off, and I'm surprised to see what looks to be a hole in the wall over his bed.

"Mr. Brachio—is your son involved with drugs?"

The question hits me on my ass. I'd recently suspected, but she'd fucking known. His own mother had known even as far back as six months ago. Not only that, she'd known where he hid it. The realization hits me right in the gut. I have to bend over, my hands on my knees, to catch my breath.

I've been so blind.

Pam

Three days after my world has been crushed once again and I'm still breathing.

I'm struggling to focus on Sarah, a single mom of two, who came to Florence House two years ago to escape an abusive boyfriend. She'd managed to get back on her feet, but the ex was still trying to connect with her after years. It's one of the reasons she still comes to me weekly; to help keep her on track.

"How did he get your number?" I ask her, already knowing the answer because Sarah had never been able to completely let him go. She drops her eyes to the floor and fidgets with the scarf she never took off her neck. "Sarah?"

Slowly her eyes come back up, filled with guilt. *Dammit.* "I'm sorry," she whispers, and my heart sinks.

"Don't apologize to me, girl. You don't owe me anything. I'm just worried about you. What happened?"

"It's just that Benji is going through a rough time. He's getting into fights at school, and the other day I caught him beating on his brother. I was at a loss and called him. I never had problems with the boys when we were with him. I thought maybe he could help."

I have to take a deep breath before I blurt out that the reason her oldest is having behavioral issues is because of her ex. The boys watched their mother getting beaten, occasionally getting in the way, and her ex didn't make any bones about slapping the kids around when he felt it was warranted either. No wonder the kids had been quiet and careful around him. They never knew what could set him off.

Christ, I'm getting tired of history repeating itself. Especially now. I know only too well what can happen with children who grow up in a situation like that. Violence can perpetuate violence.

"Tell me what's happening with Benji?" I ask instead. The truth is, I've given her the name of a great child psychologist, but she hasn't followed up.

The remaining half-hour of her session, I have to bite my tongue as Sarah does everything to minimize and justify Benji's tendency to use his twelve-year old fists on anyone who gets in his way. It doesn't matter how many helping hands I reach out, how much I try to get her to see she has become part of the problem by denying what's happening under her nose. I want to shake her, but this woman is so beaten down by life, I've tried everything to build her up, and yet we're still in the same spot we were two years ago.

Another boy who will undoubtedly end up in a place his mother doesn't want him to be; unless he gets some serious help. But other than enforcing on Sarah the importance of getting him help now, before it's too late, there isn't a damn thing I can do.

By the time she leaves, making me all the promises I've heard before, I'm wiped. Emotionally drained. I've done this for almost fifteen years and I'm running on empty. Some of these women pull through on the other side, but some, like Sarah, will slip again and again. It's not like me to believe a man is the solution to anything, but in Sarah's case, I pray that she meets one, a good one, who will use his strength to protect and love her instead of beat on her.

It's five thirty by the time I walk into the kitchen to see what to scrounge up for dinner, when the damn phone rings.

"Florence House."

"Pam?" The familiar soft voice has my heart suddenly pounding at Mach speed.

"Maria, honey?"

"I need help," she whispers and I have to strain to hear. "Anchor Motel."

Two minutes after the call is abruptly ended, I'm in my car heading to South Portland where Google Maps popped up an address for the motel. I reacted without thinking, but now I'm second-guessing the wisdom of heading out alone. I don't know what I'm walking into, I don't really want to alert the police, yet, but some back up may not be a bad idea. There's one person who comes to mind.

Mark Veldman is an ex-cop, who I met through a former resident of the shelter. He'd been involved in a sex trafficking investigation at the time. Nowadays he works with his brother in the family business, which happens to be located on the south side. My fingers have already located his number.

"Vintage Veldman."

"Mark? It's Pam. Listen, I need your help." In a few words I manage to outline my predicament, and he promises to meet me at the motel, insisting I wait in the parking lot should I get there first.

I beat him there, but don't have to wait long before he pulls into the empty spot beside me. I stay in the car and wait for him to come to me. A five foot ten black woman is not easy to miss here in Portland. New York was different, I would disappear in the crowds, but here I still tend to draw a little attention. My generally colorful wardrobe doesn't help either.

Mark leans down when I open my window. "Let me check with the front desk. See what they can tell me."

"Thanks," I say to his already retreating back.

I have my back to the building but keep an eye out in my rearview mirror. The door of the last unit, furthest from the office, opens and I watch as two vaguely familiar kids exit. One of them, for sure, I've seen hanging around the neighborhood with his Seals buddies. Before I can stop myself, I'm out of the car and walking toward the unit. The two kids, who've lit up smokes, lazily watch me coming. Punks. If they think they're impressing me, they've got another thing coming. I've seen and experienced things that would make them crap the baggy jeans, hanging almost to their knees. Idiots.

"What you want, momma?" The kid on the right, the one who hangs around my neighborhood pushes away from the wall, stepping in my path.

"Not yo momma, little man. If I were, I'd slap you upside the head so hard for smoking, they'd hear it ringing in Boston. Now move your bony butt aside." One thing I've learned from my life before I came here; you never cower. Doesn't matter if your heart is trying to squeeze out your throat, you never, ever show fear.

The kid tries to stare me down and makes a move as if to pull something from the small of his back, but I show no reaction. Doesn't mean I don't have one, it just means I'm guessing that's what he's looking for—a reaction. Well, he won't get it from me. I've played this game a little longer than he has.

After an uncomfortably long pause, he finally steps aside and leans back against the wall. Without a word, I walk up to the door and turn the handle, only to have it pull clear from my hand when someone yanks the door open from the inside. I'm shoved to the side as another youngster darts from the room running. I don't pay much attention, I'm too focused on the scene inside the room. Maria is sitting huddled in a corner on the floor beside the bed, with Christian standing over her. It takes less than a second to take in the situation. A collection of beer cans and bottles littered around the room, drug paraphernalia on the nightstand, along with an opened box of condoms. Well thank God for small blessings. But when I look back at Maria and see the state of her clothes—ripped and torn off her body—my relief is short-lived.

Christian has his arm pulled back, ready to hit her.

"You don't wanna do that, boy. Not with me as a witness," I caution him.

I almost expect the gun he pulls on me when he swings around at the sound of my voice. At the wrong end of a barrel is a place I've unfortunately been before as well, but it still doesn't stop me from swallowing hard. Christian's focus drifts over my shoulder and I sense, rather than see, Mark's presence behind me.

Before either Mark or I can react, Christian disappears into the bathroom, slamming the door shut behind him.

"He's going for the window. Take care of her," he says behind me, before I can hear the thud of his footsteps running out the door.

"Oh, sweetie," I croon softly. I sit down on the floor beside Maria, pull the questionable sheet off the bed and cover her up, keeping my arms around her shaking body.

In the distance, I hear the sound of approaching sirens. I lean my head back against the wall as I rock the young girl in my arms, wondering how to tell a loving father that I saw the tear-streaked face of his kid as he ran from a gangbang in progress.

CHAPTER THREE

Dino

"I'm not going."

I lean my head against the doorpost of Jonas' room.

After days of Gina's silent tears and Jonas' complete withdrawal, I'm starting to wonder whether I shouldn't have just lied to them.

I'd been too late to catch them before they got on the bus at school and raced home to intercept them coming off. Jonas started running to the house the moment I finished telling them what happened, and since I had a heartbroken Gina pressed against my chest, I couldn't run after him. Since then he'd basically been holed up in his room, refusing any help with clean up and not talking. I talked—I talked until I was blue in the face. The only time I got a reaction from him was when I broached the subject of drugs. My seventeen-year old son got up in my face.

"I was fourteen, Dad, the first time Mom sent me to the parking lot behind the high school to pick up some *medicine* for her. Where were you?" He'd shoved me in the chest and I let him. Stayed rooted to the spot when he ran up the stairs and slammed his door shut. Then when my little girl walked right up and wrapped her arms around me, comforting *me*—I'd never felt like a bigger failure.

Right now, I'm trying to get Jonas to come with us to Ike and Viv's for a BBQ. It's fucking freezing outside and Viv wants to barbeque. Crazy woman. A year ago, Jonas would've been all over that, although I realize now that probably had more to do with getting out of the house. Jeannie rarely, if ever, came along.

"Daddy!" Gina's voice sounds from downstairs and I take one last look at Jonas, who has turned back to his computer, headphones covering his ears. The message is clear and I don't have it in me to fight. I'd stay home if not for my girl, who needs a little bit of normalcy.

"Do me a favor, Bud? There's a basket of laundry on the coffee table that needs to be put away." I know he hears me when his eyes throw daggers in my direction.

"Coming!" I yell down to Gina as I back out of the room. Jonas doesn't even move. It's as if I don't exist. Straightening my face, I head downstairs where Gina is hopping from leg to leg, eager to get going. "Hang on, baby girl, let me grab the salads."

-

"Jonas not with you?" Viv says, when she opens the door with the baby on her hip and looks over my shoulder.

"Can't pry him away from his computer game," I reply, but from the look Viv shoots me I know she's not buying.

"I'm sorry." Her soft voice carries a world of understanding.

I watch as she hands Francessca to Gina. The smile on Gina's face is enough to crack my heart open a little wider. Not so long ago, I'd been able to make my baby girl smile like that.

"It'll be alright," Viv mumbles as she grabs the containers from my hands and motions me to follow her inside.

Until I started working at The Skipper, donkey's years ago, I'd made it a point not to socialize too much with work people. I'd seen too many personal issues creep into the work place and vice versa. It was rarely a good idea. But over the years, stepping into the kitchen at the pub has felt more like coming home than going to work. A place where I felt more connected than I did in my own house. I used to blame it on Jeannie, but I'm starting to realize it was likely as much my fault as hers. Not normally one to mince words with anyone, I avoided the problems at home.

"Beer?" Ike is standing by the open fridge in the kitchen.

"Yup."

Bottle in hand, I enter the crowded living room, my eyes drawn outside where a group of guys are standing around a smoking BBQ, drinking and laughing. Nuts. Their breath fogs against the cold outside air, yet none of the fuckers is wearing a coat. I'm still wearing mine, so with a general nod in the direction of the room, I beeline it to the sliding doors and head out to join them.

"Are you actually minding the grill or are you just trying to stay warm?"

"Dino!" Gunnar says when he turns at the sound of my voice. "Watching the meat, of course," he adds with a grin. "Real men don't get cold." I roll my eyes, taking a swig of my cold beer.

"Are the kids with you? Dex's been waiting for Jonas to get here."

Dexter, Emmy, and Caden are Gunnar's kids. Dex is the middle child and the same age as Gina, but always gravitates toward Jonas. Mutual love for gaming.

"He's home."

"Angry?" Gunnar asks, turning away from the group a little. He was there when Jonas tore through the house to find his room in shambles. He stayed while I tried to talk to the kid, but he slammed the door in my face.

"Anger I can deal with. I've seen flashes of it, but mostly he's detached, and I have no fucking clue how to handle that," I admit.

"Talk to Pam."

Gunnar's the second person to suggest that and maybe I should bite that bullet. As much as we can barely stand to be around each other, I have to admit she's damn good at what she does.

"She here?" I ask, looking inside to see if I can spot her.

"Not yet. One of her girls is in the hospital. She told Syd she'd try to pop in."

Syd is Sydney, Gunnar's wife and a good friend of Viv and Pam's. Pam has a lot to do with getting those two girls through some pretty tough times. Just like she's recently done for Ruby, another girl who was under her care and ended up working at The Skipper. It seems to be a theme. I'd put my life on the line for any of those three women. I have great respect for them, for what they struggled to overcome. It stands in such stark contrast with my own wife, who had a good life, for whom I would've done anything, but who chose to numb herself with drugs and throw her kids and her marriage away.

After shooting the shit with the guys for a bit, I head back in to check on my girl. I find her in the basement, hanging out with the other kids around the TV.

"How are you doing, Princess?" I ask her quietly, kneeling beside the couch. I lean over to give her a kiss on her head.

"Okay. Dad, can I stay over at Emmy and Dex's tonight?"

"Not sure that's a good idea, honey. Tomorrow is a normal school day."

"But I can go to school with them, Dex is in my class, remember?"

A responsible parent would nip that in the bud right away, but the barely concealed excitement on my little girl's face is something I haven't seen in a long time.

"Let me think about it. I'll talk to Syd, okay?" Gina's almost bounces out of her seat at my answer. I smile and straighten up.

"No promises, though," I caution her, but she knows as well as I do the decision is basically made.

"Thanks, Daddy." The smile she directs at me this time almost sends me back to my knees.

"Love you, baby girl."

"Love you too, Daddy."

Christ. I have to get out of here before I lose it.

Halfway up the stairs, I almost bump into Pam. With my head bent, I didn't notice her coming down.

"Hey." My voice sounds thick as I force sound past the lump in my throat. I notice her stepping back up one tread and actually have to tilt my head back a little to see her face. I'm tall at six five, but Pam's no midget, either. She's got to be close to six feet tall, which is why she can look down at me from her current vantage point. I fight the childish urge to take one step up so I can look down at her.

She has that same arrogant look on her face whenever she spots me. This time, though, her face softens when she looks at me. She actually looks approachable. Pam is a stunning woman. A true amazon, with one of the most luxurious bodies I've seen, and a beautiful, almost chiseled face, even more pronounced by her short-cropped hair, but with stone-cold eyes. I always thought her attributes were wasted on a man-hater like her, but that doesn't mean I didn't notice.

"I was looking for you." Her voice, a rich, deep alto, actually gives me a physical reaction.

"Found me."

"Clearly," she shoots back. "Can we talk for a minute?"

I'm surprised when she doesn't wait for my answer, but instead turns on her heels and starts walking up the stairs, her enticing round ass swaying from side to side. Mesmerized by the sight, I follow her.

She leads me right into the garage off the kitchen and shuts the door behind me. Intrigued, and a little on edge, I wait for her to speak. She seems nervous, wringing her hands and pacing back and forth. Very unlike her.

"Viv told me what happened at your house," she starts, and I automatically fold my arms in front of my body. A move she immediately picks up on. "Don't be pissed. She's worried about you and with good reason."

"How is that?" I snap, in full defense mode now, wondering where the hell she gets off sticking her nose in.

"Dino—please…it's not going to be easy what I have to tell you, and you're making it worse. Please trust me when I say I want to help."

I'm fucking shocked; to say the least. And more than a little worried that she'd feel the need to say *please* twice in one sentence.

In a nonverbal response, I unfold my arms and let them hang by my side.

Pam

"Did you hear about one of my girls ending up in the hospital?"

I've just come from the hospital, where Maria is being held in the psych ward for at least three days. Apparently, when she'd mentioned to her boyfriend she wanted to go back to the shelter, he felt it necessary to punish her by using her for some sick initiation ritual. The experience was devastating to her, and between the attending at the ER and myself, we felt it was for her own safety that she stay in psychiatric care for the short term.

"Gunnar mentioned something," Dino grumbles, but his eyes never waver from mine.

"She's been involved with a gang called the Seals, you know of them?"

"Heard of them, yes."

"Maria came to Florence House a while ago. She'd been beaten by her boyfriend, who happens to be the new leader of the Seals. She disappeared four days ago, and yesterday afternoon I received a call she was in trouble. I drove over to the Anchor Motel on the south side, where she said she was, and—"

"Say what?" Dino interrupts, grabbing me by the arm. "You went alone? Are you nuts?"

Something stirs me at the anger in his voice. It gets my blood boiling for two completely different reasons.

"I did not," I bite off, twisting my arm from his shovel-sized hands. "I called Mark. I'm not an idiot." I didn't bother telling him that calling Mark had been a last minute decision, I'd already been charging out like the damn cavalry.

"Well, thank fuck for small favors," he rumbles in that deep voice of his. The only thing keeping me from punching him in the face is the fact that any second now, I'll be breaking his heart.

"Anyway…I was waiting for Mark to check with the front desk when I spotted a couple of kids coming out of a room, lighting up. I had a feeling and headed over there, when the door opened and a third kid came out and ran off."

Without even hearing me say it, Dino seems to sense what is coming because, if possible, the massive man appears to be shrinking in front of my eyes. "Jonas was crying, Dino. Your boy came out of that room, but he was running away. Whatever went on there, he obviously didn't want any part of it."

"Was she raped?" his voice is faint.

"Yes, but—" Before I can clarify anything, Dino's fist slams through the wall to the side of the door. "Please, listen to me. He never touched her. He couldn't. Maria told me." I step forward, wanting to put a supporting hand on his shoulder but before I can, he turns around, his face a mask of pain.

"Tell me," he says, not even making an effort to hide his tears, his mouth set in a straight line. "Tell me everything."

The door to the mudroom opens and Ike's head pokes in, taking in the scene as well as the hole in his drywall.

"Everything alright?" He directs the question at me.

"Give us a minute? Please?" I plead with my eyes. With a nod and one last look at Dino, he pulls the door shut again.

"Christian, her boyfriend, thought it was a good idea to make Maria part of the initiation of a few new gang members. Apparently they had to watch and take turns in a gang rape."

I watch as the big man sinks down on the small step, his bald head in his hands, and my heart aches for him. I understand his pain.

"Maria says Jonas objected from the moment the three kids entered the hotel room, but Christian threatened to cut her up if they didn't participate. Apparently when Christian and the other two kids were done, Jonas couldn't go through with it. He ran out just as I walked in."

I sink down on my haunches in front of Dino, my hands on his knees. "He's a troubled kid, but he's not a bad kid, Dino. Let me help."

"Can you?" His ravaged face comes up and his eyes bore into mine.

"I sure as hell am gonna give it my best," I tell him honestly.

"The police?"

"I haven't given them a full statement yet, but I will. I'm gonna give them all I know, but I wanted you to be prepared. Whatever happens, I promise I'll do my best by your boy."

The tears that I've held in finally spill over. I literally ache for this man, who doesn't know that this is only the beginning of the agonizing path he's forced to walk.

"Good," he says, his voice cracking. "No more excuses. We're gonna do this right." Almost distractedly, he brushes at the tears on my cheek.

I carefully suggest to him we both go talk to his son and convince him to turn himself in. After a pregnant pause, he gives in.

"Come on. Let's get cleaned up," I say, trying to get up gracefully, despite my creaking knees. I reach to grab Dino's hand and pull him up on his feet. His massive body standing so close makes me feel unusually small. Most men I can look straight in the eye but with Dino I have to tilt my head back. I'm not used to that; for the first time I consider whether that is maybe part of the reason I generally bristle in his presence. My size and my attitude are usually large enough to ward off anyone I choose to, but for some reason I think neither of those do much to scare off Dino.

Shaking once to clear my head, I move past him to open the door and still holding onto his hand, I drag him past a slightly confused Ike, up the stairs to the bathroom. I scour through the small linen closet and running the tap, I wet two washcloths with cold water before turning back around. The look on his face is intense as I hand him one and use the other to scrub at my face—and hide my blush. He's always seen straight to the core of me.

From the corner of my eye, I see him mopping his own face, but his eyes never waver. They stay focused on me.

"And who looks after you?" he suddenly asks, instantly freezing my motions and with one simple question, stripping a layer of protection from my soul.

CHAPTER FOUR

Dino

The only good part of this day is my baby girl's face when I tell her she can stay the night with her friends.

Gunnar catches me coming down the stairs behind Pam, a worried look on his face. All I tell him is that I need to talk to my son and ask if Gina would be okay staying at their place.

"As long as you need," he simply says, clamping a hand on my shoulder. "We'll take care of her. We'll swing by your place tomorrow morning to pick up her stuff. You take care of your boy."

Just like that I'm leading Pam, in her car, through the streets of Portland. My house is dark by the time we get there, Pam pulling in behind me in the driveway.

Jonas doesn't have a car. He wanted one, and if not for his mother taking off with the money I'd put aside for that purpose, he would've had one by now. Luckily we've got a pretty decent public transit system that gets him around. He'd taken the bus to his part-time job at the Subway on Brown Street, but he'd quit shortly after Jeannie left.

The house is quiet when I open the door, clicking on the lights before closing the door behind Pam. Weird—having her in my house. I've never really had anyone over here, except Gunnar a few times over the years. I quietly observe Pam as she takes in my home. Nothing much to see. For the sake of the kids I never changed anything, but now that I'm looking at the place through new eyes, I notice the lack of personality and the mess.

"Jonas?" I call upstairs, but I already know there won't be an answer. Still, I go up to check his room.

"Flown the coop?" Pam's voice greets me as I come down the stairs. She's sitting on the couch in the living room, folding the clean laundry I'd asked Jonas to put away. I'm not even sure she's aware she's doing it.

"So it would appear." I'm not sure what to do with myself and start picking up discarded shoes, dirty dishes, Gina's magazines, a hairbrush, and more random items that are left around the room.

"Why don't you sit?" Pam says calmly and suddenly I'm pissed. Angry at Jonas, angry at Jeannie, and angry at Pam—but most of all, I'm angry at myself for not stepping in before he got himself into trouble. *Jesus.* I'm still doing it; using milder euphemisms to describe the gang rape my son was a part of. I sit down heavily on the coffee table and grab my head.

"I can't even…" I start, but can't finish the words. Pam places a comforting hand on my back, but I'm suddenly sick to my stomach.

I make it to the downstairs bathroom just in time to puke up my guts. I fucking hate throwing up, especially when my stomach has little in it to begin with. The instant headache burning behind my eyes is not helping, and the cold water I splash on my face only provides the bare minimum of relief.

A good fifteen minutes have passed by the time I walk into the kitchen, finding Pam rummaging through my fridge. I wasn't really expecting her to stick around, so I'm a little surprised.

"You need something to eat," she says, noticing me standing in the doorway before she turns away, cracking an egg over a small bowl.

"Not sure if that's a good idea," I point out, watching her as she pulls two pieces of bread from the toaster and dips them in the bowl. My stomach feels hollow and raw, and I'm pretty sure I won't be able to eat a thing. Pam throws me a look over her shoulder.

"Trust me on this."

The smell of the French toast she is making almost has me running for the bathroom again, but when she slides the plate in front of me, the toast topped with a thin skim of butter and a light sprinkle of cinnamon and sugar, I take a bite anyway.

We eat the meager meal in silence, standing across from each other at the counter, and I have to admit, the food seems to settle well. I glance at her when she grabs our plates and runs them under the tap before stacking them in the dishwasher. I don't think I've ever spent this much time with Pam without exchanging barbs or dirty looks.

"Why?" flies from my mouth before I can put a lid on my thoughts. She turns to me, confusion on her face.

"Why what?"

"You're being nice. It's…unusual. Confusing," I admit, watching a deep blush stain her cheeks. Now that's something new, too. The Pam I know doesn't blush, or embarrass. It makes her seem more human. I've always known there is a big heart in there, how could there not be? It throws me off to have it on display in my kitchen. We've been like dogs on opposite sides of a fence, snarling at each other in passing, so this is unfamiliar.

"I know, I…"

Just as she's about to answer, the front door slams open, and I stick my head into the hallway to see Jonas come in. He spots me and instantly moves toward the stairs.

"Don't even think about it," I warn him. "Living room, boy." I walk toward him, prepared to drag him there physically if I have to, but he's not moving at all. His panicked look is focused behind me, where I can feel Pam stepping up, putting that calming hand back between my shoulder blades. Jonas quickly glances my way before focusing on Pam again, his face morphing from fear back into the sullen scowl he usually wears these days.

"No way," he says with much more bravado than I think he feels, but when he swings around to head straight back out the door, I grab him by the scruff of his neck.

"No, buddy." I soften the firm grasp I have on the back of his neck with the sound of my voice. "No running from this one."

Pushing him ahead of me, I walk into the living room and sit him down on the couch, taking a seat on the coffee table myself. I see Pam taking a seat on the other side of the couch, effectively boxing him in.

He knows it; the fear is back in his eyes. I struggle between wanting to give him a reassuring hug and wanting to unleash my anger on him. I don't know where to start. I'm looking at my child's guilty face and it takes the breath out of me.

Pam instinctively takes the lead, drawing Jonas' attention and giving me a chance to compose myself.

"Four months ago, Maria came to the shelter I run," Pam starts in a calm voice, and Jonas immediately drops his head and shrinks back in the cushions. "She had been badly beaten and someone had used her chest to put out cigarettes. Twice Maria left the shelter to go and meet up with the man who did that to her, and both times she came back bruised and beaten. This was her third time, and I wasn't going to take her back, but when I heard her voice on the phone last night, I couldn't stay away. The fear, the agony…I just couldn't give up on her. I'm so glad I went."

My heart is pounding in my chest as Pam's voice calmly lays the groundwork. I want to rage and accuse, but I recognize what she is doing is much more effective. Jonas' head is still bent, but I can see him blinking furiously, his hands restlessly rubbing his legs.

"Maria grew up as the only child of a single mom. She never knew a father and what she knew about boys is what she learned at home. And that wasn't much good. Everything she's learned since has been worse. She's barely older than you…and not that much older than your sister."

"I didn't touch her…" Jonas' voice cracks, and I realize Pam not once had to point the finger at him. Not once did she mention his name or blame him, not a word was said about rape, but it was clear he felt the responsibility clearer than if she had. "I didn't want to. I told him no—told him I wanted out—but…he was going to hurt her."

"He did hurt her; he raped her. And so did those two other boys." Pam's words have the impact of a gunshot. I can see Jonas' body jerk in response. Then she softens her tone again. "And so did you, Jonas. You may not have been an active participant, but you were a participant nonetheless."

That is when my son breaks.

Pam

I got through.

The small moment of triumph was quickly dulled by the sobbing man-child sitting beside me. I have to remind myself this is only the first step, but I'm hopeful. I have to be hopeful we got him in time. If there's even the slightest chance of pulling this kid back from the dark turn he has taken, I will fight for it with everything I've got. I only wish I'd had it in me fifteen, twenty years ago.

Ignoring the sharp pain in my chest, I look up at Dino, who is staring at his boy with the kind of desperate love parents feel for a child who is lost. I recognize the guilt when he turns his haunted eyes to me.

"You realize I have to tell the police I saw you," I point out to Jonas, and I watch as reality hits him. Harsh, but necessary. He launches himself off the couch, but Dino is prepared.

I knew he would be. He grabs his son's hand and yanks him back down on the couch, grabbing Jonas' face in those big hands of his. With his forehead against the boy's, he speaks to him softly; "I said no running, boy." Leaning back a little he waits until Jonas' eyes meet his. "What happened…what you took part in? I won't lie, it makes me sick to my stomach, but son?" Dino lightly shakes his head. "I know you. I've seen the promise of the man you can be. You can't undo what's done, but you can do the right thing moving forward. I swear to God I will stand by you every step of the way."

I need a moment. I get up and leave the room, head straight for the bathroom, and lock the door behind me. Leaning over the sink, I splash cold water on my face, and fight off the urge to give in to my own emotions. Wiping away the single tear that managed to escape, I steel my back and head back to where Dino had moved to sit beside his son, his arm slung around his shoulders.

"No better time than the present," I announce, causing both of them to turn to face me.

-

It's three in the morning by the time Dino drops me off at home, where to my surprise, my car is sitting in the driveway.

"Ike," Dino says, noticing my reaction.

I'm blessed with the friends I've made. With a sidelong glance at Dino, a warm feeling sneaks up on me. I'd not considered him part of that circle I keep small for a reason, but this small sign of caring has me reconsider. I'm not one prone to letting emotion guide me, so I'm not quite sure what moves me to let it now, but I lean over the center console and give him a kiss on his cheek.

"Thank you."

Energy crackles in the air as he turns his stormy eyes on me, those big hands that were cradling his son's face not that long ago, now coming up to cradle mine. His mouth comes down suddenly; his hard kiss on my lips is almost bruising. I just sit there like a moron, my heart pounding so loud, I'm sure he can hear it. Even when he pulls back and whispers, "Thank you," only a breath away from my lips, I can still feel the charge bouncing over my skin.

I'm still dazed when he walks me to my door, tells me he'll call me, and leaves me with a kiss on my forehead. Unsure what to make of that, or of my own reaction to it, I push it aside and instead focus on the past few hours we spent at the police station.

-

I'd had the presence of mind to give Mark a quick call, asking him if he would mind meeting us there. An ex-Portland cop himself, I thought perhaps he could be of support. I've had enough dealings with the police force to have my own connections and go-to people, but I figured it wouldn't hurt to have another familiar, supportive, face there, both for Jonas and his father. Mark and Dino know each other, and so after the initial surprise to find Mark waiting for us, Dino quickly seemed relieved to have someone there who understood the process and could make introductions.

I was first to give my statement, and a very demure and fearful Jonas had been guided into the room after, his burdened father right behind him. With Jonas only seventeen, the detective had suggested Dino be in the room with him for the initial questioning. I'd stayed out in the hallway, declining Mark's offer to drive me home. Four hours later, Jonas had come out of the room, and with only a quick glance in my direction, was lead away down the hall by an officer. Then Dino appeared looking absolutely drained, the detective behind him with a hand on his shoulder.

"Let him stay here tonight. It won't hurt him to learn where he could end up should he continue on this path. Tomorrow we'll talk to the DA and work out a plan where to go from here. He's done the right thing, Mr. Brachio, but I'm not gonna lie—it won't be easy. I'll call you tomorrow morning when I know more, but for now, head home and try to get some rest. We'll be in touch." With that Detective Hotchkins walked off in the direction Jonas disappeared in, leaving Dino looking lost in the hallway.

Again, that pain in my chest stabbed, watching this big man torn between his need to do what's best for his son, by letting him feel his responsibilities, or to whisk him far away from here in an effort to protect him. I recognized that feeling; that's why I walked up and put my arms around him. For a moment, he just stood there, but then his arms slid around me, hands fisting in the back of my coat and his big head buried itself in my neck.

So proud, so strong, and yet brought to his knees by the weight on his shoulders. It about killed me.

The drive home had been quiet. Each of us lost in our own thoughts. It startled me when he spoke.

"The shelter or your house?"

"My house," I say after a moment's hesitation. I'd left my car at Ike and Viv's earlier and hopped in with Dino.

-

Hanging up my coat in the closet, I walk straight into my kitchen. Middle of the night, after only a single slice of French toast for dinner and a horrible cup of coffee at the police station, my stomach needs something.

Half an hour, and half a sandwich, later, I crawl into bed. The clock on my nightstand says it's close to four. I turn off the light, hoping I can catch a few hours.

Five minutes later, I click the light back on. It's no use; I can't stop thinking about Dino. Did he get home okay? He's alone in that big house; should I have stayed with him? I'm not sure why I'm obsessing over this, but I know I won't be able to stop until I know he's all right.

I scroll through my contact list and am grateful to find I have his number, even though I've never used it before. It rings three times, four, then five and I'm about to hang up when it's answered.

"No, I can't sleep either," he says, without waiting for me to identify myself.

Uncanny, how in tune he seems to be. The empathy he's shown over the years is the main reason I've kept my distance. He sees more than a normal person would, or should. He's been dead on with his concerns and care for three women I know of: Syd, Viv, and only recently, Ruby, guessing well before anyone else knew, the demons haunting them. That's why; my baggage is mine and mine alone. I've taken great care not to let my old life bleed into my current life, but Dino has the ability to bridge that gap. He's already shown it in the way he'll look at me sometimes. I've been snapping at him since the first time he spoke to me. Not because I don't like him, but because he terrifies me. With good reason, since with the single question he asked me last night, he showed me he could see all of me.

"Pam?"

"Sorry, I'm…yeah, I just wanted to make sure you got in okay," I stumble a bit.

"Thank you again," he says, his deep rumbling voice jagged. "I don't know what I would've done without you."

Irritated at the emotional response he is able to evoke, I'm a little more brusque than I mean to be.

"Nothing any half decent human being wouldn't do." I already regret the tone before the words leave my mouth, but then I hear his soft chuckle over the line.

"There she is." Amusement laces his voice. "Was wondering when my biscuit would come out."

"Your biscuit?"

"A crunchy outside, difficult to butter up, but worth every effort once her full flavor hits your palate."

I have no answer to that. His assessment both scares me and excites me. Such is the danger of Francis 'Dino' Brachio.

"Night, Dino," I blurt out instead.

"Night, Biscuit," I hear him whisper right before he disconnects the call.

CHAPTER FIVE

Dino

"What are you doing here?"

Viv is standing in the doorway, her hands on her hips, glaring at me.

The truth is, I'm going crazy at home. Gunnar forced me to take some time to sort my family out, which was a joke. Jeannie had been given the option to go to rehab, which she took, but she disappeared after three days and is currently in the wind again. Jonas spent two nights in total in jail, mostly because it took that long for the cops to pick up Christian Neve for rape and aggravated assault. With Jonas' help they were able to identify the other two who'd been there, and they'd been taken in as well.

Barnes assured Jonas that Christian would not likely be released any time soon. The guy already had a track record with the justice system, and the judge remanded him into custody until his trial.

In the week since he's been home, Jonas has barely strung a single sentence together. Before, at least we'd communicate, mostly by arguing, but now there is nothing. Not a spark, not a flicker of interest. He lets me drive him and Gina to school without complaints, and at home, he loses himself in his gaming. He barely surfaces to eat.

I've thought about taking the kids away for a short holiday, but I figure it's probably better to stick to a normal routine.

Christmas is a month away and they'll have some time off around then. First Christmas without their mom here. Maybe I'll take them away then.

"Had to get out of the house," I tell Viv, who's made her way to stand beside me. "Kids are in school and all I do is fucking twiddle my thumbs until it's time to pick them up. I'd rather do something."

"Fair enough," she says, tying her apron. She pulls a knife from the block, and runs it over the steel, while I pull out a cutting board for her.

Kitchen prep is repetitive work, but there is something comforting about it. Gratifying even, watching the bins fill with neatly cleaned and diced vegetables. Cuts of meat neatly trimmed and ready for use stacked up.

Today is Thursday, which usually means we have a special that has to stretch. I'm planning cabbage roll soup and fresh baked pesto bread. Viv get's started on cutting the cabbage, we need a shitload, and I get going on my yeast starter for the bread.

We work in companionable silence, like we've done for years, when Viv speaks up.

"I'm not going to ask you how things are— I'm guessing not great— but I saw Pam the other day, and she mentioned she hadn't heard from you."

"I called her," I say defensively. A knee-jerk reaction because I know damn well I've been avoiding her. The one time I called her was to fill her in on Jonas. She'd offered to come talk to him, and I'd cowardly told her I'd give her a call, which I hadn't.

Viv isn't buying it either. She's looking at me with an eyebrow raised.

"You guys seriously need to get over whatever the hell is going on. Something's gotta change, 'cause being in the same room with you two is exhausting with the constant acrimony," she complains before turning back to her workstation, hacking at the poor cabbage.

I'm not about to tell her that things have already changed, which is exactly why I've avoided calling. Before things may have been acrimonious, but they were comfortably familiar. Now? Fuck, now I don't know what they are. All I know is that I shouldn't have kissed her. It felt so good to have Pam waiting for me when Jonas was taken to lock up, to feel her strong arms keep me grounded. When she was about to get out of my car after I brought her home, I reacted.

Not like I've not noticed what a beautiful woman she is, because I have. She's also strong, independent, and so damn sure of herself all the time. A bit intimidating. A stunning black amazon in comparison to my petite, blonde, and very dependent wife. Guess I never allowed my thoughts to go there. Now I can't seem to keep my fucking mind off her.

So yeah, not going to elaborate to Viv on that, since I don't know what the fuck to do with it myself.

"I'll call."

Viv turns to me with a big smile on her face. "Good," she says. "I think she could really help. Her morning group session should be almost done."

"Said I'd call, girl. Don't fucking push it." I glare at her, but Viv being Viv, she just smiles back, completely unimpressed.

-

"What's for dinner, Dad?"

Gina dumps her bag on the couch the moment we walk in the door and beelines it into the kitchen, without waiting for my answer.

I'd left work at three thirty, getting to the school just in time to see Jonas and Gina walking out. Gina's face lifted a bit when she spotted me, but Jonas' head was down. It stayed that way, even when two of his classmates held him up, boys that had been to our house a few times last year, but Jonas just shrugged and shook his head, resuming his path to the car.

Once in the car, I'd tried to engage him in conversation, but he sat quietly in the back, after not even attempting to fight Gina for the front seat.

Jonas comes in behind me as I follow Gina into the kitchen. He grabs a bottle of water from the fridge and I hear his footsteps going upstairs. Back to the sanctuary of his room. I can't hold back the deep sigh and Gina, hearing it, turns around and wraps her arms around my waist.

"He'll be okay, right, Daddy?"

Poor kid. Her eyes are big and full of trust as she looks up at me, like I have all the answers in the universe. I don't. I don't have any answers, but I stroke the hair from her face and press my lips to her forehead.

"Everything is gonna be fine, Princess," I reassure her anyway, because even if I don't quite see it just yet myself, I'm determined not to fail my little girl, too. I'll do whatever it takes to live up to her faith in me.

That's why, after feeding her some of the cabbage soup and bread I brought home, and bringing a bowl upstairs for Jonas, who doesn't even look up from his computer screen when I set it down on his desk, I close myself in my bedroom with my phone.

"Hey," I respond a bit awkwardly when she answers her phone.

"Everything okay?"

The rich tone of her voice used to grate on me. Or maybe it was something else I felt then, because right now it's just soothing.

"I don't know," I admit. "He's home, he's going to school, he's not confrontational, but I still feel he's slipping away."

"Can I make a suggestion?" Her voice is hesitant.

"It's why I called you." She chuckles softly before responding.

"Your son responded well to my direct approach. I'm not really a touchy feely therapist, and to be honest, I don't think that would work anyway. Prefer not to waste time beating around the bush, if I can help it. Jonas, much like you, feels deeply but has trouble or is uncomfortable expressing." I want to argue with that, but she continues before I can. "I'd like to build a rapport with him, meet with him individually a few times, but at some point it might be helpful to see you together. I get the sense there's stuff between you that needs to be resolved. I want to see if we can't throw all that crap on the table and work through them one by one."

Therapy. It's always been a bit of a dirty word to me since Jeannie and I tried some counseling, years back. Jeannie had loved it, probably because of the constant *there-there* she was getting from the therapist. I'd sat through a few sessions, said maybe ten words in total, and was ignored the rest of the time. He ended up suggesting medication to make Jeannie *feel better*. Feeling better became the theme for her and snowballed into a substance addiction.

"Okay. I'll talk to Jonas."

"That didn't sound very convincing," Pam chuckles.

"Let's just say, if it were anybody but you, I'd have given you a different answer," I tell her truthfully.

"I think I'll take that as a compliment." Her voice, if possible, drops even deeper, and I force myself to picture her behind a desk in an office instead of in bed.

"Intended it to be," I give her, sounding gruff.

Pam

I hang up the phone, wondering what the hell just happened.

I'll be the first to admit I'm pretty damn rusty, but that sounded an awful lot like flirting. Me, the decades-long queen of evasion when it comes to anything that reeks of male interest. I've not encountered the best of examples when it comes to the opposite sex in my own life and spend all of my time helping women get out from under more like that. Don't get me wrong, I love men, or at least the promise of them, it's that the good ones I've come to know just aren't for me.

I thought that's were Dino fit. In the box labeled 'not suitable.' Of course, that was when I thought he was happily married. He's been part of my circle of friends, even though he always rubbed me the wrong way. I'm starting to think it's not so much him rubbing me the wrong way as it is him rubbing me just right.

I've had lovers over the years. A few men, who had no interest for one reason or another to get attached, but appreciated the occasional physical release. The last guy called me one day to cancel, saying he had met someone just that day he could envision a future with. He apologized and explained he wouldn't be able to pursue her in good faith if we still had a standing arrangement. Three months later, I received a brief email from him, letting me know the woman had just agreed to marry him. That was about four years ago and I haven't seen anyone else since.

I wasn't hung up on him. In fact, I was happy to see him find love. I just don't believe in it for me.

Shaking any thoughts of lovers, ex or prospective, from my head, I push my chair back and get up. I have a group starting in ten minutes and need to make a pot of tea.

Maria walks into the kitchen, just as I'm putting the huge teapot on a tray with six mugs, her face strained. This will be her first group session since she got out of the hospital, and although we've talked quite a bit since, I know she's nervous about the reaction of the other women. The timid woman is standing before me, her fingers restlessly plucking at the hem of her shirt, and her teeth worrying her bottom lip.

"Good. You can help me bring tea in." I point at the plate of brownies. "If you could grab that?"

"I'm not feeling too good," she mumbles, and I know she's looking for an out. Ignoring the tray, I walk up to her and take her face in my hands.

"Like a Band-Aid, girl. Best way to deal with things you're not looking forward to is to just dive in and get it done."

Her eyes water as she looks at me, the plea visible on her still bruised face. "They won't understand," she whispers. I chuckle softly at that.

"Are you kidding me? Those women are all in a better position to understand than anyone else. They've been there. They know."

Maria has avoided any interaction with the other residents, taking meals in her tiny room, and spending most of the past few days since she's been back lying on her bed, watching the small grainy TV on her dresser. I don't want to push her, but at the same time, I know the longer she waits facing the others, the harder it'll be.

"Let's do this." I let her go, resolutely pick up the tray, and start walking to the door, keeping my fingers crossed I'll hear her fall into step behind me. I'm already halfway down the hall when I hear the shuffle of feet behind me, catching up. I'd pump my fist, but I have a heavy-ass tray in my hands, so I smile instead. Big.

"Fucking asshole!" I hear when I walk into the room and my head snaps up. Marianne, the oldest of our residents at sixty-three, a one time country club wife and mother of two adult children, jumps up from her chair, her eyes focused behind me. *Oh boy.* I've never heard a single swear word from her lips. I have the uncontrollable urge to giggle at the short, gray-haired, normally demure woman with her hands on her hips and thunder on her face. I feel Maria close in behind me, using my body to shield her, but Marianne is not done. She walks right up to us, her eyes never wavering from her target. "Let me look at you," she says in a much softer voice.

I helpfully step out of her way, set the tray on the table, and take the brownies from Maria, leaving her exposed. The moment she has her hands free, Marianne reaches out and puts her arms around the girl. I try to ignore them while I pour tea, even though my protective instincts are on high alert.

A group like this, however small, can be volatile. Put a bunch of women in a room, and normally, I'd be the one running out the door. Still, abuse groups are on the whole a safe place, and the support of other women is a large part of healing.

Her arm still looped around Maria, Marianne guides her to the two empty seats. They sit down, but Marianne firmly holds onto Maria's hand. It warms my heart. I wasn't at all sure that she wasn't going to run at some point, but looking at her now, staring down at the much older hand clutching hers, I'm thinking perhaps she'll stick around. As incongruous as these two appear at first sight, the street kid and the country club matron, I have a feeling they'll be good for each other. Maria didn't have a very nurturing childhood and little experience with kindness. Marianne has been lost since leaving her marriage. Her two sons, both military men like their father, to whom she devoted her life, have easily cut her from their lives. Ironic, isn't it? She waited all this time, subjected herself to the soul crippling verbal and physical abuse doled out by her husband, all for the sake of the kids. The same kids who resolutely shut the door on her when she finally felt strong enough to choose herself.

I expected to be exhausted by the end of the session, but instead I feel invigorated. With my emotions all over the place in recent days, it's good to feel my own purpose reaffirmed at the sight of Maria and Marianne leaving the room side by side.

When I carry the tray into the kitchen, Brenda is standing by the stove, working on dinner.

"How did it go?" she asks when I peek over her shoulder to see what's cooking. I'm suddenly hungry.

"Well. It went well. Marianne stepped up right away and seemed to take Maria under her wing."

"No shit?" Brenda turns a surprised face my way.

"I know. She swore when she saw Maria's face. I don't think I've ever heard a single swear word from her lips since she's been here," I chuckle, thinking about the timid, perfectly groomed middle-class lady, who barely ever spoke above a whisper. "Shocked the shit out of me. She took one look at the girl and *fucking asshole* came flying out her mouth."

"Epic," Brenda says on a smile. "Wish I'd been a fly on the wall."

Before I can say anything, the phone in my pocket starts vibrating. The display shows a familiar number. "I'll be in my office," I quickly tell Brenda, answering the call as I go.

Five minutes later when I hang up, all the positive vibes I built up today are gone and a heavy feeling settles back on my shoulders. Fifteen years I've been living under a cloud. Longer, if I'm honest, but the past fifteen years I've not been able to do anything about it. Not a damn thing. I've focused all my energy on helping others where I could, because I had no way of helping myself.

I'm getting tired, though—and with every new disappointment, I can feel myself eroding more underneath the hard outer shell.

I grab my coat and stick my head around the kitchen door.

"I've got to head out. Have you got things here?"

Brenda turns from her perch at the stove. "Yup. I've got it," she assures me.

Outside the cold wind hits me as I struggle to get into my car. The bite on my skin an almost welcome sensation to focus on instead of the numbness I was feeling. Once behind the wheel, I pause for minute, not sure where I should go. I don't really want to go home, where there is nothing waiting for me.

Resolutely I turn my car in the opposite direction. I need nourishment, not only for my stomach, but also to fill the gaping hole in my chest. Food for the soul. There's one place I know I can find both.

The Skipper.

CHAPTER SIX

Dino

"Bud, can I come in?"

I don't usually stand outside my kids' doors and knock, but I don't want Jonas already irritated when I talk to him.

A surprised Jonas opens the door and steps out of the way. It makes me think of something I've heard before; if you're looking for change, start with you. Guess it worked, because Jonas isn't showing his customary scowl or blatant dismissal.

"I'm not sure where to start," I tell him honestly, as he sits back down in his chair, but instead of turning to the computer, he stays focused on me when I sit down on the edge of his bed. "Things have not been good here. Not just you." I lift my hand defensively when I see him gear up for a response. "Things with your mother…I'm not sure when it even started, but it's not been good for a while."

"No shit," I hear him mumble.

"Right. Anyway, I can't change what got us to this point, but I sure as hell can change what happens going forward. Not now, but at some point we're going to have to hash out all the crap that's been piling up." I'm about to ignore Jonas' derisive snort, but change my mind. "That right there? That's why I think we need help. You're pissed at me and I get that, and frankly, I'm pissed with you, too. We need someone to help us sort through that shit and get this damn family back on track."

The scowl that hadn't been there earlier is now firmly etched on my boy's face.

"Bud" I plead softly. "I love you. I can't sit by and let this go."

"You did fine before," he bites and I've got to admit, it hurts. Because it's true.

"And that's why I can't now," I push on. "Pam offered to help sort through this. I'd like you to talk to her."

"The social worker chick? Why?"

"Don't call her a chick, she's old enough to be your mother, so show a little respect. Pam's been more than kind to you."

"She got me locked up," he mumbles defiantly.

"*You* got you locked up," I point out. Jonas looks a little sheepish at that. "Given what she walked in on, I wouldn't have been surprised if she'd torn you limb from limb instead of going through all this trouble for you. She saw you under the worst of circumstances and still saw the good in you. I hope to God you're smart enough to appreciate that. Which brings me to the why," I say when Jonas silently stares at the floor. "Nothing you can say to her will be anything new. She knows the worst already. If there is one person you can say anything to, it's her. Besides, it'll probably work to your benefit should the district attorney decide to charge you."

Jonas straightened up, shock clear on his face. "Charge me?"

"Son, you didn't think this was just going away, did you? He may, he may not, but in the meantime you can do your damnedest to show this was a serious lack of judgement on your side, and not the beginning of a future in crime." I should feel bad, putting the screws on my own flesh and blood, but I don't. I hate seeing the tears welling in his eyes, but I meant what I said to him earlier; I will do anything. "I'll let you think on this," I say, getting up from the bed. I already have the door open when I hear him behind me.

"Dad?"

My heart does a little skip at the vulnerable sound of his voice, but I keep a straight face when I turn back to him and find him standing a few feet away.

"I'll do it," he says, a pained look on his face that almost makes me burst out laughing. Instead I take two steps and pull him into my arms. His body is stiff and unresponsive but I don't give a fuck.

"Happy about that, Bud," I mumble in his ear. "We'll get through on the other side, I promise you that."

His body, no longer that of a little boy, slumps in my hold and his fists come up behind me and clutch my shirt.

"Okay…"

-

"Can I have two fish and chips, tartar sauce on the side, for table nine?"

Matt sticks his head around the kitchen door, and I wave my acknowledgement, before diving into the cooler.

The stupid new computer that is supposed to send orders straight from the front to the small printer in the kitchen went on the fritz about half an hour ago. Right in the middle of the dinner rush. It had been a good idea, one that I completely supported, because it would cut down on the foot traffic between the pub and the kitchen. It did—for two days.

I run the halibut filets through the beer batter and drop them carefully into the fryer. I do the same with the fries on the other side. The beer batter dipped fries had been an idea that Ruby came up with. She sometimes helps in the kitchen and is constantly expanding her newfound cooking skills. She is very creative, that's for sure. I never would've thought to dip sweet potato fries into the batter, but she swore it makes them nice and easy to pick up and dip. So I had her cook them for me and was blown away.

She's revamped a lot of our regular fair with new and innovative ways to prepare and serve them, and especially overhauled the staple of fish and chips, which has become popular. In part, I'm sure, because of the chipotle she adds to the beer batter. Gunnar loves it, because anything with a little heat makes people drink more. Since we've updated the menu, beer sales in particular have gone up noticeably.

I left the kids doing homework and promised I'd be home before their bedtime, but Thursday nights are generally busy because of the special. We have enough capable hands that the kitchen keeps running even if I'm not here, but everyone has children now, and we all need an occasional night off. After that emotional talk with Jonas, I figured both he and I could do with a bit of breathing room. I'm off tomorrow night, so maybe I can convince him to watch a Bruins game with me.

I lift the fryer baskets and drop the contents on paper to drain, before arranging the food on the plates with a little fresh coleslaw. I add two little glass bowls with tartar sauce and carry the plates into the bar. It's almost eight thirty and orders are slowing down. People are settling into drinking.

The moment I step out from behind the bar, I zoom in on table nine, where, to my surprise, Pam is sitting with Mark. Mark is an ex-cop and Ruby's brother-in-law. Good guy, but something about him sitting with Pam tucked away in a booth is pissing me off.

"Fish and chips?"

Pam's head shoots up at the sound of my voice, looking surprised. I don't have a chance to question why, because Mark pipes up.

"Dayummmm, drop those babies right here." He rubs his hands. "Thanks, Dino," he says when I slide the plates on the table.

"Yeah, no problem," I respond a little distracted, before I address Pam. "I…eh… Enjoy." I walk away, ignoring the heat of her eyes on my back.

Son of a bitch. This is stupid. She used to walk into a room and all the hair on my neck would stand up straight, she annoyed me that much. These days, she still gets a physical response from me, but it sure as hell has nothing to do with my neck.

Pam

What in God's name is wrong with me?

I came here looking for some friendly distraction from the pressure on my chest and in my head. Sometimes the air feels so heavy—so thick—I can barely breathe. I bumped into Mark outside and he suggested we sit together and grab a bite. I hadn't seen him since the night I called him for help.

For some reason, I assumed Dino was at home when I talked to him earlier, but apparently not. When he walked up to the table with our order, it threw me.

Nothing's supposed to throw me. I'm supposed to be unflappable, even-keeled. It's what has worked for me for years. Stay aloof, don't show weakness, and don't lower your guard. I like to know where everyone stands, where I stand in social interactions. Until I was faced with a different Dino than I'd seen all the years before, I thought I did. The tension that's always been there, simmering between us, now all of a sudden has a completely different vibe, and I don't know what to do with that. I've always had a fairly tight hold over my emotions but lately they've slipped from my grip like loose sand. Most often in the presence of this man. He doesn't seem to fit the box I placed him in anymore.

Now I can't seem to formulate any words. Me, of the sharp tongue and the quick wit, I can't even seem to say thank you.

Watching his back retreat to the kitchen, Mark's voice startles me from my thoughts.

"I've always wondered where the animosity came from. Now I see," he says cryptically.

"Not a clue what you're talking about." I turn to him as I straighten my face into the blank mask, which has served me so well over the years. Mark seems utterly unimpressed. Being a former cop, he'd be well-versed in body language. He simply smiles and shrugs his shoulders.

"So how's the woodworking business?" I firmly direct the conversation in a different direction as we dive into dinner, and I'm able to relax a bit. It's only when I push my empty plate to the side that the subject of Dino, or rather his son, is brought up again.

"You did good with the boy; getting him to talk to police. Based on his and the girl's statements, they were able to move fast. Get those guys off the street. My sources tell me Mr. Neve won't be walking anytime soon, the deeper they dig, the more crap they unearth."

"Thank God for that. Won't see me lose anymore sleep over that little snot-nosed punk."

"I hear you," Mark agrees. "Too bad those other two were released on bail. First time offenders, coerced into participating, respectable home life…the judge wasn't gonna sit on them."

I shake my head. "I don't much care where they come from, all I know is they stuck their puny little dicks where it wasn't wanted, forcibly. And the coercion? It's bullshit. Maria told me they were hollering it up the whole time, high-fiving each other, cheering the other on. Makes me sick."

"I hear you," Mark says again, putting his hand on mine and giving it a squeeze. "How is the girl doing by the way?"

"She's…okay, I guess, considering. Hard lesson to learn, when you're not even twenty, that people are not always how you see them. The guilt she'll carry from this is not insignificant. She broke house rules, took off with a guy who was already abusive, and ended up being violated in the worst way. It's gonna be hard for her not take on responsibility for the last part of that as well."

"Do you think Ruby, or even Nina, could help?"

Ruby and her adopted daughter, Nina, are both survivors of a life filled with sexual violence. It's actually not a bad idea, but perhaps a little too soon for Maria to be exposed to that. It's a double-edged sword; these young girls, you hope they find a way to process their negative experiences and move on to a fulfilling life, but it's a fragile path. Knowing they're not alone in their experience can be healing, but sometimes adding on the horrors others have endured can be so overwhelming, they never get over their fears and insecurities.

"Maybe," I answer cautiously. "It may be too soon for that for Maria, though. Let's see how she does in the next couple of weeks and take it from there."

"Fair enough."

Mark insists on paying the bill Matt drops off at the table, and I let him, even though it goes against my grain.

"Let me walk you to your car," he offers, when we get up to leave.

"Actually, go ahead. I've got something to take care of first.
We'll be in touch." I smile to make my words a little less
dismissive than they may have come across as.

"Sure thing. Talk to you soon." Mark leans in for a peck on
my cheek before he walks out.

My reaction to Dino earlier is bugging me and I want to clear
the air. Or something. I briefly stop in the ladies' room before
heading to the kitchen. It's empty, but I hear noises coming from
the pantry in the back. Dino walks out with a plastic bin and
freezes in his tracks when he sees me standing by the table. He's
so big. An impressive mass of a man, with broad shoulders, a
solid bulk to his body, the completely bald head, and a heavy
brow. His uncommonly full lips soften the dark brooding mask
on his face. I can't stop looking at them, remembering how they
felt.

"Hey," he rumbles, after a moment, and continues to set the
bin on the counter before turning back to me. "What's up?"

What's up? I'm not so sure now. Thoughts and things to say
tumble through my mind and once again I become aware of a
crackle of energy in the air. Unfamiliar and slightly unsettling.

"Jonas," I say the first thing that finds its way to my mouth,
but I try to capitalize on it as best I can. "I just wanted to check
with you to see if you spoke with Jonas."

"That why you came?" he asks. The question is simple
enough on the surface, but from the intense way he looks at me,
I'm thinking there's a lot of information he's hoping to gain.

"I came for dinner and company to the pub. I didn't think you
were working, but since you were, I wanted to ask about Jonas."
His eyes narrow to slits. "Fine," I throw up my hands. "Things in
there earlier, felt…off. Like I said, I didn't expect you and it
threw me. I may have been awkward, or rude. Hell, I don't know,
all I know is I wanted to make sure we're good. I mean, we seem

to be getting along now…" I know I'm rambling. *Me, rambling.* But I can't seem to stop my mouth. "Talking on the phone, we were in a good place, right?…I just didn't want to… Ah, fuck it all to hell!" What in God's name is wrong with me? I turn and basically run for the door, making an already awkward situation only worse. *I hate this.*

I intend to slip straight out the backdoor and to the parking lot, but I barely get past the dumpster in the back before a heavy hand lands on my shoulder, swinging me around.

A very large and looming Dino is glowering down at me. I only have a second to consider how strange it feels to be looking so far up at a man, before his mouth slams down on mine. *Those lips.* This is not a thank-you-for-your-help kind of kiss. No ma'am. This is a full on, sizzling lip lock that has my hands come up and clutch his biceps for stability. I don't even hesitate for a second when his tongue slides between my lips—I let him in. *Son of a bitch, I'm letting him in.* The hand he had on my shoulder travels up, where he easily cradles the back of my head in his huge palm. In full control of my mouth and my head, he uses his free arm to tug me closer. I'm plastered head to toe to his body and my arms slips unwittingly around his neck, wanting to keep him right there.

Kissing this man is a full body experience, with every one of my senses fully engaged. Except perhaps my common sense…

"We're good," he mumbles against my lips when he finally comes up for air. I'm still sucking in lungfuls, or maybe that's just the panic that hits me just now.

"This is not good," I declare in between gasps, and try to push away. "I can't…this is unethical. I'm a therapist."

I feel the rumble of his chuckle coming from deep in his chest. "A therapist can't kiss? That's just sad."

"No." I thump his chest in frustration. "I just can't kiss you if I want to be able to help your son."

That has an instant effect; Dino's arms, still holding me close, drop away immediately as he takes a step back.

"Fuck," he says under his breath, rubbing a hand over his bald head. "Fuck."

His soulful eyes find mine and I want to flinch at the turmoil I see there. I loosely put my hand on his chest. "Look, whatever this is, we have Jonas to think about." He covers my hand with his before leaning in.

"All this time, I thought the tension between us was intense dislike. It's not—it's intense chemistry." He shakes his head before straightening up. "But you're right; Jonas comes first."

I should be relieved when he pulls his hand back and mine drifts to my side, but I am pissed to find myself feeling a little bereft. Both by his words and by the fact he's walking back inside.

He stops on the top step and turns back. "He comes first, but this?" he waves his hand between the two of us. "This is not done."

I'm about to protest when he stops me.

"Can't put the cat back in bag, Pam. No way I'm gonna let this be done."

CHAPTER SEVEN

Dino

"Why is she coming for dinner?" Gina asks for the fifth time today.

I hold myself back from rolling my eyes impatiently. Ever since getting off the phone with Pam this morning, and I announced we'd have a guest for dinner, she's been on my case.

It was Pam's idea, actually. She suggested it might not be a bad idea to meet under more relaxed circumstances; that it might take a bit of the weight off for Jonas. After agreeing to talk with Pam, he'd been tossing out excuse after excuse about homework and assignments needing to get done. I'm not an idiot, I knew what he was doing, but I decided to give him that play. For a while. For a week actually, but today is Saturday. When I talked to Pam earlier, and apologized for not following up with her sooner, she quickly came up with this solution.

Of course, Jonas had scrambled to come up with an excuse why he wasn't going to make dinner, but I'd laid down the law. He's not going anywhere.

Gina caught wind of it, and although I'd not planned on giving her too many specifics, my thirteen-year old is more observant than is comfortable at times. Hence the repeat questioning.

"She's coming because she's a friend," I repeat my earlier answers, but this time I add; "and because she's offered to talk through some stuff with Jonas."

"Oh," my girl says easily. "Is that about the drugs or that girl who got hurt?"

The chef's knife in my hand clatters on the counter as the wind gets knocked out of me. I'm not sure what I was thinking, trying to keep shit from my wiser-than-her-age daughter, but it's obviously been an exercise in futility.

"What do you know?" I ask her when I turn around to face her. I still don't want to give her more information than she needs to know, but I have to figure out how much she's figured out already. I watch her shrug her shoulders, pretending to be unaffected, but I can see the little frown lines between her eyebrows.

"I know he's been hanging out with a bunch of creeps and been skipping school a lot. I know he's been doing drugs, because sometimes I can see he's got weird eyes, like Mom used to get."

My heart cracks a little, when I hear my baby girl describing all of it in a matter-of-fact way, a serious mask on her face. She's too young to be exposed to this. She should be giggling with her friends and going to the mall, but instead she stands here discussing gangs and drugs like it's par for the course. It's not. It shouldn't be.

I'm reminded again that no matter how sharply I see things happening in someone else's life, I've become blind to the people in my own family, even my own flesh and blood. *Christ.*

"I know a girl was raped," she says in a much softer voice. "And that Jonas was there when it happened." Her eyes flick up at me and I'm surprised to see a little bit of fire through the tears.

"But he didn't do anything, Daddy. I know he didn't. Kids at school are just being mean."

I'm momentarily distracted by Gina's vehement belief in her brother and my heart warms at that. Then I zoom in on her last remark.

"What's that about the kids at school?" I take two steps until I stand in front of her and cup her face in my hands. I lower my voice to an almost whisper. "Baby—what is being said at school?"

"Just…they're mean," she repeats, her face crumpling as the tears start flowing. I press her against my chest and wrap my arms around her, my cheek on the top of her head.

"They're afraid to say anything to me, so they take it out on her. Saying nasty stuff about Mom—about me." My eyes come up to find Jonas standing in the doorway, an angry scowl on his face as he looks at his sister, but his eyes aren't angry; they're brimming with sadness.

Before I have a chance to say anything, the doorbell rings. Talk about perfect timing. Jonas throws a quick glance my way before turning to the door. I bend down to kiss my girl on the forehead.

"Only people who matter are right here, Princess, and I'm gonna do my very best to make sure we're all going to be okay. I promise you."

"Is this a bad time?" I hear Pam's voice from the doorway.

Gina struggles out of my firm hold, scoots past her, out the door and upstairs, with Pam watching her. When she turns back to me her normally stern face is soft.

"No. Not a bad time. A perfect time," I assure her, walking over to give her a kiss on the cheek. It's a struggle not to make it more than that, but Jonas is right behind her. "Have a seat." I wave at the stools by the kitchen island. "Jonas? Would you get

Pam a drink while I finish this up?" Without waiting for his answer, I turn back to putting the finishing touches on my mozza-tomato salad. The kids hate it, but I love it. I rip up a few fresh basil leaves, from the plants in the window sill, over top and sprinkle with a nice, aged balsamic. All the time trying to avoid listening too hard to Pam talking to my son. I can't quite make out his answers because the kid only seems to mumble, but I can hear her clearly. She's talking about everything but that fateful night. I could kiss her…again.

"So what's for dinner, Francis?" Pam's voice drifts in my direction, and I slightly wince at the use of my birth name. I still don't understand how someone could name a thirteen pound, screaming bundle of joy, Francis. Boggles my mind. My parents resorted to Frank and Frankie, but by the time I was in elementary school, I was already well on my way to being a big boy. I think it was second or third grade when the teacher had the brilliant idea to point out the largest known dinosaur and I had a name in common. It had taken only a few seconds before someone dubbed me Dino. It obviously stuck.

"Chicken stew with rice and beans, and call me Dino."

"Dad hates his name," Gina says, as she slips back into the kitchen, pulling cutlery from the drawers as she goes about setting the table without prompting. That's a new one. Curiosity seems to have been too much for her, obvious from the furtive glances she shoots Pam's way. She easily turns to Gina and a little smile settles on those luscious lips.

"Yeah? How so?"

Without further prompting, Gina happily regales the story of my elementary school teacher and Pam nods and hums every now and then. Her eyes never leave my daughter as she finishes the table and sidles up to me in the kitchen. I automatically slip my arm around her shoulder and lean down to kiss her hair. When I lift my head, I catch Pam's eyes on us. An unguarded moment that allows me a quick glimpse at a deep-seated pain I've only guessed at so far.

I'm startled at the clear longing marring her features and the shimmer of tears in her eyes.

Pam

Watching Dino with his daughter is excruciatingly sweet.

Memories of what it feels like to have a trusting, warm, little body in your arms threaten to overwhelm me. I could feel the thick tension when I walked in a little earlier, but now I only feel how thick the love is as well. Even Jonas, who's been quiet since his sister started chattering, looks at her with an expression of warm indulgence. The girl is adored, which is not a surprise, since she's adorable. However, I wonder if the men in her life see the tension at the corner of her mouth when she smiles, the strain in her eyes as she looks from one to the other. I'm curious how long this little one has played the role of peacemaker in the family.

"Hungry, Dad," Jonas announces, breaking the silence, and in the resulting flurry of activity, I have a chance to compose myself.

"What can I do?" I offer, feeling silly sitting down while the others are busy, moving around each other like a well-orchestrated ballet.

"Grab the mango chutney from the fridge? The large jar with the white lid," Dino says easily, as he passes me with a cast-iron

Dutch oven that gives off the most amazing fragrance, plopping it unceremoniously in the middle of the dining table.

The man does not have a single ounce of pretension in his body. The way he moves is easy, secure in a way that doesn't require him to draw attention to his size or dominance. Not even the shaved head, the bulk of his body, or the often menacing scowl he wears on his face detract from the fact he's an unassuming kind of guy. He just is.

By the time I get to the table with the chutney, the glasses are filled with water, and Dino is dishing out dinner. Rice and red beans, what looks to be chicken and cashew stew, making me wonder if he's deliberately picked a favorite Haitian dish for my benefit.

"Looks amazing," I say truthfully. I peek up at Dino as he slides a steaming plate in front of me. "It smells like home."

"Was aiming for that," he admits with a bit of a shrug, before turning his head. "Christ, Jonas. The way you're going at that plate, you'd think I never feed you. Wait for the rest of us, yeah?"

I stifle a snicker when I look over to find Jonas with a spoon halfway to his wide-open mouth, a good dent already in the heap of food his father served him. Gina doesn't stifle anything, she full out giggles. As one, the men in the family turn to her with equally startled expressions on their faces. The moment Gina becomes aware she is the subject of scrutiny, the smile that brightened her face dulls with embarrassment. The girl obviously doesn't smile a whole lot.

Dinner is amazing and after the brief awkwardness, conversation is pretty easy. Except Jonas, who is silent, occasionally glancing at his sister, but otherwise apparently engrossed in the massive amounts of food he's putting away. It reminds me I'm here for a reason.

"So Jonas? Your place or mine?" I jump right in and shine a spotlight on the elephant in the room. I have a feeling avoidance has sustained this family for a very long time. The only way to fix what's wrong is to put everything out in the open. The thought makes me flinch inwardly, because I'm being a hypocrite.

"Not sure," he finally mumbles, not getting any help from his father on this.

"Well, here's the deal; we can't do this at the shelter, for obvious reasons, so we're gonna have to meet in one of our homes. I come here, I might score a good meal, but you may not feel you have real privacy. Come to my house and the food's not gonna be half as good, but I'll make sure I'm stocked, and you'll be able to come and go without anyone being the wiser. Up to you." I shrug and busy myself with the last piece of chicken on my plate, making like all of this is not a big deal, when really—it is.

Dino and Gina appear to be playing along, as I hear sounds of cutlery scraping over china, but not a word is spoken.

"I'll come to you. I can always eat at home first," he finally says, a little humor in his tone.

I look up, point my fork in his direction and say, "Best be careful not to dis my cooking, buddy, or I'm gonna rescind that offer of food." If I'm not mistaken, the corner of his mouth twitches just a touch.

"Thank you for dinner." I turn to Dino as he steps outside the front door to see me off.

"Thank you for coming," he says, appearing to shuffle his feet a little. It's kind of endearing to see such a hulk of a man be somewhat bashful. "I think it went well."

"It did," I confirm before continuing cautiously, "I couldn't help but notice that Gina seemed sad when I first arrived." The deep sigh that escapes Dino tells me he hasn't forgotten either.

"She's just having a hard time at school. Kids talking." He shrugs his shoulders slightly. "She knows more than I thought."

I can tell this upsets him. Teenagers can be cruel, something I learned a long time ago. I put my hand on his arm.

"At that age, they always know more than we are comfortable with," I soothe. "Better to be straight with them. They may seem too young, but they're also resilient. It's better they learn certain things from people they care about, than from peers who are only looking for a reaction. Information is armor in situations like that."

He doesn't say anything, just grunts his acknowledgement. I get the feeling if he didn't obviously love his kids so much, he wouldn't be this accepting of advice. The silence is getting a little uncomfortable. With his head dipped low and his eyes focused on my hand, still touching him, I feel a strong connection to him and immediately pull my hand away to break the spell. Why this man? Why, after years of peaceful detachment, is he the one to get my heart racing and my emotions swirling?

As I turn to walk to my car, his hand shoots out and grabs me by the shoulder, swinging me back to face him. Before I can react, his mouth is on mine, his looming presence making me feel safely enveloped and small. My body immediately responds to the soft pressure of his lips against mine, and I don't even bother holding back the moan bubbling up. I respond to the need he brings out in me by sliding my hands around and up his back, feeling a shudder ripple through him. The heady feeling of power makes me bolder; to know I'm able to affect him as he does me, the perfect aphrodisiac. The night disappears around me as he forces the tight control out of me with the devious play of his mouth.

"Sorry…"

The muttered words, and the slam of the front door, are like a bucket of ice-cold water as we instantly jump apart. Dino's eyes are focused on the door, before slowly turning my way. Heat still lingers in his gaze, but added to that is a deep sadness, perhaps even regret as he looks at me. A clear, and somewhat painful, reminder why this was not a good idea to begin with.

"I have to…" He tilts his head to the door and I hold up my hand, not needing to hear any more.

"Go to her," I nudge quietly, before turning and walking to my car, back straight and head held high.

It takes me the drive home to talk some sense into myself. Every time he gets close to me, I'm reminded why I've done everything to avoid him in the past. He's dangerous. He brings up feelings in me that could break me. I've had decades to enforce the protective box I cram all those emotions in, but he seems to have no problem cracking the seal with just a touch. Thing is, every time that box opens, it's a little harder to lock up again, and there is stuff at the bottom, I don't ever want to experience again.

By the time I shut my own door behind me, I've got a firm hold on my feelings and have my focus back where it belongs. But as I walk through my dark, quiet house, dropping jacket and purse on the couch on my way to the kitchen, I waver. Compared to the warm, lively, and loving atmosphere of Dino's place, the lonely silence that greets me feels hollow.

Instead of the glass of wine I was going to treat myself with, I change direction and head down the hall to my bathroom, turning on the tap to run myself a bath instead.

Relaxed, a little more anyway, I pull on my comfy men's PJ pants and oversized T-shirt and head to the kitchen for that glass of wine. The plan is to veg out in front of my rarely used TV, to try and clear any lingering, unwanted thoughts from my head so I can sleep later.

I'm still flicking through channels, attempting to find anything that's not depressing the shit out of me, when I hear a knock on the door. It's conditioning that has me slide open the wardrobe closet, where I have my gun sitting on the shelf for easy access. My front door has no glass. Nothing to allow anyone from outside to peek in, but it does have a peephole. I press my eye against it to find a familiar large shadow on the other side. With one hand, I flick on the outdoor light while I take off the deadbolt with my other.

"Couldn't leave it at that," Dino's voice rumbles as I pull open the door. He steps through when I move wordlessly to the side. His hands are tucked in his pockets and his head is low, but his eyes are burning into mine. Just like that, every good intention I've built up over the past hour and a half, since I left his house, dissipates like morning fog. In a last attempt to maintain the distance that would be so much safer for me, I turn and walk straight through to the kitchen, pulling a second glass down from the cupboard. The light shuffle of stocking feet alerts me to the fact he's left his boots by the front door before following me.

"Wine?" I ask him, already pouring a healthy glassful. I catch him observing me as I hand over the glass and slip by him into the living room, my own glass waiting on the side table next to the couch, where I cuddle back in my corner. I feel the couch dip beside me as I grab the remote to turn the TV off. After taking a quick sip of my own wine for reinforcement, I put my glass down and twist my body to face him. His eyes are still on me.

"How is she?" I can tell my question surprises him from the way his eyebrow lifts ever so slightly.

"She's okay," he finally answers. "A little confused and upset with me."

"With you?"

He chuckles a little at my question. "Accused me of lying. I may have told her before you arrived you were just a friend. She was fishing."

"I am just a friend," I blurt out, a little panicked at the direction this is going, but Dino won't have it.

"Keep telling yourself that, Biscuit," he says, using that stupid nickname he came up with, and then he leans in. "We both know you were never *just* a friend."

"Look," I respond, as I pull my knees up and wrap my arms around them in an attempt to protect myself. "I thought we'd talked about this. Your kids, they've already got enough turmoil in their lives. And I'm honestly not looking for anything." I hate that my voice sounds almost pleading. Dino just chuckles as he shakes his head.

"Believe me," he says, "I know the state of my kids' lives. Mine, too. And trust me when I say the last thing I'm looking for is to get involved." *Ouch*, even though he's just confirming what I've just pointed out, having them come back at me stings. "But," he continues, "the truth is, we're already involved. We were, long before the shit hit the proverbial fan in my house, and you know it. It's the reason we steered clear; because both of us knew even then." He looks at me for a long time before taking a swig from his wine and putting his glass on the coffee table. I press myself into the corner of the couch when he twists and leans into me, his fists braced on the seat between us. "I dare you to lie about that." It's a threat—and a challenge.

The temptation is big to deny, deny, deny—but a part of me wonders why, and more importantly, who, I would be denying.

"I won't lie," I promise. "I know it's the reason the air got thick every time we were in a room together, but that doesn't change anything. Your kids—they need stability now." He scoots over so he's butted up against my shins, ignoring the distance I've tried to create by leaning his chin on my knees, his face only inches from my own.

"What my kids need is a father who is focused, and not going out of his mind with want for a formidable, strong-willed, slightly intimidating, big-hearted, and beautiful woman."

CHAPTER EIGHT

Dino

I'd warned her I wasn't just going to let this go.

There's a pattern developing that I'm determined to break through. I get close to her physically and her body responds, the instincts to get closer too strong to resist. As soon as the moment is gone, she creates distance and wrangles herself back behind that hard shell again. A constant push and pull there is only one solution for. I'm not normally one to rush in, but I am rushing now. Feet first and fingers crossed.

Not even her very defensive position, with her legs pulled up to her chest, is going to deter me. Mostly I hate being the size of a closet, but I'm grateful for it now, because it makes it almost effortless to pull her on my lap.

"Hey! Quit manhandling me," she snaps, slapping at my hands. "I'm not a bag of potatoes you can toss around." I smile at the resurrection of her sharp tongue. I've missed her attitude. It's all been tiptoeing on eggshells, by everyone.

"Trust me—I'm well aware you're not a bag of potatoes. What you are, though, is a handful." The moment the words leave my mouth, I realize I may have unintentionally put my foot in something. Pam's reaction confirms it. The half-hearted slaps become well-aimed punches, highlighted with some colorful epitaphs.

Only one thing to do; I manage to grab her by the wrists, hold them behind her back and cut off the flow of cursing by making sure her mouth is otherwise occupied. Her body instantly freezes, and I think she's settling—until she bites my bottom lip. Fucking hard.

"Jesus, woman!" I lick the offended flesh and immediately taste blood. This time when she struggles to get off me, I let her. She takes one look at me with her dark brown, shocked eyes, and runs out of the room. I get enough of an eyeful of her ample tits, bouncing under the oversized shirt she has on, to have an immediate resurgence behind my zipper. Letting out a deep sigh at my own stupidity, I lean my elbows on my knees, resting my head in my hands.

"Sit up," I hear the deep melodic sound of Pam's voice hovering over me. I do as she says. One of her hands cups my chin, lifting my face, while the other presses something cold against my lip. She tries to avoid looking at me, but my insistent staring seems to wear her down, and she finally lifts her eyes to mine.

"*I'm sorry*," she mouths soundlessly.

"That's my line," I grumble. Her hand pulls away from my face as she sits down heavily on the coffee table, holding the tea towel with ice cubes in her lap. "Look," I start and her eyes come up to meet mine. "First of all, I was referring to your personality, not your body, when I said you were a handful." She tilts her head, raising an eyebrow. "Believe I already mentioned you're a tad intimidating," I admit with a shrug. "Secondly, I didn't mean to freak you out by holding you down." At that, she lowers her head in an attempt to hide the flush of color on her face.

"You didn't freak me out," she protests softly.

"I call bullshit," is my swift reply. "I don't know what your story is, but I know you have one. I can see it."

She suddenly gets up from the table and walks out of the room again. This time I follow and find her leaning over the sink in the kitchen where she's tossed the cold compress. She doesn't move, her head stays hanging down, but I can tell by the way her shoulders tighten up that she's aware I'm behind her.

"This is why this can't happen," she whispers when I put a hand in the middle of her back. "You see too much."

I rub her back in long slow strokes, all the way along her spine, keeping my silence. One thing I've always been good at is listening, and Pam needs to be heard. It doesn't take long before she feels the need to fill the silence I'm actually quite comfortable with.

"My life…it's not what it seems. I get so tired sometimes of keeping everything together." Her voice is low and I have to strain to hear every word. "I can't…if I don't hold on to what I can control, I'll lose it."

There it is. Her vulnerability exposed. It doesn't matter what her story is, it's clear to me whatever she's carrying with her is the cause for her sometimes fierce self-protection and tight control.

"Not gonna push you for full exposure, Pam. I hope there comes a time when you can share, but I won't force it. I can promise you that."

She straightens up and turns to face me, my hand that was on her back, settling on the curve of her hip.

"This is dangerous," she worries, but I can see her resolve slipping.

"Remember I asked you who takes care of you? Let me," I offer, watching her face intently. "I'm sure there are a million reasons why we shouldn't do this, but the only thing I care about is the one reason why we should…" I bring my other hand up to cup her face and I'm encouraged when she tilts her head to rest in my palm, "…we already see each other clearly."

For a long moment she simply looks at me, searching for anything but the plain honesty she'll find in my eyes. When she lifts her head from my hand, my initial thought is that I've lost the internal battle waging in her head, but then her arms come up and circle my neck. My heart starts pounding in my chest when she simultaneously pulls me down and lifts her mouth for a kiss. This is not me taking what I want, it's her giving it to me. It's fucking amazing.

Her beautiful lips brush lightly back and forth over mine, and I struggle not to take over, relishing the feel of her soft body pressing to mine. But when her tongue slides over the crease of my mouth suggestively, I'm done. My arm slips around her back, pulling her in tighter and my hand on her hip slides up her side. She groans softly in my mouth when my palm brushes the curve of her breast, and I take that as an invitation. Pam's tits are sumptuous: large, soft, and currently unrestricted. When I lift the weight of one easily in my palm, I feel her fingers digging in my neck in response.

She likes my hands on her. *Good.* I fucking love my hands on her. With my mouth savoring hers and my thumb brushing the outline of her nipple, my other hand slips down the back of her pajama pants. Her warm skin feels like silk as I massage the soft flesh of her superb ass. Lavish and ample, my hand barely fits one cheek.

Fucking hell.

With my hands and mouth full of Pam, the rest of my body wants in on the action, and before you know it, I'm rutting my painfully hard cock into her belly.

"Please," she mumbles against my lips.

"What do you need, love? Tell me what you need," I ask, panting hard.

Instead of answering, she releases my neck and grabs the hem of her shirt. *Yes.* I help her pull it up and off, letting my eyes take in every inch of beautiful dark skin exposed. My mouth waters at the sight of her full swaying breasts, tipped with deep brown nipples.

"Magnificent."

Pam

I throw my head back the moment his lips close over my skin. The strong tug of his mouth sends electric charge straight to my core, and I almost cry at the sensation. I never realized how much I missed the feel of a meaningful touch. My hands grab at his smooth head and press him even closer to my chest. I celebrate the feeling of getting wet, without the aid of a lubricant, a feat my body hasn't been able to perform in many years.

I knew it would be good. I've guiltily fantasized about it enough over the years. But the taste of him, the electric charge his touch leaves behind on my skin, adds a different dimension to the experience I couldn't have conjured up in my dreams. I don't even care that my back is wedged against the edge of my kitchen counter, or that the blinds on the window aren't quite closed. I'm too busy feeling, too swept up in the sense of weightlessness, like I'm free-falling.

"*Christ,* you're sweet," Dino mumbles around my breast before letting the nipple pop from his mouth and latching on to its mate. A gentle but sensitive bite draws a hiss from me—the slight sting sending ripples over my skin. I barely notice his big hands both dipping down the back of my PJs, kneading my butt before slipping my pants down.

The overhead light glaring, the blinds half-open, and I'm in the middle of my kitchen—buck naked—a behemoth of a man kneeling at my feet. How the fuck did I get here?

"Stop thinking," he orders. "Just feel."

I feel every damn thing, as he lifts a leg over his shoulder, and I grab onto the counter behind me for balance. Every whisper of his warm breath over rarely exposed skin and every deft stroke of his fingers. I know what's happening, and for a fleeting second, I panic over what I must look like down there. I keep it tidy with the rest of me almost by rote, but the days of waxing are far behind me. I don't have a chance to dwell on it for long when a strong lash of Dino's tongue has my eyes rolling in my head and any coherent thought evaporates. My arms are shaking with the effort of holding me up, because my remaining leg is threatening to give away under the onslaught of his mouth.

"Holy crap…" I blurt out when I feel the blunt tip of a finger breach my entrance and slowly slide deep. Much like the rest of the man, his fingers are of a size some men would be proud to make claim to. I'm already close, and when his mouth hums around my clit while his finger plays inside me, I feel all the energy coil inside my body and spin me into an orgasm that turns every muscle in my body to Jell-O. Including the ones in my leg, which finally gives out as it buckles underneath me.

"Easy," Dino cautions, managing to guide my fall so that I end up half on his lap, half on the floor. I'm beyond caring about the picture I make, with my wrinkles, cellulite, graying hair, and lumps. I've just had the best bloody orgasm in possibly forever, and nothing is going to spoil the blissful afterglow for me. His arms come around me, and he chuckles deeply as I close my eyes and snuggle against his chest, sighing contently.

We sit like that for a bit, while I catch my breath, when I slowly become aware of my surroundings and Dino's careful shifting underneath me. *Oh my God.* I scramble out of his arms and on my feet, snatching my shirt off the floor and tugging it quickly over my head. A bit mortified, I take a quick look at Dino, who's casually leaning back on his arms, the substantial bulge in his jeans on blatant display, and wearing an amused smirk on his face. I'm at a loss for words. What does one say in a situation like this? Thank you?

"Thinking too hard again, sweetheart," he says, getting up off the floor easier and with much more grace than I was able to muster.

"I'm…" I start, but don't get any farther as his bulk crowds me back against the counter. Again. His hand comes up to brace the side of my neck, his thumb distractedly brushing along my jaw. "You…" I try again, cursing myself that my normally healthy vocabulary seems to completely elude me right now. Dino throws his head back, and for the first time, I get to witness the beautiful transformation of him when he dissolves in deep rumbling laughter right before me. Any worries I had about leaving him in his obvious…*state*, disappear as I feel my face crack into a responding smile.

"No worries, Beautiful," he chuckles, leaning his forehead against mine, his brown eyes focused. "Believe me when I say that was entirely my pleasure."

I'm not sure what to think. I'm used to a fair trade off when it comes to sex, best case scenario. In all other cases, the guy generally makes sure to get what he wants out of it. I don't know what to do with one who gives, but doesn't seem to expect anything in return.

"I've got enough to tide me over," he breaks into my thoughts, creeping me out with his ability to read me. "I'm not worried I'll be left in the cold," he adds. "I have a feeling you're well-equipped to give me the ride of my life when the time comes."

Something tells me maybe I should be a little offended at the presumptuous comment, but I don't really feel it. From Dino's mouth it sounds more like a compliment.

"Deal," I voice, as I smile up at him as he leans down for a quick kiss on my lips.

"I should get home," he points out. "Promised the kids I wouldn't be long."

"Of course," I agree, sidestepping him to tag my PJ pants, still puddled on the floor. A quick glance at the clock shows it's only ten fifteen. Feels like it's been much longer than the forty or so minutes since he got here. I follow him to the front door where he stops and turns, pulling me close.

"You gonna be okay?"

I look up at him and give him a nod before following it with the words. "I'm fine. Better than okay," I admit. His responding smile makes the corners of his eyes crinkle. I love that look.

"Good. So I'm dropping off Jonas at seven on Thursday?"

"No, actually," I say, stepping back a little. "I'd rather you let him come on his own." I watch as Dino's face grows serious and I quickly place a soothing hand along his jaw. "It's important," I emphasize. "I know you want to look after him, but he needs to learn to feel the weight of his responsibilities and that includes getting himself here and home." The sigh he releases seems to come all the way the from his toes. "Besides," I push a little further. "It's probably best for your kids if they don't see us together for the time being."

"Why?"

"You know why," I throw back at him. He knows as well as I do that kids can generally read adults like a book, and they'd instantly know something was up. They're still too raw to be able to deal with having us in their face. Or maybe that's me…

"Fine," he says curtly, but his arms are pulling me close again. "But promise you'll call me."

"You know I can't talk about what I discuss with him, Dino." I place my hands on his chest. A chest that feels so good under my hands but I haven't even been able to really touch yet.

"Not asking that, Pam. I'm asking to hear your voice." I take in his serious face and my armored heart swells in my chest. He openly shows me the uncertainly in his eyes, and the trust he offers me by doing that is humbling.

"Of course," I promise, lifting my face for a kiss, which he readily supplies before slipping out the door.

It's not until later, when I'm lying in bed and staring up at the ceiling, that I realize how unguarded and free I was around him. I can't remember the last time I felt like that around anyone. The fear of having my past exposed is always a huge concern, but the fact that Dino knows there's something, yet he won't press for the information, is enough to have me relax my mask.

Imagine that.

CHAPTER NINE

Dino

"Syd, do you mind plating that order for table three? I've gotta make a quick call."

Sydney, Gunnar's wife, is working tonight while her husband stays home with the kids. She likes coming in on Thursdays as often as she can. She's got a thing for the Thursday night special and usually comes up with the menu. In the last few years, the kitchen has gotten more and more crowded. Instead of just myself with the occasional help of Viv, now we have Syd and Ruby as well, who both have a good handle on the kitchen. It gives me a little more flexibility, which I have to say, has helped a great deal with recent changes on the home front.

I grab my coat from the hook and step outside. We've had a few flurries, here and there, but nothing with staying power. It's cold though—there's always a breeze coming off the water that seems to pick up intensity as it moves between the buildings on either side of the alley. I sit down on the step and dial Jonas' number.

"Yo."

"Bud, it's no more effort just to say hello, you know that right?" I shake my head at my son's standard answer.

"Hello, Father," he replies, sarcasm dripping from his words and tone, but I'm not going to bite. Not tonight.

"Are you home?"

"Got in five minutes ago. The brat's not here though."

"Gina's at Marcy's house, working on a project. I'm picking her up at nine thirty. There's some leftover lasagna in the fridge if you're hungry." In the background I hear the bottles in the fridge door rattle as he dives right in. "Didn't Pam feed you?" I ask, trying in a not so subtle way to find out if he kept his appointment with her. Luckily for me, Jonas is not too quick on the uptake and answers easily.

"She made roti wraps. Curried chicken was da bomb."

"So how come you're still hungry?"

"Lasagna, Dad…"

Right. I guess in Jonas' world, that is explanation enough. I feel better, though, knowing he kept his word. It still doesn't stop me from asking; "Everything go okay?"

"Fine," he snaps, confirming I should've kept my mouth shut, because he's immediately in a foul mood. "Gotta go. Got shit to do."

"With shit I hope you mean homework?"

"Duh. Hanging up, Dad."

Before I have a chance to say goodbye the line's already gone dead. A smile creeps onto my face anyway. Even with attitude, I'm grateful to have gotten more than grunts out of him, and discovered that Pam does a mean curry—I'm gonna have to get her to make some for me some day.

Since I left her house earlier in the week, I've been swamped. Gunnar and I spent two days going over the orders for Christmas. We like to get those done in plenty of time, to avoid the risk of missing out. This is the busiest time of the year for most our suppliers, and even though The Skipper is closed on Christmas Day, we're already booked up for Christmas Eve. Syd puts on a charity dinner every year, and the day after Christmas we put on a big brunch buffet, which is always well attended. So between preparations for that, regular work, cleaning and laundry at home, and driving Gina to and from Christmas concert rehearsals, I've barely had time to breathe.

I've lain in bed these past nights, tempted to call her, but I didn't want to force it. I know she's a bit hesitant about us being in any way involved while she sees my son in a professional capacity, so I didn't want to make it more awkward. But if she doesn't get in touch tonight like she promised, I'm calling.

Syd's back is turned when I return to the kitchen and hang my coat back on the hook. Her shoulders are slumped as she distractedly scrubs at a pan in the sink.

"Tired?" I ask as I walk up, putting a hand on her back. She turns her head and looks at me with a weak smile before focusing her attention in front of her again. I don't miss the glint of tears in her eyes.

"I still miss him, you know," she answers softly, and I know she's talking about her son, Daniel. The little boy died as the result of a tragic accident years ago, and Syd had gone through hell and back after. "Sometimes it hits me how good I have it— how lucky I am to have gotten this second chance at life, but inevitably the guilt follows soon after. Especially when we're coming up to the holiday season. Did I ever tell you he loved dinosaurs?" She turns a watery smile my way. "He was barely able to say 'Mama' but he would point his finger at the pictures in his book and say 'Dino.' By the time he was three, he knew the difference and managed to get his little mouth around most of the names." Her head drops, her shoulders roll forward, and her arms wrap around her middle, as if curving herself around the painful memories. I pull her away from the sink and turn her in my arms, letting her cry it out against my chest. "He would've loved you," she mumbles in my shirt.

"Because of my name?" I ask gently.

"Probably," she says on a chuckle, which turns into a sob, and she presses her face in my shirt. "Sometimes it just so difficult to breathe. I feel so weighed down by guilt, over moving on. This morning I was in Target, doing a little Christmas shopping for the kids, and I saw this set of soft dinosaur toys. My first thought was that Caden would love it. It took until now to realize Daniel wasn't first to come to mind anymore. It makes me so sad."

Caden is Syd and Gunnar's one-year-old little bruiser. Syd's pregnancy had been a bit of a surprise, and it turned out a very happy one. Gunnar has two children from a previous marriage who love Syd, but the arrival of Caden created a permanent connection for all of them. They became a family.

"Who's to know Daniel didn't have a hand, somehow, in picking that toy?" I suggest carefully. Not that I'm big on supernatural stuff, but I can't help but think if we give off energy when we're alive, that energy would still be around after we die. A soft breeze hitting your face, leaving a smile in its wake. Maybe a sound or smell that brings a memory to life. "I bet if he could've picked a gift for his baby brother, it would've been exactly that, don't you think?"

"You know I love you, right?" Syd says, as she leans back to smile up at me through her tears. I smile back shrugging my shoulders.

"Kinda partial to you too, Chickie." I give her a little squeeze.

"Do I need to ask what you're doing groping my wife?" Gunnar's voice sounds from the doorway.

We both turn in his direction and Syd's arms slip from my waist, as she starts moving to her husband, who's bouncing a sleepy Caden on his hip.

"What are you doing here?" Syd asks him, but her eyes are focused on her little boy, who immediately stretches out his arms when she's within reach. She easily takes him from Gunnar's arms into her own.

"The little man wouldn't go to sleep, kept calling for his momma, and I was kinda missin' her, too." His arms fold around his wife and child, when he notices the tears. "I'm thinking maybe Momma was missin' us, too, little man," he says, kissing the top of his son's head before doing the same with Syd.

"Are you good here, man?" he directs at me, a look of contentment on his face.

"Go." I wave my hand at the door. "Take them home." Gunnar keeps my eyes for a second, giving me a lift of his chin as he leads his family out.

I could lie and say seeing them doesn't affect me, because it does. It used to be where I was the only one with someone to go home to, miserable as it was, but now the tables have turned. All my friends seem to be getting a second chance here, and I realize I'd give my left nut for a go at one, too.

Pam

"You hungry?" I toss over my shoulder as I move through my house toward the kitchen, Dino's son reluctantly following.

I frankly wasn't sure he was going to show up, but I'm thrilled he did. Both for him and myself. Selfish, maybe, but I want a chance to pull this kid back from the sequence of bad decisions I can see him making. Call it penance for letting another boy much like him slip through my fingers years ago. By the time I saw what was happening, it had been too late for him, but it's not too late for the kid leaning awkwardly against my kitchen doorway.

I confess I put extra effort into dinner tonight. In part, I guess, because the boy's father is a chef, and he's likely used to pretty decent cooking. I'm not a slouch in the kitchen, and I can generally hold my own, but for some reason this particular meal is important. I need to win him over, even if it's with food. It's the only thing I know for sure to get a teenage boy's attention. So I mentally cross fingers and toes as I slide a plate with my curry roti in front of him and hold back a smile when he picks on up and takes a healthy bite.

Dinner is silent, and that's okay. Silence is underrated. It affords you the opportunity to assess and process your surroundings and the company you're in. Jonas isn't volunteering, and neither am I. By the time both our plates are empty, I'm pleased to see him get up, collect the dishes, and set them in the sink. It implies a level of comfort I was hoping for.

"Do you drink coffee?" I ask, as I get up and join him at the sink. "I usually make decaf, but if you need a boost, there's a few cans of soda in the fridge. Not sure what, so have a look." I turn my back and pop a pod in my coffee maker. He hasn't said anything, but I hear the fridge door open and smile to myself when I hear the hiss of a can opening.

"What am I doing here?"

They're the first words he's uttered since knocking on my door. Not a hint of the defensive attitude he displayed standing on my porch earlier. I keep my back turned and shrug my shoulders, feigning a level of indifference I don't really feel.

"To give you a chance to talk," I say almost casually.

"Why?" he asks, and this time I turn around to face him.

"Because I have a hunch you don't feel you can talk to anyone else." He takes a minute to mull it over before raising his eyebrow at me suspiciously.

"What's in it for you? You doing this for my dad?"

I suppress a smile, because I was expecting him to question my motives. This is also where it gets tricky, because I want to be as honest with him as I can.

"In part," I confess, "but also in part because I saw you in a place I know you didn't want to be. I see you as more than the sum of your actions." I pause a moment, wondering how to best phrase my thoughts. "But mostly I want to listen for me." I take my cup and start moving in the direction of the living room, listening to the fall of his footsteps as he follows me, as I knew he would. I take the couch, and Jonas slumps down in one of the club chairs across from me. His body language displaying a detachment that doesn't quite reach his eyes, which are intently focused on me. He's waiting for me to elaborate.

"You remind me of someone," I disclose. "A good kid who had some shitty things happen to him; he didn't know how to deal with. He got swept up in something he had no control over, but that changed his life. Not for the better." It's hard talking about this, but for this to work, he needs to know I come from a place of knowledge—of understanding.

"What happened?"

Oh yeah, the million dollar question.

"Let's just say he has all the time in the world to ask himself that same question. And believe me, he does."

A flicker of understanding passes over his features before he carefully rearranges them back to his preferred blank mask of indifference.

"I wasn't going to do anything stupid," he says defensively. I don't bother responding, because we both know better than that.

My silence finally gets to him and he shoots me a glance before lowering his eyes again. "I didn't know," he confesses softly. "He said I had to take part in some kind of initiation ceremony, but I swear I didn't know that's what he had planned. I freaked. I saw the girl on the bed when I walked in, and I was going to walk right back out, but then I saw the gun. I was scared."

I shove a box of tissues sitting on the coffee table in his direction, pull my legs up on the couch and sit back, quietly listening to the kid purge every sin, real and perceived. His guilt is a visceral thing, and I can see the poison of it eating at him. By the time eight o'clock comes around, he's done. We haven't even touched on how he ended up involved with people he knows are no good for him, but this is a good start. I show him the bathroom so he can clean up a little, he's quietly cried through the entire session.

"Should I come back?" he hesitantly asks when he comes out. Despite the way he phrases it, I know he means '*Can I come back?*' and that makes me ridiculously happy. This is exactly what I meant when I told Dino I wanted Jonas to come on his own. My guess is the kid has felt out of control of his life for a long time, it's important he claims it back.

"Anytime you like," I answer easily, not making a big deal of it. "I've got group sessions at the shelter on Tuesday and Wednesday nights, but any other night, just let me know." I walk ahead to show him out.

"Saturday?"

I stop by the front door and turn. "You want to come here on a Saturday night?" I blurt out before catching myself, but Jonas just chuckles sheepishly.

"Might as well," he replies. "I'm kinda grounded indefinitely."

"Well then, sure thing. Saturday it is. You going to be hungry?" I ask him with a raised eyebrow as I pull open the door for him.

"Always," he grins as he slips by me into the cold night.

The moment I close the door behind him, the sudden silence in my house threatens to swallow me. For something to do, I put away the leftovers and hand-wash the dishes, even though I have a perfectly good dishwasher. I keep my hands busy, but still my mind wanders. Jonas' visit went better than I could've hoped. The fact it didn't require a lot of prodding on my part to get him talking makes me hopeful of the outcome. And still my heart is heavy. Another boy, another time, and he was not that lucky. Funny, since he should've been able to count on me, but I was too mired in my own mess to recognize the one he was in.

The kitchen spic and span, I turn off the lights and prepare to go to bed. Ridiculous, at only nine thirty, but sleep is an excellent, albeit temporary, cure for depressing thoughts. Yet by the time I slip between my sheets, my mind is wide awake and spinning.

That's when I remember I made a promise a couple of days ago and grab my phone from the nightstand, turning the light on.

I haven't heard from Dino since he showed up here unannounced earlier in the week. No promises were made of any kind, but I still found myself hoping, more than once, for the phone to ring. I had no problems getting to sleep that night, my body still languid from the thorough and very welcome orgasm he left me with.

My cheeks burn at the realization I was stark naked in the same kitchen I welcomed his son into tonight. Something so wrong about that, and still it puts a smile on my face. It was nice to let myself go for a moment. Dino's not a man who would ever willingly hurt me. I know that. Still, it's hard for me to even imagine what it would be like to have a real relationship with someone like him. I can't grasp what it could be he sees in me. He's younger, for one, not by a whole lot but still… He's married, for another. Granted, he's separated, but as far as I know, no papers have been signed. Which brings me to my next point, his wife is blonde and tiny, and I'm…well, I'm not. I'm as far from dainty as you can get; tall, big-boned, and graying. Oh, and I'm black. It hasn't escaped me that we have some fundamental differences, but only because they're visible. I actually enjoyed the way the paler skin of his hand looked wrapped around my breast. The contrast of his bald head between my dark thighs.

Oh, for fuck's sake.

I drop the phone back on the nightstand. I've got myself all worked up now. There's no way in hell I'm going to call him in this state. I reach over and turn off the light again, when my phone rings.

"Hello?" I answer without looking, my room dark as the night outside.

"Were you going to call?"

Despite my earlier resolve, I find myself smiling when I hear his voice.

"Just about to," I lie. "Things went well, Dino. That's all I'm gonna say about it."

"I know." He surprises me with his sure answer. "Talked to Jonas already. Told me your curry kicks ass."

"It so does," I boast, my smile bigger now.

"Are you going to make it again so I can judge for myself?"

"I might be persuaded."

"I'd be happy to put in that effort. I'd start right now, if I wasn't in a driveway waiting for my daughter to get her ass out here so we can get home." His deep voice vibrates with barely contained impatience, making me snicker.

"Be happy to make it for you one time, although I don't want you to hold back on your persuasive prowess. It's quite…impressive."

The responding growl gives me goosebumps.

"You're killing me, woman. I'm calling you tomorrow, when I'm not in a car, my daughter only steps away, with a hard on that I have no chance of getting rid of any time soon."

"Night, Dino," I whisper teasingly, feeling a lot more relaxed.

"Night, Biscuit."

Moments later, with the sound of his voice still in my ear, I easily fall asleep.

CHAPTER TEN

"So can I, Daddy?"

The whole way home from her friend's house, Gina's been on about going to the movies on Saturday night. Let me tell you, the fastest way to get rid of an almost painful erection, is your daughter chattering in your ear. Especially when it involves boys. In this case, my princess and her bud, Marcy, have come up with the fabulous plan to double-date—her words, not fucking mine. *Double date?* She's way to damn young to any-kind-of-date. I'd been about to tell her that in no uncertain terms too, when I noticed her wide, hopeful smile. *Christ.* This girl will be the death of me. It's the biggest, happiest smile I've seen in…I can't even remember how long it's been.

Just like that, I swallow my knee-jerk '*Hell no*' down. Instead ask her calmly to elaborate, my hands clutching, white-knuckled, at the steering wheel. Turns out there's a whole group going; five girls and two boys. But, according to Gina, since Marcy really likes Nick, and my baby girl really likes some kid named *Trip*, it'll be almost like a date. Who the fuck names their kid Trip? What does it even mean? Was he, like, an accident?

I'm still trying to come to terms with the fact my daughter apparently is hung up on a boy whose name means either his parents are major dopeheads, or he was an oops baby, when Gina nudges me again.

"I'll think about it, girl. Okay? Maybe. I want to know how you'll get there and back, since I'm going to be working, and I'll want to have a chat with Marcy's mom."

"Okay, so I'm going over to Marcy's in the afternoon, that way we can finish the project because it's due on Monday. Then Mrs. Roper said she'd drive us to the movie theater. We're meeting the others there. Mr. Roper is picking us up after, and then I'm sleeping over at Marcy's." My daughter barely even breathes as she rattles off the detailed itinerary. It's obvious the two girls have planned it out carefully, and I can't help smile at Gina's enthusiasm. She, of course, takes it for an answer. "Yay! Thank you, Daddy!"

"Hold on," I say sternly, as I pull into our driveway and turn off the engine before turning to her. "Did you hear me agree?"

"Not yet," the little smartass fires back, the light still on in her eyes.

"If Marcy's parents are on board with these plans, and you are picked up right after the movies let out—and if you clean your room like I've asked for weeks now—I'm thinking maybe yes." The squeals that follow are deafening in the confines of the car, but the kisses she peppers my face with more than make up for it.

What can I say; I'm a sucker for my little girl's happiness.

Inside, I can see from the trail of boots and clothes, Jonas is probably in his room. His jeans are hanging from the railing going up the stairs. I pick up each item as I make my way to the kitchen and dump the lot on the floor in the laundry room beyond. The one thing their mother always did was pick up after them. She didn't cook much, and in the end she didn't clean up much either, but she always picked up the kids' junk. Always a bone of contention with me, and this is why. Seventeen years old, he should be able to clean up after himself.

I'm still mumbling to myself when I head up the stairs to check in with him. Something I haven't done enough. I aim to rectify that now. I'm surprised to find his door open.

"Hey, Bud," I say from the doorway. Jonas is not behind his computer, gaming, for once. Instead he's on his bed, arms folded behind his head, watching something on his little TV.

"What's up?" He sounds his usual, dismissive, ornery self, but I don't miss the little glance he shoots my way before pretending to be engrossed by whatever the hell he's watching.

"Just checking in—saying goodnight. I'm hitting the sack, kid. I'm tired."

I barely hear him mumble, "Night," but it lightens my heart anyway. I turn to walk out and glance back over my shoulder. "By the way, your crap was all over the house. It's in the laundry room in a pile on the floor. Take care of it."

"Whatever," he says with an uninterested shrug of his shoulders, but the moment I pull my bedroom door closed behind me, I hear his footsteps pounding down the stairs.

By the time I hit the mattress, I'm smiling; I can hear the sound of the washing machine running downstairs.

"Francis?"

I don't have time for this. The girls at The Skipper have been covering my ass lately as I'm trying to sort our shit out, so today I was determined to get there on time, and I still have to drop Gina off at Marcy's. Movie and a sleepover. Not a good time for fucking Jeannie to call.

"You know the cops are looking, right?" is my only response. If not for the fact she's still the mother of my children, I'd likely have hung up the phone. "What do you want, Jeannie?" I follow up, irritated when she doesn't react to my words.

"I'm in trouble."

No shit. "Go back to the rehab center, Jeannie. You should never have left in the first place."

"I know," she whines, her voice grating on me. "I just…I had a few things I needed to sort out first." *Right*. I'm kind of shocked at the fact I feel nothing, listening to her talk. I'm not even upset, just irritated at the disruption.

"I don't care," I convey rather callously but truthfully. "You had years to sort your stuff out, Jeannie, and I would've gladly helped you then, but you chose not to. Not even for our kids. Go back to rehab before the cops find you. You had a sweet deal going but you fucked it up. Again."

"I know, I know—I just need a little time…and some money," she says, finally revealing the true reason for her call.

"You listen to me," I snap, suddenly filled with anger. "I have two kids here who need me. Two kids you haven't even had the decency to call or ask about. Two kids who are struggling to get their feet under them because their mother was, and is, more interested in her next fix, and their father was emotionally unavailable. That is changing. My only responsibility to you is them. My *only* responsibility, Jeannie. Way I see it, you don't deserve my time, effort, or money. Not anymore. Go back, Jeannie. For fuck's sake, think of the kids." I'm almost yelling by the time I run out of steam.

"It's not much…just a few hundred," she simpers and I'm suddenly exhausted.

"Not giving you a thing, woman. You had it all. Fuck, I can't even…" I don't get to finish my thought when the phone is suddenly jerked from my hand.

"I don't ever want to see you again. Leave us alone." Gina's wobbly little girl's voice cuts me deep as she hangs up on her mother. She tosses the phone on the counter and turns immediately into my arms. Over her head, I find Jonas leaning in the doorway, his eyes focused on his sister before they drift up to me.

"Change the phone number, Dad," he says in a low voice before turning around. I hear his footsteps pounding up the stairs, while my little girl sobs against my shirt. *Christ*, she still holds the power to rip into what little balance we manage to find. Maybe Jonas is right, I should change the number. There's no telling she won't call and prey on the kids when I'm not here.

"Love you, Princess," I mumble into my daughter's hair.

"Can you drop me off at Marcy's now?" she says, still sniffling as she pulls out of my hold, and I reluctantly let her go. I feel I should talk to her, but her body language tells me she's shutting down. Maybe her friend will be a good distraction.

"Give me a minute to talk to Jonas and we'll make tracks. Got your bag packed?" When she nods yes, I suggest she loads it in the car while I say goodbye to her brother.

Jonas is at his desk when I get upstairs, his door open a crack, something he's started doing very recently. Before it would always be shut tight.

"You okay, Son?"

He swings his chair around to face me. "Not the first time she's called. I told her to fuck off earlier this week, but yesterday Gina picked up."

"Why didn't you tell me?" I try to curb my irritation as I watch him shrug his shoulders. Of course they wouldn't. She's their mother, they've had plenty of practice dealing with her shit by themselves. I swallow down the lump of guilt stuck in my throat.

"I'll get the number changed on Monday," I promise him. "Give me a call when you get home from Pam's?" Jonas nods, and before I turn to leave, I add, "And, Bud? Full disclosure from here on in, okay?"

"Sure," he easily complies. "But that goes both ways, right? What's with you and Pam?"

He takes me by surprise, especially since I don't have a clear answer myself. All I know is those chocolate eyes, I once thought ice-cold, hide a wealth of passion I've just barely had a taste of, and I crave more. Much more.

"It's complicated, that's what it is."

Pam

I don't know what's got me so distracted today. Twice already Brenda has had to repeat herself because I was off somewhere in my head. I didn't sleep that well either; woke up at three to go to the bathroom and spent the rest of the night restlessly rolling around.

"Do you think I'm getting too old for this?" I ask a question that bubbles up out of nowhere. She looks at me curiously as we work side by side at the kitchen counter, prepping dinner for tonight. We often cook larger quantities on the weekend so we have leftovers going into the week, although I have plans to take some of the jambalaya we're making home for Jonas tonight.

Now that the question is out there, I find I'm actually curious to see what she thinks. Brenda is only ten or so years younger than I am but seems far more on the ball than I've been recently.

"No, I don't," she says with conviction. "But what I do think is that you could probably stand to delegate a bit more, focus on areas you want to focus on, and leave the daily running of the shelter to Doris and myself. You don't live here anymore and yet you seem to be here every day of the week."

Doris is our latest, and youngest, addition to the team. She's qualified, if not overqualified for this job, with a bachelor's in psychology and a master's in social work. On top of that, she has experience with battered women, having worked as a social worker at Maine Medical Center. She was adamant she wanted to focus on working with women in a more long-term setting than what she'd been used to at the hospital. I'd been hesitant, but Brenda had a good feeling about her. She'd been dead on. Doris has been phenomenal. I know between her and Brenda, my girls would be in the best possible hands. Still, stepping back means more than reducing my workload. It means losing my usefulness and that looms like a dark black hole. I've made the shelter—and my girls—my life, my purpose.

"What if you focused on counseling? One-on-one, I mean? Like you do with Sarah? We've always done the group sessions, and I don't suggest to give those up, but perhaps it would be an idea to take on some other patients. Not just focus on abuse victims."

I nod, because I've thought of that. Considered that perhaps part of the reason I've never really moved on myself is because everything I hear and see every single day, keeps me mired in my own past. My mind skips to Jonas, who I'm scheduled to see at seven tonight at my place. Even Maria, who may be an abuse victim, but she's also a young girl, with her life still ahead of her. Kids like that, they still have time to make different choices, to change the course of their lives without being burdened with the weight of all the years wasted, like some of us are.

I have to swallow hard, because it's difficult; admitting I've perhaps burned myself out.

"You make a good point." I make an effort to smile. "I like the idea of a small private practice. Something I can do until I'm old and gray."

Brenda raises an eyebrow and pointedly looks at my freshly shorn, short head of silver-laced hair. "You've got half of that down already." She waggles her index finger at my head. "When are you gonna put some color in that fuzz of yours? You're way too young for that."

"When hell freezes over," I fire back, yanking on her thick braid for good measure. "And you can kiss my dimpled cheeks for even suggesting it." I slap my own ass to illustrate.

"Pass," she deadpans, a distasteful grimace on her face and I burst out laughing. God, that feels good. I don't hold back and apparently it's infectious, since soon Brenda follows suit. Before long the two of us are leaning on the counter, laughing uproariously, when the kitchen door opens and a few heads poke through the gap. The looks on the faces of Maria and Marianne only incite our hilarity.

Still on a bit of an endorphin high from the silly bout of giggles in the shelter's kitchen, I pull into my own driveway. With the knowledge Jonas will be here in less than thirty minutes, it's a little easier to walk into the dark, lonely house and flick on lights as I go. I transfer the contents of the large container into a covered baking dish and pop it in the oven to keep warm.

I've barely changed into comfy clothes when the doorbell rings. Like the first time, Jonas follows me into the kitchen, but this time he seems a bit more animated as he dramatically sniffs the air.

"Smells good. What are we having?"

I chuckle as I pull open the oven and he settles himself without invitation on one of the stools at the kitchen island. I like that he's apparently comfortable enough, or hungry enough, to do so.

"Hope you like shrimp?" I ask, as I pull down two large bowls from the cupboard.

"Yup."

"Good, 'cause it's sausage and shrimp jambalaya. You better have a steel-lined stomach, because I've added some extra heat."

He doesn't answer, but digs right in when I slide his bowl across and hand him a spoon and fork. Amused, I watch as his pace slows down a little when the heat hits. Beads of sweat break out over his forehead when I take pity on him.

"Want some water?"

"Please," he croaks out. "It's good," he adds with a little smirk.

I like a little kick to my food, especially when it's cold out; it warms me up from the inside out.

"How come you don't have any pictures up?" Jonas says suddenly, his eyes roaming the walls and the entertainment center in the living room. It's true; there aren't any pictures up. There are few to begin with and those I have don't particularly remind me of happier times, so I leave them in a box at the bottom of my closet. He looks at me inquisitively, and I decide to play it straight.

"I try to live in the present as much as possible. Pictures are reminders of the past, and not always pleasant. I bought this place not that long ago, maybe a year, and didn't actually move in until the end of the summer. I guess I could put some up, make it a little homier."

He continues to watch me closely for a minute and then his eyes start wandering the room again.

"Mom used to put up pictures everywhere," he says softly, his gaze avoiding mine. "But when I looked at them the other day, I noticed all of them were from when Gina and I were little. Mom was still smiling in those…" His voice trails off and I notice he's struggling to maintain his composure.

Even though this is a great opening for our session, I don't want to push too hard. Instead I turn my back to give him some privacy while he sorts himself out, as I quickly wash the dishes in the sink and put them away. By the time I turn back, he's facing me, the inquisitive look back on his face.

"What happened to you?" he asks. This time I'm so off guard, my hand comes up to my chest. Like father, like son. I should've guessed he's an empath like his dad. It makes sense why he tried drowning out the negative emotions, that must have been swirling around that house, with drugs and booze. He's too young to see—to feel—that much.

"Why do you ask?" I answer his question with one of my own, as I move into the living room, taking my spot in the corner of the couch.

"Because your house is not really a home," he responds with a shrug, while following me and sitting across from me in the chair. "You don't seem to have a family, and you rescue everyone."

The sudden rush of tears has me close my eyes. Seventeen years old, and his eyes are eagle sharp. This boy is an old soul and he has exposed the sum of my existence in just a few words. Just like his father did when he asked, "And who looks after you?"

"I'm sorry," he mutters, seeing my reaction. "That was rude."

"No." I'm quick to stop him. "Don't apologize. I'm just struck how much you remind me of your father. You're insightful, empathetic. It's not all that common in someone your age. I just wasn't expecting it."

His face changes from worry to curiosity. "Empathetic?"

"Yes," I smile at him. "That's when you have the ability to read between the lines of what people are saying. When you can plug in to their emotions and sometimes feel what they feel."

"Like mind reading?" he asks, a look of horror on his face and it makes me laugh.

"Not really. You're simply more attuned to people. Your father is too." The moment the last words leave my mouth, his face darkens and he lets out a bark of deriding laughter.

"Dad? He's not plugged in at all." He's angry, and I've found the focus of our session.

For the next forty or so minutes, I encourage him to get all of those feelings of anger and resentment out on the table. When I close the door behind him, I feel we've accomplished something. I'm exhausted, and not just a little bit relieved at having been able to avoid answering his earlier question.

It's only eight thirty, and although I'd love to haul my ass to bed, I fight the urge. I need to start actually living in my house, not just using it as a place to sleep. I just settled back into the couch, a soft blanket covering my feet and a glass of wine in my hand, when there's a knock on the door. I assume it's Jonas and automatically look around the room and to the kitchen island, to see if he maybe forgot something.

"Did you forget…"

I never get to finish my sentence as I pull open the door, everything happens so fast. I find myself pushed back against the wardrobe doors, an arm pressed against my throat. I don't think, I react and yank up my knee as hard as I can.

"Hey!" I hear yelled. There's another person coming in, but I don't wait; the moment I'm released I swing around, slide the door open and snag my gun from the shelf.

The two punks who stood outside of the motel room are standing in my hallway. Well, one is standing, the other is rolling on the floor clutching his crotch. *Good*. I hope I rendered his little wiener permanently disabled.

A surge of anger floods my veins and it's all I can do not to shoot the little shits.

-

"Ms. Brunard." I look up to find Detective Barnes coming through the door. I'd been backing into the living room to get to my phone, when the two managed to run, or in the case of the one kid, stumble from the house. I immediately called nine one one.

"Detective."

"I just want you to know we are trying to locate the boys, but I wanted to make sure young Mr. Brachio wasn't involved."

I immediately jump to my feet. "Listen, Detective, like I told the other officer earlier, Jonas was visiting, and I am quite positive he has nothing to do with it."

There's a bit of a shuffle by the front door, and I try to look beyond Barnes to see what's going on in the hallway, when I hear Dino's deep bass.

"What the fuck is going on?"

CHAPTER ELEVEN

Dino

"Dad…I think there might be trouble."

Fuck me. Those words are on replay in my head as I drive like a maniac. Jonas said he thought Pam might be in trouble, which is why Ike, who happened to be in the kitchen at The Skipper, is riding shotgun. All I know is some kids jumped my son as he was walking to the bus from Pam's house, and according to him, were after her next. I don't know much else, because that's when the call ended.

Pam's street is blocked off by a patrol car and the flashing lights of emergency vehicles reflect off the houses on either side.

"Easy, Dino." Ike tries to slow me down when I jump out of the car and start bulldozing past the young officer trying to block my way. I ignore both of them as I aim for a huddle of people around a prone figure on the sidewalk. I figure Ike can explain things to the cop.

"*Jonas!*"

At my call, heads swing around and the huddle opens enough for me to see my boy, his face bloody and his body too still. I drop on my knees beside him, ignoring the people jumping out of my way. I'm like a fucking bull, I'll go through walls to get to my kids if I have to.

"Hey, Bud…" I say softly as I stroke his too long hair off his forehead. His eyes are closed but he blinks them open at the sound of my voice. "Where does it hurt?" My eyes and hands are in the middle of a quick scan of his body when I'm interrupted.

"Sir? You need to step back so we have a look at him."

I didn't notice the EMTs walking up. When I try to move back to give them room, Jonas' hand snakes out and grabs my shirt.

"Dad?" his voice croaks. "Can you check on Pam?"

I've never felt so torn. "Not leaving you, Son," I answer, acid churning in my stomach as I watch the EMTs check my boy over. They strap him to a board and load him on a stretcher when a hand lands on my shoulder.

"How's he doing?" Ike's voice sounds behind me.

"I don't know. He's talking."

"That's good. Talking is good. I think Pam's okay. Cops won't let me through but assure me she's being looked after."

"Sir?" That from one of the EMTs at the back of the ambulance where they're about to load Jonas inside. "Are you coming?"

"Hell yes, I'm coming," I say, but my chest hurts.

"No, Dad…" Jonas stops me. "Please check on Pam. I'm fine—I'll be fine."

"But…" Fuck, I'm struggling.

"Please, Dad."

I lean over and carefully kiss his forehead, something I haven't done in years and tears spring to my eyes at the realization. So many mistakes.

"Ike?" I turn to the man beside me, not bothering to hide the emotion on my face. I'm proud of my son tonight.

"I'll stick with him," Ike says with an easy smile. "You good with that, Jonas?" he directs at my son, who nods, squeezing his eyes shut.

I lean down to Jonas' face again, whispering; "I'll make sure she's alright, and then I'll be right behind you, okay? Love you, kiddo."

"I'm sor…" Jonas starts, but I cut him off.

"Time for all that later," I tell him with a sharp shake of my head. Then I turn to Ike and mouth a heartfelt thank you before jogging down the street to Pam's place.

Two uniformed officers block the front steps and when I want to move between them, one of them plants a hand in the middle of my chest.

"Can't go in there, sir," he says firmly.

Like hell I can't. I shrug off his hand and try to slip by them again, one single focus on my mind—Pam. Before I realize what's happening, my arms are pulled behind my back.

"What the fuck is going on?" I struggle to get loose. "I just need to see she's alright!" I yell, frustrated when I feel the cold steel of handcuffs pressing against my wrist.

"Stop!"

I look up to find Pam standing on the doorstep. The sight of her, all in one piece and without any visible injuries, as a quick scan of her body reveals, instantly eases the pressure on my chest. Behind her, the familiar shape of Detective Barnes appears in the doorway.

"It's okay, boys. Let him go," he directs the two officers hanging on to me.

The instant they release me, I dart up the steps and pull Pam in my arms.

"Thank God," I mumble, as I feel her arms come around me.

"I'm okay, Dino. I'm okay." She takes a step back and studies my face. "What's wrong? How did you get here so fast?"

"Jonas. He called me. Said two guys got him in the street, he thought they'd go after you."

"Where is he?" She looks around me down the street.

"On his way to the hospital. Ike's with him. He insisted I make sure you're okay."

The shock on her face makes it clear she had no idea Jonas had been hurt. She suddenly swings around to face the detective.

"You! You knew he was hurt and didn't bother telling me?" She pokes a finger in his chest, making quite an imposing figure. Barnes looks a bit sheepish at the accusation and doesn't stop her when she storms inside, past him. I follow behind her and he doesn't stop me either.

Pam is rummaging in the bottom of the hallway closet, yanking out a pair of boots, she shoves her bare feet in, and grabs a heavy winter coat she shrugs on.

"Let's go," she says, grabbing my hand and pulling me back outside, where Barnes tries to block our way. "Your damn questions will have to wait, Detective," Pam spits at him, clearly infuriated. I'm not sure what exactly is going on, but I get pulled along to her driveway.

"You won't be able to get out," I suggest when she goes to unlock her car. "We'll take mine, it's at the corner."

When we get to my car, we're both a little out of breath. I start the car, while Pam buckles up and turns to me.

"How bad?" she asks, her voice thick with emotion.

"I'm not sure," I admit. "His face looks pretty bad, but I'm not sure about the rest of him."

"You should be with him," she says. It could've sounded like an accusation, but it doesn't. It sounds like guilt. I reach out and grab her hand as I weave through Saturday night, Portland traffic.

"Jonas insisted," I explain. "Wouldn't rest until I checked on you."

I don't hear anything. When I take a quick glance over at her, I can see tears rolling down her face.

"I'm gonna nail those kids," she hisses with vehemence. "Gonna nail their skinny little asses to the wall. Entitled little pricks, with parents too blind to acknowledge the miserable, puny ingrates their sons have become. I'll fucking make sure bail is not an option this time."

I feel it's in my best interests just to keep my mouth shut. Even though I want to kiss her hard right now.

When we park the car at the hospital, she waits for me to round the front and immediately grabs my hand again. Together we go in search of Jonas and Ike.

Pam

"What the heck is that?"

I've just rested my head back against the wall when Dino's bark has me shooting upright in my seat.

We've been relegated to a waiting room, where we find Ike. It appears they've taken Jonas to radiology for scans. Dino almost went off on a nurse, when she couldn't give him more information than that, and he's been pacing like a caged animal since we got here.

"What?" I look confused at Dino pointing in my direction.

"That," he hisses, stopping in front of me and tilting my chin with the fingers of one hand, while the other strokes the skin of my neck. "Those marks? Did they do that?"

I take his hand and pull him down in the chair beside me. We haven't even talked about what happened.

"Jonas had just left when someone knocked at the door. I thought he'd forgotten something and came back. Stupid, because I wasn't as careful as I should've been. Anyway," I continue when I feel his hand tighten around mine. "One of them had me pinned against the wardrobe door by the throat. I got him off, managed to grab my gun from the closet shelf, and tried to find my phone to call nine one one when the two of them bolted out of there. I'm fine," I add in a soothing voice. "I guess his hold left some marks, but trust me." I try to make light at the sight of Dino's stormy expression. "By the time that boy can swallow around his balls, I made sure will be lodged in his throat for a while, these little marks will be long gone."

Ike chuckles in the background, but Dino stares at me intensely, suddenly snagging me by the back of my head and laying a kiss on me that had my toes curling. "You kicked ass," he finally says when he releases his hold.

"Sure as hell hope so," I mumble, trying hard to not to sneak a slightly embarrassed peek at Ike's reaction to that unexpected PDA.

Before I give in to temptation, the door opens and a doctor, who looks way too young to claim that title, walks in.

"Brachio family?"

Dino stands up, instantly intimidating the young doctor to start stammering.

"I'm Doctor Weston." He sticks out his hand, which Dino pointedly ignores. "Right, well…I have some bad news and some good news," he says, unnecessarily building suspense. *Idiot.*

"Talk," Dino barks, shocking the nervous young man, who responds by fiddling with his stethoscope.

"Yes. Absolutely…we did an MRI scan of his brain since he reports having his head slammed to the ground a few times. We also did a CT scan to determine if there was any internal bleeding since he reported being kicked a few times. He's in ultrasound now and should be out shortly."

Dino growls, his frustration obviously mounting to dangerous heights, so I jump in.

"We'd like some results," I prompt, and the doctor, whose fearful eyes have been focused on Dino, turns to me in relief.

"Of course. His brain looks clear. No bleeds or swelling we can detect, but we'll observe to look for any changes. That's the good news," he quickly adds to Dino who just flares his nostrils. "The scan showed some internal bleeding, likely coming from the spleen. He's in ultrasound to confirm, but it's possible he will need surgery to have the spleen removed."

"When?" Dino bites off.

"Right away. I'll go see if he's back from radiology yet. You'll be able to see him before he's taken to the OR." Doctor Weston moves to the door, pulling it open

"You the one doing the surgery?" he calls after Weston, who's halfway out the door.

"Oh no. That will be Doctor Morton, the surgeon on call," the doctor replies before letting the door shut behind him.

"Thank fuck for that," Dino mutters, voicing my thoughts.

-

"Where's Gina?" I ask Dino when we're back in the waiting room after briefly seeing Jonas.

Dino had gone in first, when the nurse came to get him, but had returned for me shortly after. Jonas insisted he wanted to see for himself I was okay. Poor kid looked a mess, with his left eye swollen shut, a cut above his eyebrow they assured us would get stitched up in the OR, and a nose that looked to be broken. Something else they'd 'fix' while he was under, to save time. We were told his spleen had ruptured, and they wanted to move quickly to remove it and stop the bleeding. I almost lost it when I watched Dino gently stroke the hair back from his son's forehead and press a kiss there, telling him loved him, and he'd be waiting.

"At Marcy's," he answers, belatedly realizing I probably have no clue who Marcy is. "Her best friend," he adds, with a squeeze to my hand, which he's been hanging onto ever since we saw Jonas wheeled off.

Ike had excused himself maybe ten minutes ago, asking us if we wanted anything. Dino just shook his head, but I asked for a few bottles of water.

"He'll be okay," I assure Dino when the door opens and Detective Barnes walks in.

"Sorry to interrupt," he says, looking at Dino. "I understand your son is in surgery so I won't take up much of your time, but I have a few questions for both of you." At Dino's nod, he takes a seat across from us and leans forward, his elbows on his knees. "Mr. Brachio, do you know what your son was doing in Ms. Brunard's neighborhood?" I bristle, because I've already answered that question earlier, but Dino almost shoots up from his seat.

"I've mentioned that a few times already, Detective," I jump in. "Jonas was at my house, visiting, having dinner with me. Jesus, the kid had the snot beaten out of him, you can't honestly think he has anything to do with this." The detective looks at me apologetically before turning to Dino.

"I have to make sure," he clarifies. "Ms. Brunard's phone is unlisted, and I have to wonder how those two managed to find her. Your son is the only connection."

"He wouldn't have told them," Dino says in a sure voice.

"With all due respect, a lot was going on in your son's life recently you weren't aware of."

I'm done. This time I surge up from my seat. "It's none of your goddamn business, but for the sake of getting you off this dead end street; Jonas was at my house a few minutes before seven for our scheduled appointment." When the detective's eyebrows rise in question, I continue. "He's comfortable talking to me about things. He was there on Thursday night as well. Now tell me, Detective Barnes, does it make sense to you that a boy who goes to see a counselor because he struggles emotionally, would share this information with anyone? Have you considered the possibility he was followed?" His hand has come up defensively during my tirade, but he doesn't speak until I'm done.

"Of course," he says curtly, "but what you may not understand is the kind of hold these gangs can have on their recruits. This particular group won't hesitate threatening a life—a family member's life—to get what they want from an individual."

"See…that's where you're wrong," I fire back immediately. "I know it better than most." I feel the immediate scrutiny from both men the moment the revealing words leave my mouth, so I quickly push on. "What you don't seem willing to understand is that *if* Jonas had been forced somehow to pass on my address, why in God's name would he sit at my kitchen counter eating my food with gusto? Why would he spend an hour sharing the most painful thoughts and feelings with me, all the time knowing someone was waiting outside to have a go at me? That doesn't make any sense at all!"

A heavy silence settles in the room after I lose my cool. A gentle tugging at my hand draws my attention as Dino pulls me to sit back down. The moment I do, he slings an arm around my shoulders. Heavy, but grounding. He doesn't say a word, and I'm afraid to look his way, so I look at my knees instead.

"Two possibilities remain," Barnes suggests. "They either encountered him by chance and followed him, or—and this is a bit more worrisome—they've had their eye on your son the entire time. Which would imply they know where your family lives." Dino goes solid beside me. "I'll have to talk to Jonas at some point when he's recovered enough. In the meantime, until we have these two picked up, please be cautious." Without another word, he gets up and leaves.

"You jumped in for my boy," Dino rumbles beside me, and I turn to see him watching me intently.

"Of course I did. He had nothing to do with this," I sputter defensively.

"No," he says, leaning in a little. "You're not getting it. You barely know him, and yet you trusted him enough to know he wouldn't have done that." I just nod at that, unsure exactly what he's trying to tell me. "I'm his father, and I didn't believe him."

"What?" I'm confused, did he really think…

"Not about this," he clarifies. "His mother accused him of stealing from me when I found money missing. I believed her." The way his head hangs dejectedly tugs at my heartstrings.

"That's different," I offer softly, wanting to ease his guilt. "You loved her."

"I didn't," he says, surprising me. "Not anymore. Probably not for a long time." I need a minute to take that in before responding.

"Doesn't matter. Would you ever, as a parent, try to sell out your child?" I want him to answer the question himself. He's toting a lot of responsibility that doesn't belong on his shoulders.

"Of course not," he snaps, his eyes shooting daggers at me. I'll take it.

"Then why would you think the mother of your children would be capable of that?" I volley back, sitting back, letting him think on that by himself.

Shortly after that Ike comes back, carrying two bottles of water and a couple of brown paper bakery bags. He's not alone; Gunnar walks in behind him. Ike shrugs his shoulders at Dino's glare and sits down, pulling a pastry out of one of the bags and chomping down.

"Any news?" Gunnar asks, sitting on the other side of Dino after pecking me on the cheek. He doesn't mince words, doesn't go into long explanations, he's just here supporting his friend.

"Nothing yet," I hear Dino mumble, as I lean over to snag a bottle and one of the bags from the seat beside Ike. He winks at me and I can't hold back the little smile tugging at my mouth.

I've been dozing off, with the occasional rumble of voices as the guys shoot the shit, when a different doctor—presumably Doctor Morton, the surgeon—walks in the door to tell us Jonas has come through surgery. He's in recovery, but his father can see him as soon as he's moved to a room.

Dino urges the guys to get home to their families. It's coming up on one o'clock in the morning. As we're saying goodbye to Gunnar and Ike, I notice Dino hasn't suggested I head home. Nor have the other guys offered me a ride. Men will always be something of a mystery to me. They seem to be able to communicate between them without words, or effort in some cases, but become severely incapacitated in the skills of communication at other times.

It's the same now. He sits back down next to me, picks up the hand he really hasn't let go of all night, and leans his head back, his eyes closed. Never once telling me what he wants from me. I chuckle quietly, but he hears.

"What?"

"Should I leave too?" I tease him a little and laugh a little harder when his eyebrows scrunch up in confusion.

"No, I want you to stay," he says, matter-of-factly. "Unless you want to go. Maybe I can still…" He moves to get up but I hold him back.

"I'll stay. I just wanted to be sure." I put him at ease, and—if I'm honest—myself.

CHAPTER TWELVE

Dino

That's one night I never want to do over again.

We didn't have to wait long before a nurse came to let us know Jonas had been moved to a room and we could go see him briefly. I grab Pam's hand and pull her along. Not sure why, but her presence calms me, otherwise I might've put a few holes in the wall with all this pent up anger I have churning my blood. There's a strong urge to go out and hunt down those two kids who did this to my son—to Pam.

"Five minutes," the nurse said outside the door. "His roommate is sleeping."

Jonas was asleep, his face still a mess. I barely noticed the light snoring coming from behind the curtains the nurse pulled around the other patient, I'm focused on the sounds my son was making. He woke up briefly, once, just long enough for me to tell him I love him and promise to be back in the morning. We left shortly after that, Pam quietly supportive beside me.

Just like she is now, sitting in the passenger seat beside me, as I drive her home. I reach over and grab her hand again and notice how easily she slides her long fingers between mine. Effortlessly, as if we've done this our entire lives—hold hands. Suddenly I don't want to drop her off.

"Come home with me?" I hear myself asking, without taking my eyes from the road. I can feel her shifting in her seat, pinning those deep brown eyes on me.

"Dino…" she starts, her voice careful.

"Never mind," I quickly interrupt, not wanting to put her on the spot. Things are too raw right now. Too many emotions close to the surface. It's probably better. "Forget I said anything." I cringe, I sound like a fucking girl.

"What I was going to say," Pam says sternly, her hand squeezing mine. "Is that I'd like to grab a few things at my place quickly first. If that's okay?"

Stopped at a red light, I take the opportunity to glance over. Her eyes are bright in her dark face, surprising, given the long night we've had. A small smile tugs at her lips. I simply nod, bringing her hand up to kiss the back of it. I want to tell her I'm not looking for anything more than her company tonight, but I'm pretty sure she gets that.

She literally takes just two minutes before she appears with a small bag in her hand, tossing it in the backseat. Five minutes after that we pull into my driveway. The house is dark and quiet, something that's pretty rare with two teenagers. I briefly spoke with Marcy's mom earlier tonight, while Jonas was in surgery, and agreed with her that we'd let Gina have her fun tonight, and she'd bring her home tomorrow morning.

"Can I get you anything?" I ask Pam, walking into the kitchen.

"I'm good, thanks. I think I'm going to get ready for bed," she says.

"Up the stairs and to the right," I direct her. "I'll just lock up."

I watch her go up the stairs and am amazed, once again, at how easy it is with her. I check the doors and turn off the lights before following her upstairs. I sent her to my room without even thinking about it, and when I walk in, I hear the tap running in the adjoining bathroom. I strip down to my boxers and lie back on the bed, on top of the covers with my hands behind my head. The moment she walks into the bedroom, wearing old man's PJ pants and a loose tank top, I find myself smiling.

"Only you," I chuckle, as I get off the bed to take my turn in the bathroom.

"Only me, what?" she inquires.

"Make grandpa's pyjamas look sexy as shit." I don't wait for a response when I close the bathroom door behind me and the growing tent in my boxers. I could do with a cold splash of water. By the time I open the door, the tentative control I regained over my body evaporates at the sight of Pam in my bed. *Fucking hell.*

Her eyes trail down the length of my body, which doesn't really help my condition. I'm big, but perhaps not as buff as some of the other guys. A little soft around the middle, maybe, but judging from her expression, whatever it is she sees when she looks at me, she likes. She flicks back the covers for me and I get in. Without hesitation, she snuggles up with her head on my shoulder, her hand on my chest, fingers toying with the hair there, as she pulls a leg up over mine.

"Thank you," I mumble against her short hair, choked up by the easy care she shows me. Pretty fucking humbling, considering she's the one who was attacked tonight. "You're doing it again."

"What?" she asks, her breath stroking my nipple and I inadvertently shiver at the sensation.

"Looking out for others—for me, my boy." Her shoulders shrug under my arm. "Yet, it's not easy for you to let someone look out for you."

"I know," she quietly admits, surprising me.

"How come?" I tuck her a little tighter to me, trying not to get too distracted with the way her soft body molds with mine.

"Survival." Her response is as obscure as it is telling.

"Trust," I counter, feeling the instant stiffening of her shoulders as I let her know I'm on to her. "One of these days I hope you'll trust me enough."

It takes a while before she's relaxed against me again. I wonder if she's fallen asleep, as I'm about to do, when she suddenly speaks.

"You always did see right through me…"

I lift her chin with my hand, lower my mouth and slide my lips over hers in a soft kiss, without ever taking my eyes of her. When I pull back, I let my thumb stroke along her full mouth.

"Sleep," I gently prompt her. "I've got you."

Pam

"Mmmm. Don't move."

I'm not sure what time it is, just that I have a heavy, hairy leg over mine, keeping them trapped, and a strong arm holding me tight. I'm on my side with Dino behind me, his body draped over mine, holding it captive. Yet, it's the kind of captivity I don't really want to escape. His hand is possessively curved around my breast and his morning wood is pressing against my ass. Although I'm not sure it's morning wood, he felt hard against me last night as we lay talking.

It's strange, sleeping with someone. I'm not sure how long it's been since I've actually gone to sleep with someone beside me, let alone holding me. Sex, yes…I've indulged from time to time, but more as a physical release than anything else. This is intimate, much more so than I'm comfortable with.

"Need the bathroom," I whisper, both from actual need and an urge to escape.

"Mmmm," Dino groans behind me again, before kissing my neck where his face is nestled, and reluctantly letting me go.

I can only hide in here so long, once I've done my business and washed my face and hands. I even brushed my teeth, part of me hoping he's fallen back asleep, and part of me longing for something else altogether.

His arm is covering his face when I tiptoe back in. Figuring him asleep, I sneak over to the window beside the bed to peek through the curtains. It's still dark as night out there, but at this time of year, the sun takes a while to come up. All I know is, it's after two and before eight a.m.

When I move past the bed to try and find my purse, and my phone, I'm suddenly pulled down by the arm. I tumble across Dino's chest where his arms band around me tightly.

"Where are you off to?" he asks, his voice gruff with sleep.

"Just checking the time."

"It's early," he mumbles, pulling me up so my body is draped over his.

Perfectly, deliciously brushing along my skin, proving it truly is just one large erogenous zone. My brain slightly disoriented, I follow the lead of my body and let my legs fall open to cradle his hips. With my knees in the mattress, it's like my center seeks the promise I saw through the thin fabric of his boxers. His hands land deceptively casually on my thighs as I involuntarily rock myself against him, a hot flush burning up my skin.

This is not like me.

I freeze my movements and push up on his chest, trying desperately to regain some sense. Strong hands grab firm hold of my hips and Dino resumes the rhythm I abandoned, drawing a deep moan from my throat as his hot, prominent length engraves a path through my thinly covered folds.

"Feel what you do to me?" His voice is raw with need, his touch controlling. He renders me breathless—mindless—as I struggle to hang onto one coherent thought amid this sensory overload.

Each time the head of his cock brushes the tight bundle of nerves crowning my center, an electric charge travels along my skin. Goosebumps rise on my flesh and my nipples harden in response. I give myself up to sensations with my head thrown back, slowly gliding along his erection.

"Up," he croaks, pulling up on my tank top and I obediently raise my arms. He sits up underneath me and slides his hands up alongside my spine, pressing me close. My hands grab onto his head the instant his lips close around my nipple, tugging me deep into the wet heat of his mouth.

"Oh my God…" I can't hold back as he flips me on my back, his hips still between my legs and his mouth firmly attached to my breast.

"So sweet," he mumbles against my skin as his mouth travels to the other side, rolling his tongue around my nipple.

"Dino…" I sigh when his hands slip under the elastic of my PJs and work them down my hips.

"Easy, Biscuit," he cautions when my movements become urgent. "It's been a fucking long time and I don't want this over yet." I whimper when he moves off me, sitting on his heels and slowly dragging my pants down, lifting each of my legs clear.

I'm completely aware of the state of my body, but the look of reverence on his face as he traces my skin with his eyes relieves me of any misgivings I might have. Neither of us is looking for perfection. In fact, neither of us is looking, period. Yet here we are. And oh…*hello!* With an agile move I wouldn't have thought possible for a man his size, Dino has managed to ditch the boxers. One of his large paws is wrapped around his impressive looking cock, leisurely stroking, and with the fingers of the other hand he deftly plays between my legs. All I can reach in this position is the headboard, and I hold on tight, as he plays my body like a fine-tuned instrument. A little flick, a tentative brush, a languid caress, and a firm pinch have me rushing at breakneck speed toward what promises to be an earth-shattering orgasm, when suddenly his fingers drift away.

"Dino!" I hiss my displeasure, putting a self-satisfied smirk on his face as he eases himself on top of me. My hands immediately release the headboard to touch him, but he sharply shakes his head.

"Leave them," he suggests in a low voice, asking me to do more than just hold on. He's asking me to trust. When I slowly stretch them back over my head, once again grabbing the headboard, he kisses my chin, and then my nose, but his eyes never leave mine. "Thank you," he whispers, barely audible.

Settling himself a little deeper in the cradle of my hips, I feel his erection nudge at my center; I open my legs wider in invitation. I'm rewarded with another kiss.

"Next test," he mumbles against my mouth. "I don't have condoms and I'm not about to scour my son's room for them. I'm clean, babe, and I'm desperate to get inside you. You can stop me."

In his eyes I see a challenge as well as a hint of insecurity; just like that he reminds me that I have as much power as he does.

"I need a test?" I ask, my voice raspy with a need I'm struggling not to give in to. "I wasn't aware there were going to be questions." Bluster. All of it bluster, a blind man could see the hunger on my face as I attempt to feign indifference. Inasmuch as that is possible, with my legs spread wide and my arms raised well above my head, basically offering myself up.

"Say the word," he prompts, seeing right through.

"Aren't you worried about me?"

"Not even a little," he responds instantly. "Your call, Beautiful." He rocks his hips slightly, letting the head of his cock slip just inside me before pulling back. I lift my butt off the bed in an attempt to keep the connection.

"Yes." My voice sounds pathetic and needy.

"You sure?"

"Yes! Please…"

Before I can even finish, my breath is stolen from me as he fills me with his considerable girth. "Breathe, baby," he says in a strangled voice, the strain showing on his face, as he stills inside me, giving me time to accommodate to his size. The stretch is not unpleasant, but it is unexpected, and it takes me a minute to catch my breath. The entire time his head is hanging down, but his eyes are focused on my face.

"I want to touch you," I tell him, taking my hands down and curling them around his back. I slide them down until I cup his deliciously tight ass, watching the almost tortured expression on his face as he holds himself back. "Now I'm ready."

"Thank fuck," he hisses, pulling out of me excruciatingly slowly, before powering back inside. And again, the slow move out, before hammering home. I feel every ridge, every vein, every inch of his dick as he moves inside me, and each time he rams inside me, the root of his cock presses against my clit.

It's both heaven and hell. Too much, and not enough. When my body finally falls apart around me, it's accompanied by Dino's guttural grunts as he bucks his way into his own release.

Dino

Holy shit.

I'm sucking in breath like I've just finished a marathon in record time. Those damn noises she makes, the clench of her fingers on the muscles of my ass, the tight wrap of her long legs around my hips. *Christ,* I feel like my brains are leaking from my ears, I came so hard.

Still trying to regain some control over my shaking limbs, I feel her shift underneath me and realize my full weight is lying on her. I quickly push up on my arms.

"Sorry," I huff out, feeling the slight drag of my cock still half hard inside her. I don't want to leave her surprisingly tight grip on me. My forehead drops down to hers. "Did I hurt you?" I can feel her hands start stroking, soothing my back.

"No." Her husky voice is like lush velvet, rich with satisfaction, and it puts a smile on my face. "Don't look so smug," she smirks. "Or I won't tell you how memorable your moves are." I lift my head away a little, smiling down at her.

"Memorable?"

"Mmmm," she purrs, sliding a hand out from behind me and tracing the line of my jaw with her fingertips. "Quite."

"More magnificent than memorable," I tease.

"You, or it?" she comes right back, without blinking an eye.

"Us." I lean down and press my lips to her slightly stunned, opened mouth, taking the opportunity to sweep my tongue inside, tasting a hint of toothpaste coupled with the rich, creamy flavor all Pam's.

Reluctantly I pull away, and soft as I am now, I sadly slip from her body, feeling the loss immediately. I rush to the bathroom to grab something to clean her up with, but the sight of her as I walk back in has me slow down. Not a hint of embarrassment now, as she lies in my bed, one arm resting on her forehead, the other loosely folded over her stomach, and one leg still out wide with the other leg pulled up, her foot flat on the mattress. All that beautiful skin on full display.

"Beautiful," I say, as I sit down on the mattress beside her cocked leg. She quietly observes me as I gently pull her leg open and use the towel I grabbed to wipe my release from her inner thighs.

"It's the afterglow." My eyes shoot up to see her lips tilted in amusement.

"No, the afterglow makes you stunning," I clarify, watching as the amusement slips from her face and is replaced with a pensive expression.

"You mean that." It's not a question, but a conclusion that seems to surprise her.

"Every single syllable," I confirm, tossing the towel on the floor and leaning over her.

I close my mouth over hers and lick my tongue along the crease of her lips, when I hear the sound of the front door slamming shut. But it's the sound of my daughter's voice calling upstairs that hits like a bucket of ice water.

"Daddy!"

CHAPTER THIRTEEN

Pam

That wasn't awkward at all.

I've never seen a man shoot out of bed that fast. Of course, I have to admit, I was close behind him as his daughter's footsteps started coming up the stairs. I make a beeline for the bathroom, where I hung yesterday's clothes on the hook and left my bag. More importantly, where I can safely lock myself out of sight. In situations like this, it's every man for himself. Or herself. In any event, I feel no guilt as I slip by Dino's big form, digging with a touch of desperation through the dresser drawer for something to wear, and into the bathroom, locking the door firmly behind me. I hear the slamming of a drawer right before I hear the door open up and Dino's deep rumble filter through. I'm already half-dressed when a tentative knock on the door sounds. I quickly pull my shirt over my head before unlocking and opening the door a crack.

"Let me in?"

I oblige by stepping back, letting Dino squeeze his body through.

"I'm sorry."

"What are you sorry for?" I ask as I watch him lift the toilet seat. *Oh.* "I'll just wait outside," I mumble as I turn and fumble with the door before I realize I don't know who's on the other side. I'm a little freaked out by the intimacy of the situation. This entire episode I can do without. Well, except the sex part, that was really, really phenomenal. But getting caught by his little girl, and being stuck hiding in a bathroom with him peeing a few feet away from me? Yeah, that I can do without. It's a little intense.

Behind me I hear the toilet flush and the tap turn on.

"She's in her room. The other bathroom is between her room and Jonas'." I feel the heat from his body as he moves in right behind me. "I promise I won't make this a habit," he whispers, close to my ear.

A habit? That implies something long-term. And what about his kids? Jonas. That boy is in the hospital and we're hiding in the bathroom like a pair of teenagers caught in the act. What am I doing? My thoughts are erratic and I feel panic edging in.

"I've gotta go," I blurt out.

"Give me a minute to talk to her and I'll drive you. She doesn't know about Jonas yet, I haven't had a chance to tell her, but she'll want to see him right away. I'll take her to the hospital." His hands drop on my shoulders and turn me to face him. Concern is lined on his face. For his son, his little girl, even for me.

"I'll grab a cab," I say quickly. "Now's not a good time to introduce…" My voice falters while my mind scrambles to find an appropriate description for what we are. I'm not sure. We went from barely tolerating each other to this—whatever this is— and I've been so wrapped up living in the moment, I've not really thought the consequences through. "Now's just not a good time."

Dino looks at me through squinted eyes, his hands still on my shoulders.

"You're panicking," he says, matter-of-factly. I don't have to answer, I'm sure he can see it all over my face. After a moment he leans in and brushes his lips over mine. "There's a lot going on right now, so I'll let you have that play, but promise me you won't use this to keep me at a distance again. I won't let you."

"Okay," I agree, but I'm really not so sure.

Dino ends up taking Gina for breakfast, and while I'm waiting for them to leave, I call a cab. Ten minutes later, I pull the front door closed behind me.

-

"Mrs. Brunard?"

I just stepped out of a quick shower when my phone rings. I don't recognize the voice, but a cold chill slips down my back as I listen to the official way I'm addressed. Holding the towel I wrapped around me closed with a fist, I take in a deep breath before answering.

"It's Ms."

"Ms. Brunard," the man on the other side corrects himself. "I'm terribly sorry to have to inform you…"

I barely hear the rest as I sink down on the edge of my mattress, the pain in my chest ballooning to where I'm beyond functioning. All I manage is a hoarse, "Thank you," when the man stops talking, and I double over, wrapping my arms around me in an attempt to hold myself together. A low keening sound fills my ears and I realize it's coming from me.

Time stands still. I have no idea whether I've been curled up on my mattress for minutes or hours, all I know is when my phone rings, my throat is raw and my chest feels like my heart's been ripped right out of it. I push myself up and find my phone at the foot end of the bed.

"I'm sorry," I answer, after seeing the number for Florence House appear on the display.

"You're not that late," Brenda answers. "I'm just getting the group started and thought I'd give your phone one more try. Everything okay?"

I struggle to get my bearings when I notice it's getting dark outside. "Group?" I mumble, a little confused.

"Your Monday group? Pam? What's going on?"

Monday?

I take the phone away from my ear to look at the display. It's Monday, and it's a little after seven p.m., almost thirty-six hours after I left Dino's house. I struggle to remember the hours but only have vague impressions of shuffling to the bathroom before curling up in bed again. I can't even remember day turning to night and back again. Just flashes of numbly responding to my body's primary needs.

I also notice on my screen that there are a large number of missed calls.

"Pam?" I hear the tinny voice of Brenda coming from the phone I'm holding in my lap and quickly bring it back to my ear.

"I'm here," I manage, my voice sounding not much better. "Something's come up."

"Are you sick? Do you need anything?" There's an edge of worry to her voice that should warm me, but it leaves me oddly cold.

"I need some time," I say, ignoring her questions. "Can you and Doris manage?"

"Of course. You don't sound well, is there someone I can—"

"I'll be fine. I'll be in touch," I cut her off and end the call, not needing the reminder that there is no one.

Not anymore.

Dino

Three days I've tried to connect with her. Three fucking days of voice messages, texts, and calls to the shelter. Nothing. Fucking nada. The girl who answered the phone at Florence House this afternoon said she was taking some time off and couldn't say when she'd be back.

I'm not sure what happened after I whisked Gina out of the house Sunday morning, but I'm positive something did. Yes, the situation had been a little uncomfortable, but even if that had been enough to scare her off, I'm pretty confident she'd never have left Jonas hanging. He came home yesterday and I'm worried about him. He seems even more withdrawn, and I heard him and Gina fight last night, but neither will say what it's about. This morning they weren't talking and I feel at a loss, which only adds to my frustration I can't get hold of Pam.

I'm not the only one. Detective Barnes called me yesterday, letting me know that both those punks were picked up driving a stolen car the night before. Despite their parents' money and social standing, he assured me they wouldn't be let out on bail this time. He mentioned trying to contact Pam as well, but hadn't been successful and was hoping I'd be able to pass on the message.

Jonas assures me he'll be fine alone at home, and I've already taken too much time off, so I let Gunnar know I'll be in today. With Gina off to school and my boy installed on the couch with drinks, snacks, the remote, and the house phone, I head out to The Skipper. I resist the compulsion to drive by Pam's house— for the second time—but it's no use. I automatically turn left instead of right at the end of my street, part of me knowing I'll likely find her car still gone from her driveway, just like it was yesterday when I drove by twice. Borderline obsessive, that's what I've become and it pisses me off.

Sure enough, the driveway is empty, and today's Portland Press joined the previous two on her doorstep. With a frustrated squeal of my wheels, I speed away from her house, determined to get some answers today.

"Morning." A much too cheery Viv is already pulling bins from the pantry. I grunt in response, hanging up my coat and wrapping my apron around my waist. "How's Jonas?"

"Sore," I tell her, grabbing a couple of cutting boards from the cupboard. "But getting better."

"Good." She nods.

"Where's Pam?"

She turns to face me, and from the surprise on her face, I know what the answer will be.

"Pam? At work I assume," she says, her eyes narrowing slightly. "Is she okay? Ike mentioned she came to the hospital with you, but he told me she wasn't hurt. I haven't been able to get hold of her yet. Why?" She's pinning me with a suspicious glare, and I'm tempted to blow it off to avoid her scrutiny, but I can't. Something is up with Pam.

"I can't get hold of her, she's apparently taken some time off work and her car hasn't been in her driveway."

Without saying anything, Viv walks over to grab the phone and dials.

"Hey, Brenda, it's Viv. Listen, is Pam there?" I watch her face as the woman on the other end likely tells her the same thing she's been telling me. "Really? That's not like her. Did she say anything else?" The curious expression Viv wears is replaced by one of concern. "I know…odd. Are you guys managing?…All right, I'll take over the group tonight. No worries." She hangs up the phone and turns to me. "What happened? Brenda says she tried calling Sunday when she didn't show up, and all through Monday night when she finally managed to get through. She says Pam sounded like she was in bad shape." The uneasy feeling I've been trying—and failing—to ignore these past few days, takes over. "Dino? What the hell happened?"

I'm pretty sure neither Ike or Gunnar are the kind of guys to speculate out loud about whether or not there's something going on between Pam and I, although I know they noticed Saturday night.

"Gina came home Sunday morning, earlier than expected, it was awkward."

"Wait…awkward? Are you telling me Pam spent the night? With you?" Her disbelief grates on me.

"That so hard to believe? Yes—not that I owe you an explanation," I point out defensively, "—but we left the hospital late, she crashed at mine, and the next morning Gina was dropped off before we got up. Pam offered to take a cab home and I agreed. Only because I had my little girl, who had no idea yet her brother was attacked the night before and was in the hospital. It didn't seem an appropriate moment for her to also deal with…" I've run out of steam. It also doesn't help Gunnar stands in the doorway, snickering behind Viv, whose eyes seem to get bigger with every word I purge. "Pam." I finish lamely.

"I swear—" Viv fans herself dramatically as she talks. "—I don't know how much more I can take. Not only have I just witnessed the most stoic man I know suffer from flustered, verbal diarrhea, but finally—*finally*—you two have obviously come to the same conclusion the rest of us figured out fucking years ago. Alleluia!" Viv throws her arms in the air and Gunnar busts out laughing behind her.

I take in the scene for no more than a second before dousing all hilarity with cold reality.

"So where is Pam?" Repeating my earlier question has the desired effect. The silence in the kitchen is instantaneous.

"What do you mean; where's Pam?" Gunnar's face is dead serious as he stalks into the kitchen. I open my mouth to explain—again—when Viv jumps in and swiftly fills Gunnar in. Before I have a chance to weigh in, he has his phone to his ear.

"Hey, Bird," he mumbles and I know he's talking to Syd. "You heard from Pam at all?"

Apparently Syd has no clue and after Ruby shows up for her shift, she makes it clear she doesn't know either. It isn't until later that evening, when Tim walks into the kitchen with his brother Mark following close behind, that I see something other than surprise at her disappearance. Tim is as clueless as the rest of us, but I can tell Mark knows something from the way he avoids my eyes.

"Spill," I snap, as I step into his space. I'm at the end of my rope and the fact this guy clearly knows more about her than the rest of us do, doesn't exactly sit well. He brings up his hands defensively between us.

"Not my place, brother," he says, with a regretful shake of his head. Frustration, worry, and yes, even jealousy, has Mark shoved against the wall, my arm pinning him by the neck. I don't care he's an ex-cop. I don't care he's rumored to work with the FBI. All I know is that he's blocking access to Pam.

"You know," I spit in his face, while Tim is making attempts to intervene, which I ignore. "Something's happened or she would never, ever take off and let us worry. Talk!" I lean my weight into my arm, watching Mark's face get redder with no small measure of satisfaction. *Motherfucker.* I'm suddenly pulled back, Tim on one arm and Gunnar, who must've heard the commotion, on the other.

"Easy, my friend," Gunnar rumbles in my ear before turning to Mark. "As you can see, our friendly giant here has reached the end of his tether. If you have any information, I'd consider sharing." Mark's eyes dart from his brother, to Gunnar, and finally to me, before he lets out a deep sigh, his hand distractedly rubbing at his throat.

"You have to understand," he starts. "I'm guessing she has her reasons for not telling anyone. Dammit, she didn't exactly tell me. I didn't clue in until recently when I heard her last name. She's always just been Pam to me. When I heard Brunard, I knew I'd heard the name before but I couldn't place it. This weekend I caught a short article in the paper that made all the pieces fall into place. An inmate at Greenhaven Correctional Facility was found dead in his isolation cell. His name was Derrick Taylor."

"Motherfucker," I snap. "What the fuck does any of it have to do with Pam?" When Mark turns to me, it's with regret, but also anger in his eyes.

"Look it up," he says, shrugging his shoulders. "Don't make me tell you a secret she's obviously worked hard to keep. I've already said more than she'll be happy with. Don't make me sell out a friend." I meet his intense stare dead on, before I finally pull my phone from my back pocket and type, *Derrick Taylor,* into my browser. I click on the first listing and start reading until my eye catches on something.

Derrick Taylor was found lifeless in his cell at Green Haven Maximum Security Correctional Facility early this morning. Mr. Taylor, convicted in 2001 of Second Degree Murder in the death of a shopkeeper during the course of a robbery, and sentenced to twenty-five years, had been moved to the isolation

ward after a violent altercation with another inmate last month. Mr. Taylor was only thirty-three years old.

Green Haven officials indicate an investigation into the cause of death will be forthcoming.

At this time we have not been able to contact Mr. Taylor's family for a reaction. Several attempts were made to contact Ms. Paloma Brunard, currently residing in Portland, Maine, but were unsuccessful.

I sit down heavily on a kitchen chair and drop my phone on the table. It skitters to the other side where Gunnar snatches it up and starts reading. *Jesus.*

"Are you sure it's her?" I try, lifting my eyes to Mark, even though I already know the answer. I can fucking feel it in my bones.

"Positive."

"Years I've known her," Gunnar mutters under his breath, sliding my phone to Tim. "And I had no fucking idea."

None of us did. Although that's not entirely true, I always knew there was something. I just was never able to figure out what. Pam—or *Paloma*—carefully kept herself, her past, shut off from everyone.

"What the fuck?" Tim bursts out when he finishes reading. "I never even knew she had a brother."

"Son," I say quietly, as bits and pieces of conversations and impressions float back, painting a clearer picture now. Derrick Taylor is the missing piece to the puzzle that is Pam Brunard.

"Sorry, what?" Tim turns to me, looking confused.

"Pam's his mother."

CHAPTER FOURTEEN

Pam

The silence is killing me, and still I can't bring myself to turn on my phone. I never even listened to the numerous messages already accumulating.

I panicked when Brenda's call woke me. Since the warden called the morning before, I'd lost the better part of two days. Her phone call propelled me into a flurry of activity. Pushing down the urge to curl up in a ball in the shower, I washed instead. My body suddenly alive with jerky, ill-controlled movements as I dressed and packed my bags. All I could think about was being close to him, my mind not quite having processed the fact he is no longer there. His body is all that ties me to him, so I needed to be where it still is. In the Green Haven Penitentiary's morgue.

My boy.

My beautiful, cheerful, sensitive, and bright little boy, who went from a seemingly perfectly happy kid, to a sullen and troubled teen. I blame myself for not seeing it earlier. I had my head too far up my own ass at the time to recognize the happy-go-lucky smiles he showered me in were his way of lighting up our world, *my* world. All the time I was supposed to be caring for him—making sure he was happy—he was really looking after me. Until one day he stopped smiling.

Even then, I didn't want to see it. I wasn't equipped to recognize the lost soul that had taken over the body of my cheerful child. Barely able to pull out of a lifetime of poor judgement and bad decisions, myself still struggling to *adult* at thirty-four, my sixteen-year old son slipped through my fingers. Denial was easier when I worked hard to better myself, got an education, and worked nights to pay for it. I thought I had time, but it ran out sooner than I thought, when one morning the police showed up and hauled my son away in handcuffs.

I'd rolled into bed the night before after a long shift at the diner and hadn't checked to see if Derrick was home. I just assumed he was. Instead, it turns out, that just as I was pulling the covers over my ears, my son was three blocks away, putting a bullet into an innocent, whose only crime was working nights at the convenience store to take care of his family.

Too late for the pained and haunted look on my child's face when he came to realize what he'd done. Too late for the forty-two-year-old father of three, whose death served no purpose at all and left a poor family even more destitute. And too late for me to open my eyes to what I might have been able to prevent.

This is what I remember from that morning; the silence, as the noises of neighbors and traffic outside failed to penetrate. A silence that allows dark memories, regrets, and recriminations to fill the empty space. For years, after finally getting my degree, I managed to fill the ugly void by having my eyes open to everyone's needs. Yet, it was still avoidance. It was still denial. A farce of a life. None of it served any purpose because my son is still dead, and I feel guilty because part of me expected this to be the outcome.

The sudden shrill ring of the room phone on the nightstand cuts through the silence and my spinning mind. The only one who knows where I am is the warden.

"Hello?" My voice sounds alien, even to me.

"Ms. Brunard, I just wanted to see if you'd be able to come in this morning."

"Can I see my son?" I want to know. I haven't been able to get further than the gate since I first got here. I wasn't thinking, just drove five hours, straight from Portland to the facility, never clueing in that it wasn't likely I'd be granted entry in the middle of the night. I was lucky that this nondescript inn along the highway had a night watchman. I've been stuck in this room since. Called the warden's office first thing the next morning, only to be informed by his secretary that I would not be able to see Derrick until the coroner was done with him. I left the hotel number with her and have been waiting for this call for two days.

"That should be possible. I'll make sure they're ready for you after you leave my office. Is eleven fifteen good for you?"

"I'll be there," I quickly respond, looking at the alarm clock that reads twenty-two minutes past nine. Green Haven is about ten minutes away, so that gives me less than two hours to get ready.

Half an hour later, I'm sitting on the edge of the bed, tears running down my face as I take in the contents of my bags, haphazardly thrown around the room. It's clear I wasn't thinking when I packed them in a hurry. I feel hysteria bubbling up as I struggle to decide what to wear. I'm not sure why it is so important, but I really want to be dressed nice when I say goodbye to my son.

-

"I'm so sorry for your loss."

A distinguished looking man, looking more like a successful business man than a prison warden, greets me at the door to his domain. I think I manage to mumble *thank you*, as I slip past him into the room, eager to escape the scrutiny and the pitying looks of staff in the outer office.

I managed to pull something together after my meltdown at the inn, but I missed my usual carefully put-together outer armor. My face is a mess too.

"Please have a seat." He indicates a functional chair by the desk and takes a seat across from me. "Would you care for some coffee?"

"No thanks," I whisper, shaking my head lightly. I don't want anything but to see Derrick.

"Ms. Brunard, I just received the autopsy report this morning. Derrick died of a barbiturate overdose. I'm afraid it looks like your son may have taken his own life. We are currently investigating how he may have come to obtain them, but the dose he took was apparently significant enough that his death was swift."

"I don't care." The warden seems to startle at my words, but it's true. I don't care to know the *how*. I knew, when his last parole review came back negative, that he wouldn't be able to take much more. I could see even the years before that his mental health was slipping. Thirty-three years old and my son was an old and tired man, weighed down by the devastating responsibility of a man's death at his hands. Ironically, the ultimate proof of the goodness he still held in his heart, showed in his inability to live with that weight. I want to be angry with the person who put the drugs in his hands, but it's futile. I want to blame Green Haven for not monitoring him close enough, but what is the point? I should be angry with him, for giving up on himself and on me, but I can't. I get it.

All that matters is that at fifty-one years old, I'm about to say goodbye to my only child, and although I know in my heart he's at peace, the empty pain I feel is as vast as the universe.

"Do what you need to do, but I'd like to see my son."

"Of course," he answers, "I'll let them know we're on our way down.

-

I'm not sure what I expected, but the smooth, peaceful face of my son, is so reminiscent of the big-hearted, bright young boy I once knew, it almost brings me to my knees. I reach out and brush my fingers over his high cheekbones, so much like mine. His skin is cold, but still so familiar. I lean down and press my lips to his closed eyes before kissing his forehead.

"Be at peace, my boy. I'll never forget the heart of you."

I barely register the words of the warden as he leads me from the morgue, presses a box with Derrick's belongings into my arms, and walks us into the frigid air outside. Something about getting in touch with a local funeral home.

"Sorry?" I turn to him as we reach the gate to the parking lot. "Could you repeat that?"

"Of course," he says patiently, and his patronizing smile is suddenly irritating me "I was just mentioning that McHoul Funeral Home in Hopewell Junction, just a few miles west on Route 82, always does a fabulous job for our inmates."

"I don't think so," I hear behind me, the heavy voice making me wish the earth would simply swallow me up.

Dino

"Excuse me?" the self-righteous prick, who was all but patting Pam on the head, throws me a look of disdain as the gate opens up between us.

"I said, I don't think so," I repeat. "You are talking about her son, not just some nameless inmate. We'll contact you when we've had a chance to make arrangements."

Pam has not turned around to face me yet, and when I place my hand in her neck to turn her around, she makes sure to keep her eyes lowered. I take the box she's carrying in one hand and start walking her to Gunnar's SUV.

"My car…" she finally manages when I seat her.

"Give me your keys, Gunnar will get it."

Now her eyes shoot up, anger, shame, and the deepest sorrow no longer hidden. "Gunnar's here?"

"And Viv. Oh, and Sydney, too. The girls are at the motel."

"Hope you remembered to notify the mailman, the kid who mows the lawn, and oh…let's not forget the cute teller at the bank," she says, as she digs up her keys from her purse. Her defenses are instantly up as she lets the sarcasm fly, and I'm almost relieved. I wasn't sure who the beaten down woman I saw standing there was, but I know this ball-buster. I know her well.

By the time I toss the keys at a waiting Gunnar, slide behind the wheel, put the key in the ignition, and look over at her, the tears are streaming down her face. "Come here." Unclipping her seatbelt, I tag her behind the neck and pull her body closer, tucking her head in my neck.

"How?"

"A lot of worry and a little luck. It doesn't matter how or why, Biscuit. We're here, the way we should've been all along." My tone does not invite argument, and Pam wisely keeps any objections to herself as I put the truck in gear, not letting her move too far away.

It had taken a bit to find her. We'd been in Gunnar's office last night when Syd, who'd come in when Gunnar called her, suggested Pam wouldn't take off without taking care of her son first. Something Syd is in the best position to know, since she lost a child, too. None of us argued when she pulled up a list of motels and hotels near the penitentiary. It had taken Mark to pretend he was a Boston cop, working an investigation, to convince the front desk clerks to give up the information. We hit pay dirt the third call he made.

I was ready to jump in my car and go, but Viv, who joined us after locking up, pointed out we all have kids that need looking after. Ike volunteered, as did Ruby and Tim, and at eight this morning, after a long sleepless night, Syd, Viv, and I got in the truck with Gunnar.

When we arrived and didn't see her car in the parking lot, I thought for a minute perhaps she'd already checked out, but when Viv checked with the front desk, they assured her she hadn't checked out yet. The next logical step to find her was at the prison.

We couldn't get in and had been waiting for twenty minutes, Gunnar standing guard by Pam's car, and I was waiting by the gate, when Pam walked out with some suit. The moment I saw the unguarded devastation on her normally composed face, any conflicted feelings I might have had were dwarfed by just one—a deep, cloying sadness.

"Thank you." The sound of her voice startles me and I lean in to kiss the side of her head.

"For what, Beautiful?"

"For buying me some time to figure out what to do."

"You're not alone," I tell her softly, to which she lets out a harsh snort.

"That's exactly what I am now." Where normally her voice is rich and deep, now it sounds thin and raw. "Alone."

Her words make me as angry as they make me sad. There's no fucking way she's alone, but I'm not going to argue now.

There's plenty of time to get her to see that everyone, whose lives she's become an important part of, is just as much a part of hers. Family, love, friendship—none of them are a one-way street. This woman's been so focused on being there for others, she hasn't allowed anyone to be there for her. But now's not the time to point that out. Time will show her.

I reluctantly remove my arm from around her when we pull into a parking spot outside the hotel and Pam straightens up. Gunnar pulls in right beside me. I get out and go to open her door but he's beaten me too it, wrapping her in a hug just as I'm rounding the front of his car. I have to force down an irrational surge of jealousy at the sight of her head leaning on his shoulder. Before I have a chance to grab her hand like I want to, Syd and Viv—having obviously been lying in wait inside—come barreling out of the lobby and pull Pam from Gunnar's arms, herding her inside. When I try to follow, Gunnar grabs my arm.

"Let the girls do their thing, man."

I watch the three women, Pam tallest in the middle and the other two on either side with their arms wrapped around her, make a beeline to the elevator.

"There's a dinky little bar behind the lobby," he says, throwing his arm around my shoulders. "I could use a drink."

It's barely three o'clock when we sit down and Gunnar orders us a couple of drafts. Personally, I could've gone for something a bit stronger, but the beer would have to do for now.

"I know a guy who works for Hobbs Funeral Home on Cottage Street," Gunnar says, taking a good tug on his beer. "I can call him to see what it would take to get Pam's boy up to Portland."

"I can't imagine that'd be cheap. I think she'd like having him close, but who knows?"

"You okay?"

I look up at Gunnar. He's studying me intently.

"Yeah. I'm just…I don't know. Just when you think you're getting a peek at a future, shit inevitably hits the fan to mess it all up— making you question everything." It's true, Sunday morning was fucking amazing. I liked waking up with the scent of Pam in my bed and that's not all I liked. I just don't get why every time something good happens, the shit immediately has to follow.

"Are you saying this makes a difference to you?" There's a bite to Gunnar's voice I don't hear often.

"Fuck no," I quickly correct him. "Not to me. I'm here, right? No, it's her I'm worried about. *Fuck.* You know what she said to me in the car?" Gunnar gives his head a shake. "One minute she was busting my balls for showing up, and the next she sounded defeated like I've never heard her before, saying she's alone now. Like I wasn't even there. That's what worries me. I'm afraid as private as she apparently has always been, she'll bury herself so deep now, we won't be able to find her."

"No, she won't."

I swing around on my stool to find Viv standing behind me. My eyes instantly drift over her shoulder to see if anyone else came down, but she's alone.

"Where is she?"

"Syd's got her upstairs. They have something in common now."

"*Son of a bitch,*" Gunnar bites off under his breath. His wife lost her son under tragic circumstances, and he knows the pain and devastation that Syd still struggles with from time to time. This can't be easy on her either.

Viv tosses her arm around Gunnar's shoulders. "You're wife is a rock up there. She's totally got this." She gives him a little squeeze. "And you," she points a finger at me. "You need to have some faith. You never doubted me, or Syd—hell, you had Ruby's back, too—no matter how messed up we got. You always believed we'd come out the other end—and better. Now we're talking about your woman and you lose faith?"

"It's because she's his," Gunnar points out, hitting the nail on the head. Yeah, we never fooled our friends, not even when we were working hard to avoid each other.

"I could fall for her," I admit, draining my beer, when Viv and Gunnar both start laughing.

"Oh man, this is priceless," Viv snickers. "You're already down, my friend. Gone." She's still chuckling when she puts her arm around my shoulders this time.

Another round of beers is ordered, and we settle in to a practical conversation about funeral arrangements and the possible costs associated. Gunnar calls his guy at Hobbs Funeral Home, who tells him they would be able to handle the transportation.

Ten minutes later Syd calls.

"Can you come up? Room 402."

"On my way." I'm already off my stool.

"Tell Gunnar I'll be right down."

I tuck my phone back in my pocket. "I'm heading up, Syd's coming down." I don't wait around for a response and head toward the elevators.

"She's in the bathroom, but I think she needs you," Syd whispers when she opens the door for me. I can hear water running in the background. Her face looks blotchy and red and her eyes are swollen. This has got to be hard on her.

"Thanks," I mumble over her head, as I fold her in a tight hug before letting her go.

"Go gentle," she smiles sadly, slipping past me out the door.

I don't have to wait long before the bathroom door opens and Pam walks out, stopping in her tracks when she sees me. She's wearing different clothes from what she had on earlier and I can see some water drops glistening in her hair. But her shower wasn't able to wash the swollen eyes or the sheer devastation from her face.

"I'm tired, Dino," she says, her hands up.

"So let's have a nap," I answer, holding out my hand. She looks at me surprised before her gaze drops to my outstretched hand.

"You didn't come here to talk?" I hear the disbelief in her voice.

"Only if you want to. Come here, Pam. Lie down with me." I drop back on the bed without taking my eyes off her, patting the mattress beside me for good measure. Finally she starts moving.

"I'm sorry," she says as she climbs in bed beside me, while keeping her distance. I reach out and pull her closer. She hesitates only briefly before dropping her head to my shoulder and her hand on my chest.

"You have nothing to be sorry for, Biscuit," I assure her, pressing my lips to her hair. "Nothing at all."

"I'm not sure what I should do next." Her voice is faint and sounds so small. It fucking breaks my heart.

"We'll figure it out, honey. Just rest your eyes for a bit, okay?"

"Okay…"

"I've got you, Beautiful—I've got you."

"Okay…"

CHAPTER FIFTEEN

Pam

"Want me to take the group for you?"

It's been a week. Technically, it's been almost two since he died, but it's been a week since I said goodbye. A week since I found myself alone in this world, until a group of people closer than any family I've ever known showed up to prove otherwise. Every fucking day they make sure I know it. I'm starting to believe it.

That's why Viv's on the phone again. She'd been dead set against me going back to work so soon. Something Dino actually went to bat for me on. Not sure what he told her but she backed off. It was weird though, going back without even having a funeral for Derrick yet.

I haven't had the stomach to go through his box, the one Dino tossed in the back of Gunnar's truck at Green Haven. He brought it over last night. He'd been reluctant to leave me at all this past week. If not for his job or the kids he has at home, needing his attention, I swear he would've stayed glued to my side the entire time. It took a bit of arguing to get him to drop me at my house to begin with, but I needed that time. Need the chance to get my bearings. Figure out where I go from here, now that my carefully concealed past is exposed for all to see. It's a miracle I managed to escape discovery for so long.

Maybe I should tackle that box tonight. Gunnar's contact at Hobbs Funeral Home is scheduled to drive to Green Haven tomorrow to pick up Derrick's body. I don't even know what he would've wanted. For years I've gone to visit him regularly, but we still managed to become strangers. Both of us careful not to discuss how his conviction, and subsequent incarceration, affected our day-to-day life, out of concern for the other.

"Okay," I finally answer Viv. "If you don't mind, I have some things I need to take care of."

"For sure, girl. You need any help taking care of things?" I can hear concern in her forced cheer. I love her for it, but I want to do this by myself.

"I'm good. You taking the group would really help. Thank you, honey."

"Okay. No problem. Whatever you need."

I'm smiling when I end the call. More like laughing at myself, actually. Fifteen years I've been living a lie, spending my days teaching women there's no shame in where we came from, there's just responsibility for where we're going. Fuck, I've been preaching but not practicing. Who's the fool now? If I've learned anything over the past week, it's that despite my great love and admiration for the people that have included me in their life, I've so miserably underestimated them. Not one of them has questioned or called me on the fact that I've been less than forthcoming. Not one has judged or condemned me for demanding honesty and trust from them, without giving the same in return. Not one.

I push back from my desk and make my way into the kitchen, where Brenda and Doris are having tea. Both look up when I walk in. When I came back to the shelter on Monday, after being gone for a week, I called them both in my office and told them I'd had to leave town for the death of a loved one. That's all I shared, but even that much was hard for me to do. I don't do well with sympathy, it ruffles my feathers. But both girls know enough not to push for more and simply stated they'd be there if I need them.

"Viv's offered to do tonight's group. I'm going home. Make sure each of you take what you need time-wise, okay?"

"Not to worry," Brenda immediately responds. "We make a pretty good team." She nudges Doris, who is the quieter of the two, as she says it.

"We're good," Doris adds a bit more subdued.

It's hard to hand over the responsibilities I've carefully guarded for so long, but at the same time, it's a relief to be able to.

"See you tomorrow." I wave as I go to fetch my coat.

-

I stop briefly at Duckfat, a sandwich and fry restaurant only a little bit out of the way, to pick up a large poutine and a milkshake. Not the healthiest of dinners, but I figure I could use a solid base in my stomach before I get down to my self-imposed task for tonight, and I don't feel like cooking.

When I turn into my driveway, I'm surprised to find someone huddled on my porch. It's freezing out tonight and I can almost feel the snow in the air. Whoever it is must be chilled to the bone. The moment I'm out of my car, the shape unfolds itself.

It's Jonas.

"What are you doing here?" comes flying out of my mouth, before I catch myself. "You must be freezing!" I rush to open the door, and push him in ahead of me. I'm not sure what he's doing here. He just had some pretty major surgery, not even two weeks ago, and I doubt sitting in sub-zero temperatures on my porch is recommended for his recovery.

He lingers awkwardly in the hallway and I move past him to the kitchen, dropping my bag with dinner on the counter.

"I wasn't sure," he says, almost shyly as he follows behind me, still wearing his coat. "Dad told me about…well…I'm sorry," he finally says. Oddly those simple words, from this boy, hit me harder than any words of sympathy I've heard so far.

"Thank you," I manage, my voice thick with emotion and poor Jonas looks everywhere but at me. I turn my back and fight for composure before looking at him again. "What weren't you sure of?"

"It's Thursday night. I wanted to maybe talk but I wasn't sure if you still wanted me here." His voice is hesitant and I swear he's actually shuffling his feet.

Truthfully? It wasn't what I had geared up for tonight, but I can't turn him away.

"I'm guessing you're hungry?" The slow smile that spreads over his face is answer enough. "Okay, then shed the coat and I'll grab us a few plates. I didn't cook, but count yourself lucky; you're about to have a mind-blowing French fry experience. You heard of Duckfat?"

"Really?" he says when he walks back into the kitchen, his eyes seeking out the familiar name on the bag on the counter. "That place is the shit. Dad took us there once. We loved it—Mom hated it. We've never been since. Their milkshakes are something else," he ends wistfully. A lot of information right there.

"Well, it just so happens." I pull the large milkshake I ordered from the bag with great flourish and get a kick out of the look on his face. "I got large of everything, so we'll share."

I divide the poutine over two plates and pull down a plastic tumbler and straw from the cupboard, so we can share the shake.

We eat quietly, the silence a bit heavy around us, when an idea starts forming. "You know," I start when Jonas slurps the last of his drink. "Your timing actually couldn't be better." I start clearing away the dishes as I'm talking. "I could use your help with something." He follows me into the living room, where the box is sitting on the coffee table, right where Dino left it last night. I haven't even moved it. I sit down in the corner of the couch, and instead of sitting in his usual spot in the chair across from me, Jonas surprises me by taking the other side of the couch, his eye focused on the box on the table.

"So your dad told you I have…had a son?" It costs me to get the words out, but even if this only gets him thinking, it's worth pushing through the pain for. The kid is very uncomfortable, I can tell from the tight way he nods, while eyeing me carefully. I won't cry in front of him. It would send him packing. "Well—Derrick killed himself." The statement sounds brutal. I intended that, but the look of shock on Jonas' face is a bit too much for me to handle, so instead I stare at the box. "He made a mistake when he was your age—a big, life-altering mistake—and he ended up in jail. He served fifteen years and had enough. Not too long ago, he was turned down again by the parole review board. That killed all his hope—and mine." I pause for minute, giving him time to let my words settle in before I continue. But I still can't look at him. "Last night, your dad brought over all Derrick's possessions in this world. They're all in that box. I wasn't ready to open it yet, and frankly, I'm not sure I'm ready now, but I'm going to. See, tomorrow Derrick's body will be brought here to Portland, and I need to figure out what to do for his funeral. He was my son for thirty-three years and I have no idea what kind of send off he would've wanted."

It's too much, it's all too much. I stand up suddenly and rush down the hall to the bathroom before I lose it. I lean on the counter, pressing my eyes closed as I breathe in deeply through the nose, trying to keep the sob building in my chest at bay. When I feel I have it under control, I grab a washcloth, run it under cold water and hold it against my face.

By the time I walk back inside, I'm convinced Jonas bailed, but am surprised to find him sitting next to the box, on the coffee table. The lid is off and he's holding what looks to be an envelope in his hands. He doesn't look up, but rummages through the contents.

I consider whether I should be upset, but decide I'm not. I don't know if I would've been able to make that start myself. I sit down in the corner of the couch and pull my knees up.

"This is addressed to you," Jonas says, holding out the envelope to me, but I wave it off.

"Leave…" I have to clear my throat before continuing. "Leave that for later."

Jonas just nods and puts the envelope down before diving into the box and pulling out a well-worn book. *Lord of the Flies* by William Golding. The only possession he took to jail with him. It looks like he read it more than a few times, judging by its dog-eared condition. I flip through and notice a highlighted passage.

His mind was crowded with memories; memories of the knowledge that had come to them when they closed in on the struggling pig, knowledge that they had outwitted a living thing, imposed their will upon it, taken away its life like a long satisfying drink.

The significance sends a shiver down my spine. I quickly flip through a little further to encounter another marked line.

Ralph wept for the end of innocence, the darkness of man's heart, and the fall through the air of a true, wise friend called Piggy.

Tears burn my eyes but I'm willing them back. How ironic that the very book he devoured before he got involved with those kids, the book I remember cursing because at the time I thought it helped him justify his poor decisions, was also the book that clearly helped him regain some perspective. Sadly it had been too late. Perhaps not too late for some.

Jonas blinks a few times when I shove the book back in his hands.

"Here, take it, it's yours. I'd like to think that Derrick would have appreciated you having it."

"He didn't even know me," he sputters, but I sharply shake my head.

"Sweetheart…" I close my eyes and take a deep breath before continuing, "…he *was* you. It was too late for my boy, but it isn't for you. Not by a long shot. Please," I plead, pushing it in his hands. "Please take it."

"Okay," he says, hesitantly taking the book from me.

I don't say it out loud, because I'm not sure this boy could handle the responsibility, but if I have to find any kind of meaning to Derrick's death, then let it be that this living, breathing man-child, will learn enough from my son's legacy to avoid the same traitorous path.

Dino

I'm surprised to find it nine thirty when the phone rings.

"Dad?"

"Hey, Princess, what's up? I'm just gonna clean up the kitchen and will be home soon."

"I'm worried," she says, making my heart skip a beat. "Jonas left three hours ago and said he'd be home soon, but I haven't heard from him yet, and he's not answering his phone."

Dammit.

"Did he mention where he was going?" I wedge my phone between my ear and shoulder, as I shrug on my coat. Clean up will have to wait until tomorrow.

"Pam. He said he had an appointment at seven. But he's taking the bus, Dad. What if those kids…"

"Sweetheart," I cut her off, trying to put her mind at ease. "Don't jump to conclusions. I'm sure your brother is fine." I sure as fuck hope so. I never sat down to talk to him about safety, especially after his encounter with those two punks. They're locked up tight now as per the last conversation I had with Barnes, but there are more gang members out there to worry about. Of course, I hadn't considered he'd go off on his own yet, he wasn't even scheduled to try back at school until Monday. "I'll give her a call and make sure he's okay. Then I'll swing by there to grab him before coming home, okay?"

I hang up and rush into the pub where Syd's manning the bar.

"I'm heading out early. I'll come in early to do clean up but I've gotta run and get Jonas."

"Everything okay?" she asks, a concerned look on her face.

"I sure as shit hope so," I reply. "I've had about all I can take these past few weeks." And how fucking true is that, between my ex, my kids, and Pam, the weight on my shoulders is about to bring me to my knees.

I try calling Pam on my way to the car and she finally answers on the second try.

"I'm sorry," she answers right off the bat. "I never took my phone from my purse so I didn't hear it at first. Are you looking for Jonas?"

The breath I realize I've been holding releases with a whoosh. "Yes, is he there?"

"Still is," she confirms. "Sorry things ran a little late."

"Just keep him there," I order her a bit sharply.

"Of course," is her terse reply, hanging up on me. I immediately feel guilty for snapping.

The bungalow is blazing with light when I pull in next to Pam's car. Light snow just started falling and I try to remember whether there was anything significant in the forecast. I normally love this time of year. Other than right around Christmas, the pub is generally a little slower during the winter months, and I always enjoy the extra time working on plans for the coming summer season. New menu items to try out, exploring new and better suppliers, checking out the competition. None of that has happened yet, so far. Mostly because I've been behind the eight ball since even before the summer.

The front door opens before I even reach the steps.

"I really am sorry," Pam says from the doorway, a worried look on her face, and suddenly everything else loses its significance. I move to her on instinct, needing the comfort of her embrace I've missed for almost two weeks now. I've hugged her, I've even kissed her, all comforting contact—but I haven't taken anything for myself, not sure if she was in a place to give it. I need her lips on me now, though.

I cup her face in my hands and slide my mouth over hers. Need, relief, and apology all rolled into that one soft kiss. Her arms slip around my neck as she gives herself. "I was an asshole," I whisper against her lips.

"You were worried," she whispers right back.

I catch a slight movement from the corner of my eye to find my son peeking over the back of the couch, half a smirk on his face. Damn, I'd forgotten you can see clear to the front door from the living room. Pam stiffens in my arms when she realizes the same thing, too. I don't bother hiding, now that the cat is out of the bag, and pull her in for one more quick hard kiss on the lips before I walk into the living room.

"Bud, the fuck are you doing here?" I ask Jonas, taking in the mess surrounding him. It looks like the two have been busy with the box I brought over yesterday. Jonas just shrugs.

"Giving Pam a hand, that's all."

"That's good of you, Son, but I didn't know where you were, and you told your sister you'd be home well over an hour ago. On top of that, you weren't answering your phone." I try to keep my voice even, despite my anger flaring up.

"Crap," he says, slapping his forehead. "I left it in my jacket." He shoots up from the couch and dives into the hallway closet coming up with his phone. "Dead," he says, looking at the screen. The next instant his face is beet red and his eyes are big as they flick between Pam and me. "Sorry," he mouths.

I hear Pam choke off a snort. "I appreciate the concern, Jonas," she says, "but I don't expect you—nor do I want you to—weigh each word from your mouth. You should know that after tonight."

Her last comment has me curious.

"What did you guys do tonight?" I ask, noting Jonas' eyes focus on Pam, waiting for her lead.

"Let's call it a joint session, shall we?" She winks at Jonas before looking at me. "I'm glad your boy showed up tonight. He helped me go through Derrick's things and helped me figure out what he might've wanted for his send off."

My eyes go to Jonas, who looks a little sheepish under the praise. "That's right," I acknowledge, my focus coming back to Pam. "He's coming home tomorrow." She blinks a few times at my statement.

"Portland was never Derrick's home, Dino," she says softly.

"That's where you're wrong, Beautiful; it's been his home for as long as you've been here."

I see her eyes mist over right before she does a face plant in my chest. My hand comes up to cup the back of her head, and I look over at Jonas, who is observing us closely. "So what have you come up with?" I ask him, drawing attention away from Pam.

"We figured he'd probably want something quiet. No service or anything," he says, his eyes drifting back to Pam's bent head. "I figured he might've put something in the letter he left her, but she hasn't opened it yet." I watch as Jonas walks over to the table, picking up an envelope. Pam lifts her head away from my chest, throwing an accusing look in his direction.

"Traitor," she hisses, but Jonas just shrugs.

"Might as well do it when you've got two sets of strong shoulders here," my smartass boy points out. Pam's mouth falls open at his audacity, but she promptly barks out a laugh.

"Cheeky bastard," she mumbles, reaching over to snatch the envelope from his hand. I'm struck silent as I take in the byplay between these two.

Pam sits down heavily on the couch and, as if planned, my son and I sink down, flanking her on either side. Immediately the lighter atmosphere is gone and replaced by a heavier silence as Pam twirls the unopened letter in her hands.

Once again it's my boy who breaks through the tension when he snatches the envelope from her hands and unceremoniously rips it open, handing it right back to Pam.

"You looked like you needed a hand," he deadpans, and I can't hold back the chuckle. He's on a roll. Pam glares at each of us in turn, but I can see her sense of humor pulling at the corner of her mouth.

"Fine," she mumbles, taking in a deep breath before she pulls out the single, folded sheet and starts reading. My hand finds its way to rest on her leg, but I keep my eyes straight ahead. She'll share if she wants to.

The crinkle of paper accompanied by a sob has me look at her before looking at Jonas on the other side of her. His eyes are wet with unshed tears, and for a second, I question the wisdom of this heavy emotion in front of him. Then I remember what got him here in the first place, and I hope witnessing this pain will set him straight.

"You read it," Pam chokes out as she hands the letter back to Jonas. "I can't."

A quick, slightly panicked look from him flies my way before he unfolds the paper and starts reading.

"I love you, Mom. Forever. The guilt—it has left me hollow. I just don't have the energy to fight the darkness anymore. I want to set me free. Set you free. So, so stupid. May God forgive me." I can barely see my son through the sheen of tears blurring my eyes, but I can hear the hitching of his voice as I pull Pam in my arms. He sniffs loudly before continuing, "I want to be cremated. I've thought about it and I don't want you to spend the rest of your life visiting an empty shell, like you have up to now. No celebration of life, because there is nothing worth celebrating. Just toss my ashes in the wind somewhere. Just you and me, that's what I want." Jonas surprises me when he jumps up and crumples the note into a ball, tossing it at the wall. "This is bullshit!"

Pam jerks upright and both of us look at my son in shock.

"He doesn't want you to visit him? He doesn't want you to celebrate his life? That's what he wants? That's fucking bullshit!"

"Jonas!" I yell, jumping up and grabbing his shoulders. "What the hell is wrong with you?"

"Me? What is wrong with me? *He* had a mother who loved him enough to stand by him, even when he did the worst thing possible. *She* never left him!" He pulls free from my hands and points a finger at Pam, who's stepped up beside me. "But he left her. He never, not once, says anything about what she might want. Not once, Dad!" Before I have a chance to say or do anything, Pam moves between us and pulls Jonas in her arms.

"It's okay, baby," she coos at my son, whose angry tirade has ended in tears streaming down his face. This was not only about Derrick or Pam, this was just as much, if not more, about Jonas and his sense of abandonment. "Let it out, honey. Let it all out." Pam's voice seems to grow stronger with each word of comfort she utters, and I am once again in awe of the size and strength of her heart. I sit down heavily as Jonas starts to calm down.

"Tell me, what you would want me to do?" Pam asks Jonas, pulling back from him a little. He uses his sleeve to wipe his face before risking a glance my way. I nod my encouragement.

"It wouldn't matter what I would want," he says, sounding much wiser than his seventeen years. "I'd be gone. You're the one who is still here. Whatever feels right for *you* is what I would want."

If I could be any prouder of my son, my heart would burst from my chest. Pam manages a smile as she leans in and kisses his cheek.

"Then that's what we'll do."

CHAPTER SIXTEEN

Pam

Today is hard. Much harder than I thought.

Dino insisted on coming with me to the funeral home, and frankly, after the emotional events of last night, I wasn't going to argue. It had left me raw. He'd wanted to stay. When I pointed out he had a worried daughter waiting at home, and a son who needed some time to process, he tried to talk me into coming with him. I was tempted, but I've spent enough years hiding from my emotions, and going with him would've forced me to do just that. For the sake of the kids.

No—I needed a chance just to feel. To sit among Derrick's things, touch what he touched, and let it wash over me. Jonas' outburst, last night, brought up a host of thoughts and feelings that I'd suppressed long enough. Maybe it was time to let them go.

So after the boys left, Dino making me promise to call him in the morning, I made a pot of tea and sat by myself, just letting the emotions flow. I tried not to judge myself too harshly when feelings of anger and resentment bubbled up—and even some level of relief. Fear. Now that was a surprise. Fear of being alone, being no longer emotionally and genetically connected. Fear of losing my purpose, my identity. And the painful realization that the buck ends with me. I am now officially the end of the line, and I'm already two-thirds there. What do I have to show for it?

I didn't sleep much, mostly dozed on the couch, and dutifully called Dino this morning as agreed. Derrick's body was expected to arrive at the funeral home around four this afternoon, and I had an appointment at three-thirty to discuss arrangements, and he said he'd pick me up.

I'd planned to check in at Florence House, but the interruptions just kept coming. First Viv called, telling me she was on her way with Francessca with coffee and pastries. That was actually my highlight of the day, cuddling Francessca. Then Brenda called to see how things were. The bank manager was next to let me know the line of credit against the house I'd applied for a few days ago, so I could afford to lay my son to rest, was approved.

But it was the time in between, when I agonized about what I promised Jonas last night; to focus on what I want—on what feels right for me. I never realized how difficult it was not to think of others first. I'm not even sure I know what I want

Before I realized it, Dino was here and I was still in sweats. A two-minute shower and throwing on some real clothes, and I was ready to go. By the time we got to the funeral home, Derrick had already arrived. I could barely focus on the funeral director, knowing he was somewhere in the building. That's when Dino jumped in and suggested taking a ten-minute break before dragging me out to the car.

"Where are we going?"

"Fresh air," he says cryptically.

It soon becomes obvious when he pulls into the little roundabout at the light house. There's a strong wind blowing and when he opens the door for me, I'm tempted to hide out in the car.

"Come on," he urges. "I've got a blanket in the trunk."

Ducking my head against the cold, I follow him down to a bench at the top of the point. Waves are crashing against the rocks below and the wind blows sharp off the sound. Dino settles us on the bench, the blanket wrapped cocoon-like around us.

"Clear your head," he says, tucking me close to his side. "What do you feel right now?"

"Cold," I fire off instantly, earning a growl from the big man beside me.

"What else?"

"Irritated," I deadpan, which is met with an annoying chuckle.

"Very good," he patronizes. "What else?"

I move away from him and spear him with a glare. "What is this? Twenty questions?" He takes in my frown with amusement.

"Nope. I'm just trying to get you out of your head," he says with a shrug.

"What does that even mean?"

He puts his hands—his freezing cold hands—on my face and leans closer. "You can't figure out what you want because you let your mind do all the decision making. *Want* comes from the heart." His mouth comes down on mine, and right there on a bench at the top of the rocks, with cold wind chilling me to the bone, he proceeds to make my toes curl with his lips and tongue. "What else?" he insists, his mouth still against mine.

"Heat, arousal, and…irritation," I fire off, adding the last for good measure.

Dino's chest rumbles with subdued laughter as he pulls me against him. My eyes immediately drift off to the water, where the sun is starting to set, leaving bright colors in its wake.

"This is such a beautiful spot," slips from my mouth.

"Mmmm."

"I don't come out here often enough," I muse, starting to feel a bit warmer with the blanket, and Dino, surrounding me.

"Mmmm."

"You know?" I start, a thought forming. "This wouldn't be a bad place to visit from time to time."

"I agree," Dino says, stroking his big hand up and down my arm.

"Do you think it's illegal to spread Derrick's ashes here? In the wind—over the water?"

"I'm not sure," he answers, "but who would need to know?"

Fifteen minutes later, we're back in the funeral director's office, making arrangements for Derrick to be cremated without a service, as per his wishes, and we schedule to pick his ashes up Monday afternoon. We don't mention to the funeral director that we will take his remains straight to the lighthouse, where we will let him scatter to the wind—as per my wishes.

"Why Monday?" Dino wants to know when we get back into the car.

"Because The Skipper is closed on Monday," I answer. "And I think I want you all there."

"Come here," Dino rumbles, tagging me behind the neck, as he seems to enjoy doing, and pulling me toward his mouth. "Proud of you," he mumbles, and before I can even attempt to remember the last time anyone's ever said that to me—if ever—his kiss demands all my attention.

Dino

Fuck, it's been frustrating.

I crave Pam like crazy, and every time I indulge in a taste it only gets worse, but she needs this time without having me demand attention. My body won't get in line though, and the moment I'm around her; I'm like a fucking dog with its tail wagging at the buffet in front of him.

Pam decided to give her girls some time off this weekend, so she's kept busy at the shelter, and I've done the same at The Skipper. I haven't seen her, our only contact: the bedtime calls to check in, and those just cranked up the need.

It's funny; I never considered how much of a challenge it could be to care for someone who is as strong as Pam is. I'm not used to that. I've always had the role of caregiver, so my first instinct is to be the same way with her. Yet, she is so independent, she doesn't really *need* anyone to take care of her, but that doesn't stop me from wondering if she perhaps *wants* it. They say opposites should attract, but she and I are very similar. Fuck if I'm not falling for her anyway.

Despite it being Monday, I met Viv and Syd at the pub this morning, right after dropping the kids off at school. Jonas was less than excited about going back, but this being his final year, he can't afford to miss much more. Besides, he's feeling a lot better by his own admission. We talked a bit about what happened Thursday night. Well, mainly it's been me talking. He just listens and nods a lot. I'm thinking he's probably embarrassed by his outburst. It was helpful for me; gave me a better understanding where his head is at. Communication is still a challenge, though. Like me, Jonas is really not much of a talker, although it seems both of us do more than our share with Pam.

The women are already there when I enter the kitchen, both sitting at the table with mugs of coffee, and a happy Francessca bouncing in her chair in the middle.

"Leave any coffee for me?' I walk straight over to the pot, pleased to find plenty left.

At Pam's request, I'd dropped her back off at home after the meeting on Friday and headed into work. I told Viv what Pam wanted for her boy's send-off, and she went running with it. Not that that was a surprise, Viv is as much a giver as Pam herself is. But it had been Gunnar's idea to head back to The Skipper after for a celebration of life party. When I mentioned that her son hadn't wanted anything like that, Gunnar countered with similar words to the ones my son voiced the night before; that this wasn't for Derrick, but rather for Pam. I couldn't argue with that.

"What's on the menu?" I ask as I take a seat beside Syd, suspiciously eyeing the piece of paper on the table in front of her. She starts listing all the items she's written down. "Christ, Syd—that's enough to feed an orphanage," I point out.

"Not really," she replies. "We've got twenty-four or so mouths to feed. And there'll be drinking—you know there will—which means there'll be munchies."

"How'd this get to twenty-four?" I want to know.

It's Viv who answers. "She means a lot to a lot of people, Dino," she suggests. "We can't leave out the girls at the shelter, they're her family too, but they'll come straight here after."

It's clear to me that this is maybe getting a little bigger than what Pam had meant when she said she wanted us there. Regardless, there's nothing to be done at this point, since it's obvious this has become a runaway train with no way to stop it. I toss back the dregs of my coffee, and pausing a second to kiss Francessca's little cherub face, get up, and grab my apron.

"Let's get this show on the road, then."

We're up to our elbows in pastry dough and Cajun shrimp étouffée, when Matt and Ruby come stumbling in, their arms full of Christmas decorations. I'd almost forgotten we're only a few weeks away. Gunnar usually holds off decorating until the weekend of the Christmas Boat Parade of Lights, when there's a influx of visitors for the annual lights and display event in the harbor, but then he lets Syd go all out. Looks like Christmas came early.

By the time I leave to go pick up the kids from school, the pub looks like the inside of a Christmas catalogue, and smells like a New Orleans bayou café. My job is to pick up the kids, get ready, and pick up Pam to take her to Hobbs to collect her son's ashes.

It's been too busy to think much, but every now and then a deep sadness settles in. Sadness for Pam, but also for a man I'll never have a chance to get to know, who irrevocably changed the course of his short life with one, stupid, adolescent, devastating decision. Senseless.

The kids are waiting by the curb when I drive up to the school. Gina's head is bent and Jonas looks murderous.

"What's up, guys?" I ask when they climb in the car, Jonas taking shotgun and Gina, without protest for once, taking the backseat. When neither of them answer, I try to be more direct. "Jonas," I tackle my son first. "First day back, was it as bad as you expected?" He snorts his derision.

"It was fine until the brat decided to be a little bitch." As soon as the words leave his mouth, my usually agreeable little princess kicks the back of her brother's seat while hissing; "Asshole."

"Whoa." I lift a hand off the wheel and grab her ankle when she tries to haul out again. "Knock it off!" My bellow bounces off the windows and a few heads outside even turn to look at the car.

"The fuck is wrong with you two?" My voice, not quite so loud, still carries all of the threat.

"Ask her," Jonas spits out, pointing his thumb over his shoulder. "She's the one wanting to start trouble. Selfish brat."

"Enough with the name calling, already. Not gonna put up with it," I scold Jonas before shifting my eyes to the rearview mirror, where I see my daughter sitting with her arms folded over her chest, a scowl on her face, pointedly staring out the window. "What's with you? What trouble is he talking about?" I direct at her. Her eyes flick briefly to meet mine when I turn my body in the seat to look at her straight.

"Gina? Talk to me."

"It's nothing. He's making a big deal out of nothing," she says with vehemence, while shoving the seat in front of her.

"She says she's staying home, Dad. She's being selfish, she doesn't want to come to the lighthouse."

I turn my attention back to Gina, who is peeking at me through her lashes. "Well, that's easily solved," I point out. "Since this is not optional attendance, you're coming, and it's not up to you, young lady." I watch her mouth form a stubborn line so I add, "And I have to say, I'm a bit disappointed. It's important to me we show Pam some support. Life isn't always easy, but at least we have family—we have each other—but Pam only had her son, and now he's gone, too."

With that I turn my back to her and put the car in drive, pulling out into the road. My hands are grabbing the wheel tight in my attempt to hang onto my temper wanting to unleash. But when I take a glance in the rearview mirror at the first stoplight, my anger evaporates when I see Gina surreptitiously wipes away the tears from her eyes. *Ah...Jesus.*

-

"Let's go!"

I'm yelling up the stairs, for the third time in the past ten minutes. I'm not sure what Gina is doing up there, it's not like we're getting dressed up or anything. We're all to come as we are, as per Pam's instructions. Who, by the way, is probably wondering where the fuck we are. "Gina! Butt down here, *now*!"

Finally I hear sounds of movement; a door slams and finally the extra-heavy treads of my unusually defiant daughter come plodding down the stairs. Jonas is already in the car, where I sent him when it looked like he was gonna lose his shit with his sister's attitude. She's being a pain in the ass, which is something we're not used to, and I'm well aware her behavior is only a symptom of what is really going on with her. Now's just not a good time to dig into whatever it is. We've got people waiting.

-

I don't even have to prompt Jonas when we pull into Pam's driveway to find her waiting on the steps. The moment I put the car in park, he's out of the car and slips into the backseat next to his sister. Pam gets in beside me, and despite the audience, I lean over and give her a soft kiss that has her pop her eyes wide open.

"You ready?" I carefully ask, straightening in my seat.

"As ready as I can be," she responds before swiveling her head to the kids. "Hey guys. Appreciate you coming."

"No problem," Jonas says and Gina just mumbles something incoherent.

Pam turns to me with an eyebrow raised, and I give my head a slight shake; the universal grown-up sign for '*later.*'

By the time we turn onto the funeral home parking lot, Pam's hands are wringing in her lap, and the moment I have the car parked, I reach over and cover them with my hand, giving her a little squeeze.

"Want to wait here, kids? We'll be right back."

"It's okay," Pam says, her voice a little shaky. "I'll manage."

"I'm coming with you," I dictate, not about to let her go in there by herself. Before she has a chance to object, I get out, round the car, and open her door for her.

"Really, I'm okay," she mutters, as I open the front door for her.

"I know you are," I concur. "But I'm still coming in." Some of the fire is back when she rolls her eyes at me. Good.

It doesn't take long. Pam hands over a check and receives a nondescript, brown box in return. Inside is a plain urn with all that is left of her only child. The significance hits me when she walks outside in front of me, holding the box like it's her greatest treasure. I guess it is.

The short drive to the Portland Head Light is eerily quiet; all of us very aware of the fifth person in the car with us. Already, familiar cars are parked in the small lot at the circular drive. The sun has already gone down, and other than the light coming from the lighthouse itself, all I can see is a faint flickering coming from the point, where we sat just a few days ago. The kids get out of the car without a word and start walking down the path toward it. When I walk around the car to let Pam out, I notice her attention is focused on the faint light in the distance, her face a tight mask. She doesn't even react when I open her door. Not until I put a hand on her shoulder.

"Let's go, honey."

She blinks a few times at the sound of my voice and allows me to help her out of the car, the box firmly clenched in her hands.

It's quiet when we walk toward the rocky outcropping, my arm around her shoulders for support. There's a soft breeze, no voices, just the sound of the sea lapping at the rocks below. The sight of the group assembled around the bench, every one of them with a small candle in their hands, has Pam choke out a sob and I have to swallow hard. No one says anything; we're all waiting to take our cue from Pam, who is no longer attempting to hide her emotions.

Where the pavement ends, there's a dirt trail that runs right to the edge of the point. Pam heads in that direction and I follow close behind. A few steps on the trail, she turns around.

"Wait for me?"

All I can do is nod as I force myself to stand still as she continues her trek to the edge. There, she takes the urn out of the box, lifts the lid, and in a strong arc, flings the ashes to the wind and water. Her arms are outstretched on either side as her head falls back. She stands frozen like that, an image that burns itself in my heart.

It's all I can do not to rush out there and haul her back from that edge, but then I see her head straighten and her arms drop down, the urn slipping from her hand and bouncing with a clang off the rocks, and into the water below. The moment she turns around toward me, I'm moving.

Ready to catch her.

CHAPTER SEVENTEEN

Pam

It's quiet in my house. Too quiet.

I thought maybe after saying my final goodbye to Derrick by the lighthouse, I at least could force myself back into my regular routine, but it's been hard. Everyone was wonderful at The Skipper afterward, trying hard to show me their care, but the truth is, I just wanted to be home by myself. I had to brush Dino off, who'd pushed me to stay the night with him, so I wouldn't be alone, even though that's exactly what I wanted to be. Alone.

It does something to you, when the last of your blood is gone. My parents are long gone, and I didn't have a particularly close relationship with them after I ended up pregnant at barely eighteen. They never knew Derrick, nor did they want to. It still boggles my mind they could dismiss their child, as well as their grandchild, so easily. Parents are supposed to be there unconditionally, but mine weren't. I swore I'd be a better parent than that, but it turned out I had my own failings. I loved my boy to distraction but I struggled, making bad decision after bad decision. As a result, I wasn't looking out for him the way I should've been, so when he was ultimately arrested, charged, and convicted of murder, I vowed I'd stay by his side, no matter what. Like a parent should.

But here I am, my only child gone, and the rest of my life a big gaping hole in front of me.

I went to Florence House twice these past few days to try and get a handle on the Christmas preparations I normally would have taken care of a long time ago. Each time Brenda sent me home when she found me staring at the wall of my office. I couldn't seem to focus on anything without my mind drifting to that moment on the rocks, when I gave my boy over to the elements. Giving him up. I wanted to throw myself right after him. The only thing holding me back was the faint knowledge that I couldn't do that to the people behind me. The friends who'd turned out to have my back. Their children…God I don't even want to think about what it would've done to them to witness that. Yet, I think of that moment all the time.

Since then I've purposely let my phone battery drain and haven't bothered charging it. I can't handle the calls to check up on me anymore. If it wasn't Dino, it would be Viv, or one of the others. I don't want to be reminded of the holiday season and I don't want to be a drain on theirs.

Last night there was knocking at my door. I'd been sitting on the couch in the dark and didn't respond. It stopped after a while. Then again this morning, and this time I could hear Viv yelling my name, but I still never moved from my spot.

For the last few hours it's been quiet, so when there is renewed knocking on the door, it startles me. I'm frozen when I hear a scratching sound, followed shortly by the decisive clank of my lock being released, right before Dino comes storming in, Ike right on his heels.

"She's okay," he says over his shoulder to Ike, before bending over, holding on to his knees. "Christ, Biscuit. You scared the ever loving crap out of me." The familiar rumble of his voice does something to me. It seems to cut through the numbness I've surrounded myself with and makes me feel. I don't want to feel. I prefer the numbness.

In the background I can hear Ike having a conversation with someone—I presume on his phone—while Dino walks over and crouches in front of me.

"You're a mess," he says, and I flinch when he puts his hand against my face. "Let's go get cleaned up."

I let him pull me up from the couch, my legs asleep from being folded under my body for however long. I wobble a little, but his strong arm instantly closes around my waist as he walks me down the hallway to the bathroom.

"Bath or shower?" he asks, as he moves me to lean against the vanity and opens the shower curtain. I can't bring myself to answer, so he does it for me. "Bath it is."

The whole thing is like watching myself from a distance, yet every touch of Dino's hands on my body, as he undresses me, I feel straight to my soul. And it fucking hurts. I'm starting to notice other things, like the flow of the water as it fills the bathtub, the sounds of movement from my living room, a surprising pang of hunger in my empty stomach, and the smell of a body that's gone unwashed for too long.

"I stink."

"Get in the tub," Dino orders, helping me over the side. "You don't stink, you could just do with a scrub," he says once I'm seated. He grabs a loofah hanging off the plastic hook, squirts some shower gel on it, and proceeds to gently scrub my back.

"What day is it?" I ask, a little disoriented as his ministrations make my skin tingle.

"Day before Christmas Eve," he answers. "The twenty-third. I wanted to give you some time, honey, but you've been unreachable since Wednesday night."

"I'm not sure if I can do this," I whisper under my breath, but of course he hears me.

"You don't have to do anything. Nobody has any expectations, except for one thing; you have to take care of yourself, and you're not doing that right now—so I'm jumping in."

I feel a surprising surge of indignant anger at his words.

"Who do you think you are? Coming in here and pushing me around?" The smirk that curls around the edges of his mouth doesn't do much for my sudden burst of anger.

"There she is." He full out smiles before he leans in, his face just inches from mine and suddenly dead serious. "Just so you know, I don't give a fuck if you get mad at me. I'd much rather have you pissed off at me than indifferent. I know you're hurting in a way I can't even imagine, but I'll be damned if I'll let you disappear under the weight, Biscuit. I care too fucking much. We need you, Pam—but not just that, you fucking need us, too."

Dino

By the time I have her out of the tub and pull some clothes out of the drawers in her bedroom, Pam is back in fighting mode and reinforcements have arrived. Viv is standing in the doorway when Pam, who I left alone in the bathroom to dress, walks out. Viv is across the room in an instant, pulling the taller Pam in a fierce hug. For a moment she stands there, not moving, but then Pam's arms slowly come around Viv's back, and her head drops down on her shoulder.

"I'll go see about some food," I suggest, leaving the two women and closing the door behind me. I'm not surprised that despite the fact it is nine thirty on a Friday, I find Ruby and Syd already puttering around the kitchen, but there's no sign of Ike.

"Where did Ike go?" I ask as Ruby walks up and gives me a hug.

"Viv had Francessca with her, so he took the baby home. Gunnar stayed home with the kids and wants me to let him know whether we need to close down the pub today," Syd informs me.

"Can't shut the pub down today. It's gonna be packed tonight," I counter.

"Well then, talk to my husband, because he's ready to put a sign on the door."

I grab my phone to call Gunnar to tell him we need to keep the pub open. It's a perfect excuse to pull Pam out of her self-imposed exile. She may not be ready to deal with the heavy emotional demand of the shelter, but at least we can give her some safe, comfortable distraction. It's all hands on deck at the pub from here on in, and this year for the first time, I've asked Jonas to give me a hand in the kitchen these busy days. It's their first day of Christmas break today, which means they're both still in bed at home. Gina's scheduled to head over to Marcy this afternoon and spend the night there. Tomorrow is Syd's annual charity dinner at the pub, and I'm planning to have both kids there to lend a hand.

"Are Emmy and Dex gonna be there tomorrow?" I ask Syd.

"Yup," she says easily, handing me a mug of coffee and waving me to a stool. "I've got the apartment stocked with snacks and pop, and Dex is bringing over his PlayStation tomorrow, so if Gina wants to hang with him, I'm sure he won't mind."

The small apartment above the pub has served us all well over the years. Viv spent some time there when she first came back to town and was getting her feet under her. Later it was Syd who lived there for a while. In between it's served as crash pad for Gunnar or anyone else who needed a place to stay for a night.

I've even spent a occasional night, if driving home was no longer an option, but that was before things blew up with Jeannie. Aside from that, it's been a perfect hangout for any of our kids, if we couldn't make other arrangements or just wanted them close by.

Just as Ruby, who is always the quiet one of the bunch, slides a plate with huevos rancheros in front of me, Viv comes down the hall, Pam following a little slower. I can tell she's a little overwhelmed, when she sees the two women puttering in her kitchen, but quickly pulls herself together and appears to welcome the hugs she receives.

"What is this?" she asks, looking at everyone in turn. "Some kind of intervention?" Her voice has an undeniable edge and it renders the others silent. Surprisingly Ruby is the first one to speak up.

"Hardly," she snorts. "Interventions are your department, we're just here for the food and the fabulous company." The deadpan reaction is so out of character for Ruby, it has everybody burst out laughing. Including Pam. Laughing turns into a few tears, and I quickly pull her into my arms, while the other three make themselves busy with coffee, toast, and breakfast. The only three women I know who can comfortably share a kitchen without getting in each other's way or on each other's nerves.

"Are you good?" I mumble in Pam's ear, whose face is pressed into my neck. At her slight nod, I loosen my arms around her, pressing a kiss to her forehead, before I release her completely. She pulls out a stool, sits beside me, and a second later she has her own plate slid in front of her, along with a cup of steaming coffee.

While we eat in silence, Ruby scoots down the hallway and comes back with a pile of laundry in her hands. The instant Pam sees her she jumps up.

"Oh no. Don't do that, I was planning to do that later." Ruby stops her in her tracks with a stern glare and a single raised eyebrow.

"You housed me for months. Fed me. Helped me back on my feet. And yet you want to rob me of the chance to do something back? Something as silly as laundry? *Madre de Dios.* You are a stubborn one." With that she steps around Pam and disappears into the laundry room behind the kitchen.

I have to swallow down a chuckle when I see Pam's somewhat disgruntled face as she returns to her stool. I hear her mumble, "Don't have a say in my own damn house," under her breath, as she violently stabs at a piece of egg with her fork.

"Better get used to it," Viv adds oil to the fire. "Not like you're really scaring any of us, no matter how hard you try."

Instead of firing back, Pam just harrumphs and rolls her eyes, causing Syd to snort. And just like that, everyone starts laughing again. I watch Pam closely to see if the tears will follow but when she looks at me, they are dry—and warm.

-

"Why can't I just stay home?" Pam asks for the second time when we've cleaned away the dishes and I want to get going to the pub. The girls have already left in Viv's car and left me to convince Pam.

"Because—we don't want to leave you here. I don't want to leave you by yourself with nothing but your thoughts. Besides, the kids have been asking about you." Well, that's partially true; Jonas has, but Gina has barely said a word since Pam collapsed in my arms on the rocks. She's been pensive and quiet, only responding when asked a direct question.

"You're full of shit," Pam throws back. "And you don't play fair, throwing the kids in the mix."

I just shrug my shoulders; whatever gets the job done is my motto. "All's fair in love and war," I throw out and notice Pam freezing at my words. Oddly enough when she starts moving, it's to grab her boots and winter coat. She'll need them because it just started snowing.

We swing by my house to pick Jonas up, who climbs in the backseat, leans into the front of the car, and gives an unsuspecting Pam a kiss on her cheek. Threw me for a loop, too. I've always touched and hugged my kids, told them I love them, and until earlier this year, both kids reciprocated. Not so much anymore, which is why I'm a little shocked Jonas would be demonstrative like that.

"Hey, boy," Pam says with a tremulous little smile, throwing a look over her shoulder. "How are you doing?"

"Shouldn't I be asking you?" my son shoots back, putting a smile on my face. Like father like son, whether he likes it or not.

I throw a quick glance at Pam, who is rolling her eyes, and I can't hold back the chuckle, which earns me a nasty glare.

"I'm good, Jonas," she says, and now it's my turn to roll my eyes. She's full of it.

The moment we get to The Skipper, everyone, including Pam, is given prep tasks. The afternoon passes quickly, and I notice her even cracking a smile from time to time. When the pub is at full capacity, Pam helps to run orders between the kitchen and the bar, and by the time it's nearing in on ten o'clock, she looks exhausted.

"Sit down before you fall down," I tell her when she shows her face in the kitchen.

"I'm not some frail flower," she sputters indignantly, but I notice she does pull out a kitchen chair and sits her ass down.

"Not saying you are, but you've run yourself off your feet tonight. Take a break while Jonas and I finish cleaning up. We've got to get the kitchen back in shape for tomorrow night's dinner." The charity dinner is labor intensive, since the pub will be filled to capacity and everyone needs to be served at the same time. With Syd and Gunnar hosting, we'll be back here in full force tomorrow. "Am I gonna be able to get you to come tomorrow?" I ask Pam. I know I forced her today, just to get her out of her house and among people, but I hold no illusions I'd be successful doing it another time. Still, I'd like her to be here. Every year this is a family event and Pam should be part of it. She eyes me with a smirk on her face.

"You asking if I'll subject myself to another day of providing free labor?" When I don't answer and just look at her with my eyebrow raised, she finally shakes her head. "Fine," she concedes. "But I have to check in on my girls first. I'll drive myself."

I end up dropping Jonas off at home first. He just wiggles his eyebrows at me when I tell him I'll pick him up in the morning. *Pain in my ass.* Pam stays quiet in the seat beside me.

"Not sure if I'll be good company tonight," she says, breaking the silence that's been getting thicker during the drive to her place.

"Not looking for good company, honey. I'm looking for a good night's sleep, which I won't get if I'm at home wondering if you are okay. Easier this way."

"Thank you. For today, I mean," she quickly adds. "This emptiness I feel seems to swallow me up if I let it, but it's hard just to do the normal things, you know? And I don't understand why now? I managed to get through those first weeks after his death without losing myself."

"I know why," I tell her, pulling in the driveway and shutting down the engine before turning in my seat to face her. "You weren't done looking after him yet, feeling responsible for him.

That day on the rocks, when you let his ashes go, you let the purpose of everything you've done go, too. You worked hard to turn what happened with Derrick into something meaningful, and I can see why with him no longer here, it would seem the meaning is lost."

"You know why I always avoided you like the plague?" she asks, wiping at her cheeks. I do know, but I stay quiet. "I think I could sense you analyzing me. It's creepy."

I chuckle at the look of distaste on her face before leaning in to press my lips to her forehead.

"Maybe," I offer. "But I'm also dead on and you know it." I get out, round the car, and pull open her door. "Come on, woman. Let's get some sleep."

CHAPTER EIGHTEEN

Pam

"Are you okay?" Dino's deep baritone heavy with sleep, rumbles behind me.

Morning light is streaming in, and I realize I feel more rested than I have in weeks. Despite the interrupted sleep.

I'm not sure who made the first move—probably me—but somehow, at some point during the night, I found myself wrapped around Dino. Like I was looking for maximum connection, with our limbs tangled and as much of our skin touching as possible. His first reaction when he woke up was to release me and give me the distance I'd needed last night, but it wasn't distance I wanted now. Using no words, I managed to get the message across. He deftly removed any barriers between us and with his gentle hands and soft lips, readied my body for his.

The moment he pushed inside me, the tears started rolling down my face. I was afraid he'd stop, but all he did was rise up on one elbow, and cup my face with his free hand. His body never stopped moving over me, his movements strong and sure, grounding me. There was no uncontrolled passion driving our connection this time. No race for a physical release while clutching, touching, and tasting each other everywhere. This was making love in its purest form, with not only bodies, but also minds and emotions connecting. It was about me opening up enough to take what Dino was giving me; exactly what I needed.

His eyes never left mine, and I'm not sure how long we moved together before my body released the coiled tension that had built up. Instead of barreling me over the edge of a cliff, this climax washed over me like the soothing lap of warm ocean water.

"I'm good." I turn to him, stretching my limbs in the process.

"Mmmm. I'd have to agree with that," he says. "More than good, though. You are *fine.*" I roll my eyes at the cheesy lines, but do it with a smile on my face.

I take a moment to run my fingers along his face; the strong brow and nose, firm jawline, and those ridiculously full lips. That's where my focus remains as I resist putting my mouth right there and slip out from under the covers.

"Hey!" Dino protests as his hand shoots out in an attempt to grab me. "That's not fair. You touch me like that, look at me like that, and then leave me hanging? Give me my good morning kiss, woman."

I plant my hands on my hips, cock one knee and shoot him a glare full of attitude. "Woman? You keep calling me that, I might have to hurt you." The only result of my words is that his warm brown eyes now hold a twinkle, as well as some definite heat, as they track the length of my body. I turn my back on him, pretend flipping hair I don't have over my shoulder, and saunter into the bathroom, giving my ass some extra sway.

I do all this with a smile on my face. I just stood buck naked, in all my fifty-one year glory, in the middle of the room, in the harsh light of day, throwing attitude, without a lick of self-consciousness. The fact that a big hulk of a beautiful man is lying in my bed, eyeing me with unapologetic heat, helps. A lot.

I'm not sure what this is or where, if anywhere, it's heading, but I know that I have found a new appreciation for an intuitive, empathetic man. Yesterday at this time, I was completely adrift, caught in a storm of emotions with Christmas knocking on the door, making me feel my loss sharper than before. Today I feel anchored, the air stilled around me.

Because of him.

-

The day is crazy busy. From the moment we get to The Skipper, having picked up Jonas on our way, I'm swept up in a nonstop flurry of activity. It's busy, but with an easy camaraderie that envelops me like a warm blanket. A joint purpose that even has Jonas swept up. He's more talkative and social than I've witnessed from him before, and I catch Dino occasionally watching him with parental pride. It's bittersweet, the feeling it evokes in me. Somehow making my son's death more real, but at the same time making his legacy more visible. He never had a chance to give his life purpose, but perhaps I was able to. With kids like Maria and Jonas, guiding them away from a dangerous path I'm now able to recognize, because of Derrick.

The only rough spot during the afternoon is when Gina doesn't show up when she's supposed to. Dino calmly grabs his jacket and leaves to chase her down, but Jonas seems to be more upset than I would've expected of a brother. Even though he doesn't say a word. I make a mental note to have a chat with him when things quiet down a little.

Half an hour later, Dino walks into the kitchen, his face thunderous.

"Where's Gina?" Jonas asks, as his father is hanging up his coat.

"Upstairs." Dino's answer is short and does not invite any further questioning, especially since he focuses his attention on the stove right away.

"Everything okay?" I ask, maybe ten minutes later, when tension is still radiating off his back. Upon hearing my question, his shoulders slump, but he still doesn't turn around. Jonas has been relegated to the pub to help bussing the tables and Ruby just went for a bathroom break. It's just Dino and me in the kitchen. I tentatively place my hand in the middle of his back and feel his muscles tense under my touch. "Dino? Did something happen?"

"Marcy's mom hadn't seen Gina since the girls went to bed last night. She assumed the girls were still sleeping but when Marcy came downstairs, she said Gina had left early to go home. She was surprised when I told her we hadn't seen her yet."

"So where did you find her?"

"I decided to stop at home. Pulled in the driveway just as she was walking down the street, her overnight bag over her shoulder. She tried to convince me she'd just left the Roper's house until I told her I just came from there. That shut her up. She won't tell me where she went and I've grounded her for the remainder of the Christmas holidays." Finally he turns to face me. "Not sure what is going on, Pam, but something sure is. I don't recognize my little girl anymore."

I want to say something encouraging, but just then Ruby walks back into the kitchen. Instead, I resort to giving his back a quick rub before turning back to plating appetizers for the guests. I have a feeling Jonas may know more about his sister's whereabouts than he's willing to let on, and I'm determined to find out. Something is up with that girl.

Dino

I was hopeful this morning.

For the first time in perhaps years, I was looking forward to Christmas. Even before things went dramatically south with Jeannie, the holidays had been forced. Mostly for the sake of the kids, we followed traditions we'd initiated when we first became a family, hanging the stuffed stockings on the kids' doors so they could open a few gifts. In the meantime, we'd go downstairs to light candles and get coffee going before calling them downstairs. The past ten years, there'd been no grandparents or family left to go visit, so we ended up spending Christmas day in PJs, lounging around until it was time for me to pull together a festive dinner. A leisurely day that in recent years had become more of a chore than it should have been.

I hadn't looked forward to Christmas this year. Had managed to pick up a few things here and there for the kids, but it was difficult to know what they'd like. It made me realize that somewhere along the line, I'd lost touch. It doesn't help that the past month we seemed to roll from one upheaval into the next, starting with Jonas going off the rails. We haven't even put up the Christmas tree yet, which I hope to do tonight when we get home from The Skipper.

Now it would appear my thirteen-year-old daughter, the same one who just months ago would look at me like I hung the moon, has chosen the day before Christmas to cause problems.

I'm literally sick to my stomach, driving home. It doesn't go away when I see her walking down the street with her bag tossed over her shoulder. I'd suspected Marcy wasn't telling me everything she knew when she refused to meet my eyes.

"Get in," I snap at Gina when she walks up the drive, her chin tilted defiantly. She doesn't say a word and just gets in the car. No *Daddy* from my little princess today. "Where were you?"

"Marcy's," is the snappy answer and I swing my head around.

"Funny, since Marcy's mom said she hasn't seen you since last night and Marcy said you left early this morning. So I'll ask again, where were you?" I watch as shock, then guilt, flits over my little girl's face before she settles on defiance again. She lifts her little chin even higher and throws me a glare before resolutely turning her gaze out the side window. "Fine, play it like that," I tell her in a low voice. "But know that your ass is staying inside the rest of your vacation. I don't take kindly to lying, Gina."

The only fucking response I get is an incredulous snort and a shrug of her narrow shoulders, but she doesn't even turn to face me. The sick feeling in the pit of my stomach settles deeper.

The moment we walk into the back of The Skipper, Gina makes a beeline for the stairs and storms up. I head back to the kitchen, I don't have time to duke it out with her right now. I try to put it out of my mind and focus on the menu, until I feel Pam's hand at my back, reminding me I'm not alone.

It's nearing on ten o'clock when we finally file out of the pub's back door. One of Syd's stipulations for this dinner is that it's served early so that everyone can get home at a reasonable hour for Christmas Eve. Gauging by the happy smile on her face, the evening was another success raising funds for Daniel's Hope Foundation; the charity she set up in memory of her son and that helps pay medical care for children in need.

I grab Pam's hand and link my fingers with hers as we walk down the alley toward the parking lot. Jonas and Gina are walking in front of us, and it looks as if Jonas has a thing or two to say to his sister. Pam squeezes my hand to get my attention.

"Could you drop me off at home?"

"Why?" I want to know, pulling Pam to a stop. "I was hoping you'd come trim the tree at mine." A little smile tugs at the corner of her mouth as she places her other hand in the middle of my chest. It feels good there.

"I haven't been to Florence House all week. I know Brenda and Doris have everything in hand, but I should really make an appearance there tomorrow morning. Three of the residents are with family or friends for Christmas, but there are two who have nowhere to go. I don't want to leave them alone."

"What if I drop you off there right after breakfast tomorrow?" I know I sound like I'm begging, but fuck if I don't want to start my day with her right there. "We'll go grab some overnight stuff for you on the way home. What do you say?"

"But what about the kids? Do you think staying over is a good idea?"

"Jonas is old enough and no fool. I'm not sure where Gina's head's at right now, but I know I want you there. I'll sleep on the couch if I have to."

She looks at me, her eyes squinted, before patting me on the chest. "Okay, I'll stay. But I really need to pick up a few things at home if you don't mind swinging past my place." I lean down and kiss her hard in response, before tugging her along to the car, where the kids are impatiently waiting.

We swing by Pam's place, where she rushes in to grab her gear, while Jonas gives me the third degree. He seems satisfied when I tell him I just don't want Pam to wake up to an empty house on Christmas Day. Not exactly a lie, but not the entire truth either. Gina has remained quiet and when I check the rearview mirror, I notice she's following the conversation closely.

The kids try to escape to their rooms when we get home, but I won't let them.

"We're decorating the tree, guys. I'm gonna put on some hot chocolate and throw a few cookies in the oven, if you guys pull down the tree and the decorations from the attic."

Years ago, Jeannie had wanted to do away with a fresh cut Christmas tree. I conceded, because I did anything I thought could make her happy, but I really hate fake trees. Next year, we're getting a real one. If I have my way, we'll go and cut it down ourselves. For now though, we'd have to make do with the artificial one.

Grumbling, the kids head upstairs to haul the stuff down, and Pam follows me into the kitchen.

"What do you want me to do?" she asks, standing a little uncertainly in the doorway.

"First I want you to come here and kiss me, and although I'd like your mouth other places than just on my lips, with the kids upstairs, I guess I'll have to restrain myself." I chuckle as I watch Pam's face register shock before she flushes a dark rose. Her eyes sparkle as her mouth lifts in a smirk, and I think I'm in trouble. Slowly and deliberately she stalks up to me, molds the front of her body to mine, and tilts her back.

"You want my mouth on you?" she asks, her voice sultry as fuck and my crotch is immediately too tight when she teases my chest with her index finger, scratching her nail over a nipple. "Want my tongue tasting you? Want my lips stretching around you? Want to slide your cock down my throat?" Her hips roll against my dick seductively, in rhythm with each question, rendering me incapable of speech. The need to flip her around and bend her over my kitchen counter so I can spank the sass out of her is so strong, only the sound of footsteps pounding down the stairs stops me from following through. I growl deep in my chest when I see the self-satisfied smirk on her face. *Minx.*

"You'll pay," I manage right before Jonas comes storming in with the tree box in his arms.

"Where, Dad?"

"Same as every year, Bud; corner by the fireplace, in front of the bookcase." With a simple nod, he's off again and I'm left facing Pam.

"Hot chocolate is your job. I'll whip up cookies," I tell her, and she snickers when I adjust myself before diving into the fridge.

Half an hour later, we watch Jonas struggle with the lights, something that was historically my task, but I'm glad to hand over the reins for. Gina helped bring a few boxes down, but currently has her head buried in her phone. Maybe I should've taken that away from her, too. Still, she's here in the room, and although not necessarily an active or even willing participant, I'm glad for her presence. I'm even happier to have Pam snuggled up to me as we're sipping hot chocolate and tossing out instructions on placement to Jonas.

"Why exactly are we doing this?" Gina's unexpected question is sharp. It's clear she's trying to poke the bear, although why is beyond me.

Jonas swings around on his sister angrily, but before he can say anything or I can intervene, Pam's rich deep voice fills the angry silence.

"You know," she starts, not looking at anyone in particular but rather staring at the lights in the tree. "When Derrick was young and it was just him and me, I used to have a tree up every Christmas. No matter how bad our situation, and whether or not I had gifts to put underneath that year, I made it a point to have a tree. Sometimes I'd wait until the last minute, for the guy selling trees down the block, to start closing down his stand on Christmas Eve. He'd usually have a few trees left—not much, but better than nothing—and would let me drag one home. Decorations were silly things. Stuff Derrick had made in school or things we could find around the house." She pauses and I look to find both Jonas and Gina's eyes riveted on Pam's sad face. "That last year, we didn't have a tree. I was too busy...well, it doesn't really matter why. All that matters is that I haven't had a tree since then. Haven't decorated a tree since then. With Derrick gone now, I can't help but think what might have been different, if I hadn't been too busy that time; too wrapped up in what I was doing that last year. Would it have made a difference? If I'd made time for our annual Christmas decorating, would things have been different?" She surreptitiously wipes a tear from her cheek and I give her shoulder a squeeze. She turns to face Gina directly. "So you see, honey—this tree? This experience? It may not seem worth the effort to you right now, but trust me when I say that if you miss only one year, you may have to live with that regret the rest of your life—I do."

CHAPTER NINETEEN

Pam

"Wake up, sleepy."

I crack my eyes open to find Dino's deep brown ones staring at me just inches away.

I slept deep. Not sure whether it was my emotional outburst last night or the cookies and chocolate. Maybe it was the more lighthearted, but reverent, way with which we decked out the Christmas tree after. It could have been the combination of all the above, but the fact is that after the kids finally made their excuses and headed up to bed, and Dino and I silently cleaned up and followed behind—yes, Dino crawled into bed with me and I didn't stop him—my head barely hit the pillow before I drifted off.

"Merry Christmas." My words sound raw with sleep and a little thick with emotion. The corners of his eyes crinkle up with a smile, and despite the heavy sadness surrounding my heart, I feel it lift at the sight.

"The first of many more," he says, his words and the smile that accompanies them, settling deep in my soul.

My hand comes up to stroke the stubble on his jaw. There are no questions, only answers, in his eyes and I feel the need to give back.

"So far it has been nothing but rough waters, but I want you to know I don't regret being here for a minute. Taking a chance with you, stepping out of my comfort zone—you've made it worth while." I watch as his pupils dilate and his feelings are on full display. He holds nothing back. "I thought it would be scary to let this happen, but you made falling for you easy."

"I'm glad," he says, his voice a little hoarser than before. "Because I wouldn't want to fall alone."

Instead of kissing me, like I thought he would, he tucks his head in my neck and wraps his arms tightly around me. I'm not sure how long we stay like that before he releases me and sits back up on the side of the bed.

"It's snowing," he says. "Has been for a while."

Not sure what it is about snow on Christmas, but it seems to bring out the magic. I barely resist squealing as I jump out of bed and rush to the window. Sure enough, a thick blanket of white fluff covers everything in sight and more is falling.

"Why don't you hop in the shower and I'll get going on breakfast." Dino stands up and starts moving to the door when I hurry to stop him by sliding my body between him and the door. I slip my arms around his neck and lift up on my toes, reaching to kiss him. His big hand slides up my back, before cupping the back of my head, making me feel both vulnerable and safe. His mouth quickly takes over and I'm glad for his hold on me, because my knees grow weak with the barely restrained force of his kiss.

"Thank you," I mumble against his lips when he finally pulls away. One last peck before he shoves me in the direction of the bathroom, slapping my ass on the way.

-

I managed to grab a few things when I quickly packed my bag last night, but I never had the chance to wrap them. With everything going on, and being out of practice, I hadn't done any shopping for Christmas, but I didn't want to come empty-handed.

So when Dino herded us into the living room, after a stupendous breakfast of banana and Nutella stuffed French toast, I excused myself for a minute to grab my overnight bag from upstairs.

"I'm sorry, I didn't manage to get out to get you guys something," I start, walking back in the room and sitting down beside Dino on the couch. Gina is curled up in the club chair and Jonas is sitting on the floor by the tree. All eyes are on me. "I didn't even have a chance to wrap them. Gina," I turn my attention to her as I pull her gift from my bag. "My grandmother made this when I was a girl," I say as I unfold the quilt I've held onto all these years, safely stored in my linen closet. "I haven't used it since I was a teenager, but I can tell you it made me feel loved at times I really needed it. I hope it can do the same for you." I have a hard time not crying when I see Gina's eyes fill up. Her gaze comes up to meet mine, before it slips down to the blue and green painstakingly handstitched quilt in my hands.

"Biscuit," Dino's voice sounds deep and gravelly beside me, and I quickly lift a hand to stop the protest I know will be coming next.

"I want her to have it. To use it the way I was able to when times got bumpy. It would make me happy." I hold out the quilt and watch as Gina slowly unfolds herself from her chair and makes her way over, her eyes never leaving her gift.

"Thank you," she says simply, never quite looking at me, but when she sits down and smoothes the quilt around her, a little bit of wonder on her face as she studies its pattern, it makes me smile.

"I'm afraid it's a hand-me-down for you as well," I confess to Jonas as I unearth his gift. "The one thing Derrick remained passionate about was his Red Sox. Living in New York at the time, being a Red Sox fan wasn't exactly easy or welcomed, given the historical rivalry between them and the Yankees, which should show you how invested he was in his team. When he went to prison, he asked me to hold on to his favorite jersey for him. I don't know if you're familiar with him, but his favorite player was Jason Varitek. He signed Derrick's jersey outside Yankee stadium after a game one year."

"*Jesus*," Dino mutters behind me, but I ignore him as I hand the shirt over to his son, who solemnly nods his thanks before the side of his mouth tips up as he addresses his dad.

"Jason, Dad—not Jesus," he deadpans, breaking through the much too heavy atmosphere as I snicker and Gina giggles softly.

"Smartass," Dino fires back, chuckling himself.

When Dino drives me to Florence House a while later, I'm actually reluctant to leave. It's obvious Dino's kids aren't necessarily spoiled with lavish gifts, but they seemed happy with the things their father picked up for them. They'd also joined forces to get their father a gift certificate for dinner at DiMillo's On The Water, a favored floating restaurant in Portland. A sweet gift that was accompanied by a card that simply stated; *For all the times you cook for us!* Dino had been visibly moved. Jonas voiced concern that they didn't get me anything, but I quickly waved that off.

"At the risk of sounding superbly cheesy; reintroducing me to Christmas is truly the best gift you could've given me. So thank you all for that."

I think the kids were terrified things would get heavy and emotional again, because very shortly after that they disappeared upstairs to get dressed. Dino insisted they come along to drop me off and head over to the sledding hill at the Eastern Prom to work off breakfast on the slope. I have to admit, I'm a little jealous. The views of Casco Bay are fantastic from there and the sledding…let's just say I haven't been that carefree in decades. It sounds really fun.

Florence House doesn't have a driveway or a garage, it's an old, Victorian townhouse with a small, fenced front yard. Dino pulls up by the curb out front, just as Marianne and Maria step out of the gate, arm in arm.

"Hey." Marianne waves and approaches the car when she sees me, dragging Maria along. Both of them are covered in snow.

"Happy Christmas," she says through a smile, her lips a little blue from the cold.

"Merry Christmas to you two, as well," I respond in kind when I step out of the car.

More Christmas wishes are exchanged as Dino and the kids add theirs.

"What are you girls doing out here?" I want to know. A sheepish grin spreads over Marianne's face.

"Snow angels," she replies. "I've never made a snow angel and Maria offered to show me."

My eyes dart to Maria, whose eyes seem to be focused on the backseat through the window. *Shit!* I'm not sure if she actually recognizes Jonas and just as I try to close the door quickly, so they can be on their way, the backdoor opens and Jonas steps out.

"Honey, maybe you should…" I try, but Jonas is already moving toward her.

"Hey," I hear him say to her softly. Maria's eyes flit back and forth between Jonas and Marianne, who has clearly become her savior. Marianne is closer and steps in, grabbing Maria's hand. Jonas tucks his hands in his pockets and shuffles the snow a little with his foot. "I'm sorry." The words are even quieter, but stand out stark in the still air. "I know there isn't anything I can do to take back what happened—what I allowed to happen—but I want you to know that I would if I could."

Behind me I hear another car door open and know, without checking, that Dino just got out as well.

It's an awkward, painful tableau. A moment in time that seems to outline clearly how cruel life can sometimes be. Nobody knows what to say. Finally, Jonas turns his back to the women on the sidewalk and moves back to the car. I see him swallow hard as he seems to struggle to keep control over his emotions.

"Merry Christmas." The soft voice stops him in his tracks as I see Maria pull free from Marianne's hold and take a few steps closer. "If there was anything to forgive, consider yourself forgiven," she adds. "This is not your burden to carry. Just like it's not mine." She reaches out and touches his shoulder, sending a visible shock through his body. "Please."

I watch as he is unable to hold back a single tear that streaks down his face. He slowly turns around to face her. "Thanks," he says, his voice cracking on the single syllable. "You have a good Christmas, too."

"Oh for Pete's sake," Marianne pipes up, stepping between the two and very unexpectedly wrapping her arms around Jonas in a hug. "Enough with the mushy stuff. You're a little punk," she says, leaning back to look up at Jonas. "But you're an okay little punk. Now are you guys gonna come inside or just sit there freezing your asses off in the car?"

"Well, actually, the kids and I were…" Dino starts to make excuses.

"Nonsense," Marianne cuts him off. "We've got hot cider inside, and Maria and I have spent the past week baking up a storm. Enough goodies to have both of us looking like sumo wrestlers, if someone doesn't come and help us eat the stuff."

"I didn't think we were allowed in?" Dino walks up beside me and looks at me questioningly.

"Normally we don't let men in, no," I confirm. "For obvious reasons."

"Right."

"Yes, but there's no one here but us chickens, and Doris, but she's not an inmate," Marianne takes over, ignoring my protest at her choice of words and the little giggle from Maria. "We'd like you to come in. Wouldn't we?" she asks Maria, who just smiles and nods.

"Fine," I say a little ungraciously, throwing up my hands in defeat. "By all means, let's stuff our faces with more sweet stuff and hate ourselves in the morning." I start marching toward the house, leaving the rest to follow behind. Doris stands in the doorway, snickering at my scowl. "Et tu, Brute?" I fire off at her as she steps aside to let me pass.

Gone for a week and I have a mutiny on my hands.

Dino

I can honestly say, I never thought I'd celebrate Christmas inside a woman's shelter. Let alone enjoy the fuck out of it.

Marianne is a hoot. The petite woman has an attitude that makes it difficult to believe she survived decades of emotional and physical abuse. The way she mothers Maria is both heartwarming and hilarious. I notice every time Pam looks over at where the two are sitting, side by side on the couch, she gets a little misty-eyed.

"So how's about a game of Cards Against Humanity?" Marianne offers as she gets up from the couch. Maria giggles and I hear Jonas suck in a breath. I have no clue what Cards Against Humanity is, but apparently the kids do. Even Gina has a blush on her face and a slightly panicked look as she glances my way.

Pam looks as confused as I'm sure I do, but we all follow the small woman into the dining room, taking seats around the table.

Marianne sets a black box on the table and proceeds to explain the objective of the game. A word game of sorts. Everyone seems to get the concept, although Pam and I seemed to be the only ones who need explaining. Marianne takes a stack of cards from the box and starts dealing. I pick them up, one by one, and about have a fucking heart attack.

Whining like a little bitch, A big black dick, My dad's dumb fucking face, Grandpa's ashes, and *Two midgets shitting in a box.* And those are only the first five cards I pick up. I look at Pam beside me, who is clearly not faring much better. Both our eyes swing to the instigator, who looks way too pleased with herself.

"Marianne!" Pam finally manages to say in a stern tone. "I hardly think this is…"

"Oh, relax," the old bitty hushes as she flaps her hand. "Look at the kids. They've all played this before." She looks at each of them in return. "Am I right?"

All of them, including my thirteen-year-old little girl nods. *Fuck my life.*

Three hours later, my stomach aching from laughing so damn much, I herd the kids and Pam back to the car. I offered to get food to cook here, but apparently Brenda, the other woman who works here, is coming over with dinner in a bit.

I've planned an easy meal. I spend enough time in the kitchen as it is, so am throwing together a simple honey-glazed ham, with mashed potatoes, sautéed vegetables and apple pie a la mode for dessert. The kids like it. They're not big on fancy stuff, Jonas says he prefers food he can recognize.

Driving home is a bit treacherous. The roads are covered with snow and it's still coming down. Not many people out and about, and I've yet to see a plow. The five minute drive actually takes more like twenty, and the moment I pull into the garage, the kids are out of the car, and rushing into the house. Jonas a little slower than his sister, who beats him to the door.

"I forgot to ask you with everything going on," I turn to Pam, who's still seated beside me. "Did Detective Barnes ever manage to get hold of you?" The surprised look on her face is all the answer I need.

"Shit. I should've mentioned something sooner. They have those two punks in custody. He mentioned there would be no bail set this time. I'm not sure if it's because of the holidays or what, but I haven't heard from him since."

"I'll call him on Monday," Pam volunteers, sounding a little distracted. "Find out what's going on."

"How are you doing?" I ask, slipping a hand around her neck and rubbing my thumb along her jaw. "Holding up okay?" Pam had been laughing hard earlier along with the rest of us, but every now and then, I would see a shadow cloud her face. I didn't want to put her on the spot either at the shelter or with the kids listening in.

Pam leans her face into my hand and briefly closes her eyes. "I'm okay," she softly responds. "In all honesty, since Derrick was incarcerated, I haven't truly celebrated the holidays. Not like today." She sighs deeply. "It's almost like waking up from a deep sleep; everything is stiff and hurts a little from lack of use. Being so used to tamping down emotions, *feeling* this much is a bit overwhelming."

"I'm sorry." I know it's not enough, but at this point I'm not sure what else I can say. I can be here, ready to catch her, but that's all I can do. Pam is too strong and independent for anything else. Her gorgeous eyes are focused on mine, warm and caring, and together with the soft smile on her lips, she stirs up my emotions. It's rare she shows her softer side, and I'm very aware what it means that she so easily shows me.

Love is funny. Sometimes it hits you like a freight train, like with the birth of my children. The moment I held their fragile little bodies in my arms, it came at me so hard, it took my breath away. The love of friends feels comfortable, effortless, like an old pair of sneakers. Some love is hot and momentarily blinding, like what I felt for Jeannie; the instant stun of a flare that burns hot and then burns out. Then there's the kind of love that sneaks up on you. The kind you don't see coming, don't notice growing, until it is right there in your face, bigger than life.

"What is going through your mind?" Pam asks me, pulling her jacket tighter around her against the cold. I should get her inside where it's warm, but instead I lean over and cover her luscious lips with mine. Kissing her is like a hit of sugar to my veins, setting my blood buzzing with the potency of her flavor, like rich, dark coffee.

"You—you are going through my mind," I admit, when I slowly pull back from the kiss. "Constantly. I can't seem to not think about you. You're everywhere." She straightens up and looks down at her hands.

"I'm not sure if that's a good thing," she whispers.

"Oh…it's a good thing. It's a very good thing."

CHAPTER TWENTY

Pam

"How's Benji doing?"

Sarah is fidgeting with the strap of her purse she, for some reason, is keeping in a tight grip on her lap. Something is off with her today.

Christmas left me both emotionally drained but mentally refreshed. I stayed with Dino and his kids until after breakfast the day after. Although I slept in Dino's bed with him, we didn't have sex. Exactly. By the time we rolled into bed, it was late and we didn't do more than kiss and snuggle, but the next morning—apparently the preferred time of day for us both—we'd woken up sufficiently recharged to explore a little. Until distinct sounds from the hallway announced one or both of the kids were awake. Works like a cold shower.

I'd felt good, though. Still sad and a bit emotional, but somehow seeing how Marianne dealt with her first Christmas without her family, helped me to put things in perspective. That woman came into the shelter, battered physically and emotionally, and months later she is the life of the party. I never thought I would laugh that hard again, but I did. It was unadulterated, uncomplicated, and highly inappropriate fun, and we all walked away the better for it. That's why after breakfast with Dino and his family, I needed to get back on my feet. And that included taking back the groups and checking in with my clients these past few days. I've been so preoccupied with my own stuff, I feel I've left them neglected.

Sarah had sounded dull on the phone when I called yesterday, lifeless and beaten down. I forced down the guilt that wanted to bubble up and immediately asked her to come see me. I could hear reluctance in her voice when she agreed to see me today.

"He's good."

The slight hesitation and lack of elaboration has warning bells go off.

"What are the kids up to today?" I decide to try and draw her out with more general questions rather than the direct ones I usually prefer.

"Oh," she says, a little taken aback. "Well, they're actually with family. I have some family staying with us for the holidays."

"I didn't realize you had contact with your folks again? That's wonderful." She's lying and I know it. Or at least she's stretching the truth. When she first came here, she made it clear she had nowhere else to go, that her parents had turned their back on her years before and the kids had never even met them. To think that they'd suddenly show up out of the blue seemed a bit too convenient.

Her eyes look down on her hands, fiddling restlessly with the clasp of her purse.

"Sarah?" I prompt her and the truth is visible in the guilty eyes she lifts to meet mine.

"He was all alone for Christmas. He had nowhere to go," she whispers, and a feeling of dread settles in my stomach.

"Okay," I say, trying to stay calm. "So is he at your place now?" A short, sharp nod confirms my fears. "With the boys?"

I hold my breath waiting for the answer, because the bastard had not held back beating her then two little boys as easily as he beat her. She finally took the kids and left him when Benji, the oldest, had started fighting back. It had scared her. She'd been afraid the boyfriend would take it too far. Her words, not mine. In my opinion, the first time the asswipe used his hands on either her or the kids, he'd already gone way too far.

"They've been fine so far," she says, a slight whine to her voice, and I can't help the small recoil of disgust I feel. It's not fair to judge her when I haven't lived her life, but holy fucking hell, it's hard not to shake the woman for putting her kids in danger.

"Sarah," I say with more patience than I feel. "Can you honestly tell me you feel it's safe leaving the boys with him?" I don't want to put words in her mouth or add to her guilt, which is why I want her to answer the question I already know the answer to. I watch as thick tears start rolling down her cheeks, and she crumples in on herself in front of my eyes. "Honey." I lean over and put my hand on her knee. "Sarah, I need you to look at me," I say a bit sterner, and she finally lifts her eyes again. "Good. Now do your boys have cell phones? Does Benji have one?"

"He promised me he'd call if something happened," she whispers. "He was gonna keep Sam in his room with him until I get back. Phil was still sleeping when I left. They should be okay?" She asks the last—like she's asking me for confirmation.

"Call him. Call Benji right now."

Whether it's my own fragile emotions or my well-honed, hyper vigilant senses, I feel the urgent need to have the boys' well-being confirmed. Sarah is already digging through her purse, and as soon as she has her phone in hand, is dialing.

"Hi, sweetie, is everything alright?" I watch and listen as Sarah talks to her son. "Is Sammy okay?…Yes, I'll come home right now." She ends the call and turns to me with fear in her eyes.

"I've gotta go. He's looking for me." She abruptly stands up, and I barely manage to halt her with a tight grip on her wrist.

"Honey, what's going on?" I demand, standing up to.

"The kids locked themselves in the bathroom. He's trying to break down the door." The moment I release my hold on her to grab my phone, she's running toward the door.

"Sarah, wait!"

My fingers are already dialing as I run after her.

"What's your emergency?" the nine one one operator asks, as I catch up with Sarah at the front door where Marianne is blocking her way.

"Domestic assault in progress." Pulling the phone away from my mouth, I turn to Sarah who is struggling to tug loose from the much smaller woman, who by now has her pinned against the wall beside the door. "Sarah! Give me your address, honey. Now!" Shocked at my voice, she rattles off the address, which I immediately pass on to the operator before adding; "Two underage boys have locked themselves in the bathroom. Mom's boyfriend is beating down the door. Hurry!"

The moment I hear her say, "Units are on their way," I hang up, grab my coat, and snatch my car keys from the hook by the door.

"Let's go," I tell Sarah, "we're taking my car." But she's not the only one who follows me outside, Marianne is right behind her, zipping up her coat. "Where are you going, Marianne?" I ask as I unlock my doors and thank the Lord I don't need to clear snow off my car this morning. Marianne already has the backdoor open before she turns to me.

"Not going to let you go alone," she says, determination on her face as she slips in the backseat, slamming the door shut behind her.

Dino

"Gina?"

I'm supposed to be at The Skipper in twenty minutes, and I've been waiting for my girl to come downstairs for half an hour already. Ruby, Syd, and Matt were there yesterday, and today Viv, Gunnar, and I are supposed to man the pub. With Ike out of town, Viv was going to bring little Francessca and I'd suggested Gina could look after her. That way, Viv has her daughter close by, and I don't have to worry about mine all day long, wondering if she's going to stick close to home, the way she's supposed to. One of the benefits working for Gunnar, who has kids of his own, is his flexibility when it comes to our families.

But Gina's not coming down, and although I'd stopped barging in her room two years ago, I am about to break that rule. I'd knocked twice already and yelled up the stairs a few times more. I try knocking one more time, but when there's no answer I push open the door. For a minute I stand in the doorway, wondering if she'd pulled a fast one on me; there's a distinct lump under the covers but it seems too short to be a body. With two long strides, I'm by the side of the bed and reach out to rip the covers off the bed.

"What the hell?" A sleepy voice comes from my daughter, curled up in a ball, pulling the covers back from my hands. Her face is red and her eyes swollen. Worry replaces my earlier anger as I wonder what has my little girl rolled into a fetal position, hiding under her blankets. I sit down heavily on the side of the mattress and gently stroke the hair plastered to her forehead.

"Morning, Princess."

"I don't feel well," she says, when I spot her cell phone sticking out from under her pillow, the screen lit with a text message. She tries to shove it out of sight when she notices me looking, but I'm faster.

> **B**: *Can't. Supsd to look aft the brat til M gets home. Give me 1 hr? Ppmt Pk.*

"Get dressed, Gina," I bite off, looking at the guilty look on her face. "And who's 'B'?"

"Friend," she answers with a shrug, an almost bored look replacing the guilty one she wore just seconds ago. *Fucking hell.* It was just a couple of months ago I saw that exact look on her brother's face.

She rolls out of bed on the opposite side, tags some clothes from the piles on the floor, and tries to scoot by me on the way to the bathroom. Again, I'm faster as I grab her wrist, stopping her.

"Tell me you weren't planning to go against my wishes and leave the house? Lying, Princess? Since fucking when?" I take a deep breath when I notice my volume rising along with my temper. "And even if you weren't grounded, you know better than to hang out in Peppermint Park." Her eyes flare with surprise. *Yeah, honey, your old man may be ancient in your eyes but he's not a fool.* Still, she keeps her mouth firmly shut, until I finally let go of her wrist. "You've got five minutes, Gina—If I have to come up again, I swear I'll toss you over my shoulder and carry you down."

Son of a bitch. If I wasn't already late for work, I'd sit her down until I got to the bottom of this. Instead, I tuck her phone in my pocket and head downstairs.

With less than a minute to spare, Gina's footsteps come down the stairs. I'm already dressed and hand Gina her coat. She doesn't even look at me. What the hell happened to my girl?

I tried one more time to get her to tell me who she was supposed to be meeting, but she maintained her silence.

"Alright, missy; I'll be keeping your phone, since it's obvious I can't trust you with it."

"But, Dad…"

I flick my hand at her in warning. "Not a word, Gina. You screwed up and I'm done talking for now."

I try not to glance over, but in my peripheral vision I can see her staring out the passenger side window, her arms folded protectively in front of her body. *Jesus, these kids.*

When we walk into the kitchen, where Francessca is bouncing in her chair on the table, I'm amazed at the change in my daughter. With a distracted 'Hi' to Viv, Gina's entire demeanor lights up when she walks over to the baby, lifting her from the seat into her arms. It's hard to stay angry at her when I watch her giggle as the little girl slaps Gina's cheeks with her tiny hands.

"Everything okay?" Viv softly asks when I pass by her to hang up my coat. "You guys both walked in here with thunder on your faces."

"We're fine," I lie, not wanting to get into it with Gina sitting behind me at the table. Viv seems to get it and doesn't ask any more. "Want some breakfast, Princess?" I turn to Gina, watching a war play out on her face. She seems to want to hang on to her scowl when she looks at me, but the prospect of food has her wavering. Her stomach finally wins, as I guessed it would, since it's almost lunch time and she hasn't had anything, she gives me a tight nod.

I hate this kind of tension. Hated it with Jonas and hate it even more with my girl. She's only thirteen for fuck's sake, a little girl in my eyes, not this moody, secretive teenager. I throw together some cinnamon French toast and toss it in the buttered pan, while watching her from the corner of my eye. There's no scowl on her face as she makes silly faces to coax giggles from the baby. There isn't one either when Viv says something to her and she easily responds. It's clear she saves her mood for me, and I wonder what I might've done to warrant that.

After clearing her plate, Gina heads up to the apartment with Francessca to put her down for a nap. Viv just looks at me with an eyebrow raised.

"Fine?" she prompts.

"Difficult," I offer. "Not sure what's up with her."

"Hormones," is Viv's decisive response.

"She's too young."

Viv's snort has me look at her.

"For your information," she says, without taking her eyes off the dough she's kneading. "I was barely eleven when I got my period, and I remember how utterly mortifying that was in a house full of brothers. Still, I had my mom around."

"Shit. You think that's it? I don't get why she wouldn't say anything to me."

"You're a guy," Viv points out with a shoulder shrug.

"I'm her dad."

"Even worse," she chuckles. "You're the ultimate guy. The one who'd like nothing better than to keep her playing with dolls and wearing pigtails for the rest of her life, so you don't have to pulverize pimple-faced adolescent boys, who are bound to come sniffing around your daughter."

That has me thinking of the message I intercepted earlier. I wonder if it would be too late to send her to a monastery school somewhere. *Jesus*.

"You want, I can talk to her," Viv offers, and I gratefully nod yes, which gets her snickering again. I'm relieved at the thought perhaps Gina's attitude change is something as simple as getting her period for the first time. Yet, I'm not entirely convinced.

I'm putting the last touches on the goulash when the phone starts buzzing in my pocket.

"Hello," I answer without looking. I don't hear anything at first, just some scuffling in the background when a young voice starts whispering.

"Is Gina there?"

The hair on my arms stands on end when I realize it's my daughter's phone in my hand. It doesn't make me feel any better to hear a man yelling in the background, accompanied by a loud banging.

"Who is this?" I ask, reacting more to the ruckus I can hear and not his question. "What's going on?"

"I'm …it's…never mind." Just like that, the connection is broken and I take a good look at the phone. It was the same person who sent the message to my daughter earlier—*B*. I'm tempted to call right back, the boy sounded pretty scared, but I don't know what kind of situation he's in, or if I'd only make it worse.

"Viv, can you keep an eye on this? I've gotta check on Gina." Viv simply nods and I head upstairs, where my daughter is watching the little one.

When I tiptoe into the small apartment, I find not only the baby asleep in the folding crib, but my own little girl is curled up on the couch right beside her. I'm tempted to let her sleep, but I can't dismiss the fear I heard in that boy's voice.

"Wake up, baby," I whisper, trying not to wake Francessca as I sit on the edge of the couch and softly shake Gina's shoulder. "Princess, I've gotta talk to you," I try again when she pulls her shoulder from under my hand. She slowly turns her head and blinks at me. "Who is B on your phone, honey?" The question has her shoot up straight wiping hair away from her face.

"B?"

"He just called. I had your phone in my pocket, thought it was mine so I answered. He sounded scared, who is he and what's going on?" I see her face shift to worry and she puts her hand on my arm.

"Scared? Oh no…" Gina scrambles off the couch, and I follow suit, putting my hands on her shoulders to keep her in place.

"Baby, what the fuck is going on?"

"His stepdad. He beats on them. He's been scared ever since his mom let the guy move back in." Gina's rambling now, her eyes everywhere but on mine. "Benji's a good kid, Dad. He told me they got away from his stepdad once but that he's back now."

"Okay, honey, calm down." I pull Gina in to my chest when she starts sniffling. "We don't know what, if anything, is going on yet. Where does Ben live?"

"Behind the hospital, I'm not sure exactly what street it is. I've never been there."

"Here." I hand Gina her phone. "Try calling him back but keep it on speakerphone, so I can hear?" She moves into the kitchen area and I follow close behind. The phone rings on the other side but there's no answer.

"Try one more time, baby," I urge her on. This time there's an answer, and when I hear the voice my heart stops in my throat.

"Gina?" Pam says.

CHAPTER TWENTY-ONE

Pam

"Turn right."

Sarah's voice is subdued. She's been quiet the entire drive, just speaking up to give me directions to her place, her hands wringing restlessly in her lap. Marianne has been quiet in the backseat as well, all of us dreading what we might be walking into. Those poor boys, hiding from their mom's boyfriend's ire. I silently hope the police arrive before we do. I won't hesitate to barge into the house and face off with the bastard if I have to, but I'm also not an idiot; I know a few cops with sidearms will likely make more of an impact than I would.

"Oh thank God," I hear Sarah mutter beside me when flashing lights down the road come into view.

Just as I pull off to the curb, when our path is blocked by a cruiser. An ambulance with sirens blaring turns into the street behind us and continues right by us, bypassing the cop car. Sarah is out of the car and running before I have a chance to turn the engine off. Marianne is trying to keep up with her as I scramble to get out. I catch up to them when a police officer steps in our path, holding us back. Marianne has her arms around Sarah, physically restraining her, and I step in front of them, facing off with the cop.

"You cannot go through. Not until I've been assured the situation is under control," he bites off sternly.

"Officer," I try. "This woman's two underage boys are in there. We're the ones who called it in."

"I understand," he says, his tone a little friendlier as he throws a pitying look in Sarah's direction, but he doesn't budge an inch.

We're holding Sarah up, who by this time is wailing for her boys, when movement by the front door of the dilapidated little house draws our attention. Two uniformed officers drag a cuffed and shackled man out of the house, whose incoherent yelling is loud enough to reach us where we're stand on the sidewalk.

"*Sarah!* You bitch!" he yells when he spots our little huddle on the sidewalk. "You're gonna pay for this, you fucking cunt!"

The officer, who's been holding us back, steps forward to block us from the raging man's view, but not before I feel Sarah's body go completely limp in my arms. It takes everything out of me not to drop her to the ground, but between Marianne and I, we manage to keep her upright. More or less.

The moment the patrol car holding Sarah's boyfriend, Phil, whizzes by, I turn my attention to the officer in front of us. "Can we check on her boys now?"

He holds up a finger and mumbles something in his radio. He nods at what he hears back, even though I can't make head or tails of it, and indicates for us to follow him. Sarah is barely moving her feet as we march her, wedged between us, up to the front door.

The inside is teeming with uniforms, and in what looks to be the kitchen, the EMTs are attending to someone on the floor. My heart stutters in my chest until I hear Sarah call out.

"Benji!"

She pulls from our hold and runs into the kitchen, dropping down on the floor beside her son, who is thankfully moving. My eyes scan around to look for her younger boy, but I can't find him. Remembering the boys had been holed up in the bathroom earlier, I start walking down the hallway, hoping to find it. The first door is open, revealing what I think is the boys' room; a small space with bunk beds against one wall and an old dresser against the other. Dirty clothes and garbage is strewn everywhere, covering the floor and sparse furniture.

The next door is also open and reveals a filthy bathroom. Empty, at first glance, but then I hear the faint ringing of a phone. It's coming from the vanity underneath the sink, and I know I've found the younger boy when I crouch down and carefully open the cupboard. Sam is inside; his body curled into a tight ball, wedged between the side and a pile of old towels and cleaning products. Sam is small for his age and his head is tucked down, one arm covering the back of his head, a ringing phone clutched in his little fist.

"Sam?" I say as gently as I can make my voice go. "My name is Pam, remember me? I'm a friend of your mom. He's gone, honey. He's gone and your momma is here."

Carefully I put a hand in the middle of his back and I feel him shift at my touch. I don't expect to be knocked back on my ass as his little body comes flying from the cupboard and latches itself around mine. His arms are so tight around my neck, they're threatening to cut off my air, as his legs wrap themselves around my waist. He's clinging on to me like a little monkey, while I'm sitting on my ass on a less than hygienic floor, my back pressed against the wall.

"Oh, honey, it's okay. It's all gonna be okay," I coo, stroking his sweaty hair as he sobs quietly with his face pressed in my neck. He freaks out when the phone starts ringing again, and I take it from his hand, pulling him close against me with my other arm. A quick look at the screen shows; *Gina calling*.

Say what?

"Gina?" I answer quickly, trying to figure out how the hell Dino's daughter would be mixed up with this. Because there's not a doubt in my mind that's who is calling; I don't believe in coincidence.

"Christ, woman," I hear Dino's deep bark instead. "The fuck are you doing answering that phone?"

-

I stood on the doorstep as the ambulance drove off with Benji and Sarah, Marianne following right behind in my car, with Sam buckled in beside her for the short trip to the hospital. Benji had managed to tuck his brother in the vanity with his phone, right before Phil had broken down the door and pulled Benji into the hallway. He'd been enraged, and by the boy's own account, he'd endured the beating, staying mum about his mother's whereabouts, in an attempt to protect her and his little brother, who'd heard the whole thing. The cops had barged in just as the bastard was slamming Benji's head into the tile kitchen floor. He'd still been conscious and talking when the cops managed to subdue Phil and marched him outside. Still, because of the state of his face, an obvious broken arm, and the possibility of a head injury, the EMTs had loaded him up. Sam had still been clinging to me when I promised Sarah I'd look after things here, but the boy had been so distressed at the sight of his mother and brother heading to the ambulance, Marianne had offered to take him.

I turn back inside, where a familiar face had joined the responding officers. Detective Barnes had walked in, just as I was coming out of the bathroom with Sam, and had torn into the officers on the scene for not doing a better search of the place.

"Ms. Brunard, we meet again," he says sardonically, as he looks me up and down. "I hope you're alright?"

"We got here after you guys," I assure him. "Trust me, had I gotten here before, it would be that motherfucker you'd need to be worried about." He chuckles a little as he waves to a chair, indicating I sit down. To be honest, my knees feel a little wobbly suddenly and I sit down heavily. He's not the only one who was worried about my well-being. Dino had just about blown a gasket when I told him why I was there. I gave him a quick synopsis of events and made him promise to stay with his daughter, who sounded very distraught at the news Benji had gotten hurt. I vowed I'd pop in and show him my face the moment I could get away, to keep him from rushing over. From what little I've been able to gather, Gina and Benji go to the same school and got to talking a couple of weeks ago. Maybe Dino can find out a bit more.

"What can you tell me?" Barnes asks me and I give him the sequence of events as I know them. I limit myself to telling him the boys' mother and the asswipe have a history that caused her to run and hide from him earlier this year, and that she and the kids ended up at Florence House briefly. It's up to Sarah to fill in the specifics, since I'll only admit to our connection and my personal involvement this morning.

"Fair enough," the detective concedes, after trying a few times to get me to give him more. "I'm heading over to the hospital to check on the boy—do you need a ride?"

"Actually, I think I should throw some necessities together for Sarah and the kids first. I have a feeling they'll likely be staying the night there."

A bag packed with whatever I thought they might need in my hand, I follow the detective to his car. The moment I sit back against the seat, I realize with a pang of guilt, I've not thought of Derrick once since rushing from Florence House much earlier today.

Dino

There hasn't been a damn second this entire fucked up day I haven't had Pam on my mind. When she finally walks in the kitchen at The Skipper, close to ten o'clock at night, I feel I can finally take a proper breath. She looks like shit; her eyes red-rimmed and dull, her features creased with fatigue, and her proud shoulders slumped with the weight of the world. She comes in, ignores Viv, who is giving me a hand cleaning up, and walks straight into my arms, leaning her full weight against me. I catch Viv's worried eyes over her shoulder, who tilts her head in the direction of the exit.

"*Go home*," she mouths for good measure, as I stroke my hand up and down Pam's spine. I shift her body so I can push her down in a chair and grab my coat.

"Let's go, Biscuit," I tell Pam. "We're going home."

"Where's Gina?" she asks, her voice sounding as tired as she looks. *Fuck me*. I almost forgot about my daughter upstairs.

"I'll go get them," Viv interjects quickly, hurrying out of the kitchen. She'd tried to get some more information from Gina when she'd gone to check on Francessca but hadn't made any headway. Whatever is going on in my little girl's head is locked up tight.

I'm forcing some food on Pam when she's back just a couple of minutes later, with her daughter in her arms, and mine following closely behind. Gina stops in front of Pam, the worry of the day still on her face.

"Is he gonna be okay?" Her voice sounds so small, so childlike, it makes me want to wrap her up and keep her from all the fucked up mess that seems to have become part of her young life. She'd finally opened up earlier, she and Benji had become friends not that long ago. He's a year older and a grade up from her, but had got to talking at lunch break one day. Or so she says—I have a feeling there's something she's hiding from me still, but nothing she's willing to part with at this point.

"Yes, he is, honey," Pam answers her as she stands, taking my daughter's face in her hands. "He'll be just fine, he just needs a night or two in the hospital to get back on his feet."

"And Sammie?" For the first time since she walked in here, I see a smile pull at the corners of Pam's mouth.

"He never touched him, baby. Benji did a great job looking after his brother." Gina nods, swallowing hard as she tries to smile back at Pam. It's a change from the almost hostile attitude she'd been throwing around Pam.

"Let's get home," I announce, tucking my daughter to my side and grabbing Pam's hand with the other.

I've got two women in my life, who are my world—I'd better start taking care of them both.

-

"She's asleep," I tell Pam when I get back downstairs.

It's not often that I tuck my kids in anymore, both are much too old, but tonight I felt the need. Jonas may not have been in bed yet, he'd been at his desk, but he didn't object when I gave his shoulder a squeeze and kissed the top of his head. "Love you, Son."

"Love you too, Dad."

My step was decidedly lighter as I headed back down to where I left Pam on the couch with a glass of wine. She'd asked I drop her off at Florence House, where Marianne apparently had taken her car, but I refused. I didn't care Gina could hear everything from the backseat, and told Pam I needed her to let me take care of her. She didn't object, but put her head against the headrest, her eyes fixed on me as I drove us home.

"Poor thing," Pam says as she watches me approach. "She must've been exhausted."

"I'm still not sure what's going on with her, but at least I recognized my girl today," I admit, sinking down in the couch beside her.

"Why did you want me to come back here?" she asks, as I tuck her into my shoulder, propping my feet up on the coffee table. I look down into her upturned face.

"Because I've missed you," I tell her honestly. "Because, especially after today, I don't want to miss out on any opportunity to look after the people I care about most. I've been too lax on that front and I know it."

"Mmmm. Not sure if I agree," she mumbles with her lips pressed to my neck. "At least not the last part. I'm grateful for the rest. Happy you'd consider me part of that group because I care about you, too." I shift a little so I can look her in the eyes. I like what I see there.

"We seem to roll from one drama into another, but I have to tell you; if at the end I have you tucked close like this, you won't hear me complaining. Much," I add with a wink.

Pam's hand comes up and strokes along my jaw. "I'm not complaining either," she says, her eyes conveying what she's not saying. I pluck her hand from my face and use it to pull her up with me. She follows me quietly upstairs.

"I love your body," she mutters later, when she walks out of a quick shower, a towel wrapped around her torso, and finds me fully dressed in bed, my arms folded behind my head. I try not to chuckle, I know my body is no longer hard like a younger man's. Sure, I've still got some shape to my chest and shoulders, but my middle has gone soft and the hair on my chest is going gray. I'm not a pretty boy, by any stretch of the imagination, but I like that she digs my body nonetheless.

Especially when she crawls up between my legs and starts pulling off my socks, making her intentions clear as she crawls up my body. Her moves are sure as she unbuttons the fly on my jeans, and I helpfully lift my ass off the bed as she pulls jeans and boxers down at once. My cock, already wide awake at the sight of her long legs teasing me from under the towel, slaps against my belly. I make quick work of my shirt as she drops my jeans on the floor, along with the towel that was covering her.

She's not shy as she climbs over me, her ample breasts swaying hypnotically. Pam is all woman, with her dark skin, smooth as a good chocolate ganache, and her softened curves rich with age and experience.

"I love your body, too," I mumble, just before she closes her full lips over mine for a long, languid kiss, slowly destroying my restraint. My hands come up, curve around the soft globes of her ass and pull her down to where my cock lies flat against my stomach.

"Na-ah." Her lips curve in a smile against mine, before she pulls away completely. "I believe I owe you an outstanding Christmas present." I growl low in my throat. That damn sultry tease from a couple of days ago has had my imagination working overtime. The promise of her beautiful mouth wrapped around my cock too tempting.

The reality, as she slides down, her ass up in the air as her lips skim my chest and stomach on her way down, is so fucking much better. Already I feel my balls starting to draw up tight and I frantically start ticking off baseball stats of the Red Sox roster in my head before I blow prematurely. Her tongue, much pinker than her lips, peeks out between and curves around the crown. All the skin of my body tightens instantly at her touch, creating goosebumps everywhere. When she flattens her tongue and sweeps it across the bead forming on the small slit at my tip, I can't hold back the deep groan that seems to come from my toes.

With strong hands behind my knees, she opens me up and spreads me wide, using her hands as much as her mouth to have me mindlessly whimper under her assault. When she sucks me deep in her throat and swallows down on the crown of my cock, while simultaneously playing her fingers along the skin behind my balls, I arch my back off the mattress with the first surge of my release. She renders me mindless and spineless as she milks me with lips and fingers, leaving me the consistency of a jellyfish.

When I've regained some of my muscle control, I try to flip her over from where she's snuggled her body against mine, to give her some attention, but she resists.

"No, honey," she soothes, with her hand rubbing between my pecs. "You can have me tomorrow," she promises.

A promise I am planning to keep her to.

CHAPTER TWENTY-TWO

Dino

"It's coming down good out there."

I turn around, from where I'm washing some dishes at the sink, to find Gunnar leaning against the doorpost. Because of the weather, tonight had been very slow. Much, much slower than we usually were on New Year's Eve. Only five tables tonight, and they'd all been in early and left shortly after finishing their dinner in hopes of getting home safely.

The weather forecast had warned about a possible snow event, and it kept away the crowds. With good reason it looks, from the conditions outside. Thick snow covers the wharf, the wind blowing the white stuff sideways at times, causing a layer to stick even to the side of the sparse lampposts along the pier. It was going be a bitch to get home, where Pam was already preparing a late supper. It had been his idea she stay at his place again, just like she had the last few days, but it had been hers to prepare Soup JouMou, the traditional New Year's soup. Normally served on January first, according to Pam, she'd opted to start the preparations last night, for tonight's meal. Tomorrow we're scheduled to celebrate New Year's Day at Gunnar and Syd's, a newer tradition forged over the past years, courtesy of Syd, who wanted an opportunity to give back to her friends, by cooking for them. She's not allowed any of us to ever bring anything to contribute to the meal. So tonight, my kids and I will be introduced to Pam's heritage, something I'm pretty pumped about. Mostly because it shows how far we've come; having her insist on including us in her traditions.

I love her.

I've known for a while, but with life throwing new roadblocks every way we turn, there hasn't been a right time to tell her. I don't want to just throw it out there. I did that once, to the only other woman I've ever said it to, and that turned out to be way premature, because what I may have ever felt for Jeannie doesn't even reach the shadow of what I feel for Pam.

"It's disturbing how I can tell from the look on your face that I don't want to know what you're thinking about," Gunnar pipes up, startling me from my thoughts. *Crap*, I'd forgotten he was there. He's not wrong; visions of Pam's face when I bring her to climax, like I've done the last couple of mornings, put that satisfied smile on my face just now.

"Got me there," I chuckle. "So what's the plan? We have any stragglers left?"

"Nah," he says, pushing away from the door. "Arnie was the last one, and he just left with Matt. He's gonna make sure Arnie gets to his apartment okay before he heads home. I've just locked the front door and put the closed sign up."

It takes us half an hour to clean up, stock the bar for January third, when we open up again, and make sure the washrooms are at least passable until the cleaning crew comes in Wednesday morning. Not my favorite job, but then again, I don't think I know anyone who'd volunteer for that job. It still has to get done.

I wait on the step outside for Gunnar to do a last walk through. I pull my beanie down over my ears and flip up the collar on my jacket. It's fucking freezing, with the wind blowing down the alley; the snow feels like razors on my exposed skin. I don't have to wait long before Gunnar, similarly attired, steps out. Together we make our way to the parking lot through knee-deep snow, only to find there is no fucking way in hell we're going be driving home tonight. Both our cars are virtually buried, and in their infinite wisdom, the plows that went through earlier this evening have shoved a wall of snow across the exit to the street. If we want to get home, we'll have to rely on our feet to get us there.

"Fuck!" The expletive from Gunnar's mouth seems to stand out against the wind. I understand why he's pissed, he's got a longer way to go.

"Why don't you crash at mine?" I offer before another thought comes to mind. "Or just crash above the pub? Not like we haven't done that before."

"Not letting my family go to bed without me on New Year's Eve, goddammit," he bites off, obviously irritated.

"I hear you man. I hear you."

Doesn't matter what the conditions, there's nothing that would keep me from being with my family either. A family that now includes a hard-assed, smart-mouthed, incredibly beautiful, and soft-hearted woman I can't wait to turn into a more permanent fixture.

"Happy for you, man," Gunnar grunts, as we start making our way over the pile of snow to the sidewalk beyond. "Better call Bird and let her know I'm walking."

I follow suit and dive into my pocket to grab my phone, only to find it missing. Damn, I must've left it on the kitchen table. At least I hope I did. I throw a quick look over my shoulder at the dark alley toward the pub. *Nah, not going back there.* I'll be home in less than half an hour anyway, and besides, Pam's not expecting me until around ten, it's only eight-thirty now.

I chuckle as I listen to Gunnar trying to keep his wife from getting in her car and brave this weather to come get him.

Another reason why I'm happy not calling Pam, she'd probably do the same thing. I'll be damned if that doesn't fill me with enough warmth to ignore the freezing cold creeping up through my inadequate shoes.

We part ways at the second intersection where I head north and Gunnar keeps going.

"Just so you know, my phone is on the kitchen table, I'll get it Tuesday," I warn him. "If you want to get hold of me, call the house or Pam's cell; otherwise I'll see you tomorrow."

"Bring your appetite," he says. "She's been cooking since Christmas."

"Always."

With a last wave we each trudge on toward the warmth of our family.

Pam

I love the smell of JouMou.

I started last night, putting the beef in the marinade of pureed garlic, scallions, parsley, thyme, shallots, Scotch bonnet chile, lime juice, kosher salt, and black pepper. This morning I pulled it out of the fridge and already the fragrance brought tears to my eyes with memories.

I would never have done this to myself, if I didn't want to share some of me with Dino and his family, like they've been sharing with me. The therapist in me says it's probably healthier not to avoid these memory triggers, but the mother in me still wants to duck and hide. I won't let her though. If I've learned anything, it's that time is too damn short not to suck the marrow out of life at every opportunity. Even with Derrick's loss still a fresh wound in my heart, one that likely won't ever completely heal, it also has shown me that there is nothing I can or should take for granted. I'm savoring, even through my grief.

I'm inhaling the scent of the fragrant stock I just poured over the browned beef in the pan, when Gina walks into the kitchen.

"Hey, you," I casually say, as she peeks over the edge of the cast iron pot I brought over for this.

"Hey," she replies tentatively. "Smells good, but it looks like a witches' brew in that pot."

"Nah—I only stew my witches' brew at Halloween," I joke. "It's just Soup JouMou today."

"I can't live off soup for dinner," Jonas pipes up, walking in behind his sister.

"This isn't just soup, buddy. This stuff has serious substance. By the time I'm done with it it'll look more like a 'stoup'."

"What's a 'stoup'?"

"Half stew, half soup." I bite my smile as the two check out the pile of ingredients littering the counter: potato, onion, leek, carrot, squash, turnip, and cabbage. I'm not surprised at the upturned noses, because I remember being less than impressed when I first learned how to make it. I'm pretty confident they'll love it, though.

"It's tradition in Haiti on New Year's Day to have JouMou. You know Haiti was a French colony, right?" Jonas looks at me with a blank look on his face, but Gina shows a flicker of interest so I forge ahead. "The French actually started bringing in slaves by the thousands to work the sugar cane plantations. In those days, JouMou would be prepared by slaves as a delicacy for their French masters, but they never got to eat it. That changed January first of 1804, when Haiti became independent after beating out

Napoleon Bonaparte's troops in the Haitian Revolution. That day is celebrated by the Haitian people by eating JouMou."

"Cool," Jonas says, having perked up at the mention of Napoleon Bonaparte.

"So you're from Haiti?" Gina asks in a timid voice, but interest shines in her eyes.

"My mother was. I was born in the U.S.," I enlighten her. "But between my mother and my grandmother, they made sure I'd never forget my heritage."

"What about your father?"

I look at Gina, who seems a little embarrassed by her own question as she glances back from under her thick lashes, and decide to be honest. I turn back to my soup and start in an even voice; "My father was a drug addict. Mom met him at a low point in her life, and he was around just long enough to create me. Every now and then, he would come around as I was growing up. My grandmother did most of the work, raising me."

"That's fucked up," Jonas says after a pregnant silence.

"Pretty much," I agree with a snort. "Old news, though. They're all gone now and just like my grandmé taught me, I just make my JouMou every New Year's."

"And the smell makes me hungry," he says, like a typical man-child, moving straight to what's important; his stomach. "Any chance I can have a little sampler?" The cheeky grin on his face makes me laugh.

"Not a chance in hell, boy. This has at least two hours of simmering to do before I'll let you anywhere near it."

"Bummer. I'll be upstairs—*starving*—until then," he announces with dramatic flourish before stalking out of the kitchen.

Gina has been quiet throughout the exchange, and appears to follow her brother out of the room when she stops in the doorway and turns around.

"I'm sorry they're all gone," she says quietly, looking a little embarrassed. I struggle to keep the emotion from my face and words.

"Yeah, I am too, honey. I am, too." I decide to take it a little further. "And I'm sorry what you are dealing with as well, Gina. I'm sure that can't be easy, either. I know you don't particularly like me, and that's okay—I get it—but I'm aiming to stick around. I'm done losing people I care about."

Gina doesn't say anything, she just nods, turns, and disappears from sight. I turn toward the window where the night has already set in but I can still see the snow coming down steadily.

-

I pull out the *Pain*, a Haitian bread with a hint of coffee and nutmeg, and give the JouMou a final stir. Throwing a kitchen towel over the bread to keep it warm, I finish setting the table, and take a look at the clock. Depending on how busy they got at The Skipper tonight, Dino shouldn't be too much longer.

I'm pretty hungry; the few raw carrots I chewed on earlier did little to satisfy me, and the kids are likely famished as well by now. Rather than wait for Dino, maybe we should have a bite now. When I get to the bottom of the stairs, I can hear music drifting down from upstairs.

"Guys! Come and get it!" I holler up, hearing some movement in response before Jonas' head appears at the top of the stairs.

"Dinner ready?" he asks with a big grin on his face.

"Yup. Get your sister, will you? I don't think she heard me with the music on." Jonas salutes me before his head disappears again. I head back to the kitchen to put on the finishing touches.

The next thing I know, footsteps come pounding down the stairs and Jonas rushes into the kitchen.

"She's gone," he says a little out of breath.

"Sorry?" I shake my head slightly, sure I've misheard him.

"Gina—she's not in her room."

It takes one glance at the stricken look on his face to know he's dead serious and my feet start moving. I rush past Jonas and up the stairs, his footsteps following behind me. Her room is empty and I immediately rush to the window, which looks to be locked tight. A quick look outside shows the weather hasn't let up yet. It's still coming down.

"She would've gone out Dad's window," Jonas pipes up from the doorway, and this time he leads the way as we rush to the master bedroom. The door is closed but when he throws it open the cold air hits us. I rush past him to the window that's been left open a crack. I cup my hands against the glass and peer out into the night. The roof of the small porch, in front of the house, is right below the window.

"It's easy to get down there," Jonas admits, a slight blush on his cheeks. "I've used it before. I just didn't know she knew about it."

"Call her phone," I order him, as I shut the window all the way and dive into Dino's walk-in closet to grab a sweater or something. I'm going out to look.

"She's not answering," Jonas says. "I'll try Dad."

I pull an old hoodie over my head. The thing hangs halfway down my thighs but is warm. I try to ignore the panic building, as I turn to find Jonas looking at me with worry on his face.

"He's not answering either."

"Maybe he's on his way home," I try to reassure him. "Do you have the numbers for any of her friends?" That gets a shake of his head and I walk past him back to her room.

A search of her desk and nightstand doesn't result in anything helpful, and with Jonas close on my tail I head downstairs. Halfway there, I stop in my tracks and he bumps into my back.

"Benji," I whisper, half to myself and half to Jonas, before double-timing it the rest of the way, grabbing my phone from my purse on the counter. I hit Sarah's number.

"Is Benji there?" I barge right in when she answers, not bothering with niceties.

"Benji? He went out to a friend's house for a bit—why?" I feel bad about worrying Sarah, who has enough on her mind, but the thought of Gina out in this weather alone is enough to make the blood freeze in my veins. I don't even want to think about how Dino's going to feel when he gets here.

"Gina slipped out on me," I confess. "From an upstairs window. She's still grounded. I thought maybe she was planning to meet with Benji, can you call him to see if she's with him?" Sarah promises to call me right back and I turn off the burner underneath the soup.

"You stay here," I instruct Jonas. "I'm taking my phone and will stay in touch, but I've gotta go look for her." I grab my boots from the closet and start pulling them on when my phone rings.

"He's not answering," Sarah says, out of breath.

"Okay, keep trying. I'm going out there to look. Stay in touch." I end the call and tuck my phone in my pocket, looking up to find Jonas looking scared.

"What if…?" he starts. I stop him with a sharp shake of my head.

"Don't go there. Trust me, it's useless. She hasn't taken anything but whatever clothes she was wearing. She's probably just out meeting up with some friends. The two little shitheads that tried to take us down are still locked up, along with the gang leader. We haven't heard anything to the contrary, so there's no reason to let your mind go there." I can see from the marginal relief on his face, I guessed his concerns correctly. Only because my mind wanted to wander in that direction too.

"Keep trying your sister and your dad," I tell him, pulling him into a quick, somewhat awkward hug. "I'll check in."

With that I pull open the door, pull my hood tight over my head, and walk out into a virtual blizzard.

CHAPTER TWENTY-THREE

Dino

I didn't think it would take me this long, but the deep snow makes it feel like you're trudging through mud. It doesn't help that I stopped twice to help drivers stranded in the deep ruts of other motorists. The last one was an elderly lady, who was unable to get out of the bank of snow, pushed up in the middle of an intersection. That one almost took fifteen minutes to get dislodged. I advised her against trying to make it home but she was adamant. I reluctantly let her drive off, watching as the back end of her car swerved from side to side as she tried to negotiate the corner.

I turn onto my street when I find my feet suddenly moving fast, despite the frostbite I'm sure I've acquired. From a distance I can see almost all the lights on in the house, which calms me a little. I know Pam is there, keeping an eye on the kids. I'm already looking forward to the warm meal waiting. I've never had JouMou before, but did some research on it and it sounds fucking amazing.

I'm still walking on the driveway when the door opens and Jonas steps out on the porch. The look on his face has a cold fist of fear infiltrate my chest.

"Gina's taken off, Dad," he blurts out when I'm still a few steps away.

"What do you mean?" I ask, as I walk by him into the hallway.

"She's not here. Pam asked me to call her down for dinner and her room was empty. She went out the window in your room—left it open a bit."

"Where's Pam?" I call over my shoulder as I march down the hall to the kitchen.

"Out looking." I swing around to find Jonas has followed me in. "We tried calling you, Dad. I've been trying your phone and Gina's for the past half-hour."

"Fuck! I knew I should've gone back to grab it. I left it on the kitchen table at the pub."

Instead of getting warmer, I can feel the cold spreading from my chest out. I'm only half listening to Jonas as I try to remember Gunnar's number, when something he says catches my attention. *Benji.*

"What did you say?"

"Pam tried to get a hold of Benji. Apparently, he's not answering his phone either."

Fucking hell. When I get my hands on Gina, I'm going to lock her in her room until she's fucking thirty years old.

"Dad," Jonas' soft voice penetrates my anger. "Something's been up with her for a while, you…"

"Bud," I interrupt him. "We need to find her first. Everything else comes after." I feel bad for snapping at him but I need to focus on one thing at a time.

Trying a few wrong numbers first, I finally get hold of Gunnar, who sounds like he just ran a marathon.

"Not even fucking home yet, Dino," he says when he answers the phone.

"Keep your eyes open. Gina is missing and Pam's gone looking. I'm heading out there myself with Jonas' phone, since I left mine at the fucking pub. Can you take down his number?" I pass on Jonas' number and tell him my son will stay by the home phone.

"Let me come look with you, Dad," Jonas says when I get off the phone.

"Someone's gotta be here by the phone or in case she shows up. Keep trying her phone from the landline, Son. I've gotta take yours with me. Pam's out there and so is Gunnar." I pull a pair of snow boots from the hall closet and kick off my sopping wet shoes and socks. My damn toes are bloodless with cold. "Can you run up and get me a pair of dry socks?"

Jonas is back in seconds, handing me a pair of his tube socks that feel nice and warm when I pull them on. I toss off my jacket and grab the goose down one I was wishing I'd been wearing all the way home.

"Call me if you hear anything from anyone, okay?" I grab my boy around the neck and give him a quick hug, kissing his forehead. "I'll keep in touch. Love you, kid."

I walk back into the deepfreeze, wondering if I'd remembered to tell Gina I loved her this morning when I left. I hope I did.

I try to keep my mind busy, thinking about all the places she might have gone, to keep from letting myself worry about her well-being. I'm not sure how I'd be able to survive if something happened to her. I know she sometimes hangs out at the high school or the library across the street, but that is during the day. Still, it's the first location I'm going to check out.

I pull Jonas' phone from my pocket and dial Pam's number.

"Did you hear anything?" Pam answers, and I hear the shiver in her voice.

"It's me. Where are you?"

"Oh thank God, Dino. I'm so sorry. She was upstairs, I never thought to check on her. I didn't realize…"

"Pam," I stop her ramble, repeating myself. "Where are you?"

"I'm on Cumberland, just crossing Franklin. I've searched the neighborhood around the school, since that was closest, but I'm heading toward the cemetery now. I know sometimes kids like to shoot off fireworks from there on New Year's Eve." Pam sounds like her teeth are chattering from the cold.

"Peppermint Park," I half mutter to myself.

"What's that?"

"Peppermint Park is where Benji tried to get her to meet him before. Do you know where it is? It's not much more than a kid's playground with a couple of benches. You should be just a few blocks away. It'll be on your right side, but wait for me to get there. I don't want you going in alone. Stay under the streetlights." I should feel guilty for hanging up right after barking out instructions, but I don't want to give her a chance to object. Not that it really matters; knowing Pam she'll do exactly what she feels is necessary, whether I like it or not. That's why I'm going as fast as I can, walking in the street rather than on the sidewalk. It's a little faster, since at some point a plow must've come through.

I can't believe Gina took off like that. What the hell was she thinking? Thirteen years old, and roaming the streets. If it were any other kid, I'd be wondering where the hell her parents were. But this was my kid—my good-natured, gentle, and easy child. What the fuck happened? Granted, the past year has been a rough one, for her as well, clearly more so than I'd picked up on. Maybe I shouldn't have given her back her phone, but I don't like the idea of not being able to reach the kids while I'm at work. *Except I never called.*

While I was dealing with Jeannie, then Jonas, and finally Pam, I hadn't been paying attention to my daughter, assuming that she would bounce her way through life like she usually does.

Suddenly find myself at a loss. Disconnected. What kind of a parent does that make me?

Guilt and remorse eats at me as my feet, much warmer now, plod through the snow.

I don't know if it's my imagination or not, but it seems like the snow is tapering off a little as I pass by the Cathedral of the Immaculate Conception. Just a short two blocks before I hit the park.

Of course there is no Pam to be seen.

Pam

He's gonna be pissed.

Well, technically he is already pissed, judging by the tone of his voice. I don't blame him. I'd be angry if the roles were reversed as well. He entrusted me with his kids and I fell down on the job. Not the first time either.

My lungs are burning with the effort, but I get to the small park in record time. For some reason, I keep thinking that time is of the essence. I'm terrified I'll be too late and miss her somehow. Not that this is not a shot in the dark, like checking the high school was, but I had to try. I still think the cemetery is the more likely place, but I can't be sure.

Peppermint Park it is.

There are houses on either side of the park and the street side is pretty open. Toward the back, behind the slides, is a densely treed strip separating the playground from whatever lies behind. It's there I spot some movement, right inside the tree line. I stop at the edge of where the streetlamp casts its light and stare at the spot, waiting for another movement. Although the snow has slowed down, the wind is still blowing; between that and the muffling qualities of the new blanket of snow, making it hard to hear anything.

I'm about to sit down on a small wall at the edge of the park to wait for Dino, when I hear it. A soft whimper. I swing my head around to face the trees at the far edge again, but I still see nothing. Could've been an animal, but when I hear it again, it sounds distinctly human. Then I see them; two figures coming out of the trees. The smallest one, who seems to be supporting the second person, looks familiar and without realizing it, I'm already running and stumbling through the snow toward them. I'm almost there when I hear her.

"Pam! Be careful!"

Gina's voice rings clear this time and she seems to be looking over my shoulder. I whip my head around to see a big shape lumbering toward me.

"Dino!" I recognize him immediately but his attention is not on me, it's on his daughter. Dino runs right by me, straight to where Gina is faltering under the weight of the boy she's trying to hold up. I follow behind and recognize Benji when we get closer.

"What the hell is going on?" Dino's deep voice almost bellows when he pulls the boy off his daughter. He can barely keep his feet under him as Dino tries to keep him up by the shoulders.

"He's drunk," Gina admits, tears running down her face. "He didn't know who else to call. Said some older guys at the cemetery tried to force him to take drugs, but he got away and hid in the trees."

What I understand from Gina's rambling, is that Benji met with a few friends and headed to the cemetery on the other side of the trees for their own version of a New Year's party. It got out of hand when a group of older kids showed up, members of the Seals, and tried to peddle drugs among the kids. Benji was already three sheets to the wind when they got there and found himself abandoned by his so-called friends when things turned a little tense with the new arrivals. The Seals had quickly zoomed in on him, and when he said he wasn't interested in buying what they were selling, they tried to force him to swallow pills. There was some disturbance that allowed Benji to get away, and he managed to hide in the bushes, from there he called Gina.

I'm looking at Dino's face, and I have a feeling this doesn't bode well for Gina or for Benji, so I decide to jump in.

"Right. Why don't I make sure Benji gets home and you look after her?" I suggest, not even really knowing where to start with that. "We could call the cops, but I don't think it's going to do any good. They'll have their hands full tonight with this weather, and I don't want us to have to wait for God knows how long until they show. We'll be frozen solid by then. We can call them from home."

Dino doesn't even look at me. He simply marches the kid over to a bench, which is almost buried in snow, and sits him down before returning to me.

"Fine," he says through gritted teeth. "I called Gunnar on my way here and he's coming in Syd's SUV. He can take you."

"What about you?" I want to know, a little confused, but I don't get an answer. I'm about to push it, when an SUV pulls up on the side of the road.

-

It's got to be near midnight when I pull the door closed behind me. Sarah had tried to get me to stay at least until after the New Year was rung in, but I just want to get home.

What a fucked up night it had turned out to be. Gunnar dropped Dino and Gina off at home first, and other than a, "Call you," Dino hadn't said a word. No kiss—no acknowledgement at all—and suddenly it felt like the past few months never happened. Like we were back where we started. My earlier excitement at the start of a new year, in more ways than one, quickly evaporated.

I'm not sure I quite understand the shift. Don't get me wrong, I get the focus on his daughter to the exclusion of everyone else. I understand that because I've lived it. What I don't understand is his easy dismissal of me. Is he angry? Does he blame me for Gina taking off? He seemed to be able to talk to Gunnar in the front seat, while I was relegated to the back with the two kids, but he wasn't talking to me.

When we drove away from his house after dropping them off, Gunnar looked at me in the rearview mirror.

"You okay, Pam?"

The question, so innocent, represented everything that was wrong. I managed a flippant, "Yup," and quickly turned my burning eyes away from his prying ones.

He'd wanted to stay and wait for me outside Sarah's place, but I told him I had no idea what I'd find inside and to go home to his wife and kids. He reluctantly agreed and took off after helping me get a very drunk and half-asleep Benji to his front door.

The snow crunches under my feet as I walk past the hospital, in hopes of perhaps spotting a cab lingering outside the entrance. No such luck. It is no longer actively snowing and the winds have died down significantly. It's a lot more pleasant to be outside and I suddenly don't mind the walk. A plow appears to have come through the main streets, the roads are passable, and it's not too far to Dino's house where my car is still parked. So that's where

I'm heading. I have my keys in my pocket, so I can just take off—get myself home and worry about tomorrow…well, tomorrow.

I turn up his street and spot my car sitting in the driveway. There are some lights on in the house, mainly upstairs, but the front porch is lit as well. I don't see him until I actually walk up the drive, and he stands up from where he'd been sitting on the steps. I linger by the car, my plan to sneak in and drive off undetected obviously thwarted.

Dino

"How's Gina?"

I can't see her face clearly, but the sound of her warm voice only highlights what an absolute idiot I am. She should be furious with me.

"Upset, angry, a little scared, I guess. Mostly angry though—at me."

She had been, my princess, pissed off as hell. When I should have been chewing her out, I ended up getting it with both barrels from both Gina and her brother. Although Jonas did dole out his licks to his sister as well. It was messy and emotional and the entire time I couldn't stop thinking of her. Pam. The fucking house smelled phenomenal, a distinct Caribbean blend of spices and fresh, yeasty bread. She'd come here, while I was at work, spent hours preparing a meal that carries significance for her, that she wanted to share with us, and I was a giant dick. Even after she'd gone out and went searching for my kid in a snowstorm.

"At you?"

"Hmmm. Jonas, too," I offer as I slowly move closer.

"Look, I'd better get going," she says, a little uncomfortable as I approach. It makes me feel like shit.

"I wish you wouldn't."

She looks up at me. I hate the insecurity I see in her eyes. I put that there. A woman who, other than at the death of her son, has rarely shown any signs of vulnerability, is showing them now.

I round the car in a few big strides and don't stop until I have her rigid body in my arms.

"I'm sorry," I whisper against her ear. "I'm so fucking sorry. I was worried and angry, and shut down on you." When she doesn't say anything I add, "Come inside?"

A loud bang, followed by a bunch of smaller ones, has us both lift our heads just in time to see a shower of flares light up the sky. Before they dim, another bang sounds and this time a red glow fills the sky as more fireworks are set off. Behind us the front door opens and both kids step out on the porch. Jonas gives me a thumbs up when he sees us, and Gina tries to hide a smile, before their attention is drawn to the next rocket shooting off.

I look down in Pam's face, which is turned up to me, and I lower my head to press a kiss to her mouth, my eyes wide open.

"Happy New Year, Biscuit."

Her lips curve up under mine in a smile. "Happy New Year to you too, honey," she returns in her rich, silky voice.

With my arm tight around her shoulder, we watch as some unruly kids, partying it up in the cemetery, light up the Portland night sky.

CHAPTER TWENTY-FOUR

Pam

"Come for me, Beautiful."

The low rumble of Dino's voice, combined with the deep thrust of his rigid cock inside me, send me spiraling into an orgasm that has my toes curl and my body clamp down on him. The moan that wants to escape is swallowed up by his mouth finding mine, his tongue mimicking the drive of his hips between my legs. While my body is still convulsing with aftershocks of my own orgasm, I feel his muscles bunch up under my hands as he reaches his own climax. This time it's me swallowing his grunts against my lips.

I'm guessing it was close to two in the morning when we finished cleaning up and headed upstairs, following the kids, who'd gone to bed half an hour or so before. We'd eaten the JouMou and the bread, and Jonas pointed out that since it was after midnight, we'd stuck to tradition, eating it on the first of January. That made me smile.

It had been Dino who'd steered us away from discussing the events of earlier, indicating he just wanted to enjoy his family under one roof. That had softened any reservation I may have held. I knew there were things that needed to be discussed, but I felt more confident about those now that it was clear there would be a time and a place for that.

Gina had been a little subdued after she'd given me a hug and a teary apology, which is when Dino had jumped in. He'd pulled his daughter into a big bear hug, telling her he loved her, and promising her a better year ahead. It made me swallow a lump. Jonas wasn't shy hugging me, and I was reminded how much like his father he is, when he squeezed me tight and told me he was happy I was in their lives. I may have lost it a little then.

Without words, Dino had divested me of my clothes and proceeded to show me with his eyes and his body how sorry he was. It wasn't necessary, but it felt good nonetheless. Very good.

"What are you thinking?" he mumbles, his large frame still pinning me to the mattress, his face buried in the spot low on my neck he seems to like.

"That I feel safe," I tell him, surprised at my own conclusion. "In more than one way, actually," I add. "I'm not sure how long it's been, maybe I never had it, but I'm not scared of the future anymore. Or of letting myself feel." Dino pushes up on his elbows, all his attention focused on my face as I smile. "I admit, for a while last night, I wasn't so sure, but that disappeared when I saw you waiting for me. I'm grateful for your words but I didn't need them. Trust is not something I easily give, but I trust you."

"Thank you." His lips move against mine before he lifts away. "I was an ass and it had little to do with you. It was the realization I was failing as a parent." A sharp shake of his head cuts off the protest that was forming on my lips. "I wasn't watching Gina. I was too preoccupied with other things to notice she was slipping. Last night was a knee-jerk reaction. I have to get used to sharing things again. I haven't been able to do that in a long time. It was always just easier to deal with things myself. I should've talked to you."

"Stop." I cover his mouth with my fingers. "Enough of the self-recriminations. Lord knows we both have a knack for those. I still struggle with the what-ifs. I don't want to do that with you. Don't want to have regrets of any kind, and the only way to do that is to be completely open. Give you all of me, warts and all. All I want in return is to trust that when we hit the inevitable bumps in the road, you'll have my back, just as I have yours."

Dino's beautiful brown eyes turn liquid as I watch him swallow hard. "Always." His gruff voice cracks on the single word as he rolls off me and swings his legs over the side of the bed. I watch the muscles in his ass flex as he makes his way to the bathroom. Nice view. One I wouldn't mind enjoying the rest of my life.

My thoughts grind to a halt. Am I really considering that? The rest of my life?

If you'd have asked me as little as two months ago whether I'd ever consider the possibility, I would likely have laughed in your face. It doesn't seem so funny now. I just promised him all of me, and that should include the depth of my feelings. Sure, I've been trying to deny those, even to myself, but perhaps it's time to put my money where my mouth is.

When he walks back into the room with a towel in his hand, I blurt it out.

"You know I love you, right?"

Fuck. I sound like Tweetie Bird on helium, my tight voice is pitched so high.

Dino freezes a few steps into the room, shock evident on his face, and I wait with baited breath for his reaction. Fuck—any reaction. I'm about to cover my head with a pillow, my face burns so bright. I haven't uttered those words to any man, aside from Derrick, in the past thirty-some years. Maybe that's why I seem a bit rusty and tight.

I turn my face away, cursing myself to hell and back for jumping the gun. Almost instantly a familiar large hand cups my cheek and turns my head back.

"I hoped," he says, a wide grin on his face. "But now I know."

He successfully makes me forget about my embarrassment, my exhaustion, and my impromptu declaration, with a second round of inspired lovemaking.

It isn't until I collapse onto his chest, after riding him with more enthusiasm than I thought I'd be able to muster, that I realize he hasn't returned my sentiments.

My admittedly impulsive effort at full disclosure is still hanging suspended in the thick, sex-infused air.

Dino

I'm up before anyone else, despite the early hour, I finally fell into a satisfied sleep with Pam draped over me. She was already softly snoring, while I was still counting my blessings.

To hear her admit her feelings out loud took care of any lingering fear I might've had that I'd done permanent damage when I shut her out earlier. I could've come out and told her I love her too, but I didn't. I'm sure she knows I do, just like it wasn't a total surprise for me.

What was a surprise is that she told me. I wasn't expecting that until after I'd laid my soul bare. That's why I froze for a minute, letting myself feel the full impact of what she was really saying when she told me she loves me. Pam, completely open and unguarded, willingly putting herself in a very vulnerable position—and I loved it.

I never meant to make her wait, but want to pick my own perfect moment to share with her.

The kids are still on one ear, which is not news; they rarely get out of bed before ten or eleven if they don't need to. That's something they don't get from me. I like my early mornings. Apparently so much so, that even after a scant four or so hours of sleep, I'm down here impatiently waiting for the coffee to brew.

It feels good, having everyone I care about under one roof. Something I'd like to see become permanent, sooner rather than later. Won't be long until Jonas graduates and heads of to college or university, and I would love to send him off on a high note after the shit year we've had. Having Pam move in now would also provide some better stability for Gina, who is at an age where she needs a strong woman on her side.

I don't know where Jeannie is now, and it is a bit shocking how little I care. If not for the kids, I could easily dismiss her from my mind completely. But she is their mother, and not only that, she is still my wife on paper. She never went along with the divorce, she simply disappeared. I had been prepared to wait the three years of desertion that is required to get a judge to grant an at fault divorce. I could've made an attempt to get proof that she was an addict as grounds for divorce, but at the time I didn't want to go that route for the sake of the kids. She now has a record, though. Ironically, after breaking and entering my house. I haven't talked to my lawyer yet, but perhaps I should do that on Monday or Tuesday. Get the ball rolling on changing the application for divorce from no-fault, to a fault application. I'd gladly spend the money again, if it meant I could get this resolved within sixty days.

I'm actually whistling as I walk up the stairs, a coffee in each hand. Pam isn't in bed, so I march straight into the en suite bathroom, shoving the door open with my elbow, where I find her sitting on the toilet.

"Really?" she says when I calmly put our coffees on the counter and pull my shaving foam from the drawer. I lean in to inspect my scruff, when I hear Pam flush the toilet, shoving me aside with her hip and washing her hands in the sink.

"Do you prefer smooth or a little fuzz?" I ask her, as I cover my head with foam.

She grabs a towel and stands behind me, watching me in the mirror while she dries her hands. "Fuzz," she says, her head tilted to one side. "I like how it feels."

I don't even try to hide the big grin that splits my face at her words. I like it, too. I like the way my scruff leaves whisker burns on the insides of her thighs after I've had my mouth on her. I watch as she rolls her eyes in response but still her lips tilt up at the corners. She steps up behind me and puts her hands on my shoulders, turning me and pushing me to sit down on the edge of the tub. I don't say a word as she turns to pull my razor from the drawer and wedges her legs between mine, her free hand cupping my chin. I hold her by the hips and keep my eyes fixed on her face. With one long, smooth stroke she runs the razor across my scalp. I don't even flinch.

"You know I love you, right?"

Her shaving hand freezes midair as her eyes flick down to meet mine. A small smile forms on her mouth as she nods.

"Yeah," she whispers, as she strokes her thumb along my jaw. "I know."

"Good." I pull down the hand holding the razor and kiss the inside of her wrist.

-

"Morning."

Jonas barely reacts as he comes stumbling into the kitchen. He's on automatic pilot as he shuffles to the coffee pot, a fresh made one, and starts doctoring himself a mug that makes my asshole pucker. Four full scoops of sugar—my gums bleed just looking at the spoon going in each time.

"You're gonna drink that?" Pam's face looks like she's just swallowed a mouthful of mealworms. "Why not pour the coffee straight into the sugar bowl? Saves you work."

Jonas slowly turns to face her, one eye still squinted shut, but the other is open a crack.

"Do you talk this much every morning?" he asks with an edge, making me laugh out loud. That earns me a dirty, one-eyed glare.

"Nah, don't worry" Pam responds, not showing any emotion on her face. "Only on Sundays and holidays."

"Wonderful," Jonas mumbles, as he lumbers to the couch, where he sits down heavily.

I throw Pam a wink just as kid number two comes walking in. Gina used to be the same happy kid, regardless of what time she went to bed or got up. Not so much these days. Her face rivals that of her brother: squinty eyes, slack mouth, completely oblivious to her surroundings or those in it. Instead of heading for the coffee pot, my girl walks straight to the couch without any stops. With dramatic flair, she throws herself in the corner opposite from Jonas, tucking a pillow against her stomach and laying her head against the backrest.

"What's for breakfast?" she mumbles, to no one in particular.

Pam answers before I can. "I can use the rest of the *Pain* for French toast, if you like?"

At the sound of Pam's voice, Gina's head shoots up.

"Oh—Okay." It takes her a minute to place Pam before she responds.

"Jonas?"

"Hmmm?"

"Pam's asking if you want French toast, Bud," I jump in, wanting my kids to make a good impression.

"Sure," is the lackluster response.

Pam is up and rounding the counter, but she's wearing an indulgent smile. By the time she's got the first batch sizzling in butter, both kids have regained sufficient consciousness for their mouths to start working properly.

"So, Pam," Jonas pipes up. "Can we expect you moving in any time soon?" He's teasing, but I see the spatula hovering suspended over the pan. Gina's reaction is even more interesting, her intake of breath sharp, but then her eyes flit back and forth between me and the woman on the spot in the kitchen, keen curiosity in her eyes. Pam slowly lowers the spatula to the counter and wipes her hands on the towel before she carefully turns around to face us.

"That depends," she says, after slightly squinting her eyes at me when she catches me grinning. "Are you gonna be this much of a pain in the ass to get out of bed every morning?"

"Touché," he answers, a little smirk on his face.

I stay quiet throughout breakfast, just observing the play-by-play, mainly between Jonas and Pam. Of course they know each other a bit better, and I already knew he likes her, but this time I'm keeping an eye on Gina as well. She's harder to gauge. There are times I think she resents Pam being here, but then I catch her looking with something close to admiration on her face. She doesn't say much and as soon as her plate is empty, she scoots upstairs, followed shortly by Jonas.

"We're heading over to Gunnar and Syd's at three thirty. Be ready!" I call after them. It's not uncommon for Jonas particularly, to dive back into bed for a nap right after breakfast.

Pam leaves shortly after. The sun is out today and the plows just came by, making the streets passable. I clear the driveway and watch as she takes off down the street. The plan is for her to head home, get changed, and then check in at the shelter. We've agreed I'll pick her up from there between three thirty and four o'clock.

When I pull the door shut, I find Gina at the bottom of the stairs.

"What's up, Princess?" I ask when she doesn't say anything. I walk up, put my arm around her shoulders, and lead her to the couch where we sit down.

"I'm sorry, Daddy." She barely gets the words out before she bursts into tears and buries her face in my chest. "I know I shouldn't have taken off, but he was in trouble," she sobs. She's obviously talking about Ben, or Benji—whatever the hell the kid's name is. Regardless, I don't want my daughter around a kid who, at only fourteen, gets so drunk he gets himself into trouble, and then contacts my baby to come rescue him. That's not what I want for my girl. Besides, she's too young for boys.

All of those thoughts rush through my head but I can't voice any of them. Gina is talking to me now, but she won't be talking for long if I throw all that at her feet. *Jesus*. I wish Pam was here to help me navigate this minefield.

"Listen to me, girl. Your friend didn't only make a bad choice when he decided to drink himself in a stupor in the town cemetery, he made a worse decision not calling the cops when those guys approached him. Sure, he would've gotten in trouble, but he had that coming." I take in a deep breath before the resurfaced anger takes over. "But the worst one of all was when he decided to call you, when he knew damn well that could put you in danger as well. That's the part I really have trouble with, honey."

"I know, Daddy, but he's not exactly had the best examples. He really regrets it, Dad." My body reacts when I hear those words. I shift in my seat, take her by the shoulders, and move her back a little so I can look in her eyes. She seems to recognize the mistake when she sees my face.

"How do you know that, Gina?"

CHAPTER TWENTY-FIVE

Pam

"Give me that bébé."

I need some loving. Even if it's in the form of little Francessca's happy gurgles and slaphappy hands.

I noticed the change in atmosphere from this morning's breakfast, the moment I get in the car. Dino's jaw is clenched, and in the backseat, Gina's eyes are throwing daggers at the back of his head. She barely says hello, apparently lumping me in on the side of the adults in whatever is brewing between her and her father.

When I glance over my shoulder, I see Jonas just shrugs his shoulders. He's clearly in the dark on this conflict as well. A few times I try to engage Dino in conversation, but he seems limited to monosyllabic answers. I give up quickly.

With Francessca happily bouncing on my arm, I make my way into the kitchen, where Syd is spreading out a disgusting amount of food that Gunnar and his son, Dex, are eagerly sampling to Syd's obvious distress. She's slapping hands left, right, and center to everyone's hilarity. When Dex spots Gina and Jonas, he immediately leads them down to the basement where Emmy is apparently already watching a movie.

I'm glad. Perhaps with the kids out of sight, Dino will relax a little and take an opportunity to explain what the heck is going on. I'm a little frustrated when I see him disappear into the den with Gunnar, where apparently Ike is already watching the college football bowl games. That leaves Viv, Syd, little Francessca, and myself in the kitchen.

"So," Viv starts, and I already know what's coming my way. "What happened last night?" I'm a little hesitant sharing information about what I consider to be Dino's business, but I'm also well aware that Gunnar was there for part of it. He would almost certainly have shared with Syd. Since Viv was a close friend to both of us, I quickly make up my mind.

"Do you remember Sarah?" I ask the girls. Since both of them will occasionally sit in or help out with the groups, they've met her before.

"Single mom, two boys, and an asswipe of a boyfriend?" Viv says.

"That's the one," I confirm. "Gina struck up a friendship with the oldest boy and snuck out last night when he got himself into some trouble and called her." I sneak a peek down the hall to the den, to make sure no one was listening, before turning back to the girls. "It wasn't the first time she'd snuck out. I know Dino is worried about her, especially after he almost had Jonas slip off the rails."

"I know," Viv adds. "He mentioned the other day he was concerned. Personally, I think that woman did a lot more damage than what shows on the surface. Those kids were up close and personal for the train wreck that was Jeannie. I know, even before she left, she would use them as a shield between her and Dino. She knew he'd never do anything to harm those kids, which is exactly why she used them. I wonder if she's not still in the background somewhere, pulling on those strings she had everyone on."

"I only met her a few times," Syd offers, pulling down a few wineglasses and pouring us all a hefty serving. "The woman was very difficult to talk to. Somehow, she'd always manage to turn the conversation on herself. Usually some pity party about how hard it was raising those two kids, and how difficult Dino was to live with. I'll tell you, it took everything out of me not to slap her a few times." Apparently, it can still get her riled up, her face is flushed and her eyes spark fire. I can't blame her, Syd would not take kindly to anyone complaining about having kids to raise since she lost her own. It also goes to show how callous and self-involved the woman must have been to be complaining about her kids, when it was well-known by then how tragically Syd had lost her own. And of course, badmouthing Dino would not put her in a sympathetic light at all. Even if I tried hard not to like him at the time, even I couldn't help but see what an extraordinarily kind and gentle father and friend he was—is.

"Does she talk to you?" Viv asks, and it takes me a minute to realize she means Gina.

"As little as possible," I confess. I try not to take it personally, but it sometimes still stings. "You know? I know it's difficult on the kids to get introduced to another woman, let alone one who has been on the fringes of their lives for years. I may never have socialized with them directly, but there have been times we've been at the same events. They knew who I was. I'm guessing it may have been a shock to see their father with a black woman at that—at least at first—but I don't think that matters much to them."

"Pfft," Viv scoffs. "Those kids don't see color."

"I don't think so either. In any event, it's really not surprising that especially Gina, the apple of her daddy's eye, would take some time warming up to me. After all, it's been such a short time." Part of me wonders, though.

"Yeah, but you've known each other a long time," Syd points out, offering up the wine bottle. Somehow I'd managed to down most of my drink.

I'm not a stranger to girl-chats, but mostly those were with the focus on someone else, and I could easily slip into my role as therapist. It's a little different when it's you as topic of conversation. Odd, a little invasive, but also kind of nice. I think this may be the first time I actually feel a part of it, instead of looking in from the outside. That has nothing to do with them, but everything with me.

I've let down my guard and am finding that life is bumpy, it's confusing, and at times painful, but fuck if it's not also passionate, rewarding, and often incredibly beautiful.

-

I don't see Dino again until Ruby and Tim show up, just as Syd's getting ready to call everyone out for dinner. Nina, Tim and Ruby's adopted daughter, had been home for Christmas break but left this afternoon to go on a ski trip in Vermont for a few days, before heading back to university. Ruby's face is a little puffy from crying and Tim keeps his arm protectively around her.

Dino comes in from the hallway, right behind Ike, who comes straight for me and snatches Francessca from my shoulder. The poor thing got bored while us girls chatted, and fell asleep with her little face pressed to my neck. It felt good, every little puff of breath brushing against my skin. Bittersweet—the memories of long ago days when I would lie on my thrift store couch, with Derrick curled up on my chest. He'd been such a good baby. Never gave me any grief, and I remember silently promising him I'd make sure he'd have the best life possible. A promise I didn't manage to keep.

I'm so lost in memories, I don't notice Dino moving until his arms slip around me from behind. Instinctively my hands come up to hold them in place as I lean my body back against his chest.

"You okay, Biscuit?" His warm voice instantly soothes me.

"I am now," I answer quietly.

It's true. I'm not great—I can't say my heart doesn't still hurt, or that guilt doesn't still burn bitter on my tongue—but with this man at my back, I can honestly say I'm okay.

Dino

I feel bad for being short.

I'd still been raging inside when we picked Pam up. It was clear she knew something was up, but I didn't want to blow off steam in the car. The inside of my lips are already bitten raw with the effort not to explode all over Gina when I discovered she'd somehow managed to talk to the boy, sometime this morning.

When I see Pam's pained look as Ike pries his baby daughter from her arms, I know instinctively where her thoughts are taking her. She doesn't see me coming, but clearly knows its me when she immediately seeks the comfort of my body. That feels fucking great. That kind of connection, that level of trust, is something I've never felt. Getting on fifty and still discovering new and amazing things every day.

While Syd instructs Gunnar to round up the kids, and she and Ruby carry platters and pots to the massive dining table, I grab Pam's hand and lead her down the hall to the den. The game is still playing on the big screen TV, but the sound is muted.

First thing I do is kiss her—hard. She blinks when I release her mouth, licking her lips appreciatively.

"Mmmm," she purrs. "What was that for?"

"I never gave you a proper hello when I picked you up." Keen understanding lights her eyes as she realizes where I'm going with this. "I had a hard time keeping my cool—I'm sorry." I seem to be using those words a lot these days.

"What happened?" Pam wants to know.

"Gina snuck in my room before breakfast this morning and called that kid. She let it slip when she was trying to apologize to me and tell me I shouldn't be angry at Ben, or Benji….whatever the fuck his name is." I watch as Pam subtly raises an eyebrow, the expression more effective than any words would be. "Well, who the hell names their kid after a damn dog?" I sputter, quite fruitlessly, judging from her second eyebrow shooting up. "Anyway, I told her, in no uncertain terms, I don't want her associating with that kid anymore. She didn't take that well." Looking at Pam, she's not taking it too well either; her beautiful full lips are pressed tight in a harsh line. "I gather you don't agree?"

"With what exactly?" she asks, bouncing the question right back at me. Typical therapist.

"Banning her from seeing him?"

"Actually," she says, as she slips from my arms and walks up to the window, her back toward me. "I don't think that's a bad idea in the short term. Both of them have a ton to deal with that doesn't necessarily have anything to do with the other. More than most kids their age do. I'm thinking that's probably why they connected so quickly, in such a short time." She doesn't say it out loud, but I can hear the parallel she tries to draw with us, her and me, and I can't let that stand.

"Yes, things move fast in our lives, and yes, we've gone from one shitstorm into another, but I won't have you make that out to be the reason we were drawn together. You know that's not true. We've been connected for years, we just didn't want to admit it or weren't ready for it," I argue, as she turns to face me.

"Are we still talking about the kids?" she asks innocently, but with a cheeky smirk that says otherwise.

"We are. I just felt that needed clarifying."

Her smile gets even bigger as she walks back toward me, grabs my shoulders, and stands up on tiptoes to kiss me sweetly.

"So noted," she smiles against my lips before retreating. "But my point stays the same; they've clearly found someone they can relate to while their respective lives are in turmoil. And that's not necessarily a bad thing."

"Okay, you've lost me," I admit. "First you say you think it's a good idea to keep them apart, and now you say the opposite."

"But it's not the opposite. Hear me out," she implores, her hand in the middle of my chest. "You grounded Gina, understandably so, but as a result she felt forced to do something she'd otherwise never have done; go behind your back. The reason for that was Benji."

"Damn right it was. If not for him, she…" I bluster, but Pam cuts me off, shaking her head.

"Honey, that's not my point. What I'm trying to say is that at this age, the moment you forbid something, the more enticing it becomes. Perhaps, if you were to…allow them to talk on the phone once a day? She wouldn't feel forced to go behind your back. Those kids could be good for each other."

"It feels like I'd be rewarding them for doing something wrong." I can't help but point out.

"But it's not really, when you think about it. It's simply a broadening of perspective: you may be the one in the right, but that doesn't mean you can't make the punishment right for her."

"I guess," I grudgingly agree. I still don't like the idea of Gina with a kid, who obviously has little or no regard for her safety. "But in this case, the kid just seems like bad news all round."

I know I stepped over some invisible line into Pam's ire, because her eyes shoot fire.

"Okay, I wasn't going to say this," she starts, and I figure I'm about to hear what she wasn't going to say. "But do I need to remind you that there are other kids, even older than Benji, who have made not such great decisions under pressure?"

Ouch. She got me in just a single shot and she's not even naming names. I'm starting to see her point, but she's adamant to make me bleed a little.

"Although some kids were lucky enough to have a community looking out for them, others have not been so lucky." A muscle twitches in her jaw as she fights to keep her composure.

Okay, now I feel like an absolute bastard. I open my mouth to tell her I get her, but she beats me to it.

"No. I get to finish this," she snaps, and I concede with a nod. "My boy didn't have a support system, and the one parent he did have wasn't paying attention. Benji is much like that, with only his mother looking out for him, and she can barely make appropriate decisions for herself. But it's not too late for him. With some positive influences paying him attention, from us, from Gina, and maybe even from Jonas, the kid may have a fighting chance. I don't want him to end up wasting away in jail, after doing something he can't ever take back."

"Hey," I soothe, as I pull her close, tucking her head in my neck. "I hear you… I get it." I press a kiss to the short hair on her head. "You make a good point, and I'm enough of a man to concede to that."

"You're enough of a man, period," she says, tilting her head back, the sadness still in her eyes, but a smile forming on her lips.

"And you, are a bit of a wiseass, you know that?" I tease, rubbing my nose against hers.

"I am. But you love me anyway."

"That I do, Biscuit. That I do."

Pam pushes off me with a deep sigh.

"Damn, that name makes me hungry. So now that I've made you see reason, do you think you could feed me? I'm losing delicious inches off my ass standing here," she says, slapping herself on the butt. I chuckle at her antics. *There she is.*

"Can't have that," I insist, grabbing her by the shoulders, turning her around, and marching her straight down the hallway to the large dining table, where only two chairs remain open.

"I'm starving," Pam says, as I shove her chair closer to the table. "I could eat the ass of a rhinoceros." A silence falls over the table as everyone turns to look at Pam, until Ike pipes up, a grin on his face.

"I know it looks like Syd cooked every food known to mankind, but I'm pretty sure the butcher was out of rhino ass."

CHAPTER TWENTY-SIX

Pam

"Happy New Year!"

Maria is in the kitchen at Florence House, emptying the dishwasher. She rushes over, a big smile on her face and gives me a big, and very unexpected, hug.

"Same you to, girl. What has you in such a chipper mood?" The once mentally defeated girl looks like she's done a one-eighty in the past few weeks.

"I got a job!" she squeals, clapping her hands and her enthusiasm easily sweeps me along.

"You're shitting me. Where?" I smile back equally big.

"*Bean There*, the coffee shop on the corner. Seven till two, Monday to Friday, Saturdays and Sundays off, for now."

"That's fantastic! I'm so happy for you. How did that come about?" I pull out a chair at the kitchen table and sit down, gesturing for her to do the same.

"Marianne and I went for a walk yesterday and there was a sign in the window. She bugged me all night to go back there today, when they were open. The woman who owns the place is *so* nice. Said she'd seen me around before. Then she had me work this big-ass expresso machine to make a…"

"Espresso," I correct her, unable to stop myself.

"Sorry?" Obviously I've confused her and I instantly feel bad.

"It's *es*-presso not *ex*-presso. But go on," I encourage her.

"Anyway," she says, the smile back on her face. "She had me make a latte, a caramel macchiato, and a cappuccino. I didn't like the last one, but I *loved* the macchiato." I successfully hold back a chuckle when her eyes close dramatically on the word *loved.*

I have to give it to Marianne, she took this girl under her wing just a few short weeks ago, and the change is amazing. She's more animated and she's smiled more in the last ten minutes than I've seen her smile in the months since she first came here.

Ditto for Marianne, actually. I'm not sure what draws these fundamentally different women from opposite walks of life to each other, but something does, and the result is magical. A good lesson never to judge a book by its cover.

"I'm proud of you, honey," I tell Maria who, if possible, beams even brighter.

"Did you tell her?" I turn around at the sound of Marianne's voice.

"She did," I answer for her before turning back to Maria. "So when do you start?"

"Next Monday. I can't wait."

"Go get your coat," Marianne interjects. "We're gonna miss the bus otherwise." With a loud scrape over the kitchen floor Maria shoves her chair back and rushes out of the kitchen. Marianne turns to me. "We're going shopping. She needs a few new clothes."

I automatically pull my wallet out of my purse, and take a few bills out, when Marianne's hand lands on my wrist.

"What the heck do you think you're doing?" she hisses, an incredulous look on her face.

"You said she needs clothes."

"Yes, I did—and I'm paying for them." I almost chuckle when she determinedly folds her arms under her chest. A challenge if I've ever seen one.

"Don't get mad, but you came here with the clothes on your back. How will you be able to pay for it?" I ask. A valid question, I think. Marianne's eye's twinkle when she answers me.

"My clothes, and the forty thousand dollars from Fred's safe he didn't think I had the combination to."

To say I'm shocked would be an understatement. Floored is more appropriate. Mousy little Marianne is an endless source of amazement. If our lawyers hadn't already made sure there is a restraining order in place, this would be the time where I would drag her straight to the police station to put one in place. Abusers seek power, and not only had Marianne undercut her husband's control of thirty years by finally walking away—she'd added insult to injury by stealing his stash.

"You know you were playing with fire, doing that," I offer, but Marianne just shrugs her narrow shoulders.

"I didn't take anymore than what I brought into the marriage. I inherited that money when my mother passed away, two months before I married Fred, who immediately confiscated it. He's lucky I didn't grab the remaining eighty thousand he had in there."

"Holy shit. I guess so," I blurt out, trying to get my mind around the fact these people were apparently so loaded they had over one hundred grand in cash, sitting in a safe in their house. *Dayum.* "So why didn't you use it to get out of here?"

She sits down across from me at the table and plays with the salt and pepper shakers while she seems to think about that.

"It's all I have. I thought it would be enough to get a new start, maybe buy a house, but things are so much more expensive than I realized. Fred paid all the bills, I didn't even have access to a bank account anymore. He just gave me a weekly allowance."

I reach over, put my hand on hers, and give it a squeeze. "Those days are over. And for your information, forty grand is still a nice chunk of change. It's enough for a down payment on a small place and maybe some furniture." .

"Yeah?" She lifts her head and meets my eyes. "You think? But what about a mortgage? I'll need to find work, and frankly, I wouldn't know where to start. I haven't worked outside of the house for over thirty years. I have no qualifications."

Suddenly the pieces fall together. The random thoughts, secret worries, and furtive hopes all fall into line.

"That's not exactly true," I disagree, a huge grin almost splitting my face. "You have a talent. One that is proving to be invaluable." When she looks at me quizzically, I clarify. "Maria—in a short period of time you've done wonders with her. I know you have no official training, but there is nothing saying we can't give you in-house training. On the job training."

Marianne just sits there with her mouth wide open when her much younger sidekick comes skipping in.

"What's wrong?" she worriedly asks Marianne, who slowly closes her mouth only to smile wide.

"Looks like we'll both be shopping for some work clothes." Now it's Maria's turn to look confused, but Marianne doesn't explain, she gets up and starts herding the younger woman into the hallway.

"Hang on!" I call out, fishing through my purse. "Here, take my car." I dangle the keys briefly in my hand before tossing them in Marianne's direction. She surprises me yet again when she deftly snatches them out of the air, and with a saucy wink, turns on her heels and follows Maria out of the kitchen.

Dino

Thank God I have today off.

The kids are back in school, as of this morning, and I've been on the phone with my lawyer and Detective Barnes. According to my lawyer, it wouldn't take too much to change the application for divorce. But since he was due in court, and would be stuck there for the foreseeable future, he suggested I chase down the necessary paperwork myself.

I quickly check the clock. If I want to be home to catch the kids off the bus, I'd better get going.

We haven't had any snow since New Year's Eve, and even though the temperatures have remained cold enough to keep the snow from melting, the streets are mostly clear now. The drive to the police station takes no time at all, and when I walk into the building and up to the front desk, Barnes happens to be standing there.

"Mr. Brachio," he says, holding a hand out I grab firmly to shake. "Why don't you come back to my office."

Said office is little more than a cubicle with four walls, a small window, and a door.

"Have a seat." I do as he says. "It's funny you called this morning," he informs me. "I just received information this morning that the case against Christian Neve, will be tried separately from the other two boys. Neve is not only slapped with assault and rape charges, but he has some other charges pending, as well. Since the other boys were not yet eighteen at the time, he will also be charged with the corruption of a minor. Now because of that, there is a chance your son may have to testify twice, although the likelihood is great that the two other kids will plead out."

I don't know why I lulled myself into thinking that with the start of the new year, we'd leave the old one behind. It never quite works that way. I'm not an idiot, I knew Jonas, and probably even Pam, would likely have to testify at some point this year. I'm just not quite ready to deal with it only days in.

"Plead out?" I repeat, trying to process this wake up call.

"Depending on the outcome of Mr. Neve's trial, in particular on the 'corruption of a minor' charge, those two might be able to plead to a lesser offense."

"A lesser offense? They put my son in the hospital, attacked my girlfriend. There was no coercion. No corruption of a minor. They're two spoiled, entitled, rich kids, who thought it would be a good idea to intimidate witnesses with physical violence." My temper is getting the better of me at the thought of those two punks walking away scot-free, because of daddy's deep pockets. We've seen it all too many times in the news recently; money over justice.

"I hear you," Barnes says, his teeth gritting. "Trust me, I hear you loud and clear. Don't think it's not as frustrating for us, busting our asses to bring these kids to justice, only to have them walk away with no more than a slap on their wrist." He runs a hand through his hair, leaving it standing on end, the strain of the job showing in his features. "Look—depending on the outcome—there is always the possibility of a civil suit. The burden of proof is not quite to the level of a criminal trial, and at best, you would only end up with some financial compensation, but should it come to that, it's a way to maybe get some justice. For now though, they will remain behind bars until their trial."

It'll be a long four months until Neve's day in court in April.

I almost forgot what I came in here for, when the detective opens up a file folder on his desk.

"These are the arrest report and the judge's order issued to have Ms. Brachio transported to a treatment facility. I took the liberty of checking in with the facility after you called, and they have not seen her in weeks. She clearly hasn't returned."

"That's not really a surprise," I inform him when he hands me the folder. "She called me before Christmas, looking for money. I didn't give her any—clearly—but tried to get her to go back. I haven't heard from her since." I stand up and look at the file in my hand. "Anyway—thanks for this. I'd appreciate it if you'd let me know if anything changes."

"Sure thing." Barnes leads me out of his office and walks me back to the front desk. Another handshake and I'm off to the lawyer's office, feeling a lot less upbeat than I did this morning.

-

"I'm looking for an older small pickup or car. In good shape, with a bit of life left."

I'm spending the last few minutes before the kids get home calling around.

When I got to my lawyer's office, he'd just come back from court. I left the file with him and he promised he'd have the appropriate paperwork done up before the end of the week. Given that no one knows where Jeannie is right now, and she is disregarding a court order, he said no judge would have a problem granting the divorce and temporary custody.

That visit left me feeling a bit more optimistic, but it also brought home how preciously short time is. Jeannie is missing out on so much, and before you know it, the kids will be gone. Jonas will already be eighteen in a few months and going off to college not long after. That got me thinking that maybe it was time to give him a little more independence.

"Do you have a price point?" Ike wants to know.

I called him, because he knows his cars. Something that's never really had my interest. As long as it has four wheels, plenty of room for my big body, and is able to get me from A to B, I don't much care what it is I'm driving.

"I don't have a lot, can probably get my hands on three grand, max. Can you do anything with that?"

"I might," he says pensively. "Actually, I have an idea that might benefit us both. I've been trying to get Viv to let me buy her a small SUV since Francessca was born. Getting the car seat in the back of her car is a pain in the ass, since it's only a two-door, but she's stubborn. It's a great little starter car, and I bet if I told her it would go to Jonas, it would make it a shitload easier for her to let it go. Everyone benefits." He chuckles, obviously pleased with himself.

"You're a manipulative bastard, you know that?" I tell him, and it only makes him laugh harder.

"Well, hell yeah—I've had to be, how else do you think I managed to get this woman to marry me?"

"Good point," I concede with a smile of my own.

"Leave it with me, I'll have a talk with Viv. It's her car, so she'll have to come up with a fair price, but I'm pretty sure she won't be charging three grand—not if it's for Jonas."

When I hang up, it's with a lingering smile on my face.

Five more minutes until the kids get in and I suddenly feel the need to hear Pam's voice. I quickly dial her number.

"I miss you," I spill when I hear the call answered, before she has a chance to say hello. She left this morning, right after the kids got on the bus. She was planning to go to her own place tonight, joked that she may already have forgotten her own address.

I know her grief is still very fresh and that she sometimes needs to *feel* it. The best place for that is at her own house where there are no distractions, only her memories, but fuck, I much prefer her right here where I can make sure she's okay. That, and I love waking up to her in the morning. If I'm completely honest, it's in large part because she seems to enjoy morning sex as much as I do. But also because it feels right. She feels right; in my house, with my kids, it feels easy.

"Nice to know," a voice I can't place responds, startling me from my thoughts. "But I'm thinking you didn't mean me?" Amusement is evident in the woman's voice.

"Only if you're a smart-assed, tall, buxom, beautiful, ebony queen by the name of Pam," I fire back.

"Ahhhh—that would be a no. There's no way my skinny, five foot three, blindingly white ass could pass for that. You've got Doris." She finally introduces herself as I snicker at her cheek.

"Doris, nice to meet you. I'm Dino and I'm looking for Pam."

"Doris and Dino? Hell no, that would never have worked. It sounds like a Cartoon Network show. Let me get…oops, here she is." I hear rustling as the phone apparently changes hands, and then Pam's rich husky voice comes over the line.

"Hello?"

"Biscuit, I've gotta say, you have a way of surrounding yourself with arguably the most entertaining chicks I know."

"Are you calling Marianne a chick, too? Damn, she'll be tickled pink when she hears that." Pam is feeling good, I can tell by the lift in her voice.

"I may have told your Doris I missed her," I confess. "I meant it for you." A deep chortle comes over the line.

"I miss you too, honey. And I'm sure Doris appreciates the sentiment. How's your day?"

I haven't told Pam yet about my plans to fast track my divorce. I don't want her to think I feel obligated for her sake. I don't. Not entirely. For the most part I'm just ready to tie off loose ends and find some stability. Hopefully with Pam.

"It was good. What about yours?"

"I've had a surprisingly productive day, with a few interesting developments," she says, piquing my interest.

"Care to share?" I prompt.

"I would, but I think I'd rather wait till I see you. What I can tell you, is that there's some change coming."

"Tease," I return. "I'd keep my bit of news to myself just to spite you, but I suck at secrets. The kids'll be home soon so I have to be fast, but just spoke with Ike. He's helping me get a car for Jonas."

"That kid's gonna be beside himself; he'll be happier than a pup with two tails. That's great, Dino. I'm happy you're showing him a little trust."

I never really considered that, but I guess I am. Maybe it's time for me to prove myself to him instead of the other way around. Show him a little faith.

CHAPTER TWENTY-SEVEN

Pam

"Do you want me to stay home?"

I can barely hear Dino through my tears. I'm not sure what happened, but waking up this morning I felt a strong wave of sadness.

He'd come over on Wednesday night after work and had been excited to hear about my plans to hire Marianne on. He just nodded, with a knowing smile on his face, when I'd told him I thought I was ready for some more time to enjoy life. Ironic how his keen insight once seemed like a threat to me, but now feels like the warmest acceptance.

Over the last few days, the guilt started niggling at me. I was safe, hopeful, and even happy, and somehow that went down the wrong way. It's so fucking frustrating to understand exactly what is happening on a conscious level, but to be unable to control it. I'm starting to plan for a future; one that suddenly seems possible. Inevitable, even. But for the death of my son, I wouldn't be here. But for the early end to his sad life, I would likely still be hiding in my work, purposely keeping to myself. It makes for conflicting emotions, like being caught between a rock and a hard place. I know the only way is forward, but it fucking hurts.

Dino noticed the change in my mood last night when I got here, but he didn't push. He'd asked me to bring a bag for the weekend. I'd been looking forward to it, so I did my best to enjoy the family's banter. This morning though, I can't hold back the tears, the loss of my child cutting through my morning drowsiness.

"I'll be fine," I assure him. "I'm gonna have a quick shower and pull myself together."

Dino leans in and kisses the tears from my cheeks before moving to my mouth, chasing the last of my tears away.

"I'll get some coffee going," he says, swinging his legs over the side, giving me an eyeful of glorious ass, as he bends down to pick some sweatpants off the floor. A little wistful sigh escapes me as he pulls them on. His amused eyes meet mine over his shoulder. "You liked that, huh?"

"Hell yeah. I may be mopey, but I'm not dead."

"Oh, honey, I can vouch for that. You scratched the fuck out of my back last night," he says with a cheeky grin, as he pulls a shirt over his head.

"Whatever." I dismiss him with a wave of my hand, but inside he makes me feel lighter, and I have to bite back a smile when he blows a kiss before disappearing down the hall.

-

I stayed.

He asked me to, and I didn't have it in me to fight it. I wanted to stay. My house feels lonely. The only reason I keep going back there is because I feel I have to. That it's too soon to spend so much time here, but the truth is that I like it. I like the music filtering from Gina's room, the sound of gunshots as Jonas has his PlayStation on too loud. It's lived in, comfortable, with family pictures on the walls and throw pillows on the couch. I actually appreciate the fact that Dino makes no attempt to hide the fact that Jeannie lived here. It's important for the kids to know that even though their mom is pretty fucked up right now, she was and is still part of this family.

I've never really been invested enough in any kind of entanglement to feel jealousy, but even now that I am invested—fully so—it's apparently not part of my 'make-up.'

After Dino left this morning, I actually spent some time on his computer, looking at the value of houses in my area. Just to get an idea, should I decide to sell at some point. *Crap—who am I kidding?* At this point I'm pretty sure should Dino asked me outright to move in with him, I would. I'm over fifty; I'm past the point of caring what it might look like to the outside world. How many of us get another shot at building a future at this time in their life?

"Don't look a gift horse in the mouth," my grandmé used to tell me, when I would complain about the bags of second hand clothing a neighbor would drop off for us. It seems appropriate here. Just because someone has discarded something, doesn't mean it can't be the perfect fit for somebody else. Like Dino and his kids are a perfect fit for me. I just need to know I'm one for them too. Jonas and even Gina—although a little less obvious—seem okay with me being around. They've been downstairs a few times, Gina even watching some TV while I was on the computer. When I'd asked her if she wanted to run the store to pick up some things for dinner with me, she hesitated for a minute. She looked as if she wanted to, but ended up giving her head a quick shake before disappearing upstairs again.

"What are you cooking?"

Jonas walks into the kitchen and lifts the lid off a pot of the jambalaya I'm making because he liked it so much last time. I'm not sure about Gina, but I'm pretty sure if she doesn't like that, she'll like the mango crème brûlée I'm putting together for dessert. Jonas turns to me with a smile on his face.

"Is that the same stuff you cooked before?"

"It is," I confirm, but before I can elaborate, the door bell rings.

"I'll get it," Jonas says, already walking out of the kitchen. I keep stirring the custard in the double boiler I was excited to find in Dino's cupboard until I hear Jonas' raised voice. I can't tell what's being said, but I'm worried about who he might be having words with. I quickly turn off the burner, move the pan off the heat source, and go check.

I recognize the bedraggled looking woman on the doorstep; Jeannie. Her son is bent down, his face in hers as he loudly tells her to "*Fuck off!*"

"Jonas!" I call out, my heart aching at the flinch on the woman's face at his words. But the moment she spots me, the sad teary look on her face morphs into an angry, calculating sneer.

"What do you think you're doing in *my* house?" she hisses, clearly not pleased to see me. I can't say I blame her; I'm pretty sure I wouldn't be happy either, finding a strange woman with my children. Then again, I wouldn't have bailed on my kids like she did. Even when a good case could be made to walk away from Derrick at some point, I never could.

"Pretty sure it doesn't qualify as your house anymore. And if I remember correctly, you're not allowed to come here," Jonas answers for me, and I put a calming hand on his shoulder. This is looking to get ugly unless I can calm things down.

"It's okay, Jonas," I tell him, but that just seems to anger his mother more.

"Don't tell my son what to do! If you think for one minute you can come in here and take my place, you're in for a surprise. Dino will welcome me back with open arms; he'll do anything for his kids." The last is almost spit at me, the venom obvious in her voice.

"You're wrong…" an unexpected soft voice comes from behind me as Gina steps around me and places herself in front of me.

"Baby," Jeannie is suddenly all smiles for her daughter. "I came to see you. I thought you were coming to visit me last week?" Gina shoots a quick glance over her shoulder at her brother and me.

"What the fuck, Gina?" Jonas turns on his sister. "Have you been talking to her?"

"I…I didn't want to…" The poor girl is close to tears. "She came to school—I didn't know what to do."

I don't notice Jeannie stepping over the threshold until she grabs Gina hard by the upper arm, shaking her. "You didn't want to? That's not what you told me!" The woman is screeching now, and I take a step closer when I notice the wild, dilated look in her eyes. The stupid bitch is high as a kite.

"You'll want to take your hands off her, Jeannie," I caution her.

"My daughter, and I can damn well do what I want." I didn't expect her to listen to me, but I also didn't expect her to put her other arm around the crying girl and start backing away toward the door.

Jonas makes a move as if to step in, but I quietly caution him. "Jonas, no. Go call the police, honey." He looks at his sister and then at me before stalking past me into the house. Jeannie's eyes flick back and forth between Jonas' retreating back and me. Gina struggles in her arms. "Let her go, Jeannie. You're hurting her," I plead, hoping to moderate an already explosive situation.

"I have a right to see my babies!"

"Not if you're hurting them, Jeannie. Look at your daughter—she's scared." I'm inching closer as I talk, ready to grab for Gina should Jeannie drag her down the porch steps.

Slowly I sidestep until we've almost reversed our positions, her back is now mostly turned to the front door, and I'm blocking the steps. She blinks her eyes a few times before she lowers her eyes to her daughter, only to have them come up again to me.

"You don't belong here," she repeats to me, but her voice is wavering a little. Her eyes dart around, slightly panicked when she realizes I've blocked her path. The woman is tripping on something and I'm worried about her.

I try to keep a straight face as Jonas steps out behind his mother, he's a good head taller than her already. "The cops are on their way." Hearing his voice, Jeannie swings around, finally letting Gina go. She makes a beeline for me, her arms wrapping tightly around my waist and burying her face against my chest. The poor child is sobbing uncontrollably.

"Mom," Jonas says softly. "You need help."

Dino

Jesus what a clusterfuck.

When Jonas called, I could immediately hear from his voice that something was wrong. I had my coat on before he finished telling me what was going on. Ruby rushed me out of the kitchen, telling me she'd cover for me.

By the time I get home, there are two patrol cars out front. I can see Jeannie in the back of one of them. I ignore her and instead rush up the steps and into the house, where I expect my kids to be. They are. I'm surprised to find Gina on the couch, leaning into Pam. Jonas is sitting at the table, talking to two officers. When he sees me, he indicates his sister with a chin lift. Taking the direction, I lower myself on the couch beside her. The moment my ass hits the seat, she swings around and buries her body against my chest. My arms protectively curl around her as she mumbles *sorry* over and over again through her tears..

"It's okay, Princess. You're okay," I soothe her, my eyes finding Pam's over her head.

"Hey," she says on a tight little smile.

"Hey. Thanks for being there for the kids. What happened?" Jonas told me the gist of it, but I wanted to hear it from Pam. Instead it's Gina who answers, her voice muffled by my shirt. "I can't hear, baby." She lifts her head and looks up at me through tear-filled eyes before leaning her back against Pam, who tucks an arm around her. Whatever my daughter has to say, she clearly needs the support. I'm not sure whether to be upset or happy about that. "Gina?" I gently prompt Gina.

"She was at the fence at school with Ben's mother, calling me over." I can see Pam's face tighten at that tidbit of information. "Well, Mom was, Ben's mom was arguing with him. I didn't know what to do. I tried to ignore her, but she started crying, and I felt bad. She said she missed me and that she wanted to see me. I told her I'd think about it, just to get rid of her, it was embarrassing—she was embarrassing. That's when Ben started talking to me." Her eyes look up from under her lashes and she lightly shrugs her shoulders. "I'd noticed him before, but he'd never actually said anything to me."

From the tone of her voice I can tell that '*notice*' is a euphemism for '*crush*' for a thirteen-year-old.

"Go on," I encourage her, reaching out to sweep her bangs off her forehead.

"Anyway, so a few days after that, Ben asked if I'd come to his house after school."

"Wait." I lifted my hand to interrupt her. "Where was I? How come I didn't know this?" Gina's face turns beet red

"You were at work. Jonas was out with his buddies," she says timidly, before going on the defensive. "It's not like you guys noticed whether I was here or not," she says and it cuts. Because the truth of it is, I didn't really notice, I just assumed she'd be home; sweet, easy, and compliant.

"Carry on, baby," I prompt again.

"Anyway, it was weird. Mom was there with some other people, one guy was hanging off her, and I'm pretty sure they were hammered. It looked like some kind of party and made me uncomfortable, so Ben got me out of there. He said he was sorry, he didn't know his mom's boyfriend and his buddies would be there. Mom followed me outside, being all nasty that I was leaving and making me feel guilty. So I gave her my number so she could call."

I'd given Gina a cell phone after Jeannie left so we could keep track of each other. Jonas had had one since fifteen, but we'd always thought Gina was too young.

"She called me only once. It was during my lunch break, and she wanted to know if you were working. Said she needed to talk to you. I didn't think anything of it, Daddy. It was the day she broke in. I'm so sorry," she says as she breaks into tears again. Things become a little clearer to me. Her slow withdrawal after that, her moodiness. She felt responsible and it made me even angrier with Jeannie.

"Listen to me. That had nothing to do with you. Your mom—shit, honey—there's no easy way to say this; she's a mess. She's not well and hasn't been for a while. If she wanted in the house so bad, she would've done so regardless. That's not on you, it's on her—and on her addiction." Gina keeps her face pressed to Pam's side until she lifts my little girl's face with her hand.

"Listen to your dad, Sweetie. He's right. Nothing about this is your fault. Just get it all out," Pam urges her.

"After that I ignored her calls and they stopped for a bit." Gina sits a little straighter and wipes her face on her sleeve. I want to reach out and pull her close, but she seems to feel safe with Pam at her back, so I resist. "I didn't hear from her again until the week before Christmas. I didn't check call display when I answered, and it was her. She told me she was sorry, begged me not to hang up and that it had all been a big mistake. She wanted to see me, so she could make it right again. Said she missed us terribly and had Christmas presents for us all, but that she was afraid to come to the house to drop them off. She sounded so sad. I told her I'd meet with her on Christmas Eve. Ben said he'd go with me when I told him, said he didn't want me going alone. She told me to meet her at the Dunkin' Donuts."

"On the south side? Main Street?" One of the police officers, who'd obviously been listening in, piped up, startling us all. Gina looked at me, and I gave her a little nod before she turned to the young man again with a nod of her own.

"Across from the Knights Inn," she confirms. "When we got there, she seemed upset Ben had come along. She tried to get me to come to her room—at the motel across the street—so she could give me the gifts, but insisted Ben wait for me at Dunkin' Donuts. I told her I didn't want to and she got so mad, the manager came to see what was going on. It was embarrassing. Mom started crying and making a scene again, when Ben told her we had to leave. Then she asked when she'd see me again, I told her maybe after Christmas."

Gina's hands fiddle restlessly with the hem of her sweater, as she continues to explain that she and Ben had gotten into an argument over that on the way home on the bus. They'd not talked over Christmas, and when he messaged her on New Year's Eve, wanting to see her to talk things out, she just *had* to go see him, despite the fact she was already grounded.

The officers ask a few more questions about what happened when Jeannie showed up at the door, before getting ready to leave. The car that had Jeannie in the back is long gone by the time I show them out.

"You may want to contact Detective Barnes," I suggest to them. "He knows what happened before, knows about Jeannie. She walked away from a court-ordered stint in rehab and has been on the lam since."

Back inside, Pam has disappeared into the kitchen and Jonas is now sitting beside his sister on the couch. Both look up when I walk in and sit down on the coffee table in front of them.

"Okay guys, here's the deal; we've got a lot of shit going on in our lives, and it sometimes easier just to keep things from each other. Let's not do that anymore. I don't care if it means we get into arguments from time to time, I'd much rather that and resolve it, than feel the rug pulled out from under me every time I turn my back." Both kids look guilty and that is not what I want. "What I'm trying to tell you is that the sure way to get through whatever life tosses at us, is to stick together. All of us."

"Does that include Pam?" Jonas asks, a smirk on his face. When I turn to see Gina's reaction, she just seems curious.

"Damn right it does. Which brings me to my next news; I've put things in place to expedite the divorce." I watch the kids' faces drop, but in light of my earlier lobby for honesty, I figure they should know where I'm at. "You know your mom and I have not worked for a long time, that's not new. I can't blame it all on the addiction, although it is a big part of it. The truth is, I will always love what your mom gave me—you two—she made me a father and that's something I'll always be grateful for. I hung in there this long because, despite the fact I may not have loved your mom the way I should have, I sure as hell love the family we created. With all my heart."

"And Pam, too," Gina adds quietly, a tentative smile on her face.

"Yes, Princess; and Pam, too."

CHAPTER TWENTY-EIGHT

Pam

"Keep your door unlocked tonight; I need to talk to you."

I don't know why his words have a flock of butterflies going ballistic in my stomach, all of a sudden. It's not like we don't talk or see each other almost daily. There's something about the way he announces it this time, like it's of utmost importance.

For the past month or so, my life has felt suspended. Transitional, in a way; leaving my old life behind, and looking forward to my new one, but I'm just not there yet. Ever since I overheard Dino talking to his kids, the day their mother was hauled away in the back of a patrol car, I've been waiting. I'm hoping he's just been holding off on moving forward to give the kids a chance to get used to the idea of sharing their life with me. We may have been emotionally ready for it that quickly, but it was a bit much to ask the kids to accept such a quick transition.

I'm ready, though. I've already spoken to a real estate agent to get an idea of the current market, and he's been blowing up my phone, wondering when I'll be ready to list the house. Funny how I was so sure at the beginning of the year, but with time passing have started questioning things. Not my feelings; they're clear as glass. And not really Dino's feelings either, he tells me he loves me every chance he gets, and it never fails to leave me feeling lucky. No—it's the worry that the mess with Jeannie earlier this year, has made him a little leery at the thought of tying himself to another woman. I wouldn't blame him, an experience like that is enough of a deterrent for a lot of people to make that kind of commitment again, but it happened just as I had made up my mind I was ready for it. What if that incident got him thinking, and he decided not to want to take the risk again? Where would that leave me?

Despite the fact I've always been the one shying away from any kind of commitment, I'm not sure if just sharing parts of our lives would be enough for me. I want it all; the kids, the daily grind, Dino—I need all of it.

"Where are you?" Marianne says, as she walks into my office at Florence House. "You look miles away." Not miles, only a few short blocks, actually.

"Just thinking," I smile at her, making a decision on the spot. Regardless of what he has to tell me tonight, I'm ready to make a move forward. Ready to put everything on the line for what I want. "Are you still looking for a place?" I ask her, waving her to one of the chairs on the other side of my desk.

"I am. Although I've had little success thus far. I think once I can say I've worked here a little more than just a few weeks, I'll be taken a bit more seriously."

It's tough, getting back on your feet after you lose everything. I know, I've been there a few times as well. In fact, I don't think any of the women I know have managed without at least a small nudge in the right direction or a helping hand. Viv, who was able to connect with Gunnar, an old friend of her brother's, who was able to set her up with work and even a place to stay for a bit. After that it was Syd's turn, who was perhaps worse off than any of us when she took a leap of faith and took Viv's proffered hand. Just last year it was Ruby. I wasn't sure she'd ever be able to adjust to a regular life or trust anyone again, but she accepted a job from Syd and Gunnar, let Viv help her settle in her old apartment, and even allowed Tim to guide her the rest of the way.

Paying it forward.

It starts with one simple kindness and grows exponentially from there. I've seen it, I've experienced it, and I whole-heartedly believe in it. Something that doesn't have to cost much to give, sometimes no more than simple thoughtful gesture, but can be of immeasurable value to someone else.

"I have an idea," I forge ahead, putting myself out there. "I'm thinking of selling my house. It's a beautiful little place, not very far from here, I bought two years ago."

"Why are you selling?"

It's a valid question, but one I'm not sure how to answer. Still I try.

"I bought the place because I thought I needed to put down some roots, other than the shelter. I'd been living there for well over the decade. With Derrick in jail, I'd allowed myself to live in limbo. When the time came that he could be considered for parole, I realized I didn't have a place for him to come to in case he'd be released." It still feels a little weird talking freely about Derrick, when all these years I'd kept him a secret. Marianne shoots me a compassionate smile. She may not have lost a child to death, but that doesn't mean she doesn't understand the pain of loss. "So I bought us a house. A place to start new. Except things didn't turn out that way, and without him, that house can never be a home to me."

"So it doesn't have anything to do with that scrumptious behemoth of a man and his fabulous kids?" she asks with a twinkle in her eyes.

"Oh, I'm not denying that. They are why I realized it wasn't about me being unable to settle, but about the house not being the right one for me to settle in. Not without Derrick," I freely admit before getting back to my point. "But just because it's not the right place for me to put down those roots, doesn't mean it can't be the perfect spot for you and Maria. It's not big, but it has everything you need, plus it's a short bus ride from the shelter, and in the summer it's a comfortable fifteen or twenty minute walk. What do you think?"

"It sounds wonderful, but Pam, you realize it doesn't change my problem; the banks still won't want to talk to me," she points out, and I realize I left out an important part of my plan.

"You won't need the bank. You can be renting to own. We can get a proper contract drawn up, which I suggest we do for both our sakes, in which we can hammer out the details. I've already done a bit of research into fair market value, but I strongly suggest you do the same and figure out what you'll be able to do month to month. We'll make sure the contract keeps the arrangement entirely separate from our working relationship or our friendship." I smile, pleased with my plan.

"You're serious…" Marianne says, a bit shell shocked and I chuckle.

"Completely."

I burst out laughing when she jumps up and starts doing some kind of victory dance. Next thing I know, she's digging through her purse, pulling out her phone.

"Guess what?" she half yells into the phone, and I'm guessing she's talking to Maria. "We've got a house…No, I'm not kidding, Pam's giving us her house."

I shake my head as she walks out of my office, chattering on the phone, pulling the door closed behind her.

I'm still smiling when I dive back into the accounting program, entering the expenses for the first month of the year. I've barely got two entries done when the door slams open, and

Marianne strides right back up to my desk. She places both hands on top as she leans in.

"For the record," she whispers with a serious face. "Thank you. You are a true lifesaver." I nod, but when she starts moving to the door, I call her back.

"Marianne," I wait for her to turn before I say, "so are you."

Dino

All the way through the dinner rush, I think about the cryptic message I left with Pam. I could tell she'd been a little taken aback, and I know I've been skirting around some issues, causing her to be a little unsure where she stands. I plan to remedy all of that tonight.

Last month, when it became clear Jeannie was going to be charged, I saw an opportunity and contacted my lawyer right away. With a little help from Detective Barnes, I'd been able to get in to see her, and have her sign off on the divorce and uncontested claim for custody of the kids my lawyer had quickly drawn up. I don't feel guilty capitalizing on the fact she had clearly hit rock bottom. I'd do anything for my kids. I promised her if she completed rehab, and got herself back on her feet, I would not stand in her way if she wanted to see the children. She'd cried, apologized, pleaded, and I listened to it all—until she started mouthing off on Pam. That was the end for me and I made it clear.

"That woman has done more for those kids, in the short time she's known them, than you have in all of their lives. For Christ's sake, Jeannie—she had to jump in to protect the kids *from* you."

My lawyer jumped in then, stopping me from doing any more potential damage. He pulled me aside and reminded me why we were there. She ended up signing, though.

The wait after that was long. I had a hard time not jumping the gun but it felt important to close one chapter out before starting another. Better for the kids, but also fairer to Pam. This afternoon I finally got the call that the divorce certificate was signed, which is when I called Pam right away. It's time.

By the time I'm driving to her place, I've got to admit I'm a little nervous. It's not that I think she doesn't love me, because I know she does. Hell, I want to bet she loves my kids too, judging from the way she is with them, and more importantly, the way they are with her. I just don't know if she's ready to share a life with me, with us.

She's left the outside light on when I pull into the driveway, and I grab the cannoli I made for her this afternoon from the passenger seat. The door is unlocked, and inside, I'm surprised to find the house in complete disarray. There are boxes everywhere, and for a moment my heart stops in my throat. What if she's leaving?

"Pam?" I call out, not seeing her anywhere.

"Here." Her head pops up from behind the counter in the kitchen.

"What are you doing?"

"Packing."

"I can see that, Biscuit, but packing for what?" A brief look of insecurity flashes over her face before she masks it with a big smile.

"I'm renting out my house to Marianne and Maria. This is not home for me, it never was." She's almost whispering on the last words.

"I thought…" I let my voice trail off as I rephrase carefully. "I mean; how did you know?"

Her eyebrows shoot up when I ask her that. "I'm confused," she says. "How did I know what?" I realize this is going to hell in a handbasket if we don't start communicating. It may not be the way I envisioned it, and I'm certainly not looking forward to possibly getting shut down, but here it goes.

"Come sit down with me for a second." I go into the kitchen and pull her up off the floor before leading her to the couch. I have to move a few boxes to make room to sit. "I'll tell you why I'm here first, and then maybe you can explain to me why you are packing. Deal?" A tight nod is my only answer, I better make this good. "If it were up to me, I'd have asked you to move in with me the first time I got to kiss you. Or maybe when you cooked for me. I definitely wanted to when you cooked for us, sharing a little of your heritage with the kids and me. But each time something would happen—life would happen—and I didn't want it to seem like it was just for convenience. That's why, when Jeannie showed up that day, as a pretty drastic reminder that I had some things unfinished, I realized I didn't want to ask until those were taken care of. You deserve a man who is yours in every way you want him, and a house no other woman can lay claim to ever again." Pam's eyes are tearing up a little and I take that as a good sign. "My divorce became final today. I already talked to the kids a while ago and they are on board. Which means, Biscuit, that I am now in a position where I'm able to offer you all that I have and all that I am."

I'm getting worried when she doesn't say anything for a while, and only shock registers on her face, but then her lips spread into a blinding smile.

"I might just take you up on that," she says, her voice a little rough. "It seems only fair since I was planning on offering you all of me, if you'd have me."

I let out a relieved breath and lift her on my lap, where her arms automatically find their way around my neck and her forehead comes to rest against mine. "I'd be honored."

My hands, settled on her hips, slide up, skim the side of her breasts and slip around her back, pulling her closer.

"Give me that beautiful mouth, honey. Let's seal this deal."

Still smiling, her lips close over mine in a kiss that starts slow, sweet—but quickly picks up heat as our tongues slide and tangle, while hands touch and explore. When Pam lifts her head, both of us are breathing hard. She grabs the edge of her T-shirt and lifts it over her head. No bra. Her breasts, full and heavy with dark brown nipples, sway level with my face, and I can't resist the temptation. I lift the weight of one in my hand and bring it to my mouth, tracing the areola with my tongue, before sucking the peak between my lips. A moan has me lift my eyes to look at her face; her head thrown back, eyes closed with lips slightly parted. Her hips unapologetically undulate, her heat seeking out the hard ridge of my cock. She's raw, uninhibited, and yet almost majestic as she unleashes her passion. She leaves me breathless.

With a sudden need to be inside her, I let go of her nipple with a pop, and firmly grab her hips.

"Up, honey." She looks a little dazed at first but then moves quickly off my lap. I tug her sweats and underwear down to her ankles and she easily steps out of them. *God,* she's gorgeous: her beautiful dark skin almost gleaming, her curves rich and soft. I lean forward to press a kiss on her soft stomach, still bearing the marks of the child she lost. Her hands find my head and hold me in place.

"I love you," I mumble against her skin.

She places her hands on my face and lifts it up, her eyes burning down on me.

"I know…I'm so blessed. I've been touched with the glow of love growing around me for years. Was happy for each of my friends finding and fighting for theirs. I just never thought it was in the cards for me." Her long fingers stroke over my scalp and her eyes trace my features. "It's the most astonishing, exquisite feeling; I never believed I would one day feel the heat of it on my skin."

I reach behind my back, pulling my shirt up and off. She takes a step back and I get up, unbuttoning my jeans and pushing them down my hips. Her eyes track down the length of my body, such as it is. I don't have a sculpted body, by any stretch of the imagination, but you wouldn't know by the way Pam is looking at me.

"You're right," I tell her, reaching out to grab her hand. "It is."

My heart may have softened, but my cock is possibly harder than before. With a quick tug, I pull her body flush against mine, wrapping her tight in my arms before falling back on the couch, her body landing on top of mine.

Her knees settle on either side of me as she shifts to line up over my dick. When I feel her wet heat sink down on me, I struggle to let her take the lead, my hands clutching her hips so hard, my fingers sink in her flesh.

"You make me insatiable," she breathes heavily, riding me, my thumb working her clit.

"Feel…free…to use and abuse me,…Biscuit," I pant as my hips buck underneath her.

-

I trail my fingers down her spine to the top of her ass.

"Are you sleeping?"

We eventually ended up in her bed, after removing more packing boxes to the floor. Her body is tucked up against mine, one of her long legs and an arm pinning me to the mattress. I can't see her face, but I love looking at the way her skin stands out in contrast against mine.

"Not yet," she mumbles against my chest.

"How about we move these boxes to my house this weekend?"

"Sounds like a plan." Her voice sounds like she's smiling, and she snuggles in closer when I kiss the top of her head.

CHAPTER TWENTY-NINE

Pam

"Hand me that one."

I point at a box at the far side of the bedroom.

Gina volunteered to help me put away my stuff in the master bedroom, while her father took Jonas for an errand. Dino, at some point in the past few days, had managed to repaint the bedroom a beautiful slate gray and had somehow replaced his old bed with simple, raised box spring and mattress. A gorgeous burgundy red tufted headboard is mounted on the wall and simple grey and white sheets and pillows cover the bed.

I was shocked when Gina opened the door for me, revealing the transformation inside. Dino's arms snuck around me from behind, and with his lips moving against my neck he asked, "Do you like it?"

All I could do was nod, moved by the significance of the gesture.

"How did you manage this?"

"I've got friends." He kisses my shoulder before releasing me. "There's room in the dresser and the walk in closet for your stuff," he said, before heading back downstairs.

With Gina's help I've got my clothes tucked away and am down to two boxes with toiletries and linens. Gina, who has been quiet but helpful, hands me the one that goes in the bathroom. The vanity has a stack of drawers on either side of two sinks and it looks like Dino cleaned one out for me. I'm feeling myself getting excited now. Earlier I'd been too busy to let the reality of this new situation settle in, but now that we're getting down to the last boxes, I'm feeling almost giddy.

We spent the past few days apart; I was busy packing and sorting, while Dino had the pub and obviously had also been working on the house. We did talk on the phone a few times, trying to sort out which pieces of furniture to keep and which ones to let go. Dino suggested I should go ahead and change whatever I wanted, but I gently reminded him that it wasn't just his call; his kids live there too. In the end it was Viv who came up with a good point when she was helping one night.

"Don't dismiss the importance of making that house your home," she said. "They've lived there since the kids were little, so no matter what furniture is in the living room or what cups they're drinking from, it'll still be their home, but you might need an occasional reminder."

It helped. I decided on keeping my couch, which is large and comfy, and can fit us all easily. Also, since a few nights ago, it's my favorite piece of furniture. A perfect reminder of the start of our life together.

"Where did I put those box cutters?"

"Here you go," Gina says, handing them over, and I quickly slice through the packing tape.

"Thanks. Okay, if you grab that last box—it has some towels and sheets in it—and see if there's room in the linen closet for them. We'll be done in no time, and maybe we can whip up a batch of cookies or something before the guys get home." Gina doesn't say anything but the little smile on her face, as she goes to fetch the box, tells me she likes that idea. Girls and cookies, there's no way you can go wrong with that.

I'm putting away my hair products in the shower when I notice her hesitate just outside the door.

"Did they fit?" I ask, referring to the linens. Her eyes shoot up from the bottles in my hand to my face and she quickly nods. "You know," I say as I arrange my products on the little shelf. "Some of those pretty sheets I have? The ones with the vines? They won't fit the new bed. Too small. But you have a queen-sized bed, right?"

"I think so," she says, a hopeful sparkle in her eyes.

"Good. Then those are yours, if you want them." I decide with a shrug. "Not like Jonas is going to want those on his bed, right?" I'm trying not to make a big deal about it, but I'm still pleased when I hear a soft giggle escape her.

"Why do you need a different shampoo?"

Ahhh, so that's what she was looking at. I grab the bottles off the shelf and sit down on the side of the tub, indicating with a tilt of my head for her to join me.

"Feel my hair," I say, bending my head down a little so she can touch it. It takes her a minute, but finally she lifts her hand and gingerly touches my short curls.

"It's soft," she says, sounding surprised.

"Not normally," I explain. "It's bristly and a bit rough to the touch, which is why I use a relaxing shampoo and conditioner. I also put a mask on my hair every week, just to keep it soft. It still curls, but not as tightly." Gina's hand comes up, this time to touch her own long dark strands. "African American hair often is different than your hair, for instance. It tends to twist around itself as it grows, which is what causes that kink and makes it feel bristly. A lot of women choose to straighten their hair or go to a hairdresser to have it done. I don't have long hair, so I just use this. It seems to do the job."

"Mom had special stuff too, for shine. She let me use it, but Dad just buys the two-in-one stuff. In bulk," she says the last with disgust in her voice and it makes me smile.

"Well, you're welcome to use my shampoo and conditioner any time you like, but I'm thinking you have such gorgeous thick hair, we should get you something that is perfect just for you. Maybe tomorrow we can pop in to Walgreens? See what they have for your hair type?"

"Sure," she says, sounding casual enough, but she can't keep the pleased look off her face. Just like that I've fallen head over heels for this kid, too.

"Perfect. It's a date then. Now how about those cookies?" I quickly return the bottles to the shelf and lead the way out of the bathroom before I get all mushy over the poor kid.

We've barely got the first batch in the oven when the front door opens, and Jonas is yelling through the house.

"Gina! Pam! Come look at this!"

Dino

"Where are we going?" Jonas asks the moment I pull out of the driveway.

I'm glad I never mentioned anything about a car when I first talked to Ike last month. The kid would probably have been hell to live with, testing his patience like that. It had still taken Ike a few weeks before convincing Viv she needed a new vehicle. Of course, then it had taken them a few more weeks to come up with something that would meet Viv's esthetic demands as well as Ike's safety and reliability ones. Yesterday when he showed up to help put the new bed together, he pulled me aside.

"Picked up Viv's new car yesterday, a Toyota RAV. I've had her old car looked over. Had an oil change, tire alignment, and brake service done; it should be good to go. Want to give it a test run and hit the DMV before it closes?"

We got the title signed over and since I had to get to work, we left the car at Ike's for us to pick up this afternoon. That's where we're going.

"We have to stop by Ike and Viv's for a minute, but first we have to pick up that package at Maine Photo Works." I try to keep my cool but the truth is, I don't know which of the two I'm more excited about.

"Shit, that's right," Jonas says. "I'd almost forgotten about that."

I chuckle to myself. Typical teenager; his mind only able to retain stats he reached in Call Of Duty and little else. I'm pretty proud when he came up with the idea.

"She's gonna love it," I tell him when we tuck the package in the trunk of my car and make our way over to Ike's.

Jonas doesn't suspect a thing when Viv pulls the door open with Francessca on her hip. He walks right past his new car without even blinking an eye, too focused on the baby. Both my kids seem to be enamored with babies. All babies—not just Francessca, but Syd and Gunnar's little guy, Caden, as well. That's why I'm not surprised when he plucks the baby from Viv's arms and walks past her in the house, leaving Viv grinning after him.

"He doesn't have a clue, does he?" she observes, before following him in.

"Not a one," I mutter, filing inside after her.

We're sitting at the counter in her kitchen, having a coffee, when Ike walks in with bags of groceries and throws a wink my way.

"Hey, Jonas," he says, drawing my boy's attention before tossing him a set of keys he easily catches midair. "Mind moving your car out of the driveway? I've got more shit in the back of mine and I'd like to back it in."

It's pretty fucking funny to see the range of emotions playing out on his face, until he finally settles on one. With a big yelp, he jumps off the stool, his fist in the air. Poor Francessca, who was half dozing in her bouncy chair startles and starts crying. Before Viv can react, Jonas is already on his knees next to the baby, cooing and kissing her head.

"Sorry," he mouths with a wince at Viv, who just smiles and waves him off.

"Go check out your wheels, buddy," she tells him and he rushes out the door, leaving me standing beside the stool.

For a second I feel a bit of a let down, but it passes quickly when the next moment Jonas comes running back in, not stopping until he has me in a tight squeeze.

"Love you, Dad. I won't disappoint you."

My arms come around him, one hand cupping the back of his head, the way I did when he was little.

"You can't even if you tried, Son. You make me so proud." I swallow a huge lump from my throat but can't keep the thick emotion from my voice. "I love you, Jonas. Now get out of here and make sure you're home at five for dinner."

This time I follow him out the door and watch from the front steps as he backs his first car out of the driveway—narrowly missing the mailbox—and driving at a cautious speed down the street. I watch him until he turns the corner and disappears from sight.

I feel an arm slipping around my waist as Viv steps out beside me.

"I don't even want to know what that feels like," she says with a shudder. "Watching your kid drive off for the first time."

"Not helping, Vivian," I growl low in my throat, only to have her laugh in my face.

"No worries, you big lug. You'll be sure to have the last laugh on this one."

Ten minutes later, I pull into the driveway, only to find my spot taken by Jonas. Didn't quite think that through—not with Pam's car filling the other half of the driveway. *Fuck me.* By the time I back up and park the car at the curb, Pam and the kids come rushing out of the house. They don't even see me as they circle his car—not until I get out of the car—then Gina spots me first and comes running. I'm still reeling from the fact that my son, who for the first time has the freedom to go wherever he wants with whomever he wants, chose to drive his brand-new car straight home to show Pam and his sister. It both says something about how he feels about Pam and his sister, and about his priorities. Both please me to no end.

I barely have a chance to brace myself when Gina jumps in my arms, smiling from ear-to-ear.

"Hey, Daddy!"

"Hey, Princess." I slowly lower her until her feet hit the ground, wondering what I did to deserve this type of greeting. The minute I let her go, she runs back to the car. Jonas opens the passenger side door and I watch her climb in. *Oh fuck.* I watch as he rounds the hood and opens the driver's door, while Pam watches on.

"Wait a minute!" I call out, my feet eating up the lawn until I hit the driveway. "What are you doing?"

"Taking Gina for a drive?" he answers. I can almost sense the mental eye roll I'm sure he performed at the same time.

Yeah, that's what I was afraid of.

"Not sure that's a good idea, Bud."

"Why not?" Gina fires from a rolled down window.

Pam sidles up to me, slipping an arm around my waist. "What is worrying you?" she whispers under her breath, her amusement still audible.

"She's too young," I hiss back, which apparently amuses Pam even more, judging by the loud snort.

"Dino…" I feel myself being turned toward the front door, Pam firmly leading me. "She's just gonna go for a drive around the block in her brother's new car." I look down at her and see understanding shining in her eyes, even though her mouth is still twitching. Twisting my head around, I'm just in time to see my son getting behind the wheel, buckling himself in. *Thank God.* Gina seems to be giggling at me as Jonas slowly backs out of the driveway.

Pam

"That was delicious. You cooked—I'll clean up."

I get up and start collecting plates.

The kids returned after only ten minutes, and I managed to keep Dino distracted with some heavy petting right there in the hallway. It was a pretty big day for all of us, it seems, and the atmosphere around the dinner table was good-natured.

I'm in the kitchen, washing some dishes in the sink and lost in thought, when familiar arms slip around my waist from behind, and Dino leans his chin on my shoulder.

"You coming in any time soon?" A little shiver runs down my back as his breath ghosts against the shell of my ear.

"Almost done," I return, but he reaches around me and turns off the tap.

"Come on, Biscuit. The kids want to watch a movie," he says, as he steps back and holds out a towel for me to dry my hands.

"Should I get some snacks?" I ask, not able to remember the last time I sat down for a family movie.

"Honey, we just finished dinner. We'll grab something later." He grabs my hand and pulls me into the living room, the TV not even on yet. Instead, both kids watch me walk in with barely veiled anticipation, and I look around for what I might be missing. *What the hell?*

That's when I spot it, and my knees want to buckle, but clearly Dino was prepared. I barely notice him pulling me against his chest, I can't drag my eyes away from the large framed picture they've centered on the wall of family photos.

I remember that day like it was yesterday. It was the beginning of the end. A moment I have called up and treasured more than just a few times in recent months. Derrick's graduation from middle school; a time when my clever boy was still applying himself, before he got swept up in the disturbing dynamics of high school.

He'd just finished his graduation speech, selected because of his outstanding academic performance, and jumped off the stage, clear into my arms. We'd both been on such a high that day. One of his teachers had taken the picture and had sent it to me. All these years I thought it was lost.

Yet here it is, enlarged, hanging among pictures of Dino's kids growing up.

"How?" I manage to get out, although it's more of a sob.

"Jonas found it stuck inside the back cover of Derrick's book. He wanted to frame it and give it to you for Christmas, but it was pretty creased and damaged. Gina was the one who suggested taking it to Maine Photo Works. She'd seen their ad in a magazine, promoting their services and one of them was image restoration."

"Oh my God."

"We tried to get it back before Christmas, but they said they needed more time. Since it wasn't gonna be ready on time anyway, we figured we might as well have it enlarged," Jonas pipes up, and I turn my eyes to him. He has his arm around his sister, who is leaning against his shoulder. She's quietly crying and I realize my reaction may have upset her.

"Gina, honey…look at me, baby." Slowly her eyes come up. "I'm not upset—these are happy tears."

"I know," she says, smiling through her tears. "So are these."

-

"You know what I don't get?"

Dino turns to look at me.

"I looked for that picture for years, wanting the visual with the memory, and all this time Derrick had it. He never told me."

The kids went upstairs earlier after I gave them both big emotional hugs. Dino and I are sitting on the couch, just looking at the family wall, where the picture of Derrick and me should look out of place—except, it doesn't.

In the picture, his arms are wrapped around my waist and he has his head tilted back, laughing with his mouth wide open, his eyes fixed on me. I'm holding him close, looking down on him with obvious pride, also smiling wide. A happy moment, among a wall full of happy moments.

"Think about this," Dino says, pulling me closer. "Maybe he needed it more than you."

"You think?"

"I do."

"Dino?"

"Hmmm?"

"Thank you." I lift my head to look at him.

"You're welcome, beautiful, but like I said earlier, it was all the kids' idea." I smile and shake my head.

"No, honey. Thank you for bringing me home."

Suddenly I find myself flipped in the air and land draped on top of Dino, his arm banding around me and a happy grin on his face.

"Biscuit," he murmurs, stroking my face with his palm. "I should be thanking you. The past months have been chaos and you've had my back. You maintained common sense, offered a voice of reason, and provided me quiet shelter in the storm. I'm a selfish man; I love you and am not ashamed to admit I need you here. And you brought this couch…it was a no-brainer."

EPILOGUE

Dino

I watch my son as he shakes hands, accepts hugs and kisses, and listens to words of advice and wisdom.

This is a send-off party for Jonas. We'll be driving him to Boston tomorrow, where he'll be attending Boston Architectural College. He'd agonized long and hard, especially since sometime during this summer he and Emmy, Gunnar and Syd's oldest, had become a couple. She is scheduled to start at the Maine College of Art, right here in Portland, and is planning to live at home. It was tempting for Jonas to choose a local college in Portland, so he could stay closer to Emmy, but ultimately he realized his acceptance into the BAC was an opportunity he shouldn't pass up on.

"Tough?" I turn to the side, finding Mark raising a bottle of beer to his lips.

"Tougher than I thought," I admit." It scares me that I can't keep a close eye on him. Temptation is everywhere on college campuses, especially in a big city like Boston."

"He's a good kid. For what it's worth, I think he'll be alright. It's not like he's across the country, he's a couple of hours away at most. You can drive there, meet him for lunch, and be back before dinner. It may help him stay rooted, make it easier for him to resist getting swept up in anything bad." Mark shrugs his shoulders and takes another swig of his beer.

"He's right, you know?" Pam says, walking up behind us and slipping her arm around my waist. "We'll talk to him regularly, let him know we're still right there, even if it's not in the same house. He's grown up. Even more so now that he has Emmy. Those kids have a lot in common."

We watch as Jonas tags Emmy as she walks by, pulls her close, and drops a quick kiss on her mouth. Mark chuckles beside me. I follow his gaze which is focused on Gunnar, standing behind the bar and glaring at my son.

"I bet he's growling," Pam, who spots him as well, points out. Mark chuckles even louder.

Gunnar had not been a happy man when Emmy introduced Jonas as her boyfriend. Not happy at all. I'd steered clear of him for those first few weeks, not wanting the confrontation I was afraid was coming. It was inevitable, though. I'm protective of my boy, proud of him. He's not made the best decisions, but he owned up to them, faced the consequences, and has done everything right since. On the other hand, Gunnar was looking out for his little girl, his firstborn. I don't think any boy would've been good enough in his eyes.

The confrontation had come one night when Syd and I were cleaning up the pub, and Gunnar stormed in the backdoor.

"Told you that kid would be a bad influence on her!" he yelled at Syd, ignoring me completely, even though it was my son he was referring to. "I caught Emmy checking out colleges in Boston. She gonna give up her future for that punk."

I hadn't even realized I was moving until Syd stepped between, a hand in the middle of my chest and one in Gunnar's, physically holding us apart.

"Enough!" The voice coming from her small frame was impressive. "Weeks I've watched you two circling around each other and over what? They're good kids, both of them with a good head on their shoulders." She proceeded to read us both the riot act. Pointing out that we should be glad that if anything ever happened with the kids, they'd have a support system like no other to help them out. She made it clear that we were the ones behaving immaturely, not the kids. "How many years have you been friends? How many years have you had each other's backs, been part of the other's family? You've seen that boy grow up, Gunnar. You know that boy almost as well as his father does. And you," she said, poking a pointy finger in my chest. "You should give him some slack. You of all people should know what it's like to worry your little girl is going to get hurt."

I swear she made me feel three feet tall that night.

If I'm honest, I don't really blame him for calling Jonas a punk, I just reacted. I've called Benji a punk—fuck, I've called him worse—and he didn't deserve that either. And he's just Gina's friend—at least I fucking hope so.

I look around the pub, which is closed for our private party, and see only familiar faces. Matt is helping Gunnar man the bar. Syd and Ruby are fussing around the buffet table they set up along the far wall. Pam and those two prepared too much food. Tim and Ike, still the best of friends, are sitting at the far end of the bar, talking with Arnie, who is as much part of The Skipper family as anyone else. We've got Gunnar's mother sitting in a booth with Tim and Mark's parents and Viv's mother. The older guard.

Claudia, Mark's girlfriend, is laughing at something Viv's youngest brother, Dorian, says, while her oldest brother, Owen, is trying to teach Nina to play darts. Nina is Ruby and Tim's adopted daughter, who is going into her second year of college. Dex, Gina, and Ben are watching from a nearby table, laughing every time Nina's darts miss the board and clatter to the ground.

We make up a colorful community. Family, really.

A large, diverse and dysfunctional family—but I've never experienced so much love in one room. Despite the different cultures, life experiences, differences in race, and preference, we all seem to fit.

I look at my son, who is now smiling and talking with Pam, his arm loosely around Emmy's shoulder. Pam's eyes come up and meet mine. Everything I see and feel is reflected there. The corner of her mouth pulls up in a little lopsided smile.

Pam

I cried yesterday.

Hell, I cried the day before, too. Sitting around a table at The Skipper with my girls on Saturday night; Viv, Syd, and Ruby. Women who have become as close as sisters to me. Women I can share everything with: worries, pain, joy, and victories. And the circle is only getting bigger. Marianne and Maria, two more victims turned survivors—two more women who wake up each day, surprised to find themselves stronger than the day before, despite the hell they had to walk through to get here. There's Sarah, whose path has been more like a twisted mountain road, with lots of hairpin turns and deep valleys, but even she is finding her feet. Her sons now holding all of her focus. Sarah's discovered the power of sisterhood is stronger than the hold one man can have over you. She's even started paying it forward by being a sounding board for Jeannie; who came out of rehab only two months ago and is still struggling to get on her feet. Hers will likely be a lifelong struggle, but she's trying hard. I've been in touch with her a few times; while still in rehab, and since she's been out. Dino doesn't know I've kept her informed on the well-being of the children. Something that seems to have given her a focus, too. She knows it's up to the kids, but she wants to get well enough to maybe be in their lives again one day. I was able to help her find a halfway house; an environment where she'll be able to start building a life of her own, yet still have the security of monitoring and support. A place to start. That's all any of us need.

I sat there with my girls, looked at the pub full of people, who all somehow had become an important part of my life—who'd collectively pulled me from solitude and made me feel part of something bigger—and I cried.

I don't think I've cried as much in my lifetime as I have in the past ten months or so. A lot of sad tears, but even more happy ones. I've been alive.

Even saying goodbye to Jonas was with mixed feelings.

We'd driven to Boston in two cars yesterday. Gina had gone with Jonas in his car, and Dino and I followed behind, both cars loaded full. He was staying in a residence hall his first year, something Dino had insisted on. Living with other students would give him an opportunity to make friends in a relatively safe environment. Jonas didn't object, because it came with a place to park his car at low cost. Something that was at premium in Boston.

He had a room to himself in an old, rather ornate building, where the rooms were larger, but the downfall was shared bathroom facilities. Not that Jonas cared much, he was too excited about the gorgeous, tall bay window that allowed him a view of beautiful Chestnut Hill. The residence hall is short ride from campus on the bus that stops right in front. He doesn't really need his car to move around Boston, in fact, it's easier without, but having it there gives both him and Dino a sense of security. The ability for him to come home whenever he wants or needs to.

Once we have him settled into his room, we head over to Fenway Park. I'd managed to score some Red Sox tickets, with the help of Gunnar. I thought it would be good idea to end the day on a fun experience for us all. Hoping to add something positive to what would otherwise just be a pretty sad affair. I'm glad I did; we had a really good time at dinner and the whole game experience was a blast.

"I love you, Pam," he'd whispered in my ear when we said our goodbyes out front of his dorm.

"Me too, baby. Me, too," I sniffed before holding him at arm's length. "Be smart, be careful, and be safe, boy. I hear anything else—remember—I know where you live."

I carried the sound of his chuckle and the sight of his bright smile all the way back to Portland.

Damn, I'm proud of the kid; he struggled a little during the Christian Neve trial this summer, but he never wavered. He stayed on the straight and narrow. Luckily, after the guilty verdict came down on all counts, including corruption of a minor, the other two kids opted to plea to a lesser charge, as expected. We talked about the possibility of a civil suit, but for the sake of closure for all of us, we decided not to. We needed to collectively move past it. So I'm happy Jonas is doing just that, going off to college. That doesn't mean I'm not sad he's moving to Boston.

The house will be quiet without him. Hell, it already is.

Gina left on the school bus this morning, leaving silence in her wake. At least she'll be home this afternoon.

"What are you doing?" Dino sits beside me on the couch, fresh from the shower.

"I'm listening."

"To what?" he wants to know.

"Still air…" I reply, sorting my thoughts and feelings while I look at the family wall. "Before, the silence was absolute, the air thick and heavy, making it hard to breathe. Now, the house is quiet but the air is still—peaceful with the knowledge the kids are safe—and vibrant with the echo of their voices. The sound is full of promise—Hopeful."

Dino's arm pulls me tight to his side and his lips brush my forehead.

"You know I love you, right?" he whispers.

"I do," I tell him, lifting my eyes so I can study his rugged face, softened with true emotion. "I hear it…I see it, and…I feel it." I take one of his large hands and press it between my breasts. "Right here."

THE END

NOTE FROM THE AUTHOR:

My Portland, ME, novels have been labors of love. This fourth and final story rounds up this series and features, arguably, perhaps the strongest of the women I've portrayed. As with the other novels in the series, the root of the story is a true life story, but the focus is not on the tragic events, but rather on the way our heroine copes with the turmoil in her life.

As daughters, mothers, partners, and/or wives, women tend to carry not only the weight of their own demons on their shoulders, but those of loved ones around them as well. We have a tendency to repress our own pain, identity, grief, struggles, and end up placing others' needs above our own. That struggle is real, as it is for Pam, our heroine. Caring for others becomes our purpose, our reason for being, and is often our coping mechanism.

I've personally gone through a struggle like that, although I thankfully have never had to grieve the loss of a child. For me, it was my health that started to fail, making it impossible for me to continue working and costing me my mobility. I found myself at a loss; my children grown and no longer in need of my care, and I was no longer 'productive' or needed. It took me three years of wrestling with depression to find some foothold again. It required digging deep to figure out what my purpose was—who I was.

I needed to reinvent myself many times over, every time I lost the ability to continue on the path I was on, but I found *me*. Not better, not worse, just different. And I'm happy where I find myself; not despite of all that went before, but in large part because of it.

Strength.

We all have an infinite supply of strength that sometimes needs new and creative ways to access. In the end, though, we're all still standing, a little worse for wear, but never more secure or confident with our place in the world.

Character cannot be developed in ease and quiet. Only through experience of trial and suffering can the soul be strengthened, ambition inspired, and success achieved.

(Helen Keller)

ACKNOWLEDGEMENTS:

As always my readers come first! I am so grateful to all of you who've either read my books from the beginning, or have only just discovered my writing. I love connecting with you via social media, email, messages and most of all, at one of the many signings I've attended. Your feedback is always amazing and inspires me to do more…and better!

I'm privileged to have a phenomenal group of people who offer their continuous support in my Barks & Bites. You lift me up, you cheer me on and you have my back. All the damn time! I love you guys!

My amazing beta-readers who are not afraid to speak their mind, set me straight, and press me for better. You are indispensable. Joanne Thompson, Chris Alderson Kovacich, Debbie Bishop, Nancy Huddleston, Pam Buchanan, Sam Price, Deb Blake, Lena Konstantinos, Catherine Scott, Kerry-Ann Bell, Tracy Meighan, and Rebecca Stacy. I love you all.

My amazing editor, Karen Hrdlicka, who always makes me look so damn good! A brilliant brain I can always count on to bounce my ideas off. There are few I trust to guide me as much as I do you. I'm so blessed to have you by my side, and look forward to our future projects! Love you to bits!

My agent, Stephanie DeLamater Phillips, who is perhaps not always immediately visible, but who has quietly managed to garnish me a fabulous contract with EverAfter Romance for all my currently published works. Thank you for all you do behind the scenes, my lovely! I love your face!

I have to thank all the awesome blogs who pimp, promote, push and review my books. Your time, your enthusiasm, your support, is absolutely imperative. I adore you all and hope you know how much

I appreciate all of you!

Dana Hook; what can I say about this woman? She is an advocate for upcoming authors. She is my talented partner in Rebel, Edit & Design. But more than that, she is my own personal "Asshat" and I love her like a sister. You've put up with me for five weeks, and held my hand through three signings, electronic mishaps, and seven seasons of SOA. I love you Opie! And asshat! So hard, it's not even funny.

My family rocks. They put up with my erratic schedule and my frequent absences when I travel. The house is still here, every time I come home, and everyone (and the dog!) is well taken care of. Mark, Sanne, Stijn, Justin, Nicole, thank you all for allowing me to evolve, the way you have. I love you so much.

Mom, you are the best and most supportive person in my life. You read every word I write, and never hesitate to tell me how much you enoy it. Love you, Mama.

ABOUT THE AUTHOR

Freya Barker inspires with her stories about 'real' people, perhaps less than perfect, each struggling to find their own slice of happy, but just as deserving of romance, thrills and chills, and some hot, sizzling sex in their lives.

Recipient of the RomCon "Reader's Choice" Award for best first book, "Slim To None," Freya has hit the ground running. She loves nothing more than to meet and mingle with her readers, whether it be online or in person at one of the signings she attends.

Freya spins story after story with an endless supply of bruised and dented characters, vying for attention!

Freya

https://www.freyabarker.com

http://bit.ly/FreyaAmazon

https://www.goodreads.com/FreyaBarker

https://www.facebook.com/FreyaBarkerWrites

https://tsu.co/FreyaB

https://twitter.com/freya_barker

or mailto:freyabarker.writes@gmail.com

ALSO BY FREYA BARKER

CEDAR TREE SERIES:

SLIM TO NONE

HUNDRED TO ONE

AGAINST ME

CLEAN LINES

UPPER HAND

LIKE ARROWS

HEAD START

PORTLAND, ME, NOVELS:

FROM DUST

CRUEL WATER

THROUGH FIRE

STILL AIR

NORTHERN LIGHTS COLLECTION:

A CHANGE OF TIDE

A CHANGE OF VIEW

A CHANGE OF PACE

(Coming soon!)

ROCK POINT SERIES:

KEEPING 6

CABIN 12

(Coming soon!)

SNAPSHOT SERIES:

SHUTTER SPEED

FREEZE FRAME

IDEAL IMAGE

PICTURE PERFECT

(coming soon!)